FATAL COURAGE

SHADOW FORCE INTERNATIONAL

MISTY EVANS

ROMANTIC SUSPENSE AND MYSTERIES BY MISTY EVANS

The Super Agent Series
Operation Sheba
Operation Paris
Operation Proof of Life
The Blood Code
The Perfect Hostage, A Super Agent Novella

The Deadly Series
Deadly Pursuit
Deadly Deception
Deadly Force
Deadly Intent
Deadly Attraction (coming 2016)
Deadly Affair, A SCVC Taskforce novella (coming 2016)

The Justice Team Series (with Adrienne Giordano)
Stealing Justice
Cheating Justice
Holiday Justice
Exposing Justice
Undercover Justice
Protecting Justice

Shadow Force International Series
Fatal Truth
Fatal Honor
Fatal Courage

The Secret Ingredient Culinary Mystery Series
The Secret Ingredient, A Culinary Romantic Mystery with Bonus Recipes
The Secret Life of Cranberry Sauce, A Secret Ingredient Holiday Novella

ACKNOWLEDGMENTS

Another wonderful adventure for me, writing Fatal Courage and learning about the world of medicine, the business of terrorism, and weaving an intricate storyline where a good guy might be bad...or he might be a bad guy who excels at making people believe he's good. Which one is Elliot? Honestly, it wasn't until I was done with the first draft that I knew myself. That's where gratitude to Adrienne Giordano comes in. She gave me the idea for Elliot's character. Thank you, my friend and awesome brainstorming partner.

Thanks, also, to the Rockin' Readers, my street team/review crew, who are always there for me, like an extended family. You guys make this journey fun and exciting. Often when I'm writing, I picture all of you in my head.

A special shout-out to Maria Mercedes, who volunteered to share her name with Beatrice's midwife. You'll be reading more about Beatrice, Cal, and Maria in the upcoming novella, FATAL LOVE, starring the new baby. Girl or boy? Readers get to decide, so check out the end of the story to find out where you can cast your vote.

The white room meditation mentioned in the story comes via my son, Ben, who also turned me onto Tibetan singing bowls. Kids these days. <smile>

By the way, for those who love Jax, a piece of trivia. The name Sloan is Gaelic and means "warrior". I didn't know that when I picked his name, but it sure fits.

A huge thank you goes out to my yoga sister, Gloria Rumpf, who told me about her midwife and the foot trick to induce labor during our teacher training. I had to use it, G. Great story! To all of my yoga teacher training classmates (Gloria,

Julie, Kayla, and Sonya) and our beloved yoga teacher (Pam) —I owe you my sanity. I was writing this story during our training period and preparing for my sons' graduation as well as my move to a new state. I met my edge many times over and handled it with your love and support. Thank you, yogis!

As always, I am indebted to my editors, cover artist, beta readers, and formatter, who take my lump of clay and make it shiny and pretty. I couldn't do it without all of you, or without Amy Remus, who does a fantastic job keeping me organized.

To Mark,

who is always salty, and free with the curse words.

A group of former SEALs, abandoned by the United States and labeled as rogue operatives, who now work as a black ops team performing private intelligence, security, and paramilitary missions for those who have nowhere else to turn.

Fate whispers to the warrior 'you cannot withstand the storm'; the warrior whispers back 'I am the storm.'

~ Anonymous

CHAPTER ONE

Jaxon Sloan wanted to stuff burlap in his ears.

Techno dance music filled the air. The entire Chicago nightclub pulsed, the rhythm beating against his eardrums and making his eyes cross.

He used to love this type of music, the deep throb that reminded him of sex. After his stint in Morocco with a certain female CIA operative, he lost his love of the hard-driving, electronic music. These days, he preferred the sensuous tease of finger symbols, flutes, and frame drums.

Not even the sexy women grinding it out on the dance floor in front of him were enough to distract him. He should have had a hard-on from all the tight bodies on display, the luscious hips and full racks undulating under the flashing neon lights. Red lips, fuck-me pumps, skin, skin, and more skin everywhere he looked.

She's not here.

He knew what that meant.

No Ruby, no hard-on.

Story of his fucking life.

Forcing himself to tune out the hellish music, he scanned the crowd again. He'd spotted her rental outside. She had to be here somewhere.

Restroom?

Bar?

Private room upstairs?

His gaze darted to the reflective mirrors over the dance floor. The club boasted a private suite with two-way mirrors, a personal bar, and giant flat-screens. Tonight's renter, a gangster named Augustus "Little Gus" Nelson, had recently dipped his toes into the international terrorist trade.

A soft, involuntary growl rose from Jax's throat. The thought that Ruby might be with Little Gus, using her inimitable charms as well as her CIA training to pump the king of the South Side black market for information made him want to draw his weapon and shoot the mirrored glass overhead.

Pull your shit together.

Beatrice, his boss at Shadow Force International, was always warning him about his temper. Too many times in his thirty years of life, it had gotten him into major trouble.

But then, he sort of liked trouble.

Hell, he *loved* trouble. Trouble meant confrontation, swinging fists, and sometimes a one-night stand with a beautiful, belly-dancing spy.

Dropping his gaze, he analyzed various ways to get into that suite and find out if his intuition was accurate. The only reason Ruby was here tonight had to be Little Gus. She was supposed to have her ass planted behind a desk, spending her probation time from the Agency assisting the local Feds with counterterrorism cases. No fieldwork. No undercover assignments. Just good old-fashioned paper shuffling.

Yet, she was here, in this club, frequented by the gangster. If Jax knew anything about the CIA's former golden girl, Ruby wasn't here for the apple cosmos and Calvin Harris music.

Maybe she's meeting Hayden.

And wouldn't that make his night? Snagging Elliot Hayden, Ruby's former partner, currently a federal fugitive, would be one fucking big feather in Jaxon's cap. Hell, he'd barely received his orders to go after Hayden three hours ago. If he wrapped up this mission for Shadow Force International before sunrise, he'd be on the fast track to running his own SFI team. Beatrice would be so unbelievably impressed, she might even congratulate him and give him a raise.

Sweet bonus, that. The head of Shadow Force International teams was one hard woman to impress. Even harder to get in good with.

Plus, Hayden was a scumbag. Taking him down—again—would feel pretty righteous. How the fucknugget had escaped federal prison was beyond Jax. He feared Hayden had had assistance from a pretty brunette who could talk her way into and out of anything.

Including Jax's bed.

Although, to be fair, in that one night of mind-blowing sex, they'd christened every piece of furniture, the floor, and the shower, spending little time actually in his bed.

Whoa. His gaze snagged on a young woman making her way onto the dance floor in a clingy red number that draped over her curves like hot fudge over ice cream.

He couldn't see her face as she danced alone, raising her arms over her head and shimmying her body. She was blond instead of brunette, but he knew that body well. The shimmying started at her fingertips, moved down her arms, her chest, her belly. It ended at her hips with a figure eight sway, back and forth, back and forth, her hips hitting that certain spot...and Jax knew.

Knew.

Like a straight shot of whiskey to his stomach, his system reacted. His fingers twitched; sweat broke out on along his hairline. The hard-on he should have had earlier jumped to attention.

Goddammit, Ruby.

He'd seen the belly dancer moves before, in the privacy of a steamy Marrakech bedroom, nothing touching her skin except for the see-through hip scarf with gold coins hanging low on her hips. He still remembered the way the coins were sensitive to every move she made.

Ting, ting, ting. The remembered sound infiltrated his ears, blocking out the driving dance music, the rise and drop of her exquisite hips flashing through his mind.

His hard-on grew.

The memory of her dancing over him shook him to his core. The way she'd laid him on his back and kept those hips moving, the *ting*ing mesmerizing him as much as her movements. She'd lowered her head to take in his jutting tip, then shook her hips, jingling that scarf. Inch by slow inch, she'd taken more of him into her mouth, undulating her hips in a belly dance he'd never forget in a million years.

There was no one like Ruby McKellen.

Every man, and many of the women, in the general vicinity stared at her on the dance floor, those enchanting hips and high, bouncing breasts impossible to resist. Another growl rose from the depths of Jax's chest.

Eight months since Marrakech. Mosques, medieval gardens, maze-like alleys. Sex and betrayal.

His last mission as a SEAL.

No, he didn't need to see Ruby's face to know it was her on the dance floor. *Hips don't lie.*

Hers were like a fingerprint. Unique. Unlike any other woman's in the world.

But when she whirled around, moving toward the center of the dancers, her stunning face confirmed it.

She's here.

And she was undercover.

The wig, the way she was purposely trying to draw the attention not only of all the people around her, but of the man sitting behind the mirrors upstairs...

Jax's body moved forward, striding onto the dance floor before the next pump of bass, his large frame colliding with people in his way. A woman reached out and ran a bold hand down his arm.

"Hi handsome." She grabbed onto him and slowed him down. "Dance with me?"

She was a striking redhead with big green eyes and a wide mouth. Those eyes that told him she wanted nothing more than a dance and some sex. Another time, he might have given her exactly what she wanted.

Not tonight. Even though he hadn't had a woman since Ruby, and his dry spell was screwing with him, he had a job to do.

Removing the woman's hand from his arm, he gave her a charming smile. "Save me one."

The redhead pouted and he moved on, his attention once more on the spy dead ahead.

As if she felt him bearing down on her, Ruby scanned the crowd. She'd picked up a partner whose hands angled for her hips, but she danced away, her gaze, and then the rest of her, colliding with Jax.

Ruby McKellen was no amateur. If she was surprised to see him, it didn't show. Her facial expression didn't change except for an almost imperceptible widening of her eyes. Her body kept moving...right past Jax.

Oh, no, honey. You're not getting away that easy.

As her new partner tried to follow, Jax cut in front of him. Over the music, he heard the guy balk. Felt a hand on his shoulder.

One quick uppercut and the guy bent over, sucking wind. Jax patted him on the back. "Stay away from her or the next time you come within spitting distance, I'll pull your heart out through your throat."

By the time he turned around, Ruby and her mind-blowing hips were slipping off the dance floor.

***

She'd almost blown it.

Ruby's pulse hammered in her ears. Her legs, in the four-inch heels, wobbled as she half-ran for cover.

That's what Jaxon Sloan did to her.

Every damn time.

Get away.

She scooted past a dancing couple, dodged a groping hand, and slid off the dance floor behind a woman slightly bigger than her. Her undercover training kicked in, her brain commanding her breathing to slow and her body to move less erratically.

Less like prey.

Seeing Jax out on the dance floor had shocked her system from head to toe. The months—they felt like years—had slogged by and suddenly he was here. An apparition. A ghost of her failure, come back to haunt her.

Heading for the rear of the club, she didn't dare look behind her. She'd nearly keeled over from a heart attack right there in the middle of everyone on the dance floor.

What was he doing here? How did he know she was in Chicago?

He could have blown her mission. *Again.*

Worse, with her little slip, she'd almost let him. After all of her training and twenty-one missions with only that one, single failure, she knew how to handle surprises. Nothing tripped her up.

Except Jax.

Tall, dark, and forever full of himself, his sudden appearance had thrown her but good. For a second, she'd thought her subconscious had wished him into being. She'd been thinking of him—couldn't get the man out of her mind even after all this time. With every move of her hips as she danced, she'd thought of him and their time in Marrakech. The way he'd touched her, the way he'd made her moan his name and beg for more.

She hit the back hallway, signs for the restrooms pointing to the left. Ruby went right.

Her pulse returned to normal and she dodged into an office doorway to avoid being seen by one of the owner's goons. The back entrance was only a few steps away. Her car waited in the parking lot.

The goon disappeared and Ruby started forward, then stopped. Now that she was thinking more clearly, she had to consider the consequences of bailing. A part of her didn't want to go—it wanted to confront Jax. Yell at him. Tell him to get the hell out.

Or maybe, take him back to her place.

Ah, hell.

Yep, she'd nearly flaked out on the dance floor when she saw him in the flesh, his smoldering dark eyes eating her up. Her heart had frozen in her chest, her limbs suddenly quivering with anticipation.

That's what happened when you'd been fantasizing about a guy for months and then he showed up looking even better than he did in your dreams.

Fantasy. That's all he was and that's how he had to remain.

Mission first and always. She didn't have time for distractions. Elliot was counting on her. The Agency was breathing down her neck.

The last person on the face of the earth she wanted to talk to—regardless of the fact he was the only man who'd ever chiseled his way past her solid walls—was Jaxon Sloan.

As she stepped out from her hiding place, Jax's deep voice stopped her in her tracks. "Are you running from me, Ruby?"

Running. That's exactly what she was doing.

Not that she would ever let him know that.

A shiver slid down her spine from his simple nearness. The music continued to beat in the background, snapping at her nerves. "I don't run from anyone." *Liar.*

"Sure looks like that's what you're doing."

She whirled around to face him; her breath caught.

He'd trapped her under a broken overhead light and the shadows around the former SEAL made him look even bigger and more badass than she knew him to be.

Swallowing the tightness in her throat, she stomped on the lust bubbling up inside her. Never had a man affected her the way he did. Never had anyone gotten under her skin like he had. His presence, his voice, ignited like dry kindling inside her.

"What do you want?" She forced her voice not to betray the

wild emotions riding her. She was an operative for God's sake, deceiving the enemy was second nature.

And Jaxon Sloan was definitely her enemy.

He was also the one man who saw past her duplicity every time.

His eyes swept over her, lingering on her hips for a second before coming back up to her face. "You know what."

"No, I really don't, and I can't be seen with you. You'll blow my mission." She brushed a strand of hair from her face. "You're good at that as I recall."

He didn't flinch, didn't so much as blink. The barely-there light from farther down the hall caught on the scar on his temple. "You're not working a legitimate mission, so knock it off. Whatever this is, it isn't important."

"Isn't important?" Clearing Elliot's name was her *only* mission. Sure, she was in Chicago to help the FBI with a counterterrorism case, but that was only to make her boss happy. Little Gus had connections she needed for Elliot. "Of course, that's what you'd say."

She turned her back on him, the past anger surfacing as she headed for the back entrance, but that was good. Anger kept her clearheaded. Anger suffocated her tangled emotions.

Anger would keep Jax at a safe distance.

She'd have to come back another night to see if she could get to Little Gus.

Two strong hands grabbed her by the arms and spun her around. Jax pinned her wrists to her sides and pushed her against the wall. "Where is he?"

She jerked her wrists away, only because he allowed it. He could probably crush every bone in them with ease. "Who?"

"You know who."

He smelled like cedar and warm rain. Her mind went back to that night in Marrakech, the soft rain starting after midnight, falling outside as he did wicked things to her body.

Concentrate. "I have no idea what you're talking about."

His liquid brown eyes, black in the shadows, narrowed and his head tilted slightly. For some stupid reason, she wanted his hands on her again. "Are we really playing this game?"

"I'm not playing a game. I don't know who you're talking about." *Shut him down. Get away, before you become a blubbering, lusty bitch.* Oh, right, too late. "Get out of my way and don't come back here to harass me again."

She tried to leave him, but his arm shot out, his hand resting on the wall near her head and stopping her.

He leaned in, studied her face. His full lips beckoned. "You're lying."

"I know you think that all I do is lie, but that's not true."

She'd told him the truth that night and then she'd betrayed him by taking Elliot's side when everything went south. He'd returned the favor by "proving" her partner was a traitor.

Elliot wasn't a traitor any more than she was. Jax had it all wrong. If only she could make him see that.

Proof. She was going to get proof of her partner's innocence. That's why she'd been here tonight, trying to get in good with the biggest gangster the South Side of Chicago had ever seen. He had the connections she needed.

Jax's face was inches from hers. His gaze dropped to her mouth, slid back up to her eyes. "You honestly don't know, do you?"

"Know what?"

A tense silence ensued. He still wasn't sure.

His proximity—so close she could raise her lips an inch and kiss him—was doing strange things to her. Like making her think about kissing him.

Down girl! "Jax, honest to God, either tell me what this is about or get out of my way."

"Elliot escaped."

The words buzzed inside her head, blurry, indistinct. "What?"

"He was in the medical ward after a fight and somehow ended up exchanging clothes with a guard and walking right out of the place. The guard is in serious condition, by the way, from a blow to the head."

My God. If she hadn't been backed up against the wall, she might have staggered. "Elliot would never do that."

His eyes challenged her. "See that's where you and I disagree. You think Elliot is this great guy. I know he's a miserable, lying traitor who will do anything to cover his ass."

Her jaw tightened. "There has to be a reason he would bail like that. He knew I was working on clearing his name. Why would he run?" On the heels of that unpleasant thought, came another. "Why didn't my boss notify me about this?"

"Probably because the CIA knows you're sympathetic to the douchecanoe."

Her exasperation morphed into outright annoyance. Mostly because he was probably correct. "Why do you care? Why did you come here to tell me this? To rub it in that you're right about my partner?"

"Ex-partner. He's not worthy of the ground you walk on, and no, I didn't come here to remind you he's a worthless goatwaffle. I came here because I know you're the first person he'll run to for help."

"That's sweet, but he's not stupid, and again, I don't understand why you care if he does come running to me for help. You made sure he went to prison after Marrakech, but he's no longer your problem, is he? He really was never your problem. You made him into a traitor, so while I'm sure it upsets you that he's escaped, the Agency will find him. Go back to your life and forget about him. Forget about me."

The words tumbled out of her mouth, even as her heart clenched. She didn't mean it. If anything, she wanted the opposite. To the man who'd probably slept his way around the world, she wanted to be the one woman he would never forget.

The clean-shaven SEAL of six months ago was gone. He'd grown a short beard since she'd last seen him and her fingers itched to touch it. To feel the scratch of it against her skin. His focus—so intense it made gooseflesh rise on her arms—dropped to her lips. "I will never forget you."

Bam. He'd read her mind.

Her heart stuttered. "Jax…"

He laid a finger against her lips. "Hear me out. I didn't come here to fight with you, Ruby. I know you're running an unsanctioned mission to find proof Elliot was innocent of the charges I brought against him, but you need to switch your focus and help me find him. He will come to you. You're the only person that ever believed he was innocent to begin with, and while I respect that kind of loyalty, you could be in danger. You think I ruined your career? Honey, let me tell you, if you in any way assist a federal fugitive—this federal fugitive—I'll make damn sure your ass lands in a prison cell next to his."

Threats. Nice.

Her stuttering heart hardened. Thankfully, she was speechless. If she tried to say anything, she'd probably lose it, so she shoved at his chest, pushing all her emotions into it.

Her shove met a brick wall.

Once she'd loved his solidness, his strength. Currently, she found it annoying as hell.

Like everything else about him.

Training, dammit. Ruby could hear her boss yelling in her ear. *Don't let him see he got to you. Turn the tables on him.*

Taking a deep, cleansing breath, she set her face to neutral, dropped her hands from his chest. "I'm not helping you hunt down my partner, which is not your job anyway. You're obsessed with Elliot because you're jealous of him. Why won't you own up to that?"

He traced her jaw with the same finger that had silenced her. "You think I'm jealous of Elliot Hayden?"

Her body shivered at the intimacy and she smacked his hand away. "You and I had a one-night stand, Jax, that's all it was. One night. You wanted more and I refused. You thought you'd snap your fingers and I'd fall at your combat boots, and when the shit went down with Elliot and Abdel, you expected me to side with you. I didn't and you still can't believe it. You don't respect the fact I'm loyal to my partner. You're jealous of him."

His chuckle was low and soft, raising goose bumps along her skin. "You want to know why I'm here watching your backside and asking for your help with Hayden?"

This should be good. The man was in total denial over his true motivations. "Why?"

"Because, honey." He rubbed the pad of his thumb over her chin, raising more gooseflesh. "The CIA hired me to hunt him down."

CHAPTER TWO

Either Jax's closeness was screwing with her brain, or he'd officially gone wacko. "Why would the CIA hire *you* to hunt down Elliot?" Ruby asked.

A noisy couple passed them. Jax waited until they'd disappeared down the hallway to answer. "They're keeping Hayden's escape under wraps for the time being because they think he may have had insider help. They don't know who or what is involved, could be one of their own. Your boss contacted my boss and requested me personally."

That was crazy. He was no bounty hunter; he worked for some bodyguard service these days—a waste of his talents if you asked her.

But no one cared what she thought and she hadn't missed the insinuation that the Agency thought she was the insider. "While your previous SEAL training makes you a good tracker, you're a bodyguard now. The Agency has plenty of people better equipped to find Elliot."

A derisive snort. "You always knew how to attack a guy's ego."

"This isn't about ego. If the Agency hired you, there's a reason."

"Maybe because I know Hayden." He brushed a finger along her jaw again. "And I know you."

It was her turn for derision. Ignoring the heat flooding her lower belly, she jeered at him. "Whatever you think you know, you're wrong. No one sees the real me. No one. That's why I'm so damn good at my job."

"Is that so?" His finger strayed to her throat, her collarbone, traced the edge of the V of her dress, dancing across her considerable cleavage. "Correct me if I'm wrong, but I know how to make you howl at the moon, sweetheart."

Gah. He would bring that up right now, trying to tilt her off center again. The full moon in Marrakech that night had been so beautiful, hanging, it seemed, right over their hut. The light coming through the window had created a perfect rectangle on the floor, where he'd laid her down and taken her. He'd teased her mercilessly with his tongue and fingers, bringing her right to the edge of her release, but never letting her go over until she'd begged him. Pleaded with him. He'd promised her earlier that evening that he'd make her howl and she'd scoffed at the idea. On the floor of the hut, in that bed of moonlight, he'd fulfilled his promise. She'd howled his name at the low-hanging moon when he'd finally given her what she wanted.

The rains had come shortly after that, sheltering them from the outside world. There were days, moments, she wished they'd never left.

She should have been out hunting down Mohammed Izala, and instead, she'd stayed inside the world Jax and the rain created. She ignored her mission. She had Izala's coordinates, had a SEAL team waiting off the Strait who could capture him once she'd flushed him out of hiding.

But instead of following the lead her boss at Langley had sent her, she'd stayed in bed with Jaxon Sloan.

The worst of it was, even with everything that had happened since that night, she wouldn't go back and change a thing.

Jax's other hand slipped down over her hip, giving it a squeeze. He rubbed the silky material of her dress between his fingers, lifting it higher, brushing a leg against hers.

Her breath flew out in a rush, his touch was like no other. She couldn't resist—even now, her body had a mind of its own. Melting into him, lowering her resistance.

Can't breathe…

Have…to get away.

He knew her body inside and out after their one night together, but he didn't know the first thing about the rest of her. Shoving him away, she slid from the wall and gulped a lungful of air, keeping one hand out as if that could hold him at bay. "I'm not helping you find Elliot."

She turned on her heels and hustled for the back door.

Adrenaline carried her, her ears peeled for the sound of him telling her to stop, her body anticipating the feel of his hands jerking her back.

He didn't come after her, didn't call her name.

Which was oddly disappointing.

At the door, she chanced a look back over her shoulder, saw him standing stock-still, one hand resting on the wall where she'd just been, his gaze on the floor. His muscled arm was covered with tattoos.

"Oh, and one more thing," she said, letting her gaze roam over him. It could be the last time she ever saw him. She wanted to make sure she remembered every detail. "I don't believe you're a bodyguard."

He didn't look up, didn't even acknowledge her. She burst out the door, setting off an alarm, and headed for the parking lot.

The night was warm. Too warm. Beads of sweat broke out along the back of her neck as she passed the couple from before getting handsy with each other near a black SUV. She wiped at a droplet of sweat that tracked down her neck.

Just like Marrakech.

No, it wasn't. Nothing compared to the heat of Morocco. Not even a muggy night in Chicago.

She placed her thumb on the rental car's digital lock and a second later was inside, pushing the start button. The Ford hybrid came to life and she jetted out of the lot.

Elliot escaped. Why? Why would he do that when he knew she was working at clearing his name? Tonight's meeting with Little Gus would have put them one step closer…but now she was stalled again, thanks to Jax.

The man made her crazy. He was too big, too handsome, too assertive for his own good. To top it off, he was smart.

Damn smart.

Intelligent men did her in every time. Add a quick wit and a delicious body and she was screwed.

In all her years, she'd never found such a mix in any other man. The drop-dead gorgeous ones were full of themselves and never tried too hard even if they had a decent IQ. The overachieving geniuses, so focused on their minds, rarely paid attention to their looks.

But not Jax. No, siree. That man had it all—the looks, the smarts, the wordplay…she loved every minute with him, even when they were at each other's throats.

The Marrakech mission had been like that. She'd found him annoying and overly confident when they'd started on their quest to pick up Abdel Al-Safari. A chemical weapons expert who contracted his services out to various terrorist groups, he had once worked for Saddam Hussein, eventually finding his way to Izala and the Moroccan 5.

She and Elliot had been assigned to covertly get him out of Morocco and to a secret facility in Spain for interrogation, but because Izala was a cunning, brutal terrorist, the Pentagon had insisted they take a Special Ops team with them.

A team of one, it turned out. While the rest of Jax's team waited for them at the Strait of Gibraltar, Jax had accompanied her and Elliot across the African landscape to Marrakech. They'd picked up Al-Safari from the Moroccan spy agency and began the arduous task of moving him covertly out of the country.

Except on that fateful night, Al-Safari killed himself while Ruby and Jax were tearing up the sheets.

⌖

Since little Gus liked raucous, DJ-driven clubs rather than the sports bars and craft-beer pubs closer to his stomping grounds, Ruby wound her way out of downtown, past the tourist sites on Michigan and into the grittier section of the city. Traffic was moderately light, the Loop seeing more action than the streets. A nice change of pace, since, like any large city, Chicago had far too many cars and stoplights for her liking.

She also didn't appreciate the car tailing her a block back.

Jax or Elliot?

Or was it someone else?

Too many enemies to count these days.

Losing the tail took her a few extra minutes, but it felt good to put her tradecraft to work rather than her body, and she lost the tail without any problem, taking off her wig at the same time.

If only clearing Elliot's name were so easy.

Her apartment was modest, the most she could afford on her current salary. She parked in the tiny parking lot, the edges nearly overrun with wild bushes and trees, and secured her compact Sig Sauer into its holder on her thigh. Security wasn't the greatest in this area, but the place rented by the month, and since she didn't know how long this would take—plus her salary had been halved with her probation—she had to take what she could get.

Elevators were claustrophobic, so she took the un-air-conditioned stairs. Her modest one-bedroom was on the third floor and a little cardio would burn off the last of her adrenaline high. The place allowed dogs and the smell of old urine and stale beer met her nose. Nerves still on edge from Jax's appearance and the beat of the dance music still ringing in her ears, she nearly collided with her neighbor Dan as she went to open the third floor fire door.

He and Woodstock, his Pug mix, came flying through the heavy door and nearly toppled Ruby. She hit the wall with her back and Dan looked as surprised as she was.

"Sorry," he called over his shoulder. His long, thin, red hair flew out around his head as he and the dog descended the stairwell. "Pee emergency!"

Ruby laughed as the fat Pug and her skinny owner barreled down the stairs. Not a lot of green grass around the place, but the overgrown lot behind the building served as the dog park.

Rubbing the back of her neck, Ruby continued on to her apartment door. The carpet in the hallway was worn, her door labeled 7. She hadn't brought a purse so she dug the key from inside her bra.

Her fingers hit something out of place.

She grabbed it and pulled it out.

A piece of paper with a cell number written in Jax's heavy, solid handwriting.

Damn it all to hell. How had he managed that? Slipping his number in her bra while they were in that dark hallway?

She chuckled in spite of herself. The former SEAL had some skills. Even his tailing of her car hadn't been too shabby. She was a CIA agent, after all. She'd had as much, if not more, training than he had on evading the enemy.

Shaking her head, she let herself into the apartment, tossing her key and wig on the table just inside the door.

The place was cooler than outside, but not by much. She turned on a living room lamp and headed for the fridge.

Standing in the pool of light from the refrigerator, she considered her options.

Water or water.

Crap, she'd forgotten to buy wine again. Hell, at this point, she'd settle for Kool-Aid. Anything cold and wet would do.

The refrigerator's motor kicked in, reminding her it was probably an original to the place. Hot air seeped out from under the door, blasting her toes.

Closing the fridge door, she opened the freezer. Maybe the ice cream fairy had taken pity on her and brought her some double chocolate chunk.

Nope. Her fairy, the bitch, had let her down again. No chocolate ice cream. Just ice cubes.

The cold blasting her face felt damn good though. After her encounter with Jax, she needed to crawl into a freezer to cool off.

Too bad she couldn't stand in front of the fridge all night. A cold shower would have to do. Taking an ice cube from the tray, she held it against the pulse at the base of her throat, closed the freezer door, and turned around.

Her heart froze and it had nothing to do with the cold trickle of water from the cube in her hand. In the shadow of the kitchen doorway, backlit from the living room lamp, stood a broad man.

In his hand, he held a knife.

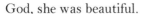

God, she was beautiful.

Elliot Hayden stood for a moment in the doorway and stared at the woman in front of him. The kitchen was dark except for the sliver of moonlight coming through the tiny window over the sink. It sliced across her dark hair, startled eyes, and the pale skin of her neck.

He'd counted on her to free him from prison. She'd hadn't been able to get the job done, and he'd taken matters into his own hands.

Her hesitation lasted only a second. Blood red fingernails tightened on the ice cube. She drew back and hurled it straight at his face.

Instinct made him flinch, the ice cube sailing past his ear and hitting the wall. "Ruby, it's me."

She already had her gun out—a pixy of a thing—and she trained it on him. The tiny, black weapon appeared harmless but in his partner's hands, he knew it could take off both of his

balls with one shot. Her face screwed up as she held him in the
gun's sight.

Her voice came out suspicious, incredulous. "Elliot?"

He raised his hands in the air in a show of surrender. "You
were expecting Santa Claus?"

The gun lowered. She looked as if she were seeing a ghost.
"What...what are you doing here? How did you get... It's true,
isn't it?"

"What's true?"

"You broke out of prison."

"You really think a low-security facility like Moretto could
hold me?"

Her hands hung at her hips, the peashooter tapping against
her thigh. "I was working on getting the evidence we need to
get you out legitimately."

Leaning a shoulder against the doorjamb, he chuckled. "This
isn't exactly the homecoming I fantasized about."

She reached over and flipped on the light over the sink. Her
gaze slid over him and the stained and torn clothes he wore.
"You thought I'd be happy to see you?"

He'd been masquerading as a homeless man and it didn't
surprise him she hadn't recognized him at first. His face was
covered with dirt and a few days' worth of beard. The clothes he
wore, he'd stolen out of a homeless person's supply. They were
a size too big and covered in grime.

The disguise had worked well. He'd added a cane and a limp
to his public appearances. Amazing how people looked right
through you when you were one of the discarded.

He blinked to adjust his eyes to the harsh light. "Free of a
faded orange jumpsuit and chains? Yeah, I guess I did think
you'd be happy to see me."

Her shoulders drooped. She stared at the floor for a moment,
wrestling with her conscience no doubt, then walked over to
him. "I *am* glad to see you, you idiot."

He laid the knife on the counter and opened his arms. "I've
missed you so much."

She went into the circle of his arms and he hugged her. They
stayed that way for a long moment.

Partners. They'd been through everything together from the
moment they'd both joined the Agency. The Farm, their first
assignment, months in foreign countries under false identities,
all of it. When her grandmother had passed away—a woman

Ruby had been very close to—he'd been by her side back here in the States the whole time. When he'd broken his leg during a rough mission in Germany, she'd showed up for every one of his rehab treatments to egg him on and make him strong again. They'd been inseparable, right up until their last mission.

That bastard Sloan. He'd taken her away from him. Made Ruby doubt him.

He'll pay.

"Why did you do it, El?" she asked softly, her head on his shoulder. "I know it's taken longer than expected, but I would have gotten the evidence eventually to get you freed."

Eventually. What a useless word. "Jimmy Shine."

She reared back, searched his face. "Jimmy Shine? What about him?"

The fellow CIA operative had gone Hollywood a year ago and ended up getting his hands slapped by his former employer when they'd exposed the fact Shine was disclosing classified information to reporters. He'd ended up in Moretto Federal Prison too. "He's my new cell mate."

"You're kidding."

Elliot shook his head, toyed with a strand of her hair. "It was a calculated move. The Agency wanted him to take me out. I couldn't even close my eyes for fear Shine would shank me while I slept."

Confusion clouded her features. "I can see him wanting revenge for himself, but why would the Agency tell him to take you out?"

He grabbed her shoulders gently. For all of her skills and talents, she still was innocent when it came to the type of betrayal they were dealing with. Unfortunately, he couldn't divulge just how deep that betrayal might run. "Think, Ruby. They believe your boyfriend Sloan. They think I killed Abdel and was selling secrets. I know too much. *You* know too much. About Marrakech, about the Moroccan 5. I didn't realize they would go to any lengths to keep us quiet, but they will, Ruby That's why I came here—to get you. The Agency plans to dispose of us both. We have to go dark. Disappear. For good."

She broke his hold and stepped back. He could see her calculating mind hashing over the logic, the options. "First of all, Jaxon Sloan is not my boyfriend, and secondly, what does the Moroccan 5 have to do with this? That mission was closed eighteen months ago."

"All of our previous missions are a political land mine." He needed her help. Needed to get her out of here, out of Chicago, and definitely away from Sloan. That guy was probably in on all of this. "You need to trust me. Grab your go-bag and let's hit the road. I'll tell you everything once we're away from here."

Another step back. "I'm not leaving. I'm close to getting in with Little Gus, and he can find Deuce for us. You told me if we find Deuce, he can help me clear your name."

"Deuce is in the wind, you know that. And his word won't hold up against Jaxon Sloan's. You know that too."

"But you said…"

"I only told you to track Deuce down to give you hope." Couldn't she see that? He hated the hurt in her eyes, the hopelessness. "The only way to get the US government to drop the charges against me is if your boyfriend renounces his testimony. He won't, but it doesn't matter. The Agency is after us, regardless. Homeland, too. They've deemed you and I dangerous. I had to come and get you."

Her tone was flat. "What does this have to do with the Moroccan 5?"

Should he tell her? Maybe if he gave her something, she'd give a little too. "Al-Safari. I turned him."

"You what?"

"I turned him into an asset when we captured M5. He was working for me in Marrakech."

Her brain made quick work of the fact he'd lied to her. That he was still not telling her the meat of the story. He waited for her to slap him, to yell at him. Instead, she stayed emotionless. "Doing what exactly?"

No wonder the Colonel loved her as much as Elliot did. Their boss and his training had turned Ruby into the perfect spy. "I'll fill you in once we're out of here and somewhere safe."

"Did this have to do with finding Mohammed Izala?"

He nodded.

"You lied to me?"

"It went deeper than Izala."

She crossed her arms over her chest and said nothing, waiting.

"I was under orders."

Her expression went hard. "You should go, Elliot."

What? Didn't she understand? "You're coming with me, right?"

A shake of her head. "I'm going to find the evidence that

clears your name and I will use it to get Jaxon to renounce his testimony, but I'm not going on the run with you. What kind of life would that be? Always running, always looking over our shoulders." Another shake. "I won't do it. I will clear your name and then, by God, I will hunt down Mohammed Izala and bring him to justice."

"Ruby." He reached for her, but she angled away from him, coming into contact with the fridge. "I can't leave you alone. They'll kill you. You have to come with me, and you can't take on Izala on your own."

Her eyes narrowed. He could practically see steam coming out her ears. "El, you know I love you. You're the older brother I never had, but I will not go on the run with you."

Anger and disappointment warred in the pit of his stomach. Brother? He'd never wanted to be her brother, couldn't she see that? She would never understand what he'd done in Marrakech or why, but he was a true-blue American through and through. He would never betray his country. Never purposely place her in danger. "Ruby, I'm looking out for you. Like a good *brother* would do."

"I get it, El, I do, but I'm not giving up. The Agency can come after me if they want, but they'll fail. I know what I'm doing and I know I can fix this mess. If you're innocent, I will prove it. You have to believe in me."

"Of course I believe in you." Did she still believe in him though? A slice of pain went through his heart. "You and I are the best of partners, aren't we?"

She was silent for a second too long. "We were. We will be again."

"Then come with me."

She shifted her weight, glanced away. "There's something you should know. Jax is looking for you."

A cold, creeping sensation wormed its way into his belly. "*What?*"

"He found me at the club tonight, told me the Agency is keeping a tight lid on the news about your escape. They've hired him to hunt you down and bring you back as quickly and quietly as possible."

Goddamn bastard. "He came running to you before the ink was dry on the order. Big surprise."

"He said I was the first person you'd ask for help." She bit her lower lip. "He was right."

"Because you're my *partner* and you're in danger."

"I can appreciate your current mindset and I understand why you're here, but if you're not going to fill me in on the details about you and Al-Safari, you should go. I'm on probation. I can't harbor a federal fugitive, partner or not."

"I can't believe I'm hearing this. Who saved your ass in Bagdad? Jakarta? Athens?"

"You did, and I saved your ass just as many times. But you and I both know you can't run from the Agency. We can fight your conviction and bring new evidence to light through legitimate channels. I can clear your name, Elliot, but you have to let me do it my way."

That was just it. She couldn't clear his name, no matter what she believed. "They'll kill you."

"If they wanted to silence me, they would have already done it. The Agency may do a lot of shitty things in the name of freedom but they don't kill their own for acting on orders."

God, this was not the way he'd imagined this would go. "Next, you'll be calling the cops to report me."

"I would never do that."

"Wouldn't you? Kinda sounds like you don't have my back anymore, partner."

He picked up the knife and turned on his heel. Time to get out of here before that bastard Sloan showed up.

Ruby was on him before he got to the door. She grabbed his arm and slid in front of him, blocking his exit. "Promise me you'll turn yourself in."

Gritting his teeth, he gently shifted her out of his way. "No can do, Rubes. The CIA isn't going to take me down."

He jerked the door open, meeting her pretty brown eyes one last time. "Watch your back, kid. I won't be there to cover your six anymore."

"Wait."

Hope rose in his chest as she ran for the bedroom. Had she changed her mind? Was she coming with him?

Emerging a moment later, she carried a small blue duffel bag in her hand. Her go-bag.

Yes!

"Take this," she said, holding out the bag. "There's cash, some burn phones, a weapon."

Shock rippled through him, crushing the hope. He loved her so much, the thought of walking away from her undid him.

But he had to. She wasn't coming with him, no matter how badly he wanted her to.

"Thanks." He took the bag; at least it was something.

He was almost through the door when she threw her arms around him and hugged him for an all-too-brief moment. "Be careful, El. I'll keep working the case, and I swear by all that's in me, I will clear your name.

For a moment, he let her hug him, let his feelings for her rush over him. It was the one thing that had kept him going in prison. The one thing he'd allowed himself to feel. "I'm innocent, Rubes."

"I know you are." She went up on her tiptoes and lightly kissed his cheek. "I'll prove it."

A moment later, he let himself out the service door downstairs and faced an unwanted future without her.

Chapter Three

Jax sat watching Ruby's apartment building from the parking lot at the back of the building. Lights went on and off behind closed curtains, but no shadows crossed in front of the windows. Hard to tell if she was alone or not.

Spies. *Pain in the ass.*

He'd followed her from the club. At least most of the way. She'd lost him somewhere around Wacker Drive—what a name for a street. Like most big cities, Chicago's downtown was a maze and he'd never been here before. Ruby, however, had grown up in a suburb called Oak Lawn, southwest of the city.

His navigational skills were spot-on most of the time, thanks to his SEAL training, and 'lost' wasn't in his vocabulary. He didn't get lost in major metropolitan cities any more than he got lost in Middle Eastern deserts or South American jungles. It just didn't happen.

So when he got turned around in some shady South Side neighborhood, he knew he'd been had by one petite CIA operative.

He was good, but she was better.

And didn't that stick in his craw.

Thanks to the CIA chief who'd hired Shadow Force International—and him, specifically—to hunt down Elliot Hayden, Jax knew Ruby's temporary address and had already checked it out. He'd considered picking the lock on the door and letting himself in, but he knew the spy would have some kind of personal security in place. She was adept at electronics; she probably had sensors on every window and both exits. Not wanting to tip his hand and let her know he was looking for her, he'd kept his lock pick in his medical bag and waited. She'd come home from her day job, consulting with the local FBI counterterrorism group, and left for the club shortly afterward.

Her consulting job was simply a way for the CIA to make her lay low while she was on probation. They didn't want her at Langley and couldn't put her back in the field. She was one of their top UC operatives, but because they suspected she'd lied about her partner's actions—and maybe had played a part in his treasonous activities—they'd had no choice but to do something. They couldn't prove she was guilty, but in the CIA, you were never innocent. Until they'd vetted her allegiance to them and were once again assured of her loyalty, she was forced to lay low and consult.

He bet it ate at her. She probably wasn't sleeping, barely eating. He'd only spent a few days with her in Morocco but he'd seen how obsessed she got when on a mission.

Along with the lock pick in his bag were fake IDs and passports for both of them. The Central Intelligence Agency didn't want word to get out about Hayden's escape trick, and although they were in the business of covert operations, someone higher up in the US government hadn't trusted the Agency to bring Hayden in alive.

Jax's boss, Beatrice Reese, had been rather furtive about the client as well, but that was to be expected of the genius who'd formerly worked for the NSA in a special operations group that had tried to silence her. Her reach within the international intelligence world was long and deep, and she knew things that got you killed; Jax had no doubt that was why she'd changed her name and given herself a new identity before taking over Shadow Force International for the founder, Emit Petit.

When she'd called him into her office to tell him his next assignment was in Chicago, she'd been as direct as always. There was no "hi, how ya doin'?" with Beatrice. No lead-in to the mission. Just the facts, plain and simple, and the assignment.

"Elliot Hayden escaped the Moretto, Pennsylvania low-security prison three days ago," Beatrice had informed him. "You're to hunt him down and bring him back. His first target will be Agent Ruby McKellen."

"Target?" Jax had nearly come out of the seat. "As in wet job?"

"Not to kill her. To ask for assistance in staying off the radar."

Jax's too-tight lungs had relaxed a fraction. "Right. Of course. He has no money, no weapons, no ID."

"And she believes he's innocent."

Jax had shaken his head and rolled his eyes. A juvenile move, but he couldn't help it. Ruby always brought out the base side of him. "She's completely blinded by her loyalty to the jackass."

Beatrice had studied him for a moment, a light coming into her eyes. "The three of you worked closely on your mission in Marrakech, I understand."

Her source for this assignment had probably told her more than he cared to know. "Ruby and I did our jobs."

"And Elliot?"

"Killed a man in cold blood. A terrorist the US wanted to interrogate."

"Agent Hayden claimed the man came at him, tried to use his weapon against him to kill him and escape."

Jax's blood had boiled, just like it had that night when he'd realized what Elliot had done. "Hayden's a fucking liar. He didn't want that man interrogated for a reason. A reason that made me sick. It's all in my report to Justice."

Beatrice had glanced at her computer screen as if checking her notes. Which was pointless, because she had a near perfect memory of everything she read. "You claimed the man who was killed, Abdel Al-Safari, was the go-between for Hayden and a leader of AQIM, Mohammed Izala. That Hayden was selling US intelligence secrets to the Izala camp."

AQIM was a Sunni Islamist group associated with Al-Qaeda. These days, AQIM wanted to show ISIS they were still top dog and Al-Safari had been running a dangerous game, dealing with both AQIM and ISIS. Hayden had recruited the man as an asset, then found other, more lucrative uses for him.

Jax's cell rang, breaking his reverie. He fished out his phone. "Speak of the devil," he muttered to himself when he saw the caller ID. "Hey, boss. What's up?"

Even though they were on secure lines, Beatrice used his Rock Star code name. "I have new intel for you, Megadeth. A source Elliot Hayden might contact."

She'd told Jax she believed Elliot was too smart to go to Ruby since everyone assumed that's exactly what he would do. Beatrice had told him she would contact some of her sources to find other people Hayden might go to. One of her sources being former operative Zeb Riceman, who sometimes helped out with SFI missions.

Jax figured that's what Hayden was counting on—that no one would pay much attention to Ruby because they believed she was too obvious. "I'm all ears."

"Rory and Emit ran TracMap and found that Elliot Hayden did four years in the army with a man named Keon James."

TracMap was a creation of Emit Petit. A people-mapping program that showed relationships between people and groups they belonged to. The former Navy man and founder of the Rock Stars, which was simply a front for Shadow Force, knew his stuff, from weapons to computer software programs. Probably why Beatrice had gone to work for him.

"Upon completion of their military terms," she continued, "Elliot was recruited by the CIA while James stayed with the army. Two years ago, James was recruited for Army Africa and a new program called African Horizons. Army Africa works on infiltrating and taking down Al-Shabaab in East Africa, Boko Haram in Central Africa, and the Islamic State terror group in the north. Keon James joined the Military Intelligence Brigade and was stationed in Morocco."

All the lights went out in Ruby's apartment. Jax sat forward, keeping a close eye on the fire escape at the back of her apartment. "Hayden and James kept in contact, I take it?"

"A source tells me Keon James was good at getting inside the local groups and getting them to trust him. While his superiors thought he was gathering intel for them, he is suspected of actually setting up his own network to sell intelligence secrets."

"Hayden was helping him?"

"I can find nothing to confirm that. My sources claim Elliot Hayden was an outstanding operative and the commendations in his folder corroborate that fact. I asked a mutual friend of ours to do some digging and he found one connection that suggests the two were working together outside of their job parameters."

Their mutual friend had to be Zeb. The old spy had as many, if not more, nefarious connections in the world than Beatrice, and seemed to be the one person who could always find the needle in the haystack.

"Keon James disappeared about three days before your mission in Marrakech," Beatrice said.

Ruby hadn't emerged from the building. At least not from the rear fire escape. From his angle, he could see her car on the side of the lot, and that hadn't moved either.

"What is the mutual connection James and Hayden had?" Jax asked.

"Al-Safari."

"No shit. That doesn't do me much good, does it, since he's six feet under."

"Focus on Keon James."

"You said he's in the wind."

"The army believes James was kidnapped or killed by one of the terrorist groups he'd supposedly infiltrated, but if Hayden and James are guilty of selling secrets, what do you think happened to James? His disappearance occurred three days before Hayden killed their mutual friend."

Jax turned several ideas over in his head, struck on one he liked. "Someone found out what James and Hayden were up to, and they needed to shut down the operation and cover their tracks."

"That would be my assumption." Her voice was warm, like she was proud of him, and that was damn rare. Her intellect might be off the charts, but her emotional responses were usually unreadable.

She might have been NSA once, and a so-called analyst at that, but damn if he believed that was all she'd been. She was a spy at heart.

He heard her typing, the click of keys muted in the background. "A few minutes ago, I located a man matching Keon James' description. He goes by the moniker Deuce. While in the army, Keon was known as Deuce because of a bet he made while playing poker."

"Where is he?"

"Chicago."

Sweat dotted his forehead as he sat in his hot rental, his mind circling with new understanding. He'd assumed the CIA had assigned Ruby to Chicago to get her away from Langley. Apparently, there was more to it than that.

Ruby had requested Chicago.

He'd known she was working an unsanctioned mission to clear Hayden's name, and now it all became clear.

She was looking for Deuce.

But why? If Keon James was guilty of the crimes Hayden

had been charged with, how would that clear Hayden's name?

Another option, one that sat like acid in his stomach, took hold. Was Ruby searching for James because she was taking up the reins of Hayden's operation?

Should have bugged her apartment.

Hayden had disappeared off the grid the moment he'd escaped Moretto. Not one sighting of him in the past forty-eight hours. The spy was damned good at his job and it was going to take every one of Jax's skills to bring him in.

No Moretto when I'm done with you this time, Hayden. This time, I'll make sure you go straight to Supermax in Colorado.

Ruby was the key to making that happen. Hayden would show up here, Jax was sure of it. The only way to catch the spy was to get a listening device in that apartment so he'd know when Hayden came to her for help.

Thing was, it might also prove Ruby was in on the whole blasted mess.

His gut crawled. "I need a photo of James and any other info you can get for me."

"Sending it to your phone," Beatrice said. "Your friends in Chicago are running TracRec to see if they can get a facial match and location. They'll be in contact as soon as they get a hit."

His "friends" were Emit, the founder of SFI, and Rory Tephra, a man who'd once been a SEAL, then done assassinations for the CIA. Rory's last gig had been taking out Beatrice. Somehow, she'd turned Rory around and he now worked for them.

Weird shit.

TracRec was another of Emit's creations. Emit, Rory, and Colton—a former SEAL whose real name was Colton Bells—were all in Chicago setting up the new Midwest Rock Star Security headquarters. The building had been purchased and was undergoing some serious security upgrades before they opened the doors and began taking clients come the first of the month.

TracRec mimicked the government's satellite surveillance program. It used traffic cams, ATM cams, and a host of public surveillance cameras as well to find suspects.

"Roger that."

"Need backup?" Beatrice asked.

"I'm good. I'll haul your boss's butt into it if I need a wingman."

Humor laced Beatrice's voice. "He could use some field time. Cal says he's getting soft."

"That's what happens when you spend your days creating high-tech software instead of jumping out of planes."

They shared a laugh and disconnected.

Reaching over, Jax opened his medical kit. His new ID said he was Jackson Hughes, MD. Once upon a time, he'd planned to take the oath to do no harm. Then he'd ended up in the SEALs and tallied twenty-seven kills.

When his SEAL days came to an end after Marrakech, Beatrice had offered him a job with Rock Star Security, the front for Shadow Force International. The Rock Stars were real—a band of former SEALs who'd been kicked out or had willingly left their teams and wanted to put their skills to work in the commercial sector. The bodyguard business was lucrative and booming, hence the expansion into Chicago. They already had a lineup of clients waiting for the office doors to open.

Jax had gone for irony when picking his Rock Star name: Megadeth. Rock Star Security gave him purpose again. He put Marrakech far behind him. The rejection of his family, his SEAL team, and even Ruby behind him.

When Beatrice asked him to join the Shadow Force Team, a black ops team performing private intelligence, security, and paramilitary missions for those who had nowhere else to turn, he'd wrestled with the idea. He liked doing security work, liked protecting this clients. Yet, he missed fieldwork, missed getting his hands dirty.

So here he was, ready to play Dr. Hughes while digging out a Shadow Tracker, a small GPS he could slap under the wheel well of Ruby's rental car. He found a couple of tiny listening devices and collected them as well.

Hiding one in the palm of his hand, he exited his car, locked up, and went to pay Agent McKellen a surprise visit.

<hr />

She was going back to the club.

Pulse knocking around after Elliot's visit, Ruby considered her options as she stared at herself in her bathroom mirror.

Call her handler and turn El in.

Go with him.

Go back to the club and get that damn information from Little Gus.

Call Jax.

No way. That last one wasn't an option. He could be the last man on Earth and she wouldn't give him the satisfaction.

Jax and satisfaction. If that combo didn't conjure a whole host of unbidden memories.

Stop it. She wiped at the eyeliner that was smudged under her eye. Jax wanted Elliot's head on a platter. She was not going to let that happen.

The three of them had been good together. Until they weren't. Elliot was like her brother, smart and always looking out for her. He'd taught her the craft in ways Langley had never thought of. Always cool and levelheaded in the tight places and the most dangerous moments, what he'd said was true. She tended to jump first and get her ass in trouble. Elliot had always been there to bail her out.

He was, without a doubt, the best spy she'd ever worked with, and she'd worked with a few who would sell out their grandmothers with a straight face.

Jax, on the other hand, was bold and egotistical and didn't back down from anything. The opposite of finesse. Not that he couldn't deceive or use his charm to get what he wanted. He had some skills she admired, and his SEAL training had taught him plenty of subterfuge, but his abilities were more physical-based. Undercover operatives relied on their mental skills and cunning as much as anything. They were actors. She was an actor. There was an art to being an agent. It took more brain than brawn.

Of course, Jax could be sneaky, i.e. the handwritten number he'd snuck into her bra while he'd been distracting her with that very physical body of his.

Ugh.

How could I let myself be sidetracked by him?

She knew how. He might have made her crazy, but her body wanted him. He was like French pastries to a woman on a diet.

Her diet had lasted a long, long time.

And now he'd come along and tempted her, offering her an unlimited supply of his special brand of pastry.

Ruby licked her lips.

Enough. She had to quit thinking about him. Elliot was out there on the run and she needed to get back to the club before

Little Gus was too drunk or too high to give her the info she needed on Deuce.

Her hair was limp thanks to the heat and humidity, so she flipped her head upside down and gave it a quick spray with her super hold hairspray. She couldn't bear putting the wig back on. She blotted her damp skin, reapplied eyeliner, and touched up her lips.

Good enough.

Her Sig was once more secured in its holster, her cell phone hidden away as well. She'd just started to turn off the living room lamp when someone knocked at her door.

Had Elliot come back? She rushed to the door and checked the peephole.

God Almighty.

She closed her eyes. *You've got to be kidding me.*

Didn't this guy ever give up?

She couldn't exactly ignore him, but the thought held appeal. Knowing Jax, he'd bust in anyway.

"What do you want?" she said through the door. "I already told you, I don't know where he is and I wouldn't help you find him if I did."

"Testy. You need some sleep, Ruby, or maybe something else. I can help with that last one, you know. Work that stress right out of you."

God, yes! Her nipples puckered at the thought. Steadying one hand against the door, she mentally scolded her traitorous breasts. "Go to hell, Jaxon. Please."

He chuckled. "Are you going to open the door or are we going to have this conversation in front of your neighbor. His dog is cute. Fat, but cute. He might wonder about you if I start talking louder and saying things like…"—his voice rose an octave—"I know how you like that spot on the back of your neck kissed. How it sends you into orbit. And how about the inside of your thigh. Oh, yeah, that's a favorite, isn't it, Ruby?"

"I hate you," she said more to herself than him as she unlocked the door. Jerking it open, she saw Dan letting himself and Woodstock into their place across the hall. A frown creased his forehead, so Ruby smiled and waved at him while speaking to Jax through gritted teeth. "Stop acting like a child."

His bold eyes met hers. "Let me in."

Be strong. "No."

A smirk caught at the corner of his mouth. "Why not?"

"Because, like I just said, I hate you."

"Is everything okay?" Dan called.

Woodstock strained at the leash toward Jaxon. Dumb dog, she should be barking at him. Growling. Instead, she looked at him with her big, liquid eyes and panted like he was her favorite dog treat.

"Fine," Jax said, giving Dan a casual wave.

Ruby kept up her fake smile as she spoke to Jax under her breath. "We're not fine. You need to leave."

He swung those sultry eyes back to her. "But I have something you want, Ruby."

Boy, did he. There was a whole beautiful glass case of pastries in that gaze, in his teasing tone. "And what would that be, Jaxon?"

"I know how to find Hayden."

"Is that so?"

Dan tugged Woodstock through their door. A second later, it closed and Ruby heard the flip of the deadbolt.

Thanks for ruining my one normal relationship. "Then I suggest you run along and go find him."

She started to slam the door shut, but he stopped it with one beefy arm. His eyes narrowed. "He was here, wasn't he?"

"What? No."

"Damn it." He pushed into the room, forcing her back, his gaze scanning her small apartment. "You were hiding him here. I can't believe it. He was right under my nose and I let him get away."

How did he guess Elliot had been there? "I was *not* hiding him."

His gaze swung to hers, his eyes hard as chunks of coal. "But you've seen him, haven't you? You've talked to him."

For the second time that night, she needed to kick a man out of her apartment. Something about that seemed wrong since she hadn't had a relationship—outside of that one night with Jaxon—in years. "You can't just force your way in here and accuse me of aiding a federal fugitive."

"The hell I can't."

The small space seemed even smaller as he circled the living room, checked the kitchen, bedroom, and bath. He took up too much space.

"Happy?" she asked as he returned to scowl down at her. "I

told you he isn't here. He's far too smart and savvy to come to me for help."

"He's clever, I'll give you that, but he's also in love with you. Love makes people do stupid things."

Her chin came up. Jax didn't know the first thing about real partnerships. What she and Elliot had wasn't that kind of love.

"I wouldn't know."

He shook his head. "Such a liar."

Yes, she was. Came with the territory. But not about this. She and Elliot were partners, not lovers.

Maybe it was time to go on the offensive. Do a little intel gathering. "So how *are* you going to find Elliot?"

"I have a lead. A guy who goes by the name of Deuce. But forget about it." He opened the door and strolled through. "I'll figure it out on my own."

Deuce. Shit. "You have contact information for that guy?"

Jax glanced back over his shoulder, turned and leaned an arm against the doorjamb. His face came within inches of hers as he studied her reaction carefully. "We could work together, Ruby. Share our intel."

Never in a million years.

She bit her lip, considered her options.

Go back to the club and hope like hell she would attract Little Gus's attention.

Stay here and flirt with the man whose attention she already had.

Hard choice.

She stepped back. "Why don't you come in, Jaxon?"

CHAPTER FOUR

On his loop of the place looking for Hayden, Jax managed to stick three bugs around the small apartment.

He hoped like hell Ruby wouldn't find them. Knowing her, she probably did a sweep every night before she went to bed.

He'd made sure to put one as close to that bed as possible.

Which was probably a straight shot to Torture Land. Hearing her moving around in bed would only fuel his already out-of-control fantasies.

He just hoped she went to bed alone.

Because if not, then he would have to kill someone.

"Who's this Deuce person?" Ruby said.

She stood near the door, arms crossed over her breasts. He couldn't tell if she was pissed or curious. Maybe both.

"You tell me. Isn't he why you're in Chicago? You're looking for him, right?"

Her lips thinned ever so slightly. "I'm in Chicago helping an FBI special taskforce with counterterrorism."

He plunked down on the worn sofa that must have come with the place. Ruby didn't seem like the midcentury, green-tweed-with-cigarette burns kind of person, but beggars couldn't be choosers, right? "You were at that club tonight looking to score a meeting with Augustus "Little Gus" Nelson, who just happens to know Deuce, aka Keon James. Is that part of your counterterrorism gig?"

Her features remained stoic. "I went to the club to have a drink and dance. Having a good time is not illegal."

"Cut the crap, Ruby. I know about your personal mission to

clear Hayden's name and I know that Keon James and your partner were working together to sell military secrets."

"What?" She scoffed. "You always think the worst of everyone."

He stared at her, let her words hang out there, and propped his feet on the coffee table. It wasn't untrue. He did tend to think the worst of people because people constantly disappointed him. In big, big ways. This, however, wasn't about what he thought. It was about evidence. Proof. The connections between Elliot Hayden and Keon James couldn't be ignored.

"We both want to find this Deuce guy," Jax said. "Let's work together."

She chuckled, a hard, humorless sound that echoed off the ceiling. "The last time we worked together, I lost my partner and ended up on probation. Why in the hell would I work with you again?"

Ouch. Bitter much? "Did Hayden try to get you to help him when he dropped by?"

"I'm not helping Elliot. I didn't even know about his escape until you told me."

"So you said. Hard for me to believe, but okay, I'll give that one to you if you admit you're in Chicago to find Deuce."

"What do you know about him?"

He refused to show his irritation with her non-answer. "I know he's an old army buddy of Hayden's and that he's suspected of selling intelligence secrets. An equal opportunity traitor, sounds like. He also knew Abdel Al-Safari, which seems like a damning coincidence, don't you think?"

She chewed the inside of her cheek. "Deuce can clear Elliot's name, so you go ahead and find him."

"Is that what Hayden told you?"

Her dark eyes locked on his. "Do you know where Deuce is?"

"I'll have his exact coordinates soon."

"But you haven't found him yet."

"Neither have you, apparently."

A buzzing came from her thigh. She reached down, drew up the hem of her dress, and gave him an eyeful of leg. His pulse hopscotched as he took in all of that smooth, sexy skin and the holster she had strapped there. A compact Sig Saur rested in the black holster along with a cell phone.

She pulled out the cell, caught him ogling her leg and gave him a sneer. Then she stomped off to the bedroom where she shut the door with a sharp *whack.*

SEAL training had taught him how to move his big body soundlessly. He avoided the creak in the floor he'd noticed earlier and scooted over to the closed door, setting his ear against it to listen.

"Yes, sir," he heard Ruby say. "I understand...no, I didn't know until tonight. I'll keep an eye out... Yes, I understand how this could affect my future."

There was a long pause as whoever was on the other end of the conversation—her boss at Langley?—rambled.

There were more 'yes, sirs' and 'no, sirs', Ruby making out like she was a team player and would never contemplate rocking the boat. Jax mentally scoffed. If the person on the other end knew Ruby at all, they had to know this was an exercise in futility.

"Sir, if you would just let me—"

She was interrupted again and Jax could almost feel her frustration through the wooden door. The sound of her heels pacing across the worn carpeting filled the silence on her end as she listened.

Suddenly, she was saying her goodbyes, her voice close to the door. With quick, yet still soundless movements, he scooted away, heading for the kitchen.

He grabbed the fridge door and opened it like he'd been looking for something to eat when she jerked the bedroom door open and stomped out.

Nice ploy, but the fridge was empty. He closed it and hurriedly opened the freezer.

Ice cubes. That was it.

What did she eat?

"What are you doing?" she demanded from behind him.

"Ordering pizza, it looks like," he said, facing her. "Where's the food?"

She grabbed him by the arm and tried to angle him toward the door. "You can grab something on your way home."

Kicking him out, was she? He rooted his feet in place, her body slamming into him. "We need to discuss what we're going to do when I locate Keon James. Could be a long night."

He threw in a grin, partially to irritate her, partially because she was still attempting to get him moving out of her kitchen and toward the door. He wasn't going anywhere, but he did like the touch of her hands on his back.

She gave up, throwing her hands into the air and letting out an aggravated noise from the back of her throat. "Fine. You want pizza, there's a good place three blocks from here. Deep-dish, Chicago-style pizza that weighs about six pounds. But they don't deliver." She leaned against the counter and started peeling off her strappy heels. "You have to pick it up."

"What's their number? I'll order one and we'll go get it."

She combed her fingers through her hair and rattled off a number. "I'm going to go change clothes."

He ordered, feeling smug about her surrender, and then looked for plates.

None.

How was she surviving?

At least there were paper towels. He'd worked with less.

She materialized from the bedroom in sweats, and damn, if she didn't look just as appetizing in them as the slinky dress.

Not that he would have minded if she'd kept that little number on. He had some pretty clever ideas on how he'd wanted to work her out of that barely-there dress.

Progress was progress, though. She was finally willing to work with him.

"Is there a convenience store nearby?" he asked. "We need drinks."

"The pizza place sells 2-liters."

"And you have no glasses to pour the pop in."

"True. There's a Hop-n-Shop right around the corner."

"Cool." He headed for the door. "We'll hit that first, then snag the pizza."

She flopped down on the couch. "Can you do it? I'm beat. I'm going to wash my face and close my eyes for a minute."

Right. "Don't screw with me, Ruby."

Her gaze met his, and he saw the utter exhaustion in her eyes. "I'm not, Jax. It's been another long day in a string of long days. I'm tired and hungry and it would be nice to sit here for a moment and veg out."

He almost believed her. Her shoulders were slumped, her face drawn. He wasn't used to seeing her vulnerable. That primal urge to take care of her kicked in. "Don't even think of leaving."

She gave him a tiny smile. "I'm too tired to leave. I'll make a list of ideas of what we should do to find Elliot while you're gone."

He fished his keys out of his front pocket. "I'll be back in a few."

Downstairs, he let himself into his car and waited.

Five minutes later, he was rewarded for his patience when Ruby left by the front door.

It was easy to fake out Jax.

Ruby had thrown on sweats over her dress and made sure not to mess up her makeup. She skipped the wig, fluffing her hair with her fingers. She knew if she played the exhaustion card and looked the part, the male in Jax would come to the rescue.

She had to get back to the club and find Little Gus. Tonight. She couldn't stand the thought of Elliot running around alone and on the lam. Not that he couldn't take care of himself, but the sooner she got the proof she needed, the sooner she could get his ass off the streets and back where it belonged.

Working beside her.

Even though he'd lied to her, she knew he was a good agent. A good man. There was more to the story; once she cleared his name, he could come home and they would hash it out.

She sped through the streets of Chicago, wondering where Elliot was. The tall buildings and street lights felt like home to her since she'd grown up in the area. For someone who hadn't, it could be an overwhelming place. A dangerous one too.

While she loved her job and the travel it required, she'd missed this place. Memories of baseball games with her brothers and trips to the Shedd Aquarium with her mother filled her head. Her dad, a history professor, had taken her on weekend jaunts to all the old buildings and historical sites.

The art, the food, the museums and libraries—for her, Chicago wasn't just a city. It was the hum of life under her skin. It was friends and family and happiness.

Tonight, it was risk and uncertainty. For her, for Elliot, even for Jax.

Ugh, how that man got under her skin. When he was in the same room, she couldn't think, couldn't breathe. Her brain cells went on hiatus around him while her hormones went into overdrive.

Jax was risk, uncertainty, danger. Three things she typically thrived on, which was why she'd let down her guard with him in Marrakech. They'd grabbed Al-Safari and their cover was intact. Izala had no idea they were in country, stealing his right-hand man out from under his nose. All that was left was to get Abdel out of the country and for her to confirm Izala's location so her boss could call in the SEALs to take him out.

She'd nailed her twenty-first successful CIA mission in the field and was on a high, ready to go after the big fish—Izala—next and make it twenty-two. Jax was there with his bedroom eyes and sexy swagger, offering her a one-night stand, a no-strings attached interlude. It was better than champagne. Better than another honorable mention in her file at Langley. She'd been working her ass off for five years with no time for relationships. Seriously. Five *long* years.

The one night she let herself lose focus, the one night she allowed herself to seduce and be seduced by the most gorgeous man she'd ever met, she'd nearly lost everything she'd worked for. She'd certainly lost her mind.

Never again.

The nightclub came into view and Ruby found a parking spot a few blocks down. It was nearing midnight, but the streets were lined with partygoers, coming and going from the clubs and restaurants lining the streets. Hopefully, Little Gus was still inside Club Z and hadn't moved on to one of the other places nearby.

Ruby locked her car and headed for the back door and pounding bass of the club. A couple of college-aged guys going the opposite direction made some lewd comments about her and invited her to join them. She ignored their stupidity and kept going.

One of the boys didn't take the hint, and jogged up behind her, grabbing her by the arm. "Hey, baby, come on. You're obviously looking for a good time and me and my buddies can give it to you."

How original. Ruby snatched the fingers on her bicep, gave a jerk and twisted. Bones and tendons popped, the kid howled, and next, his knees kissed the pavement.

"How's that for fun?" she asked, releasing him and continuing on.

Swearing and whining followed after her. She turned the corner to the rear entrance and saw a shadow move in her peripheral vision—the club's beefy bouncer, a gold nose ring flashing under the pale glow of the backdoor light.

She stopped, held up her hand with the club's stamp on it. He knew her after she'd been here three nights in a row and had slipped him some cash to ask around about Deuce. He nodded at her, then glanced behind her. "The friend you was asking about?" he said, his dark skin damp with sweat.

A tingle of anticipation touched the base of her spine. "Yes?"

He cocked his head toward the door. "Got here a few minutes ago."

Damn. Thank God, she'd come back, regardless of what Elliot had said.

Dipping into her bra, she found the fifty hidden there and slipped it to the bouncer. "What's he wearing?"

"Don't worry," the bouncer said, tucking the tip out of sight. "He'll find you."

"He better." She winked at him, but it was a promise, not a flirt. "Or I'll be back for that."

He eyed her as if wondering whether or not she was serious. A lot of other men had wondered about her warnings as well, and a few of them had learned the hard way that she never made idle threats.

Inside, the party was going strong, the flashing lights on the dance floor keeping an erratic rhythm with a hip-hop, techno dance song. Ruby skirted the floor, looking for her target.

She only had one picture of Keon James, aka Deuce, and that was of a clean cut guy in an army uniform from three years ago. Elliot had told her Deuce didn't look anything like that anymore, but he didn't have a more recent photo. James worked a lot of undercover assignments for Army Africa and had changed his appearance accordingly. The last time she'd seen Elliot, he'd claimed the guy currently had an afro and beard, and wore three crosses around his neck. One for each of his friends killed in battle.

Deuce had disappeared right before the Marrakech fiasco, and while Elliot claimed it was because Deuce feared Al-Safari would blow his undercover identity, Ruby worried that he'd been part of the double-cross that had landed Elliot behind bars.

A double-cross Jax knew nothing about and Ruby couldn't prove.

Yet.

She made her way to the bar, waiting, waiting, waiting for Deuce to find her.

Nothing happened.

As an undercover agent, she was used to staying in the shadows, watching people, blending in rather than standing out. But if she wanted to find Keon James before Jax found her again, she had to get things moving. Like her hips.

Which meant another trip to the dance floor.

Her travels through Europe had taught her many things. The one tool she had found most useful was the ancient art of moving her body.

The musical number was a slower, grinding hip-hop song. Not her favorite, but it would do. She was just about to slip out to the dance floor when a hand landed on her waist.

For a split-second, she thought Jax had already followed her back to the club. She turned to tell him to bug off and found herself staring into the coal-black eyes of a man she assumed was Keon James.

"Heard you were looking for me," he said, the smell of beer wafting from him.

A sense of relief took root in her belly, but his expression didn't bode well. "I'm not here to cause you trouble, I just need to talk to you for a moment."

His pause was long, calculated. His hand prodded her away from the crowd. "Let's go."

She tried leading him outside, but he stopped her at the storage closet near the manager's office and shoved her inside. The scent of cleaning products chuffed at her nose.

"Elliot Hayden needs your help," Ruby said under the florescent light. "You knew Abdel Al-Safari and what he was doing with—"

Deuce's afro shuddered slightly as he shook his head. "I'm not doing nothing for Elliot Hayden and you best stop asking people about me, you hear? I've got terrorists gunning for my ass as well as the US Army and you come sniffing around here, bringing trouble with you? What kind of bitch are you, anyway?"

"Who's after you? Which terrorist? Izala? Why didn't you go back to your headquarters and have them reassign you?"

A long finger pointed at her nose. "I couldn't go back. There was shit going down in our unit and I couldn't trust anyone. My head was on the chopping block and Elliot knew it as well as I did. He can tell you. Hell, he was probably behind it, that two-faced son-of-a-bitch. He promised if I got in good with Izala, that when the shit hit the fan, the CIA would take care of me. Now look. Here I am, on the run, and I can't trust nobody. Izala's coming for my ass, sure as shit."

"You trusted me enough to talk to me."

"I know who you are, bitch. Elliot didn't take care of me, so now you're going to."

"What do you mean?"

"I mean, you're going to get me out of this fucking mess or you're going to die tonight."

Nice. "You're going to have to explain to me exactly what this 'fucking mess' is before I can help you."

Deuce made a grab for the door handle. "Ask your partner."

"Wait." Ruby jammed her foot out to stop the door from opening. "My partner broke out of prison and is on the run. I can't ask him, and I need your help to clear his name. I know he was running Abdel Al-Safari as an asset. Were you in on that?"

"Clear his name? You've got to fucking be kidding me. After what he did, you want me to help you clear his name? You got balls, lady."

He shoved her backward, smacking her into the metal shelf. "If he's out of jail, you tell him I'm looking for him. And you get one of your bosses to guarantee my safety, asap. I'll tell them everything they want to know, but I need help. Like yesterday."

"Deuce, wait," she called as he went out the door, but the words were lost in the heavy bass echoing in the close quarters of the hall.

One minute he was threatening her life if she didn't help him; the next he was running away. Elliot had done a similar thing. Could this "fucking mess", as Keon had called it get any weirder?

She started to follow him, her heels sliding on the greasy floor, when she suddenly found herself surrounded by the three boys from earlier.

The one she'd put on the ground led the posse. "Well, well, look who we have here."

Seriously? She didn't have time for this. Deuce was disappearing up the stairs that led to the private suite behind the mirrors. "Move, Junior. I have business with someone."

The boys formed a wall of testosterone. Junior rubbed his hands. "Business? Like fucking some guy in the storage closet?"

He glanced at his buddies. "We tried to take you somewhere nice for a party, but hey, whatever. Storage closet it is."

There was a lot of stupid grinning and posturing like the three of them were going to take revenge.

So not going to happen.

Roughing up Junior outside was one thing. Beating up him and his friends inside the club where there were cameras and witnesses was another. She didn't need trouble with the owner of the club or the cops.

"Alrighty, boys." She cocked a finger at them. "Follow me."

It was like leading frat boys to beer. Hopped up on their own stupidity, the three of them practically salivated as they trailed after her.

All she had to do was get them inside the storage room, bust their balls, and lock them in. Thirty seconds tops.

Which might still be too long. But if Deuce had gone upstairs, he hadn't left the building yet. She still had a chance to talk to him.

"I wouldn't do that if I were you, boys," a deep voice said from the shadows near the back door. A hulking frame emerged and Ruby saw a smirk on Jax's face. "She'll eat you up and spit you out."

Junior sneered. "Shut up, old man." His good hand dropped onto the top of Ruby's shoulder. "Get your own. She's ours."

"You really shouldn't have said that," Ruby murmured.

And then, as expected, all hell broke loose.

CHAPTER FIVE

Old man, huh? Apparently Jax needed to teach these fuckwits a lesson.

"Take your hand off her, half-pint," he said and got the exact reaction he was hoping for.

The kid took his hand off Ruby all right.

And took a swing at him.

Poor kid didn't stand a chance. Not only did Jax outweigh him by a good thirty pounds—all muscle—but the way he telegraphed his punch, the fucker had never been in a real, down-and-dirty street fight in his life. On top of that, Jax had already smelled the alcohol fumes wafting off the kid and his friends from three feet away.

So as half-pint went roundhouse on him, he grabbed the kid's fist and used all of that drunken, angry momentum to smash the fist into the wall.

The kid crumpled in a heap of screams. *Baby.*

As Jax whirled around to take on the next boy, he saw he didn't have to.

Ruby's high-heeled foot was in one of their stomachs. The flat of her hand was connecting with the other one's nose. She was stretched out end to end, like a ballet dancer for the single flash of a disco ball, and then, *bam.* Both culprits ended up on the floor.

Brushing her hands together, she did a causal glance over her handiwork. Her targets had joined their friend, writhing, crying, and bleeding at her feet.

"Clean this up, will you?" she said, heels clicking on the tile floor as she headed for the stairs.

"Where are you going?" he called, jogging after her.

She spun around and pointed a finger in his face, speaking barely over the music. "Do not follow me. You've already screwed up enough of my life."

Yowza. Harsh. The burn of guilt lit up his solar plexus. *Don't let it show.* "Your pizza's getting cold," he said and grinned.

She huffed out a breath and circled back toward the stairs. "Stop following me, Jaxon. I'm not helping you."

Keep dreaming, honey. "What did Keon James say to you?"

His words brought her up short on the bottom step. She seemed to think about it for a moment, then glanced over her shoulder at him. "I'm not sure."

What the hell did that mean? He leaned closer, making sure she heard him. "That was him in that room with you, right? What did he say?"

She started climbing again. "Don't worry about it."

Jax went after her, ignoring her stint of complaints about him tagging along. Two young women dressed in sequins and not much else came down the stairs, slowing to smile at him.

"Hey," one of them said.

He smiled and nodded back. "Ladies."

Giggling ensued. Ruby stomped back down a stair and smacked him on the shoulder. "Pay attention here."

"What?" he said, warming to the fact she was jealous and hated him paying attention to anyone else. "You told me to get lost."

Sequins 1 and 2 continued on, shooting him 'come-find-us' looks over their shoulders as they descended to the dance floor.

Ruby was on the step above him, which, thanks to her heels, brought her eye-to-eye with him when he stopped gawking at the sequin sisters and turned to face her.

"You're pathetic," she said over the music.

"And you're jealous."

Outrage fired in her eyes. She started to spit some of that at him, but bit her bottom lip instead. Then she turned on her heel and jogged up the stairs, skirting other club goers.

Jax stood, watching her hips sway under the slinky dress as she hustled away from him. Since when did Ruby not have a comeback?

More people were coming and going, creating a traffic jam on the stairs. Over the side of the railing, he saw a couple of security guys escorting the three fuckers he and Ruby had leveled out the backdoor of the club. The kid with the bloody nose was yelling and swinging a finger in his direction. He gave the kid a salute. *Lucky you didn't end up with more than a broken nose.*

If he'd had his way, all three of them would be in the hospital.

Whoa, buddy. Take it down a notch.

As Beatrice kept reminding him, he couldn't let his anger management issues cause problems for SFI.

Managing his anger was the least of his worries at the moment, and really, since the source of his immediate anger was hightailing it away from him straight into a clusterfuck of trouble, what choice did he have but to go after her?

Taking the stairs two at a time, he caught sight of her dress in the crowd on the terrace overlooking the dance floor.

I should have gone after Deuce myself instead of hanging back to watch Ruby's six.

When that stupid kid had touched her, all of Jax's instincts had gone ballistic. Talk about anger flooding his system and making him see red. Ruby could take care of herself; she'd proven that. But something inside him drove him to protect her anyway. That caveman in him—that's what she'd called him when she'd dressed him down in front of the Justice Department the day he'd given his testimony against Elliot.

Yeah, he was jealous of the bastard. So what? Elliot had been Ruby's partner for five years. Five years of being with her day in and day out, learning her secrets, sharing her life. They might not have ever done the nasty, but Jax knew Elliot had tried. That he would keep trying to get Ruby into his bed.

One night with Ruby and all of Jax's instincts had gone straight to possession central. She was the drug in his blood he couldn't shake. No amount of abstinence was going to clear his system. No prescription for another drug would do the trick. He wanted her, now and forever.

Up ahead, she looked back over her shoulder and caught Jax staring at her. Her eyes narrowed and she mouthed something he couldn't read. Probably another threat to stay away, go home, leave her be.

Not happening.

Tweaking his big body sideways, he sidestepped a couple making out against the back wall. Ruby stopped in front of a door with two security guards in front of it. Both men were Jaxon's size, wearing navy blue suits and sunglasses.

Ruby said something to one of them and the guy shook his head, motioned for her to get lost.

Ruby being Ruby, no wasn't in her vocabulary. Turning up the wattage, she smiled seductively at the guard and Jax stopped, hiking himself up against the wall to watch.

Her red lips moved and she gave the guard a pout with a little exaggerated hip jut. Nothing about the man's demeanor changed overtly, but Jax saw it anyway. The way he paused, hesitated, for a fraction of a second.

Ruby raised her hand and ran a finger along the suit's collar, slow, seductive, as she spoke to him.

The man caught her wrist and leaned down to bark something in her face.

Time to stop this before she gets into real trouble.

Jax had just stepped forward when the crack of a gun echoed through the club.

Bam, bam, bam!

The music came to an abrupt stop. Screams ripped through the club, echoing off the high ceiling. People ran; shoving, tripping, jumping over others.

In the commotion, Jax lost sight of Ruby.

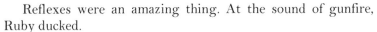

Reflexes were an amazing thing. At the sound of gunfire, Ruby ducked.

As he drew his weapon, the guard knocked her backward, out of his way. Her right ankle went sideways and she tumbled into a couple passing right behind her.

In their panic, they tripped her. She hit the floor hard, a grunt escaping her lips from the impact and sharp pains shooting from her palms up into her wrists. Hands and feet pummeled her as people ran past her, over her. The air was knocked out of her lungs, one of her shoes was knocked off her foot, and something heavy hit her in the back of the head.

In her peripheral vision, she saw the door open, a host of booted feet stampeding out of Little Gus' private party.

Who had fired the shots? Had anyone been hurt?

She curled up, making herself as small as possible and tried to scoot to the wall. Above the din of frightened, hysterical club goers, she heard Jaxon yelling her name.

"Ruby!"

Bam, bam, bam. More gunfire. Fresh screams and stampeding feet reverberated around her. Half of the lights suddenly went out.

A return *pop, pop, pop* mimicked the earlier gun rhythm. A second shooter returning fire?

While her body tried to hide, her brain analyzed. Gang related? Or something else?

In the dark, a hard shoe connected with Ruby's ribcage. The air flew out of her lungs, and she curled tighter, rolling to her right.

Where is that damn wall?

She had to get her back to it, find cover.

"Ruby!"

Jax's voice broke through the chaos like a bell, a beacon in the maelstrom.

"Here!" she yelled, finally touching the sweet, cool solidness of the wall and sitting up against it. Raising one hand above her head, she waved it for all she was worth as legs blurred past her in the darkness. "I'm here, Jax!"

The shooting had come from her left, from the second private suite. Not the one Little Gus had been in. At least she thought that's where it had originated—the acoustics in the club resonated to accentuate the music, causing sound to play tricks on the ears.

For a half a second, she thought she caught sight of Jax, fighting upstream against the onslaught of the crowd, a wave of arms and legs surging toward the stairs.

Ruby's left elbow tingled and she felt a warm, sticky substance running down her arm. There was no time to worry about the cuts and bruises covering her body—she needed to get out.

Her analytical brain cut through her flight impulse. Where was Deuce? Had he fled with the rest of the crowd?

A part of her wondered if he'd been involved with the shooting.

A man in front of her went flying to the side. Jax appeared. "Ruby. Jesus, are you okay?" he said bending down.

In the distance, she heard sirens wailing. The last of the upstairs crowd made it down, and Ruby's stomach cramped, her entire body throbbing with pain.

Jax's hands felt her arms, her shoulders, her thighs, checking her for injuries. "You're bleeding."

The place fell silent as the last of the people downstairs pushed out the front doors. Ruby lowered her voice. "That's what happens when you get trampled."

Calloused fingers lifted her face as he stared down at her. He was backlit by the emergency lights and she couldn't see his face clearly. Didn't matter. Urgency screamed in his voice, his touch. "Can you walk? We need to get out of here."

She nodded, not sure he could see it as he hoisted her up. "Where's the shooter?"

Then, whoopsie daisy, she careened to the side, her balance completely off, the fact she was missing a shoe not helping the situation.

Jax caught her, pulled her close to steady her. "It came from up here," he murmured. "We need to haul ass in case the shooter is still here."

"Deuce was up here. I need to make sure he's all right."

"Forget about Keon James. He's probably long gone. We'll catch him later." He slid an arm around her waist. "Let's go."

"Are there casualties? We can't just walk away. We could help whoever was shot until the ambulance arrives. If the shooter is still here, we can catch him."

"You're injured. The cops can handle it."

He dragged her forward, keeping an eye over his shoulder.

"There was more than one," Ruby said, losing her other shoe as she hobbled along. The ankle she'd twisted didn't want to cooperate. "I heard two distinct guns."

"Me too." Jax brought her in closer. "They probably went down the fire escape, but one or both perps could still be up here."

He smelled good, like a spice bomb of cinnamon, bergamot, and rich leather. He felt good too. She tried not to let her mind go there, but her body was a traitor. She leaned into him, soaking up his rock-hard solidity as he steadied her down the stairs.

They were only a few feet from the front entrance when Chicago Metro officers rushed in, guns drawn.

"Hands up!" one of them yelled.

Jax and Ruby stopped in their tracks. Ruby raised her arms, and damn her left one hurt like a son-of-a-bitch, but Jax didn't loosen is grip on her.

"Jaxon Sloan, Rock Star Security," he said. "ID's in my right back pocket. I have an injured woman here, and your perps were upstairs, but they're probably long gone by now."

The cops swarmed around them. "Down on your knees," the lead officer demanded.

Through the glass window, Ruby saw press vans pulling in and people with cell phones videoing the whole thing. *Crap.* So much for low profile.

She didn't want to announce to the whole world she was CIA, but with six guns pointed at her and her vision swimming, she had to do something before she keeled over. "I'm Agent Ruby McKellen, consultant with the FBI. Contact Special Agent in Charge Richard Timms and he'll confirm my identification."

"She needs medical attention," Jax said.

The lead officer—his badge read Officer Perkins—repeated himself. "Down on your knees. Now!"

"Oh, for God's sake." Ruby started forward, ready to get in Perkins' face when she was hauled back by Jax.

"Do what he says, Ruby." His voice was low, controlled. "The sooner we resolve this with the authorities, the sooner we get back to your mission."

Sighing, she let him help her down to her knees. He kneeled next to her, both of them raising their hands.

They were pushed down to their stomachs. One of the officers ran his hands over her body, searching her for weapons.

"What do we have here?" he said, pulling out her Sig.

She clenched her teeth. She didn't like other people touching her weapons. "My gun, and once you call SAC Timms and clear this up, I'm going to shoot you with it."

The man laughed as he handed the gun to Perkins, who bagged it.

"Make sure to test her hands for gun residue," Perkins said as Ruby and Jax were hauled to their feet.

The officer who'd patted down Jax had found his ID and was on the phone verifying it.

Jax stood stock-still. "Your perps are getting away while you harass us, officer. Mighty sloppy work for Chicago PD."

Perkins snorted. "Is that so? Club security claims you and your girlfriend here beat up some customers and were looking for a gang lord. They were about to kick you out when the shots were fired from up there, where you two came down from." He pointed to upstairs, back to Ruby. "She's packing a gun. Not hard to put two and two together."

They were herded toward the front door. Perkins leaned in as they passed by him. "I suggest you two get a good lawyer ASAP."

Jax stopped, kept his gaze facing forward. "And I suggest you run for cover, because when Ruby's done putting a slug in your ass, I'm going to follow it up with another half dozen."

CHAPTER SIX

Jax was released from jail just before sunrise, emerging onto State Street in the humid morning air. Shadows danced over the concrete; a big, black Caddie idled at the curb between several white police vehicles.

As Jax walked over, Emit boosted off the side of the Escalade, his mirrored aviators reflecting Jax's image back to him. "This is not how I'd planned to introduce Rock Star Security to Chicago."

Even though Jax thought he'd done a kick-ass job controlling his anger and frustration at the club shootout, he'd earned a fine. Threatening a police officer, even if the guy was an idiot, meant that not only did his phone have a voicemail from Beatrice chewing him out, the founder and chief of SFI was waiting to pick him up from jail.

"I'll pay the fucking fine," Jax grumbled, looking around. "How's Ruby? *Where* is Ruby?"

Emit cocked a thumb at the backseat. "Feds got her out almost immediately, but she spent the last few hours at Mercy getting checked out."

The sharp edge of anger filed across Jax's skin. "How bad?"

"Mostly cuts and bruises. A bullet winged her elbow."

Shit. He refrained from punching the Escalade. "Any leads on our shooters?"

Emit glanced at two officers coming out the entrance, the breeze lifting a section of his blond hair. "I'll brief you at headquarters."

Jax climbed into the backseat, found Ruby with her head

leaning against the headrest and her eyes closed. Her elbow was bandaged, her left cheek bruised and slightly swollen. "Coffee," she said without even looking at him. "Stat."

Emit, climbing into the driver's seat, nodded. "Could use a bucket of the stuff myself."

One pit stop at the local coffee shop and they were on their way to the new Chicago branch of Rock Star Security, aka Shadow Force International, Midwest Division.

Traffic was light at this hour and they made record time getting out of the heart of the city. The new headquarters building was under construction and several contractor vans were already parked outside when they arrived. Bulletproof windows were going in, new wiring for the extensive security system Emit wanted, and Rory was overseeing the installation of the new computers.

The meeting room sat two dozen people. Cushy leather chairs surrounded a glass tabletop. Individual pop-up computer touchscreens were stationed at every place so no one had to crane their neck to look at a screen on the wall.

Jax helped Ruby into one of the chairs. Someone had loaded a side table with coffee carafes, pastries, and fruit. Jax's environmentally friendly cup was empty, so he refilled it and snagged a heaping plate of food to bring back to the table.

Ruby, dark circles under her eyes, ignored his offer of a jelly-filled donut for a cluster of grapes instead. "I need a shower and a couple hours of sleep, Emit, so can we get on with this...whatever *this* is?"

And whoa. Ruby sounded like she knew Emit. As in *knew* knew him. Not like he'd simply picked her up from the hospital because she needed a ride.

"This," Emit said, sipping his coffee as he fiddled with the touchscreen at the head of the table, "is a debriefing and client intake meeting."

"Client?" Ruby and Jax said at the same time.

"Yes. *Client.*" Emit glanced up and pinned them both with a hard look. "You're all over the news and YouTube after your little escapade last night. Ruby, you're in deep shit with the Feds and your own agency, and neither wants to touch you right now, much less provide security for you. So guess what? As of 0200 hours this fine morning, you became a Rock Star Security client."

She sat back, a flustered noise coming from her throat.

"You've got to be kidding me. I don't need a bodyguard."

Emit glanced at her elbow. "I'm well aware that you have the skills to defend yourself, but you ruffled the wrong feathers last night and someone shot at you."

"You don't know they were shooting at me," she fumed. "It could have been totally random."

Emit continued as if he hadn't heard her. "Between Beatrice filling me in, and you and I having our talk this morning at the hospital, I can tell you, you're in need of security. Your former partner is on the run from the government and there are a lot of people questioning your loyalties at this moment. I don't know who took that shot at you, but there are plenty of players on the game board. Your employer specifically requested I keep you safe and off the grid for the time being."

Jax grinned. This was good. Really good.

Ruby opened her mouth to protest, but was interrupted by a noise in the hall. A *thunk, slide, thunk, slide* was accompanied by two male voices.

"Where's your wheelchair, man? That puppy is sick. I don't know why you want to kill yourself on those crutches when you can ride in style."

Jax recognized the voice and felt a jolt of awesome. Colton Bells, codename Shinedown, was in town to help Emit get the Chicago branch up and running. Colton had been all over the place recently—DC, San Diego, and a few compass points in between. The former SEAL never stayed in one place long. Jax suspected that was due to the fact nasty people were looking for him.

"Shut up, punk," Rory, the former SEAL-turned-assassin-turned-SFI computer expert grumbled. *Thunkslide.* "A couple more months of therapy and I'll be able to take you with one hand tied behind my back."

Jax rose and met the two at the door. "I'm surprised you haven't killed him in his sleep already, Rory."

Rory grunted and shifted one of his crutches to shake Jax's hand. Colt gave Jax the manly version of hug—a chest bump and a pat on the back. "Righteous undercover work last night, brother."

"Fuck you," Jax said good-naturedly. "It was Ruby's fault."

"Hey," she complained from behind him. "I told you to leave me alone. If you hadn't followed me back to the club…"

"You might be dead," he interrupted.

Emit pulled a chair out for Rory as he introduced the mad computer scientist. He also introduced Colton to Ruby, using his code name only. Standard protocol. Because of the sensitivity of most of the SEALs' backgrounds, clients never knew real names. Ever. "Let's get to work, people," Emit said.

Once settled, Rory updated them. "Police believe the initial shots were fired into the ceiling on the second floor." He poked at his touchscreen tablet and a series of photos came up on each of their monitors along with the official police report. "Agent McKellen, you were on the second floor at the time of the shooting, correct? You told the detective who interviewed you that you didn't see anyone with a gun, or anyone fire a gun. That true?"

Ruby's head jerked up and she gave Rory a narrow-eyed glance. "Of course it's true."

He nodded. "Just checking, Agent. Don't get your undies in a bunch. It's not like CIA operatives don't fudge the truth at times to law enforcement members."

Ruby gave Jax a frown. He shrugged, completely seeing Rory's point.

Another tap of Rory's tablet brought up a video. "Surveillance footage from inside the club is sketchy since the owners purposely only have two cameras. One trained on the bar area and the other on this hallway upstairs."

The video showed the long hallway filled with people from the night before. The lighting was bad, making it nearly impossible to ID anyone. A rainbow of colors flashed in time to the music, the strobes sending a wave of light over the crowd on the balcony and going up and down the steps.

A blue beam of color rolled across the ceiling and fell on a woman in a tight dress with dark hair.

Ruby.

"This is the twenty seconds or so of footage leading up to the first shots fired," Rory said.

"How did you get all this stuff?" Ruby asked.

Rory scoffed and gave her a look that said *seriously?*

Jax leaned close to her and murmured. "He's a former spook."

"Oh," she said, eyeing Rory with new respect on her face. "Cool. I think."

The scene played out, Ruby making her way up to the guards standing outside the private room Little Gus had rented for the night. Somewhere behind the two-way mirrored glass on the dance floor side, her target had probably watched her.

Jax felt the slow burn of irritation under his skin as Ruby flirted with the guard. At one point, he wanted to look away, forced himself not to.

A flash at the edge of the camera, the reverberation of the shots, panic.

Ruby went down.

It was only a video. Ruby was okay, sitting right next to him, but he still gripped the arms of the chair, fighting the instinct that suddenly shot through him. *Get to her.*

He gritted his teeth. *I should have been closer, should have been right next to her.*

Rory stopped the video. "Any idea who the shooter might have been? Why he fired up at the ceiling?"

"Whoever he was, he wanted to clear the place," Jax offered.

Ruby rubbed her forehead. Her phone kept going off, and even though she had it on silent, he'd seen her checking it and disregarding the calls. At one point, she'd told him it was her mother, who'd seen TV footage of Ruby being arrested and had freaked out. "He wanted to stop me from talking to Little Gus."

"Who did?" Emit said.

"I don't know." She stared at the screen a moment, shrugged. "Deuce?"

"Keon James, aka, Deuce," Jax supplied to the others. "Beatrice believes he has strong ties to Elliot Hayden and I was looking for him, trying to get a lead on Hayden." He turned to Ruby. "What did he say to you in that supply closet?"

She closed her eyes for a second as if debating how much to say, how much to cooperate. She was tired—exhausted, if the strain around her eyes said anything—and maybe she was finally realizing a little help wasn't the worst thing in the world.

Her eyes opened and she rubbed the top of her thigh. "From what I know, Keon James, aka Deuce, was helping Elliot with an undercover assignment in Morocco. He disappeared right before the Marrakech fiasco, and Elliot claimed it was because Deuce feared Al-Safari would blow his undercover identity. Last night, he said a bunch of stuff that doesn't make sense to me, but it may be why he didn't want me talking to Little Gus."

Emit rocked back in his chair, pulled a coiled up Twizzler from his front pocket. Guy was addicted to the strawberry twists. "Like what?" he said before taking a bite.

Ruby also sat back, rubbed her eyes. Her mascara was smudged so badly that rubbing her eyes made no difference in the raccoon circles under them. "He said a terrorist was gunning for him—a guy by the name of Mohammed Izala, whom Al-Safari worked for. Keon also claimed the army was after him too. That he couldn't go back to headquarters or his unit because he couldn't trust anyone. He said his head was on the chopping block and Elliot knew it."

She swallowed hard, stared at the screen in front of her, avoiding all of their eyes.

She was holding back. Something had disturbed her. "What else?" Jax said.

She blew out a tight sigh, fiddled with the edge of the table. "He claimed Elliot promised him that if he got in good with Izala—a leader of AQIM—that when the shit hit the fan, the CIA would take care of him. Last night, he told me he believed everyone was after him, and Elliot had..."

"Had what?"

She stared at the table for a long moment. "He believes Elliot double crossed him."

Jax's convo with Beatrice the previous day poked his frontal lobe. "Hayden must have been running both James and Al-Safari. The two were buddies, working together with Hayden, feeding intel to Izala and anyone else who would pay for it."

"Wait...how did you know Elliot had turned Al-Safari into an..." Ruby stopped herself. "Never mind. You obviously have intel even I don't have. Anyway, we don't know what the three of them were doing."

"Mr. James was killed last night," Rory said, matter-of-factly.

Ruby went a paler shade of flat-out fried. "Killed?"

Rory touched his tablet again, a crime scene photo appearing on their screens. Keon James, lying on the ground, two bullet holes in his forehead. "His body was found in the alley behind the club shortly after the two of you were arrested."

"Oh crap," Ruby whispered.

Jax stared at the bullet holes.

"Double-tap to the head," Colton analyzed. "Execution style."

"Two to the head, one to the heart," Rory confirmed. "Assassin style. *CIA* style. Someone put two slugs in him from behind, rolled him over and put another in his heart."

All eyes swung to Ruby. She sat up straighter, gave Rory the hairy eyeball. "The CIA isn't the only one who uses that type of kill pattern."

"True," he agreed, "but Keon James wasn't killed in the crossfire by some amateur gang banger. A skilled assassin purposely put him down. Since he was dealing with the CIA, odds are one of them took him out. One of them...oh, say, such as Elliot Hayden, who escaped from prison a few days ago?"

"Elliot didn't kill him," Ruby insisted, but her voice was weak. "That's ridiculous."

Seemed pretty damn coincidental to him. "Elliot wanted to shut him up about their operation. Makes perfect sense."

Ruby came out of her seat. "Elliot is not a killer!"

"Okay, okay." He grabbed her wrist and tugged her back down. "We're just brainstorming here. If not Elliot, who? Why would they kill him? Because he knew too much about something? So he wouldn't talk to you or anyone else?"

Ruby's gaze dropped to the table once more. Silence enveloped them for a moment as they gave her the chance to implicate her ex-partner. Or anyone for that matter.

She didn't.

Jax's frustration grew. He needed one of those goddamned Twizzlers so he could bite off the end.

"Another tidbit of info you might find interesting," Rory continued. "Keon James and Augustus Nelson—aka Little Gus—were almost stepbrothers. Nelson's father and James's mother lived together for six months back in the day. The boys formed a close bond according to a citation made in Nelson's child services file that was created after his father was shot and killed. Nelson was ten when he went into the system. He asked repeatedly to see his brother Kee. The social worker made a note that Nelson had no brother named Kee. He was probably referring to Keon."

Ruby looked up. "So that's how Little Gus had the contacts in the Middle East. Keon James was his point man."

"Looks that way," Rory said. "Nelson was taken into police custody early this morning and questioned, but the interrogation was interrupted by an Agent Brown, supposedly from Homeland. You heard of him?"

Ruby frowned and shook her head.

"Me either." Rory sent them another video, this one from inside the police station. A man in a Cubs hat and a navy blue car coat was escorted to an interrogation room, then seen leaving with Nelson in cuffs a few minutes later. "The guy's good. Kept his face off camera and who knows what was tucked under that coat of his, but the officer on duty claimed his Homeland credentials were legit."

Emit played with a new twist of red licorice. "We don't have enough facial points for TracRec, but we're running the guy's build and gait through the software to see if we get a hit. We've matched people on less."

Nothing changed in Ruby's demeanor—and maybe it was his overactive imagination, or the fact his body was so tuned into hers—but Jax was sure she contracted ever so slightly. Like she'd bit into a piece of Emit's licorice.

The video looped and Colton paused it at the moment Nelson was herded out of the room by Agent Brown. Nelson's eyes were wide as saucers, his face drawn. "He look scared to you?" Colt said quietly to Jax.

Damn straight he did. "Fuck, yeah."

Rory continued. "Before Brown took off with Little Gus, the guy told the detective interviewing him that Keon James and Elliot Hayden were both set up by someone."

"Who?" Ruby said.

Rory shrugged.

"Confirms what Deuce told you," Jax said to Ruby.

The gears in Ruby's head were spinning if the laser gaze she shot him was any indication. That or she was morphing into Agent McKellen right before his eyes, her spy persona clicking into place.

Color returned to her face, her hand steadied as she took a sip of coffee. "Sounds like nothing but conspiracy theories at this point. Unless we have hard evidence or a name, we're at a dead end."

The hard line of Rory's set-in-stone, non-smile eased a bit. One corner actually lifted as if amused at her challenge. "If I had to guess, Agent Brown swooped in just in time to keep our boy from giving up the goods. Question is, did our buddy Brown here kill Keon James to silence him too?"

Emit chewed the last of his candy, swallowed. "Or did Elliot Hayden kill him?"

A buzzing came from Ruby's thigh. Jax raised a brow at her.

"My phone," she said. "Could someone point me to the ladies room?"

She'd flipped on the ringer to use it as an escape.

Agent McKellen was definitely back. Was it her mother again, or someone more important?

Emit stood and showed her out, returning a moment later to drop into his seat. "I don't like it. Jax?"

Jax had turned over the idea in his head a dozen times already. "Ruby's right. Intel is only as reliable as the source it comes from. All we have at the moment are theories based on a couple of random accusations by two men who may or may not have been involved in illegal, potentially traitorous activities with Elliot Hayden."

But what if Hayden is innocent?

Jax shoved the ugly, unwanted thought away. "Little Gus Nelson is a known criminal whose word is suspect since he'll lie and rat out anyone to save his own skin, and Keon James faked his own death and is AWOL from the army. On the other hand..."

Colton grinned. "Conspiracy theories are fun."

Crazy motherfucker.

The corner of Rory's mouth did that lift thing again. "We do have legitimate links between Hayden, James, and Nelson, the fact that James was point-blank assassinated, and some mysterious agent from Homeland kidnapped the man everyone wants to talk to. Those aren't coincidences."

"Agent McKellen's life could definitely be in danger," Emit said. "Get her client paperwork done, Jax. Rory can send it to Beatrice."

"Jax has to find Hayden," Colton volunteered. "I'll hang with Ruby."

The hell you will. "Ruby will refuse our help," Jax said, "and besides, she can take care of herself."

"That's good," Rory said, staring at his tablet. "Cuz she's heading out the back door right now."

<hr />

"Yes, sir," Ruby said into her cell as she hustled out the back door of Rock Star Security. The sun nearly blinded her and she had to put her hand up to shade her eyes. One of the guys replacing a window on that side of the building stopped what he was doing to grin at her. "I'm on my way to the office as we speak. I was only released from the hospital a little bit ago."

Director Timms was not happy. Not happy at all. "You have

some explaining to do, Agent McKellen. Serious explaining."

She had no car. It was still back at the club, and she didn't have time to pick it up, go home, and clean herself up. Plus, her former partner was running around impersonating Homeland Security and fucking with the only source she had left who could help her clear his name.

All her brain seemed able to do was spin in what-the-hell-is-going-on-here mode.

Yet, the ever-confident, efficient Ruby rose to the surface like the trained agent she was. "I don't blame you, sir. Just let me state that I appreciate you calling the station last night to make them aware of my reasons for being at the club."

"Last night? It was two in the morning and you had no business being at that club, McKellen. Which is why you are one lucky agent and you're going to get your backside into my office and explain to me exactly what you *were* doing at that club before I ship your ass back to Langley and wash my hands of you."

"Can't a girl go out once in a while?" She chuckled, hoping he would follow suit, chalk it all up to her personal life. He didn't, a tense, impatient pause hanging between them. A bright yellow blob caught her eye. She waved at the taxi. "I can explain everything, sir, I assure you."

His response was to hang up.

Alrighty, then.

The taxicab slid up to the curb and Ruby bare-footed it across the warm concrete. The vision of Elliot in that stupid coat and Cubs cap replayed on an endless loop in her brain. The cap was from her go bag. It was like he was flipping her off.

Or egging her on.

Definitely some kind of sign or signal, but what?

He'd always challenged her. Forced her to go beyond her comfort zone and live up to being the CIA's Golden Girl.

But this...this was reckless, even for Elliot. What the hell had he been doing? How had he come up with a legitimate Homeland ID?

Jax's voice stopped her mid-stride. "Where are you going?"

Raising a finger to the cabbie, she glanced back. Jax was two days or more past a shave and sporting circles under his eyes. His hair was unkempt as if he'd been running his fingers through it.

As a ray of morning sun sliced across his face, brightening his eyes, he was still the best-looking man she'd ever laid eyes on. Certain female parts below her waist purred to life.

One hand instinctively went to her lower abdomen. "To work. The director of the FBI Chicago field office just called to chew me a new one. I have to go."

Behind Jax, the contractor working on the window openly ogled her.

Yes, I'm an agent. She gave him a sneer. *And, no, you don't stand a chance with me.*

"I'm going with you."

Like hell he was. She took a step closer to him and lowered her voice so Mr. Eavesdropper couldn't hear her. "This isn't Take Your One-Night Stand to work day. I'm in enough trouble as it is. The last thing I need is you tagging along looking like…" She waved a hand at him.

He looked down at himself. "Like what?"

Like sex on a come-to-momma stick. It wasn't fair. He'd been through a traumatic night just like she had and he looked as delicious as ever.

"Hey, lady, do ya want a ride or not?" the cabbie called with that distinctive Chicago accent.

Ruby peeled her eyes off Jax and hustled toward her escape. She needed to get home and check her computer. Long ago, she'd put a GPS tracker inside the lining of her go-bag. She needed to know where Elliot was. "I'll call you later," she said to Jax over her shoulder.

"So do you know Emit?" Jax called. "I mean like, did you know him before today?"

"What?" She grabbed the taxi door handle. "No. I've heard of him. Who hasn't? He's one of the youngest billionaires in the country and your merry band of rock star security agents aren't exactly keeping a low profile."

A black SUV—the same tricked out one that had picked her up that morning—slid to a stop in front of the taxi, blocking it in.

Jax stepped forward, grabbed Ruby by the arm, and leaned down to see into the cab. He handed the driver a folded bill. "Got her covered, man. Thanks."

The cab driver absconded with the tip as Jax guided her to Emit Petit's Escalade.

"I don't need a ride."

"Really?" Jax snickered. "That's why you hailed a cab?"

The balls of this man. Whatever. When she ripped them off, it would cripple him. "Look, I have no shoes, I look like I've been run over by an elephant, and I smell like a cross between the hospital and a roadside bar. I need to go get my car, get home, and change my clothes before Director Timms calls my boss at Langley and gets me fired."

The passenger side window rolled down. Rory cocked his head at the backseat. "Get in."

Jesus, these people were pushy. "You don't understand."

Emit leaned around Rory. "I'll square things with Timms. You're our client now because your life could be in danger. We'll get you to Timm's office after we take you to your apartment to clean up. While we're at your place, we'll give you an upgrade in security and make plans for where we're going from here."

"My life *isn't* in danger."

"Yeah, it is," Jax said, opening the door and boosting her inside.

She ended up squashed between the guy Emit called Shinedown and Jax. Shinedown gave her a grin and handed her a small plastic coffee cup with the Rock Star logo plastered on the side. "Just go with it," he said.

He was cocky like Jax, but not as big and broad. More athletic, like a runner or basketball player. Sandy hair, dark green eyes, and a dimple in one cheek when he grinned.

Lord have mercy.

What choice did she have? She'd sent Elliot away, Deuce was dead, Little Gus in the wind with a Homeland agent who in reality didn't exist.

Or had Elliot been playing her all along? Was he working for Homeland as well as undercover with the CIA?

Don't be ridiculous. She and Elliot had no secrets. If he worked for Homeland, why would he work for the Agency too?

Before she could buckle in, they were moving, blending in with traffic. Rory played on a laptop, Emit dialed up a classic rock station. Morning commuters clogged the streets.

Timms is going to kill me. And when he's done, the Colonel is going get his turn.

The head of the spy group had once held Ruby in his esteemed grace like she was the Royal Scepter in the Queen's Crown Jewels.

Not any more. Now, she was his star operative who'd failed.

The Colonel didn't do failure. He wanted the best and only the best in his elite army of operatives. She was lucky to still have a job, even if she was on probation.

One call from Timms and the tight rope she was walking would snap.

Ruby fiddled with the coffee cup. She had to admit, the coffee inside was good. Really good. She needed the caffeine if she was going to get through this crazy-assed day. "This really isn't necessary," she said over the music to Emit.

"You're all signed up," Rory said, hitting the enter key on his keyboard. He handed a bracelet to Jax. "Welcome to Rock Star Security, blah, blah, blah. Jax, who you will refer to as Megadeth from this point on, is your security agent. Your personal information is confidential, etcetera, etcetera, and all that other bullshit. Thank you for your business."

"She didn't sign the release form," Shinedown said as Jax secured the bracelet around her wrist.

She tried to resist the bracelet, but she was holding the coffee and could barely breathe, much less move away, since Hulk and his little brother, who was only little compared to Jax, were book-ending her in the seat.

Rory wiggled his fingers. "The wonders of modern technology. I lifted her John Hancock from her hospital release form which was scanned and imported into the hospital database fifteen minutes ago."

Ruby wasn't all that surprised. Impressed? Maybe a little. "You forged my name?"

"Forgery?" Rory sounded as if she'd insulted him. "I prefer the term skillful manipulation."

The bracelet, a pretty gold number that had Rock Star imprinted on a gold plate, jangled on her arm. She glanced at Jax. "Megadeth? Really?"

"You don't like heavy metal?" He shot her a grin. "Let me guess, you're a country fan. Taylor Swift, I bet."

"Taylor Swift is a pop cross-over. Personally, I like contemporary jazz."

"What?" Shinedown grimaced. "Nobody likes jazz."

Jax leaned forward to look around Ruby. "I like jazz."

"Dude." Shinedown shook his head. "You gotta get out more."

The two of them continued to rag each other about music selections while the coffee in Ruby's stomach turned to acid. Was that *really* Elliot in the Cubs hat and long coat or were her eyes playing tricks on her? Had he offed Keon James and kidnapped Augustus Nelson?

The real question was why. Why had Elliot snuck out of

prison? What motivation would he have to kill Deuce, the one man he'd claimed could prove his innocence?

None of this made sense.

Thirty seconds later, the club came into view. In the early morning light, it looked sad, empty, yellow crime scene tape draped across the entrance and back exit. A couple of reporters were out in front, using the tape and the desolate atmosphere of the place as a backdrop for their follow-up stories.

She pointed toward the rental. "That's my car, down there."

Emit pulled the SUV up behind the Ford and idled. "We'll follow you to your place."

Jax opened the door, scanned the area, and held out a hand to her.

As Shinedown bailed out the opposite side, doing his own scan of the area, Ruby juggled her coffee and slid across to that big hand waiting for her. The hem of her dress caught on the leather and rolled up, revealing her leg holster with its pockets containing her gun and her phone.

Jax's gaze dropped down and did a slow perusal from her bright red toenails, all the way up to her gun.

"Stop gawking," she said, snatching the hem of the dress down as she set her coffee cup in his hand.

He switched the cup to his free hand and grabbed her elbow, helping her out of the vehicle. "Hey, you're the one laying that leg bomb out there. You can't expect me not to look."

She landed on the sidewalk, a gritty rock digging into her left heel. Her right ankle was secured with tape and felt pretty stable. Picking the rock out of her heel, she took a moment to look over the building. Questions with no answers continued to swirl inside her head. What if Jax was right? What if Elliot wasn't the man she believed him to be?

What if he *was* a killer?

If only she could get inside and do her own assessment of the place. But really, what was there to look for? Deuce was dead after firing off a weapon inside the club. The police had no witnesses, no surveillance video, no suspects.

The only thing Ruby could do at this point was to play along with Jax and his Rock Star buddies and hope that Elliot contacted her again.

She needed answers, and by God, she was going to get some.

CHAPTER SEVEN

Beatrice lay on a collection of pillows and bolsters in her office and felt like a beached whale.

Her pregnant belly was a giant mound pointed at the marbleized ceiling above her, her back finally finding a smidgen of relief from the tight band that seemed to circle it 24/7 these days.

"That's right," Trace Hunter said, adjusting a folded blanket under her neck, then a pillow under her knees. "Close your eyes and relax."

Close my eyes.

Relax.

Right.

Like that was going to happen. She could close her eyes, sure, but relaxing? How did one relax when your baby was three days overdue, your husband was consulting at the White House on a secret program for God-only-knew what, and the founder and CEO of the business you were in charge of was in Chicago, getting the third Rock Star office up and running?

Not to mention he'd taken your computer guru with him, and your system's software had taken a timely dump last night, which meant client files, employee files, and your daily calendar had all disappeared. Poof!

Trace's deep voice cut through the ever-jumping thoughts in her monkey mind. His handsome face swam into view as he leaned over her. "Beatrice, you're thinking again."

Imagine...Trace Hunter, super soldier and elite SFI operative, teaching her yoga and meditation techniques. A waste of his skills to be certain, but she had to admit, he'd been a godsend in the past couple of weeks. A few daily stretches, some simple breathing exercises, and twenty minutes of restorative poses with her eyes closed had lowered her blood pressure and kept her off bed rest.

No way she could handle being stuck in bed until this baby—her first, and quite possibly her last at this point—decided to make his entrance.

Three days late. How many more?

Stubborn. Just like his dad.

His dad who called or texted her hourly, afraid she would birth the kid without him.

Another reason her blood pressure was on a merry-go-round. Cal's project was top-secret and she didn't like secrets. In her opinion, nothing good had ever come out of the Oval Office. She doubted anything good would come out of it this time.

Along with her distrust of the government came a healthy distrust of all agencies associated with it. The CIA had hired Shadow Force International to hunt down Elliot Hayden and her computer system had done a Chernobyl meltdown all in the same day.

Coincidence?

I think not.

Omen was more like it.

Good thing she didn't believe in nonsense. "You're goddamn right I'm thinking, Trace." She had a business to run and a child to deliver. "You should have gone with Jax."

"Cal assigned me to you while he's playing nice with the new president. Deal with it."

She wasn't sure who was more annoying—her husband or his stand-in. Since Trace was here and within striking distance, she took out her frustration on him. "You're the super soldier. Why didn't he and Emit send you to talk to President Milton?"

"After I shot the previous leader of the free world, it didn't seem like a good idea."

Sighing, she closed her eyes. "I taught Jax that 2 to 1 breathing exercise you suggested. The white room visualization as well. He said it helps."

"Of course it helps."

"I don't think he's actually tried it. He only said it helped to get me to leave him alone."

"Quit worrying about Jax and Cal. The only thing you need to think about is yourself and your baby."

"Don't you know some yoga poses to activate labor?"

"Will you relax for ten minutes if I promise to show them to you later?"

Langley was breathing down her neck about Jaxon catching Agent Hayden. Mostly because Jax's face had been all over the news that morning and Hayden was still in the wind. "Did you read the file on Elliot Hayden?"

"Yes."

So like Trace to be succinct and irritated all at the same time. Of course he'd read the file after she'd told him to. As a SEAL, and later as the former president's number one cleaner, he'd been a good soldier, following orders to the letter until the president had ordered him to take out an innocent pregnant woman and her child. He'd refused, and ended up going head-to-head with his commander-in-chief.

But Trace was still a good soldier. He did what she asked.

Most of the time.

She pictured the white room. Trace had told her to imagine a waterfall, but that hadn't worked for her. The white room did, giving her a visual blank slate during their daily restorative appointments. The window looked out over a garden. Today, her busy mind saw a hummingbird flitting around a trellis covered with purple flowers. "Anything stand out to you?"

"Nope."

Come on. Give me something. "You have nothing else to add?"

She heard nothing from him for a long moment, the clock on her fireplace mantel ticking off the seconds as she wrestled with her urge to open her eyes.

Outside the white room's window, she saw a shadow. "Trace?"

Exasperation laced his reply. "The fact Hayden's file is clean is what stands out to me."

She knew where he was going, what his gut was telling him. Her high intellect agreed. Still, she wanted him to verbalize it. "How so?"

"The file's been scrubbed."

Bingo. She'd seen plenty of personnel files in her job with the NSA. Good undercover operatives often stepped outside the box to complete a mission. High-risk missions were unpredictable, perilous. They required people who broke rules and gambled with fate. Those types of people were the exact types the CIA and NSA hired. The risk-takers. The gamblers. The ones who knew the rules and broke them anyway.

Like Agent Ruby McKellen. "His partner, McKellen. Did you read her file?"

Trace picked up her right hand and began doing acupressure on her fingers and thumb. "Yep. Her file is...messier. I don't think it was scrubbed. She's the real deal."

There were advantages to being a beautiful woman with the smarts to analyze and manipulate. Several reports in McKellen's file mentioned she had used her feminine attributes to get intel. Harmless flirting from the sounds of it, but McKellen often used her attributes as a means of distraction while her partner accessed whatever—or whoever—the two of them were after. "Is it possible Hayden let McKellen do the *messy* stuff in order to keep his own nose clean?"

"Possible, yes. Probable is more like it."

There was more, but he wasn't saying it. She peeked at him under her eyelashes, saw the consternation lining his face. "Something's bothering you."

His steely blue eyes met hers. "*You're* bothering me. Now, close your eyes."

A heavy sigh left her mouth. Her body was relaxing, even if her mind continued its spin class. She shut her eyes, trying to soak in the acupressure. "Most operatives work alone. Hayden and McKellen's teamwork has been outstanding, so the Agency kept them together. They posed as husband and wife on multiple occasions."

It was all stuff he already knew from their files, but she wanted to get him back to thinking about the case and not about her. Being the center of attention made her uncomfortable.

"Hayden's not much of a partner if he made her take all the risks," Trace said.

"Maybe he didn't. That's why his file is scrubbed."

Trace moved to her other side, so quiet, so fast, she didn't even realize it until he lifted her left hand and began applying pressure. As the only soldier to survive Project 24, his superhuman skills were a thing to behold.

"Or he screwed up royally," he said, "but they didn't want to break up a good thing. They erased it from his files and kept both of them in the field doing their Mr. and Mrs. Smith routine."

She'd seen the movie he referred to. It was decent entertainment, but any operative worth her salt would have taken out her partner in his sleep, not called attention to herself or ruining a lovely house in an effort to gun the man down. "Or

Hayden's been doing off-the-books work that his partner may or may not have known about."

"Like what?"

Her garden visualization was turning stormy. "When I worked for NSA, we were often given a legitimate assignment with a second, secret assignment layered under it."

"Had a few of those myself." He released her hand, laying it next to her. "So Hayden gets double duty, but McKellen is left in the dark about it."

"Help me up," she said, popping her eyes open. "I need to call Zeb."

"You have ten more minutes of relaxation."

Trying to roll to her side, she sent a mental apology to the baby. "If Hayden was working subsequent secret operations, he may be a severe liability to the Agency. You know what they do to liabilities."

Trace sat back on his heels, but put a hand on her shoulder, keeping her down. "You think they hired us to go after Hayden because they want him dead?"

"They hired Jax, specifically. The man who reported Hayden to the Justice Department, who ended up putting him in prison for crimes against the nation. A black mark on the CIA's already shaky blotter."

"They know Hayden has information that could get them in trouble with Congress, and he's not about to go down peacefully when Jax finds him."

"Exactly."

Trace shook his head. "Fuckers. They've put Jax in a no-win situation so he takes out their man and they keep their hands clean."

"Which is why I need to call Zeb first, then Jaxon."

She tried to shrug off his hand, but he was stronger. "You stay put. I'll handle this."

He stood and stepped around her, heading for her desk. "What's Zeb's number?" he asked, snatching up the handset.

"He's on speed dial. Number 3."

Trace nodded and punched the button.

<hr />

A reporter rushed them as soon as she recognized their faces.

Jax saw the blond bombshell heading their direction before Ruby did. "Incoming, six o'clock."

Ruby checked for the danger over her shoulder, then jammed her finger onto the car door's lock. "Get in."

Lucky for them, Emit, Rory, and Colton were idling behind the car. Jax hand-signaled Emit; he nodded, and the next thing they all knew, the reporter found a big, black barricade in the form of a Cadillac Escalade between her and her quarry.

Ruby gave Emit a thumbs-up before she slid into the driver's seat. Jax did the same, tucking himself into a tight ball to fit into the passenger seat. "Could you have rented a smaller car?"

The engine revved and Ruby made a smooth squeeze between Emit's Caddy and the car in front of them. "Hey, not all of us are ex-linebackers."

He shot her a look. "You ran a background check on me?"

"Please. It was a lucky guess."

Lucky guess, his ass.

Still...she'd looked into his background. She'd wanted to know more about him. He grinned. "State champs my senior year."

She merged into traffic, heading for her apartment. "And you were scouted by several major universities, yada, yada, yada."

Jax checked the sideview, saw Emit trailing them. "You *did* do a background check."

"Nothing that in-depth. Maybe a Google search. You accused my partner of treason after all."

"Speaking of... Who was that on the video from the station?"

Her fingers clenched slightly on the wheel. Because of the traffic or because he'd hit the nail on the head?

She checked her side mirror, changed lanes. "I told you and Emit, I've never heard of Agent Brown."

Lying, but not lying. "But you know who the man is *posing* as Agent Brown, don't you?"

"What? No."

God, he hated it when she lied to him. "Ruby."

She glanced over at him, gave him a WTF smile. "Jax, I'm just as invested in this as you are."

"Yet, you continue to keep intel from me. I get it, Elliot is in some deep shit. Deeper than I realized. Maybe the guy isn't guilty, he's simply trapped in a game he can't win."

She nearly rear-ended a camper in front of them. As she

stomped the brakes, the front of the car nose-dived, then snapped back up. "Did you just say what I think you said?"

He huffed, not appreciating her incredulous tone. "There are a lot of things that don't add up, and if I screwed up, and Elliot is innocent of killing Al-Safari, or there's more to the story than he admitted because he's in a goatfuck with the CIA, or Homeland, or whoever, then I want to make it right."

She focused on her driving again, a frown creasing her forehead. "That's mighty noble of you."

"I'm a noble guy."

She snorted. "No, you're not."

Silence fell like a blanket between them, Ruby seeming lost in thought. Or maybe she was simply concentrating on the horrible traffic.

One thing for certain, she was right. He wasn't a noble guy.

Fifteen minutes later, they pulled into the parking lot behind her apartment building. That guy he'd seen yesterday with the dog was sitting outside, a cigarette dangling from his skinny fingers and his eyes hidden behind tiny John Lennon sunglasses.

Emit and the others parked beside them and Emit got out. Jax rolled down the window. Humid air engulfed the car.

"We'll canvas the place first, make sure it's clear," Emit said, handing him an earbud.

Jax popped it in and tapped the button to turn on the comm. "Roger that, boss."

Emit and Colton headed for the apartment.

"Wait," Ruby called out. "Don't you want the key?"

She held it up, the metal key flashing in the sun. Colton turned, grinned as he walked back to her. "Aw, what fun is that? We'd rather use our awesome skills to break in."

"You need to get out more if breaking and entering is your idea of fun," Ruby said, dropping it into his hand.

Colton lowered his head to flash his grin at Jax. "I like her." He switched his gaze to Ruby. "Any time you want to take me out for some fun, I'll clear my calendar."

Jax rolled his eyes and flipped Colt off behind Ruby's back.

Ruby tapped the steering wheel as Emit and Colton made their way inside. "This really isn't necessary," she said.

Jax tapped his comm to turn off the mic and touched the bracelet on her wrist. "You're a card-carrying Rock Star client, Ruby. Your safety is our highest priority."

"Your boss wants to bug my place in case Elliot shows up."

"Yeah, about that..." Jax glanced over at John Lennon Junior and debated whether telling her the truth was a good idea, but what the hell? He needed her to trust him and the best way to gain that trust was to be honest.

She glanced at him, eyes narrowed. "You already did, didn't you?"

JL Junior watched him and Ruby. In his ear, Jax heard Rory, still in the Escalade, humming a Beatles song.

"I was sent here to hunt down Hayden, and I knew he would come to you. You were uncooperative, so..." He shrugged, letting her fill in the rest.

She opened a compartment under the armrest between them and pointed down. What Jax saw inside made him shake his head.

All three of the bugs he'd placed inside her apartment were nestled inside with some change and a hair clip. He'd never had a chance to turn on his phone's app to listen in last night and Ruby had found every one them.

All three were flattened, tangled messes. "You stepped on them?"

She was smiling. "I imagined your pretty-boy, linebacker face as I ground my heel into each one."

Liar.

She loved that he'd bugged her place. He could see it in the way her eyes danced. She loved that she'd found them and ruined his plans, because like every spook he'd ever worked with, Ruby loved *the game.*

The strategy, the bluffing, the deceit. The one-upping everyone else. It made her blood pump faster, her senses heighten, her brain work out multiple scenarios like a chess game.

In essence, she was a con man, addicted to the adrenaline rush.

He knew the feeling. The first time he took a football in for a touchdown, he was only ten years old. Ever since, he'd been chasing that elusive feeling. All through high school, into college, hitting the gridiron harder than anyone on his team, making the hail Mary plays time and time again.

Not to win the game. Not because he counted on the football scholarships to get him through his first four years of college.

He did it because it felt good.

Better than good.

Eventually, he couldn't meet the demands of school and football. The call to be a doctor had been strong, but he missed the rush of playing sports. Leaving med school and joining the Navy had met his next quest for that high.

He'd found it, ending up a SEAL for four years. Four glorious years of pushing his body and his mind to the limit.

Until Marrakech. Until Ruby.

One night with her and nothing felt the same. The rush, the high that came from being with her, turned his addiction into something completely different. One he still didn't understand.

The need thrummed just under his skin with every sway of her hair, every smile, every look she gave him.

Colt's voice came over the comm, jerking Jax out of his mind travel. "We're in."

Jax relayed the info to Ruby as he scanned the area. He wanted to talk about Elliot again, but bringing that up seemed like a good way to ruin their current truce. Over at the picnic table, JL Junior was finishing his smoke. "Your neighbor sure is nosy."

Ruby glanced over the guy. "Dan's just lonely. Woodstock is all he has."

"Woodstock?"

"The dog. That's her name."

"How original. A hippy with a dog named Woodstock."

"You're so cynical."

She said it with humor, but she was right. He *was* cynical. Angry. Hurt.

Addicted to a drug sitting right next to him, close enough to touch but still completely out of reach.

He wanted her back in his life. Not just for another one-night stand. He wanted to date her, think about something long-term.

Spies didn't do long-term.

Ruby was talking again. "...and he's not a hippy. Dan's a geologist. Works with rocks and stuff for one of the universities."

"No wonder he doesn't have friends."

"Jaxon." A reprimand.

He turned to her, as best as his big body could do in the compact car. Truce time was up. "Ruby, who was that on the video?"

She opened her mouth to answer, then shut it with a shake of her head. "If I tell you what I'm thinking, you have to swear not to go off half-cocked or tell anyone else until I confirm it."

Shit. That could only mean...

Emit's voice interrupted him. "Place is clear, but someone left Ruby a message. You better get up here."

Jax clenched his teeth, trying to hold in the expletives on his tongue. He tapped his comm to open his end. "Roger that," he growled.

Rory was already out of the SUV, fighting with his crutches.

"It appears *Agent Brown* is two steps ahead of us," Jax said to Ruby. "He left you a message upstairs."

Before he could open his door, Ruby was out and running for her apartment.

/

Chapter Eight

Ruby's breath caught in her throat the moment she swept through the door.

The place was destroyed.

The couch had been upended, the cushions slashed. Her few personal items—books and papers—lay torn and trampled on the floor. The flat screen TV had been ripped from the wall, a crater in the center where someone had stomped on the screen. Her laptop was missing from the desk; the drawers had been yanked out and dumped.

Emit emerged from the kitchen, a bug scanner in hand. "The place is a wreck, but there are no listening devices or hidden cameras. Any idea what they were after?"

Me.

It was a total gut reaction—she had no real basis for thinking someone was after her, but since the near miss at the club and now this...

"The laptop, maybe." Her voice sounded strained, giving away that she didn't believe it. "It was on the desk."

He walked to the desk, stepping over the scattered drawers. "What was on it? Anything top secret?"

"Of course not."

Jax came up behind her and whistled under his breath as he pulled up short. "Fucking A. What the hell?"

Ruby steadied her shaky legs and moved farther into the living room, avoiding the broken glass from a mirror that had been jerked from the wall. "There was nothing classified on my laptop," she said to Emit.

"You'll need to do an inventory," he said, snapping a picture with his phone of the destruction. "Jewelry, cash, weapons. See if anything else is missing.

Shinedown appeared in the doorway from the bedroom, holding up a pair of sneakers. "Better put these on."

Ruby accepted the shoes and slipped her feet into them. She bent down to collect the papers, mostly to give herself something to do. Her fingers felt stiff, her mind cataloging what was mostly bills. Water, electric, Internet.

"Hey," Jax said softly as he bent down to help. He reached out and took the pile of papers from her hands. "Why don't you grab a shower and a change of clothes? I've got this."

"This wasn't Elliot. He wouldn't do this."

"Is it possible he was looking for something?"

"Like what?"

"Like something on that laptop?" Emit supplied.

"There was nothing important on there, and why would he trash the place if all he wanted was the laptop?"

The logic made sense; she could see it in Jax's face. If it was a simple grab-and-go, there was no reason to vandalize the apartment. It didn't make sense.

Unless someone was trying to throw them off track.

Or scare her.

Jax apparently followed her train of thought. "They might have taken the laptop to make it look like a robbery. Or trashed the place to make it look like a random B&E when they were after the laptop."

"But why? I didn't have anything of value intel-wise. To Elliot or anyone else."

Shinedown scooted the flat screen over to the side. "Maybe they think you do."

"Or maybe you do," Emit added, his sharp eyes sizing her up, "but you don't realize it."

Her brain hurt. Literally hurt as blood pounded against her temples. "Whoever did this was looking for Elliot. I'd bet my last paycheck on it, which may be coming sooner than I'd hoped if I don't get my ass to Director Timm's office."

She kicked a torn cushion out of the way, made eye contact with Jax, and cocked her head toward the bedroom.

He followed her through the debris, then stood with her as they surveyed the damage done to her bedroom. The pillows had been split open, the mattress as well. The lamp from the nightstand had been tossed to the floor, breaking the bulb and damaging the shade. Her sparse collection of clothes and shoes lay scattered across the floor.

"This looks personal to me." Jax eyed the deep gashes in the mattress. "Whoever did this is sending you a strong message, but you're right. This wasn't Elliot. This was someone who's after him."

Someone who meant business. If she'd been here, no telling what they might have done to her.

But who were "they?"

It was time to stop pulling her punches. She needed help, and like it or not, help was standing next to her. "I need to show you something."

She went for her cell phone, saw Jax's eyes tracking her leg again as she hoisted her hemline and pulled the phone from its case on her thigh. Let him stare. She liked the fact that he couldn't take his eyes off her body when she showed it to him.

Sick, but whatever. He made her feel good about herself, even if he did gawk. He wasn't like the men who only cared about her sexiness. He treated her with respect, even when he was mad at her. And she'd hurt him, she knew that. Regretted that.

Unfortunately, it came with her job.

She couldn't get close to anyone. Not without risking her operative status and, possibly, their lives.

No way she would do that. Her job meant everything to her, but risking the life of someone who felt something for her was out of the question. She'd become an agent to save innocent people, not to put them in the line of fire.

Entering her password, she tapped an icon to open the GPS tracking software that would link her to the transmitter she'd hidden in her go-bag. Several seconds passed as the software did its thing, bringing up a map of the area and scanning for the transmitter.

Come on, come on. Where are you, El?

The map shifted, zooming out. Finally a red pin dropped onto a spot. Quite a ways from where they were, but stationary. Stationary was good.

Turning the screen so Jax could see it, she hoped Elliot was immobile because he'd found a place to crash. The other options— kidnapped, dead—weren't pleasant to consider. "He's there."

"Who?"

"Elliot. I gave him my go-bag to help him out. I had a GPS tracker hidden inside the bag."

Jax's expression lightened. "Well, I'll be damned." He screwed up his forehead and squinted at the map. "Where exactly is that?"

She used her fingers to zoom in. The spot was several hours west of the city in an area she'd never been to. "I don't know, but we're going to go find it as soon as I clean up."

Jax nodded. "I'll help the guys while you shower. We'll put security on the place, but tonight, you're going to a safe house."

She didn't like that idea, but night was still hours away. Maybe they would find Elliot and clear up what was going on by then.

"Give me fifteen," she said, and snatched some clean, if wrinkled, clothes off the floor on her way to the bathroom.

She only wished washing away this mess were as easy as washing off the night's grime.

Ruby was in the shower and it took all of Jax's concentration to work on cleaning up her apartment while Emit and Colton installed listening devices and cameras. His brain would much rather shut down than think about her luscious body standing under a stream of hot water.

Because, it seemed, his brain as well as his dick were hardwired into the Ruby Fantasy Channel. *All Ruby, all the time.*

Along with the lust, rage burned under his skin. The look on her face as she'd viewed the damage had nearly done him in.

The fact of the matter was that she'd barely shown any sort of emotion. A slight hitch in her chest, a hard swallow, the tiniest pinch between her eyebrows. But to him, tuned into her every gesture, her every breath, it spoke volumes. Random or not, even the most hardened person felt violated after a break-in. It scared you, shook something deep inside you that went back to your childhood. Security. Safety.

Ruby hadn't shown it, but it had shaken her too. "I'm going to fucking kill whoever did this," Jax said as he scooped up broken glass from the floor.

"Who *do* you think did it?" Emit asked.

He dumped the dustpan into the garbage, the glass tinkling as it fell. "No idea."

Colton tested a camera angle, adjusted it. He'd hidden the tiny thing inside the smoke detector. "You don't think it was this Agent Brown guy?"

Jax stretched his back. Ruby's compact car was the size of a sardine can. It felt like it had squished his spine into half its size. "Agent Brown is Elliot, so no, I don't think it was him. He already visited her and she gave him her go-bag to help him out. If he'd been after something, he would have gone for it then. Plus, he's just not the kind of guy to do this." He waved a hand at the destruction.

"Wait," Emit said. "Elliot impersonated a Homeland agent and took Augustus Nelson from the cops?"

"At this point, I'm not all that sure he was *impersonating* anyone."

Emit screwed up his face. "You think he's working for Homeland?"

"As a CIA agent, he's already under their umbrella. What I can't figure out is if he's Homeland undercover inside the CIA or he's CIA running a deep undercover op on his fellow operatives for Homeland."

Colton squinted. "Trying to follow that makes my head hurt."

"Why would Homeland insert one of their own into the Agency?" Emit pondered.

Jax wondered the same. "Only thing I can think of is that they suspect a mole or traitor high in the ranks. Fits with what James said to Ruby."

Emit nodded. "How does that tie into James and Nelson?"

"No fucking idea," Jax said, "but my gut's telling me Elliot may be innocent of the charges I accused him of, or there's at least a damn good reason he did what he did."

Emit shoved desk drawers back into their respective places and stuck a bug under one of them. "If he's Homeland, why didn't they tell Justice to drop it and not pursue prosecution?"

"Maybe he found out something he shouldn't have and Homeland wanted to shut him up," Colton volunteered.

Jax shook his head. "The only good way to shut him up would be to kill him, not send him to a country club prison."

"We need to talk to Beatrice." Emit tossed Jax one of the tiny listening devices and pointed at the door. "She's better at cyphering out conspiracy theories than I am."

Jax placed the bug on top of the mirror next to the door. "I'm due to check in with her anyway."

In the hallway outside, he heard the click of dog nails on the stairs. The jingle of keys.

Dan.

"I'll be right back," Jax said.

He caught John Lennon Junior unlocking his door. "Hey, man."

Dan glanced up. "Yes?"

The dog growled for half a second, then wagged its tail.

"Jaxon Sloan." He held out his hand while Woodstock sniffed his boots. "I'm a friend of Ruby's and she says you're a good neighbor. Her place was broken into sometime between midnight and seven this morning. You hear anything weird? See anyone suspicious?"

"Broken into?" Dan's bloodshot eyes swung right, then left, as if the boogie man was about to jump out at them. "Is Ruby all right?"

"She's fine, she wasn't home, but her place is a disaster. Got any ideas who might have paid her a visit?"

"Jeez, I've no idea, man. I never heard anything, never saw anyone other than Mrs. Lieberman downstairs when I took Woodstock for her walk this morning."

Wow. All the crashing and banging around that must have happened and Dan heard none of it? *Dan needs to lay off the weed.* "Mrs. Lieberman, huh? Do you think she might talk to me? Which apartment does she live in? Are there any other neighbors up here that might have heard something?"

"Nah, just me and Ruby on this floor. Mrs. Lieberman is one floor below mine. She's a nosy old gal, but nice enough. She's out of town for the weekend. Was packing up her car when I saw her this morning. Said she was going to visit her sister in Michigan."

Damn. "Who lives in the apartment below Ruby's?"

Dan urged Woodstock into the apartment and half slid into it himself, blocking the doorway. "No one that I know of. It's been vacant for a few weeks."

"All right, thanks. Do you have a number for Mrs. Lieberman?"

He shook his head, edging the door closed. "She doesn't have a cell and I don't even know her sister's name. Sorry."

The door shut, leaving him alone in the hallway. Somehow Jax had the feeling Dan wasn't sorry at all.

He was the nosy one from what Jax could see, but Jax almost believed the guy had been out cold while Ruby's place was being tossed.

Still. Wouldn't hurt to keep an eye on him. Run a background check.

Ruby was fresh from the shower, dressed in a white blouse and faded jeans, when he got back inside. "What were you doing?" she asked.

She smelled like some flower and looked ten years younger with all the makeup scrubbed off her face. "Asking Dan a few questions. What's his last name?"

She pulled sunglasses out of the purse hanging over her shoulder and propped them on her head. "Why?"

"Last name is Hughley. He's clean," Rory called from the kitchen where he'd set up his laptop on the tiny table. "I already ran facial rec and got his name. Nothing in his background but some unpaid parking tickets and an arrest at a protest march against gun violence in DC in 2000."

Well, that fit, didn't it?

Ruby crossed her arms and looked at Jax dubiously. "You suspect Dan is in on this?"

"Doesn't hurt to vet those around you, and I wanted to know if he saw or heard anything suspicious last night."

"Did he?"

"Nope. You ready?"

Emit held up a hand and spoke to Ruby. "I called Timms and explained what was going on—not the details, since we're not sure who we can trust—but enough for him to give you some space. Whatever story you're going to tell him, I'd appreciate being privy to it since he may decide to confirm it with me."

"Copy that," she said, pulling out her car keys. "I don't plan to tell him any more than necessary at this point."

Ach. He had to ride in that blasted sardine can again. If only he'd grabbed his car at the club. "We'll be in touch as soon as she's done with Timms."

Emit nodded. "We'll lock up."

Ruby and Jax headed out, Jax following her down the stairs and outside.

"Are we really going to see Director Timms?" he asked.

She slid into the driver's seat and started the car. "Nope," she said as he folded himself into the car and buckled up.

"Didn't figure."

She handed him her phone with the red pin still dropped in the same place on her GPS map. "We're going to find Elliot and figure out what the hell is going on."

CHAPTER NINE

Ruby slowed the car to twenty miles an hour and leaned forward to look through the windshield at the abandoned building looming off to her right. "Are you sure this is the place?"

Jax held up her phone where the red pin sat almost directly over the pulsing blue circle that represented her car. "We're here."

Pottersville, population 613. Nearly two hours west of the city and a good twenty minutes from any reasonable suburb. They were in the boonies, complete with endless cornfields and county roads.

Overhead, the skies had turned dark, grey clouds roiling like bubbling smog. Here and there, lightning popped, followed by the deep bass of thunder.

The car's headlights lit up the metal side of the Potter Feed & Grain Mill, the red writing on the building faded to a dull rust as Ruby turned into what had once been a parking lot but now was overgrown with weeds.

Jax was poking at her phone with his long, lean fingers. "According to the Wiki page on this town, the two biggest attractions are the cemetery and a Christmas tree farm."

A good place to hide out if you wanted to disappear. "Long way from Chicago," Ruby muttered out loud.

"Wouldn't Elliot want to get away from the city?"

"How'd he get here? Stolen car?"

Thunder boomed in the distance as Jax shrugged. "Hitching a ride is risky when your face has been on the news. You think he turned Little Gus loose and hotfooted it here?"

Her phone rang. Jax showed her the screen. "The Colonel" showed on caller ID.

Speaking of having your face plastered all over the news.

"Don't you think you should answer this?" he said. "The guy's called you twice since we left your apartment."

"Let it go to voicemail."

Which was a bad, bad decision. One she would get her ass kicked for.

"Who is he?" Jax asked. "Boyfriend?"

She'd wondered when he was finally going to break down and ask her. "My boss. The real one. The CIA's director of operations."

"You call him Colonel?"

"Only behind his back."

She drove around the north side of the building where the parking lot ended. No other vehicles were anywhere, but then she didn't expect Elliot to leave his getaway car in plain sight.

Jax hit the decline button and the call went to voicemail. "Why?"

She parked close to the back door and killed the lights. A fat rain drop splattered on the windshield. "You know how in the Navy, you have your basic seamen, then the next level of experienced seamen, and on and on up the ranks until you get to the highest level, the SEALs?"

"Yeah."

"We have something similar, a graduated level of operatives. The highest one is sort of secret army, like the SEALs. We call our boss Colonel as an inside joke."

"A secret army, huh?" He smiled. "That's cool."

"It *is* cool, but the Colonel doesn't like screw-ups, and after my mug was all over the morning news, he's not calling to tell me my probation is over and I'm back into his elite group."

"Ah, shit," Jax said, as if it were only now dawning on him. "You're blown, aren't you?"

Ruby sighed. "I had a lot of makeup on last night, but yeah. I'm guessing since a few million people in the Windy City alone have seen my face in connection with the shooting last night, which has now gone to the national news channels as well as all over the Internet..." She drew an imaginary knife across her throat. "My undercover days are most likely over."

"Well, that fucking sucks."

Was he smiling? "You don't believe that," she accused. "You're happy my UC job is in jeopardy."

He met her gaze head on. "It's risky, dangerous work. You're a good operative, but I can't say I'm not relieved that you won't be going undercover again for awhile."

She wanted to be pissed at him, found she didn't have the energy. "Let's just find the GPS tracker."

Jax popped his door open. "And Elliot."

Right. And Elliot.

She didn't really believe El was inside. He'd no doubt found the tracker and dumped it here to lead her on a wild goose chase.

If that was the case, she was out of ideas. Unless she could find Augustus Nelson, her leads were gone.

Stepping out of the car, she took her gun from a shoulder holster and checked the chamber. Several cold raindrops fell on her face, her hands.

Across from the abandoned feed mill, acres of cornfields stretched out, most of them unplanted. A tall silo, shedding tiles from its sides, stood like a sentry over the dry fields of old broken stalks and weeds. One lone oak tree stretched dead branches toward the sky, its massive trunk still solid and sturdy, while a branch the size of a small tree had broken off and lay at its base.

Jax naturally fell into the lead position, which annoyed her, but as she pointed her gun upward and sidled up to the opposite side of the door, she was glad for once to have him with her. Tiny town, deserted old building, a storm moving in. Being out here alone, with no way of knowing what was on the other side of this door, would have been unnerving.

Jax's big body moved with grace, his face calm. He glanced at her, did a couple of hand signals to let her know his plan, and when she nodded her understanding, he nodded back.

But he didn't move, three fingers in the air, ready to count them down.

She waited. Still he didn't move, his eyes locked on hers, intense, powerful, earnest. Heat shot across the couple of feet between them into her chest, down her legs. She reminded herself to breathe.

Lightning flashed in her peripheral vision, but she didn't flinch, didn't look away. Jax was there. He would keep her safe regardless of the threat, just like he'd done last night in the club. Just like he'd done that morning, cleaning up her apartment, interrogating poor Dan.

One side of her lips lifted. She couldn't help it. As annoying as he was, he was also one of the bravest men she'd ever met.

He saw her half-smile and returned it. One by one, his fingers fell.

One.

Two.

Three.

She expected him to try the door handle, but he didn't. Instead he kicked in the door, barreling through and sweeping his gun from side to side as she followed.

Dark. The interior was too dark with little outside light able to get in, even with the broken windows.

And it smelled. Badly.

Before her eyes could adjust or she could reach for her flashlight, Jax turned his own on, illuminating the open, barn-like interior.

Someone had gutted most of the machines, although a few still stood anchored to the back wall and concrete floor. Another wall held various tools, chains, and shelves of rusted cans and miscellaneous stuff. A pile of pallets domed in the center of the floor, a weird red ball sat off to the side, as if a child had been in here playing and had suddenly run away.

A chill played tag up the vertebrae of Ruby's spine. "Elliot," she called. "It's me, Ruby. We know you're in here."

Her voice echoed in the space, bouncing off the high ceiling and loft, falling back onto her.

A beat passed. Another. Not a sound except those coming from Mother Nature outside.

She knew there wouldn't be an answer. Elliot was too smart for his own damn good.

Where's the go-bag?

Perhaps he'd simply removed the hidden GPS tracker and hid it somewhere. Dropped it into the mess of pallets or stuck it in one of the machines.

"I'll check upstairs," Jax said, heading for a set of steps at the back of the building.

Ruby dug out her flashlight, flicked it on, and began examining the lower floor more carefully. The place smelled of mold, old wood, decay. Mice had made the place their palace, leaving droppings everywhere.

No wonder it smells.

A desk, chair, and bulletin board in one section had been the office. There were still papers on the desk, a bulky computer screen from the early 90s. A wastebasket full of candy wrappers and Mr. Pibb cans. Probably something had died in there, its rotted smell adding to the place's fragrance du jour.

Behind the desk was a file cabinet. An old-fashioned, three-part receipt book lay open on top, the pages aged and yellowed.

Moving around the room, she heard the sound of Jax's footsteps progressing softly above her in a similar right to left trajectory. Rain came down harder, pelting the metal roof. Wind whistled through the broken windows high above, driving in rivulets of water that ran down the walls.

Sweeping her flashlight over the shelves, she kept an eye out for her bag. There were feed sacks and rags, pieces of rope and tools she couldn't name.

She moved to the back of the building, swiping cobwebs out of her way and looking over the first machine. Jax appeared at the top of the stairs. "You better come see this."

His tone ignited an unsettled twisting in her belly. "What is it?"

He didn't answer, disappearing into the loft's shadows.

Please don't let it be Elliot. Please...

The stairs groaned under her feet as she took them as quickly as her vision allowed. She hit the landing at full speed, but pulled up short. The smell was more intense up here, a hint of metal mingled with the scent of fresh, rain-soaked air.

Not metal.

Blood.

Jax was standing in the corner, flashlight spotlighting something on the floor. She couldn't see over a collection of cardboard boxes and giant metal canisters between them, but as lightning flashed outside, it lit up the loft and she saw the look on Jax's face.

Oh no.

It was the same look she'd seen that night in Marrakech when they'd discovered Al-Safari's body, Elliot bent over it.

Ruby jetted around the barricade of boxes and barrels and ran up to Jax's side.

Looking down, her guts twisted in a knot and her knees gave out.

⌒——◆——⌒

The man lay face down on the floor, his body wrapped in a

blood-soaked car coat. His head was hid underneath a Cubs baseball cap, and his wrists were bound with twine.

His flashlight beam showed Jax the dead man at his feet wasn't Caucasian.

Not Elliot.

Good thing he'd put his weapon away already because Ruby's knees buckled and Jax had to grab her to keep her from going down.

The feel of her body against him ignited rioting all over his. "It's not him," he said, holding her close and rubbing a hand over her back in comforting circles. "It's not Elliot."

She clung to him, hands clenching his shirt, her jaw working into his shoulder. "Are you sure?"

The guy had a good deal of blood on him, but he was definitely too dark-skinned to be Elliot, who was as pale as the Moroccan sand. "Yeah, I'm sure. This guy's black or Hispanic or a mix. I need to turn him over and get a better look."

Ruby swallowed hard and broke the embrace. "This is a crime scene. I should call it in and we should, you know, back away and not disturb anything. We may have already destroyed evidence."

Jax turned his flashlight back toward the man's body. "There's a lot of wounds. A lot of blood. He was tortured before he bled out."

Ignoring Ruby's protest, he bent down next to the body, reached in to check for a pulse, even though he knew damn well there wouldn't be one.

"Anything?" she said so quietly he almost didn't hear her over the storm.

Jax found the guy's carotid and let his fingertips linger for a moment. Dropped his hand and shook his head. "Nothing. Body's cool to the touch. He hasn't been dead long, but he's definitely dead."

Behind him she swore. "Is it Augustus Nelson?"

"Only one way to find out."

Jax grabbed the man's shoulder and rolled him over enough to see the face while Ruby shined her flashlight on him.

As the cap fell off, Jax saw there wasn't much discernible about the face. Someone had beaten the guy to a pulp. Both eyes were swollen to the size of golf balls, the cheekbones were caved in, and the jaw appeared broken.

Definitely tortured.

"Holy Father Christopher," Ruby mumbled. "He looks like he got hit by a tank."

"His overall body proportions seem correct for Nelson, but I can't be sure."

"It's him," she said, spotlighting a patch of skin on the side of the neck.

Jax looked closer and saw nothing but dried blood covering the spot she was focused on. Blood had run from the man's ear and temple, down the side of his face and neck. "How do you know?"

"There." She leaned over his back and pointed to a place slightly covered by the coat's collar. "See that? The edge of the cross tattoo on his neck. I recognize the curlicues. They have spikes on the ends."

Drawing the collar back, Jax saw what she was pointing at. "What the hell did you do, Elliot?" he said to no one in particular.

Outside, the wind changed direction, rain suddenly driving in a broken window to their right.

"You really think Elliot did this?" Ruby said over the noise.

"Torture someone enough to kill him? No." This wasn't Hayden's style. He was a CIA agent, and regardless of Ruby's beliefs, he was trained to put a bullet in someone, but this was something else. "I think someone's messing with us. You're sure that was Hayden on the tape leaving with Nelson?"

"Pretty sure. I couldn't see his face because of the angle of the camera, but it looked like his gait, his general body proportions. Plus, he was wearing the cap from my go-bag."

"He has to be working with someone."

Ruby bent down beside him. "Someone who wanted to shut up Nelson."

Jax checked the pockets of the coat, Nelson's jean pockets. Empty. "First, they wanted information. That's why they tortured him."

"Or maybe it was personal," Ruby mused. "Like you said it might have been with me."

The only person associated with both Ruby and Nelson who would be extracting some kind of personal revenge had to be Elliot, didn't it?

But this wasn't him. None of it. He was highly intelligent and sneaky as hell, but not brutally violent. And he loved Ruby, Jax was sure. Hurting her would be the last thing Elliot Hayden would ever do.

Unless he'd had a mental breakdown. Prison, even country club prison, could make a person lose their shit.

Ruby flinched as a bright bolt of lightning cracked nearby. "This storm is getting serious."

"Let's take some pictures for reference and we'll go downstairs and call the local cops."

She stood and brought out her phone. "That will tie us up for awhile. We don't have time for the cops."

Jax held the body so she could take pictures of the face, then he allowed it to return to its original position, facedown. "We'll call it in anonymously. My cell is a secure line."

"Mine too. I still don't like using our cells."

"Paranoid, much?"

"You would be, too, if you knew the shit the CIA and NSA do."

He conceded with a nod. "I'll call Emit. He'll take care of it."

Thunder boomed so hard, it shook the building's walls. Both of them flinched this time. The wind roared around the windows. "Let's get downstairs," Jax said, taking her by the elbow.

She was still playing with her phone. "I don't know about you, but I don't have service."

Jax stopped at the top of the stairs, checked his phone, saw he had no connection either. "Must be the storm. It's knocked out transmissions or a tower is down."

Ruby glanced back. "So now what?"

"We ride the storm out and head to town when it's over. We'll either find service or a pay phone."

The creaky stairs were drowned out by a rapid-fire *pingpingping* against the metal walls and roof. "Is that hail?" Jax called over the noise.

"Must be," Ruby yelled back as she made it to the first floor. "It better not damage my rental!"

If he'd had Wi-Fi, he could have checked his weather app. Instead, he followed Ruby as she danced around the debris in the middle of the floor to the window above the desk.

"Oh, man," he heard her say. The window didn't allow much of a view, the hail, wind, and sheeting rain obscuring the parking lot.

She turned to him, her face concerned. "How safe do you think we are in here?"

Safe? In this old building? The way it was creaking didn't exactly scream stable. "Why?"

Ruby opened her mouth to answer but nothing came out as the sound of a long, wailing siren pierced the chaos of the storm.

She raised a finger and cocked her head toward the window. "That," she said.

Jax listened closer, heard the wailing continue, reminding him of the air raid sirens he'd heard a time or two in combat. He wasn't from the Midwest, but he had a sneaking suspicion he knew what that was. "Shit on a stick, please tell me that's not what I think it is."

"Yep." Ruby squinted out the window, looking up. "That, my friend, is a tornado siren."

CHAPTER TEN

Ruby didn't move away when Jax stepped behind her and wrapped an arm around her waist. She did squeal a little when he lifted her off the ground and spun her away from the window.

God help her. The wind was roaring and the hail was smacking the roof and, hopefully, Jax didn't hear her whimper of fear.

She'd faced terrorists head on. Gang bangers and some pretty righteously mean bastards as well. Hell, she'd been underground in a tunnel when it had blown up.

Not much scared her like hearing a tornado siren.

Growing up in this part of the country, sirens were a part of every summer. For two weeks every July, she and her siblings would spend time on their grandparents' farm near Galena. They'd help their grandpa with his prize garden, swing on the porch swing in the evenings, watching fireflies. There was a stream nearby where they went swimming and sometimes caught fish.

Ruby always threw hers back.

It was an idyllic two weeks except for the storms that always rolled through.

The tornado that had killed her grandfather had come at dusk, the sun slipping below the horizon and disguising the fast moving clouds. They'd heard the siren go off in the nearest town, five miles away, the air so still on the front porch, Ruby's grandfather had waved it off. The crops and garden were dry from lack of rain, and Grandpa McKellen had sniffed the air.

"Probably pass us right on by," he'd said. "Just you watch."

By the time their grandmother had sent the kids into the cellar, sheer winds generated by the approaching tornado had split the willow tree in two. One massive side of the tree fell into the house. Ruby's grandfather, sitting at the kitchen table, had died instantly.

Jax hustled her across the floor to the back of the building where the machines sat forgotten and tucked her between a grain bin and the back wall. Squeezing his body in with her, he drew her down into a squat.

She couldn't see anything, his massive body blocking out what little light there was as he hovered slightly over her, prepared to protect her from the storm.

The storm inside her was equally as strong, her heart and mind in turmoil, her body eager to curl up to Jax's solidness and hold on for dear life.

The simple act of breathing became a challenge, the air in the room seeming to be sucked out by a giant vacuum. White noise roared in her ears; the ground under her feet trembled.

Her hands found Jax of their own volition, grabbing onto his shirt, his arms, wrapping around his chest. The smell of his soap and his sweat cut through the other smells. The weight of one of his hands on the back of her neck brought her head to his chest. Over the awful noises of the storm and her own mental chaos, she thought she heard his heartbeat, steady and strong like the rest of him.

The timing was wrong, the train wreck of her career, her life, continuing to lurch further off the tracks. Yet, something made her fingers snake up his chest, his neck, then touch his firm jaw. She felt more than heard him grunt, sensed his face turning down to look at her.

The feel of his cheeks, his lips under her fingers made her even bolder. She wanted him so much in that moment—this protector, this incredible man who made her toes curl and her blood run hot—that she stopped thinking about her job, her loyalties to the CIA and Elliot, to her own insecurities about relationships. Even to her fear of tornadoes.

She had nowhere else to be in that moment, no deadlines, no undercover op. The storm raged around them, uncontrollable and wild, and in that moment, she wanted to be like the storm. Wanted to let go of her fears and the maelstrom of her life and be wild and reckless.

Her fingers found their way into his hair, tickled his earlobes, traced a rivulet of water running down the back of his neck.

She felt him shiver under the stroke of her hand.

And then the hand holding the back of her neck drew her closer. In the dark, she felt the soft glide of his lips against hers, the taste of his tongue as she sought it with her own.

Muscles rippled under her hands as she brought her fingers to this shoulders, dragging him closer until their chests bumped. His tongue swept into her mouth, deepening the kiss.

The air she couldn't find before now flooded her lungs as she gasped at the fresh sensations surging through her veins, firing up her blood. She'd been so lonely since Marrakech. So *alone*.

Ruby knew how the poor, old building felt, all alone, no longer necessary. She'd felt that way since Marrakech.

People came and went in her life. No big deal. It was the life of an operative. Friends, family, co-workers, most of them never knew why she kept her distance. Why she never looked back.

Being on her own had never bothered her. She liked being independent, not tied down to a desk job or a steady relationship. Elliot had been her one long-term alliance—a partner she had trusted with her life, her very soul.

And then Jaxon Sloan had come along and changed everything.

Clinging to him in the midst of a tornado, she didn't want to let go. Couldn't stand the thought of being alone. She'd never given her heart to anyone, yet somehow, on the worst mission of her life, he'd slipped under her skin, gotten into her blood, her very atoms.

The howling around them faded into the background as his hands found their way under her shirt, up to her bra. He thumbed her nipples through the soft lace and Ruby panted into his mouth, shifting her weight back on her knees so she could fumble with his belt buckle.

He broke the kiss, caught her hand and drew it away. She felt the vibration of his chest as though he'd said something, but she couldn't hear him above the roar in her ears.

Then he was pulling her under the nearest machine, flattening her to the ground with his heavy, muscled body. One hand tangled in her hair, his fist gathering the tresses and tugging on them until she arched back, exposing her neck to him. The other hand went between her legs, cupping her, his thumb rubbing her sensitive spot through her jeans.

He dropped his lips to her neck, kissing, sucking, running his tongue along her vulnerable throat. Teeth scraped against her skin, nibbled her earlobe, sending a fresh, white hot zap of electricity down to her lower belly, between her legs.

She arched even higher, rocking against his hand. Above them, rain lashed against the building. Ruby vaguely heard the sound of a tree splitting, a crash.

She whimpered again, but not from fear.

The rhythm Jax was building was oh-so good, and she wanted more, more, more. Wanted her jeans gone and his fingers inside her. Wanted *him* inside her.

Molotov cocktail. That's what Elliot had called the two of them on their mission in Morocco. Fire and fuel. A dangerous, unpredictable bomb ready to explode.

"Jax," she called, reaching for his belt buckle again. Could he hear her? "I need you. *Now.*"

Lightning flashed, the illumination under the machine minimal. Still, she saw the look on his face, the desire there warring with the need to protect her. They could die here, in this storm, in this awful abandoned building in the middle of nowhere. How long would it take someone to find them?

His lips came down next to her ear. "You sure about that? Right now?"

He thought she was crazy.

Maybe she was, but the sound of his voice, intense, rich, bold, asking the question while at the same time daring her to give him exactly what he wanted, spurred her on.

Grabbing his shirt lapels in each hand, she gave a hard yank.

Buttons flew. His shirt opened, revealing his massive chest. She reached out and ran her hands over his pecs, down to his stomach.

She heard the growl from his chest—loud and primal. He popped open her jeans and unzipped them.

The torture was exquisite as he stared into her eyes and slowly, slowly, slid his hand down to her panties, cupping her fully with his palm, completely ignoring the raging storm around them.

A finger pushed the fabric aside and dove between her folds, his thumb finding her clit. At the same time, he brought his mouth down on hers, his tongue shooting between her lips.

The double assault bowed her back once more, her cry caught by his kiss. Her hips jerked under his hand, allowing him deeper access and a fresh rhythm built quickly between them, sending her up, up, up, spiraling like the wind outside.

Her release came so quickly, she felt like the tree outside, splitting right down her middle. She flew apart, Jax's name screamed into the raging whirlwind.

On the heels of her orgasm, a second scream, violent and untamed, ripped through their surroundings.

Jax had snuck into strongholds in enemy territory, survived windstorms in the desert, pulled himself out of quicksand, and gone mano-a-mano with terrorists who thought they owned the world.

But never in his life had he brought a woman to orgasm during a fucking tornado.

Probably not the best idea he'd ever had.

But it was Ruby and she'd clung to him and kissed him and ran her fingers across his face and he was one hundred percent fucked.

Because they both knew he'd give her any damn thing she wanted, any time she wanted it.

Even in the midst of a tornado.

She was insane. So was he. Put the two of them together and boom. Fireworks, explosions, shitass craziness of every kind.

He couldn't say no to her. She lit the fire in him in a way no one else ever had, ever would. He needed her brand of drug in his veins. Needed her in ways he'd never imagined.

Now she lay under him, panting, completely undone as an ungodly screech rent the air. Jax jerked a look back over his shoulder and saw the right front corner of the roof split. Half a second later, it was clawed away by the storm.

The number and intensity of curse words that fell from his lips were lost in the midst of rain and debris that came through the open roof as he lifted Ruby up and tucked her into a ball farther under the bagging machine. His body instinctively wrapped around hers.

Rudely ripped from her post-orgasmic haze, she protested, but her objections were cut short as she realized what was happening and how truly fucked they both were.

She shouted something, her mouth working, and he could actually see her face since they had a new source of light. The words, however, were sucked away on the wind, her hair blowing around her face. He brought his hand to the back of her head, and motioned for her to duck as he pressed her head down, leaning over her.

He didn't think the roar of the wind could get worse, yet it did. Even as covered as he was, rain and other things pelted into his back. He prayed to whatever god there might be that the hand tools that had been laying on the shelves didn't rap him on their way by.

From the next harsh, piercing noise behind him, he guessed another piece of the roof went bye-bye. Within seconds, his backside was completely soaked and he felt a shift in the air around him. The air was pressing on him, and then, suddenly, it wasn't.

Instead, it reversed and he felt a sucking sensation in his lungs, his gut. If there was a god, he was reaching down, about to grab Jax right out from under this machine.

Shit. *Better hold on.*

Yanking his belt off, he tied it around the end of the machine and then around Ruby's wrist. "Hold on!" he yelled into her ear as the sucking sensation gripped hold of him and started to pull him out from under his hidey hole.

Quick as the lightning flashing overhead, he wrapped one arm around the machine leg and his other around Ruby.

Her arms went around his neck, her legs around his waist. The added weight grounded him and he would have breathed a sigh of relief if he'd actually been able to breathe at all.

Because that hand of God was sucking every last bit of air from the place.

A piece of wall broke free and went flying off into the abyss outside. Then another. The bagging machine trembled, its legs scooting a couple of centimeters to the right.

Don't you dare, you piece of shit.

It trembled harder. Ruby tightened her grip on him even more. Jax clenched his teeth and held on for all he was worth.

Next thing he knew, the hand of God finally caught up with him. His ass lifted off the ground.

Airborne. Even with Ruby sitting in his lap.

If she hadn't been wrapped around him, she would have fallen flat on the ground, then been swept up by the wind. As it was, she clung to him and he clung to the machine and they seemed to float there for a moment.

A long, agonizing moment, where her hair wrapped around his face, covering his eyes and his muscles strained beyond their edge, his heart nearly exploded from fear.

Don't let Ruby die.

Don't let Ruby die.

The refrain echoed over and over in his brain. His lungs cried out for oxygen. His body tried to find the ground.

Stupid goddamn idiot!

Why hadn't he paid attention to the weather report? The impending storm? The fact that when they'd heard the siren go off, he hadn't taken it more seriously and gotten both of them the hell out of there?

But where would they have gone? Cornfields weren't known for their storm cellars.

Ruby's cheek grazed his and something inside him calmed. His heart was still flipping out, his brain still beating him to a pulp for his foolishness, and yet…his body shifted to a different state as he felt her grounding him, even in the midst of near death.

A piece of her hair fell from his eyes and he fought the force of the wind to shift his head enough he could see her. She was looking up, up into the storm threatening to end them as they continued to be lifted off the floor.

And there it was. That thing he loved about her. Fearlessness, ballsiness, courage.

Her eyes were wide open, cheeks rosy. There was no alarm in her features, but more of a reverence. As if God were truly there, looking down on them, and she was standing in awe of His power.

In the face of death, she looked…peaceful.

That's when he knew. If he died today, right here with her wrapped in his arms, he'd be at peace too.

It was a blissful thought for a moment. Then his survival instincts—good guys that they were—kicked in hard. No way, no how, were the two of them dying here today.

Using all his might, he cranked the arm holding Ruby around, twisting, twisting, twisting until…

Yes! He grabbed the machine leg with that hand. Two points of contact, and a whole lot more leverage, might just be the ticket to their survival.

The sucky part was, he couldn't hold onto Ruby and the machine leg at the same time. He had to rely on her. She had to keep her body clinging to his in order to keep her safe. The sensation was akin to skydiving with a partner. He'd done tandem jumping a time or two, never much cared for it. Until now.

"Don't let go!" he yelled and saw her head nod.

Inch by inch, he crawled his hand down the machine leg, the machine itself still scooting across the floor ever so slowly as the suction worked it over.

As long as it didn't lift off, they could ride this out.

That was when he felt the machine shudder, the leg he was hanging onto suddenly hovering above the ground.

CHAPTER ELEVEN

A ghost was chasing him.

Elliot came to in the middle of a cornfield, rain pouring down, and a crushing pain in his thigh.

Above him, angry clouds swirled, lightning flashed. The wind was insane. Raising his head and blinking through the sharp wind, he saw green weeds twining their leggy bodies around dead corn stalks left over from the previous fall. The field he was lying in was fallow and unplanted.

Dead. Abandoned.

Like me.

His head pounded, the cold rain shocking against the heat of his brow. Shirt plastered to his chest, he felt for his weapon and found it missing.

How did I end up here?

He'd been at the old feed mill, questioning Nelson, hiding him. He thought they'd escaped, that they were free from the tail he'd had since the police station.

Convincing Nelson he couldn't go back to Chicago had stretched his already thin patience to the breaking point. The stupid gang banger didn't understand. The man hunting both of them wouldn't stop until he had what he wanted—Elliot's head on a platter.

Elliot had given Nelson one of the phones from Ruby's go-bag and explained their options. There was no going back to Chicago. Not until the ghost was dealt with, maybe not even then.

The man who wanted Ruby would keep sending his minions.

Leaving Nelson to stew, Elliot had gone in search of food and water. Even in the middle of nowhere, he couldn't exactly walk into a gas station and grab supplies without fear of being recognized. His last disguise as a Homeland official was too out of the ordinary in a small farming community.

The mill's office had provided a pair of overalls and a new hat. Elliot liked the overalls—they were loose and provided plenty of pockets for his weapon, the phones, and the cash Ruby had given him. The hat—well, he knew nothing about fertilizer companies, but like the overalls, the dusty, worn, ball cap advertising Dow would allow him to keep his face partially hidden and keep him from attracting notice if he was lucky.

It was still impossible to be inconspicuous in a small town where everyone knew everyone. A place where no one was in a hurry and everyone wanted to chat.

Sure enough, when he'd hit the local gas station and grabbed some water and two sandwiches, the first thing the clerk did was ask him if he was from around there.

Elliot had been quick on his feet like always, pulling his rain drenched hat farther down on his face. "Nah, just passin' through," he'd told the old geezer. "On my way to the city."

A siren had gone off in the far distance, followed by another. "You might want to find you a place to hunker down," the clerk had said. "Find you" had sounded like *fine-jew.* "Nasty weather headed our way."

Elliot had thanked him and hustled out, pretending to be worried about the approaching storm, rather than the man hunting him down.

The ghost had been close on his heels. By the time Elliot had gotten back to the abandoned mill, he'd already been there.

Sirens were once again going off, the long wails making him think of demons in hell, keening for his soul. Pushing himself to a seated position, Elliot wiped water from his eyes and saw a nasty, swirling mass far away in the distance.

Ah, hell.

The tip of the fat tornado raced along the ground, sending detritus into the air in all directions. Even this far away, Elliot felt the energy crackling and hissing along the ground, in the air.

His vision was slightly off from one too many blows to his head from the ghost, so he squinted to try to clear it. Realized what he was seeing. Where the tornado actually was, the path of destruction it was taking.

The mill.

Only a few minutes ago—or had it been longer?—he'd run away from the mill. Images of Nelson's tortured body flashed through his mind. All that blood...the man's screams...

Had Nelson told him? Told the man about Elliot? About Ruby?

No way to know. His brain couldn't remember exactly what had happened.

Didn't matter. He had to go back.

Because if by some chance, Nelson was still alive...

Ruby.

The ghost was here for her.

Ignoring the righteous pain in his leg, Elliot forced himself to his feet and started running.

He took two steps and fell flat on his face, one foot twisting around a broken corn stalk. As hail began to pelt him, he lost consciousness.

Ruby's body felt like it might implode one vertebrae, one organ at a time.

One second, she was holding onto Jax for dear life as the heavy machine he'd tied them to began to come off the ground.

The next second, the severe wind died with no warning, sending them and the machine back to the ground with a hard thump.

Her back hit first, then her head. Jax came down on top of her, a dead weight knocking the air from her lungs and crushing her into the concrete floor.

An "ooof" left her mouth and she realized she could actually hear herself. The horrible wind tunnel they'd been in was gone. The only sound meeting her ears now was the soft fall of rain pinging on the machines, the shelves, the floor.

Jax lay for a moment on top of her, his eyes closed, his mouth sucking in oxygen. His hair was matted, water rivulets running down his forehead, his jaw.

His eyelids flipped open and he zeroed in on her face. "You all right?"

His voice was gravelly and rough. Probably from the amount of dirt and rubbish he'd ingested. God knew, she'd eaten a bit of that herself.

"I can't…breathe…" she choked out.

"Jesus, sorry." The startled look on his face made her smile as he jerked himself up off of her, his one hand releasing its grip on the machine leg somewhat reluctantly. "My arm is asleep."

She laughed, a bubble of hysteria riding just under her breastbone. "I can't believe we're alive."

He chuckled too, leaning on one elbow, his long legs stretched out beside her. "I've saved quite a few people in my time—bullets flying, dark of night, never knowing where the next bad guy is hiding—but never like this. This is one for the books."

She had to agree. Reaching up, she brushed a piece of straw off his face. "Thank you."

He shot her a knowing glance, followed by a smirk. "For saving your ass or giving you the best orgasm of your life?"

She buttoned her pants, then struggled to sit up. Her hair hung in wet strands and she ran a hand through it, her fingers getting caught in multiple tangles. The hysteria filling her chest subsided a bit. Her brain came fully online. "It was good, but I wouldn't qualify it as the *best* orgasm of my life."

He sat up next to her, helping her with the tangles. His fingers did more damage than good, but it felt nice to have him close. "Is that so? I barely touched you and you exploded."

Oh, my God. Were they really arguing about the significance of her orgasm right now? "I'll grant you that I won't soon forget it under the circumstances, but really, it wasn't the best of my life."

The best had been in Marrakech. When he was inside her and had made her come multiple times in the span of a minute.

Yeah, *that* was the best.

Of course, she'd been easy then too. He'd been flirting with her, staring at her, touching her here and there the whole trip into Morocco. It had been like extended foreplay, the way he knew exactly how to make her blush, challenge her, make her feel sexier than she'd ever felt before.

When she'd finally given in and kissed him, their first lovemaking had turned into a fast, furious pounding against the wall of her hotel room. What had followed had been hours and hours of the best sex she'd ever had.

His finger and thumb cupped her chin, turning her head so they were eye-to-eye. "Maybe the best is yet to come."

She really shouldn't lead him on. What she'd felt for him during the storm was the tip of the iceberg. If she let her feelings run wide open, they'd both careen over the cliff and blow their careers—as well as their hearts—to oblivion.

But, sweet Jesus, it just might be worth it.

It was wrong, but she grinned through the rain running down her face. "Maybe."

The hope she shouldn't have given him was evident on his face. It promised her a future filled with hot, head-banging sex.

The anticipation was almost as good as the actual sex act.

Almost.

He helped her up and they surveyed the damage. In the distance they heard the rumble of thunder, much less menacing than before. Ruby did her best to smooth her hair back from her face, but it was pointless. It would take her hours to get the disaster under control. Her gun was missing and a quick sweep of the area revealed the Sig was gone.

Damn, and that was her favorite handgun.

She pointed upward to the loft. Half of it was gone, along with the stairs that had led up to it. "Think the body is still there?"

Jax, standing over at the hole left by the tornado, stared outside at the spot where she'd parked the rental. "Nope."

Ruby huffed out a sigh and went to look at what he was staring at.

The breeze rattled the lone wall panel still intact and she inched her way past it, worried it might let loose of its tenuous hold at any moment. Through part of the opening, she saw the oak tree had indeed split in half, a massive piece of trunk and a scattering of branches visible on the ground just beyond the building.

She stopped next to Jax and peered out.

Her body recoiled. Augustus Nelson lay sprawled, his limbs torqued at unnatural angles, across her rental car.

Which was on its side, glass and car parts scattered around it as if a giant having a tantrum had picked it up and smashed it against the ground.

"So much for having Emit make an anonymous phone call."

"Yeah," Jax said, hands on hips as he glanced at the horizon. "I think we're in for another long night."

"Well, if I hadn't already ruined my last chance at getting my old job back, this would have done it anyway."

"We couldn't have called it in, Ruby. We had no service." Jax drew out his cell phone. The case had a crack in it and it was drenched, but still seemed to work. "I've got one bar."

Better than nothing. She slipped a hand into his, lacing her fingers between his bigger ones. "Guess we better alert the authorities."

He tugged her close and her body bumped against his. "Emit first. He can smooth things over with the local PD."

He made the call while Ruby stared at Augustus, his cuts and bruises now on full display.

There's no way Elliot would have done that to a person. Not even someone he hated.

A flash of something in the branches of the part of the oak that was still standing caught her eye. Her mind whirled with the possibilities as her go-bag, the fabric rent and stuck on a dead branch, fluttered in the breeze.

CHAPTER TWELVE

"THEY WH...WHAT?" Beatrice sputtered into her office phone.

"Don't freak, B," Emit said through the speaker. "Both of them are okay. The tornado got close, but they rode it out. Under some machine from what I understand. Jax's arm is a little screwed up from holding onto the thing, but he claims it's minor."

Good thing her office chair was behind her with Trace standing nearby on alert because her legs turned to Jell-O at the thought of Jaxon and Agent McKellen riding out a tornado hanging onto some feed mill machine. Trace, thank goodness for his superhuman reflexes, got the chair under her before she fell to the floor.

No wonder Jax hadn't returned her phone calls. "Jax would say he was fine even if he was bleeding out. I want them transported to the emergency room, asap."

"They're in Bumblefuck, USA," Emit countered. There isn't anything more than a local clinic, and at the moment, as I understand, they're at the police station giving their detailed accounts of what happened."

"Police station?"

"There was a casualty. Not from the tornado, but..."

"What happened?"

"They found Augustus Nelson, aka Little Gus, at the building. He'd been tortured and beaten to a pulp."

"How did they find him?"

"Ruby gave Elliot a bag with a GPS tracker sewn into the

lining. They told me they were going to see Director Timms, Ruby's temporary boss, at FBI headquarters. Instead, they followed the signal to the feed and grain mill."

Beatrice leaned back in the chair and rocked, trying to reduce her blood pressure that was skyrocketing again. She glanced at Trace, who was listening intently. She would deal with Jaxon's duplicity and impertinence later. "Elliot Hayden killed Nelson?"

"Jax doesn't think it fits with Hayden's MO. Nelson might have had info to clear Elliot's name, according to Ruby. Doesn't make sense he would off the guy."

Trace tapped his lip with a finger. "Unless he got the info and realized Nelson was a problem. If Hayden didn't kill him, who did? Who led Jax and Ruby to that building?"

"You think it's a setup?" Beatrice asked Trace.

"Don't you?" he said.

Beatrice went back to the phone and Emit. "Are Jax and Ruby suspects?"

Emit sighed. "At this point, I'd say they're the only suspects. I called Director Timms for the second time today to vouch for Ruby, but he refuses to accept my reasons for why she went AWOL. He doesn't know Hayden's escaped and therefore has no idea why she'd be tracking him. She needs someone at the CIA level to explain the situation to Timms and the PD in Pottersville, and clear her name."

"Langley won't do that," Beatrice said, rubbing her temple. "They don't want anyone to know Hayden escaped—not Timms and especially not a group of small town police officers with absolutely no top-secret clearance."

A long pause ensued. "Well, then, it looks like Jax and Agent McKellen may be hanging out in Bumblefuck for awhile."

Great. Just what they all needed. "I'll get them out and back to Chicago."

"How?"

Beatrice ignored the concerned look Trace shot her. "Let me worry about that. You, Rory, and Colton stay on Hayden's tail."

"B, don't do anything…"

"Stupid?" she interrupted him. "You aren't seriously going to call me that, are you?"

"I wasn't calling *you* stupid, just warning you not to do anything you'll regret."

She wasn't about to. Jaxon Sloan was as much her family as

the baby inside of her, and the baby was making no moves to join the world anytime soon. "It's a little over two hours to Chicago. Even if I go into labor, Jax has assured me I'll be in that state for longer than two hours, so you needn't worry about me having the baby in the plane."

She disconnected, grabbed her laptop, and stood. "Ready the plane," she said to Trace. "We're going to Bumblefuck, Illinois."

TWO HOURS LATER

"Don't leave town," Jeremy Rolands growled.

The Pottersville PD's chief looked, Jax thought, a lot like Santa Claus...white beard, a belly that strained the buttons on his shirt and crystal blue eyes. "I may be wanting to talk to you two again. Soon," the man added, giving Jax the stink eye.

After a couple of hours in an interrogation room, someone— Beatrice? Emit? The Colonel?—had called good ol' Santa Rolands and gotten Jax and Ruby off the hook.

Not that they were completely out of hot water, but at least their identities had been confirmed and they were being released. No overnight stay in the single cell inside city hall tonight.

Ruby, who still had dreck in her hair, narrowed her eyes at the chief. Her wet shirt clung to her breasts and made it infinitely hard for Jax to concentrate. "Where exactly do you expect us to hang out? Is there a Holiday Inn hiding in this village?"

"Look, girlie—"

"Girlie?" Ruby huffed.

Jax kicked her under the table. Not hard, just to remind her that they needed to make nice to the officer and vamoose.

"We'll figure something out," he said, smiling at Rolands as he held his shirt together in the front where all the buttons were missing. He stood, his soggy pants leaving wet marks on the chair. "You have my cell number. Give me a call, Chief. We're glad to help."

"You haven't been any help at all," the old codger said. "But I know all about you government types. I got a brother who thinks he's God's gift to the world cuz he used to work for the spook house."

Ruby tilted her head as Jax grabbed her elbow and drew her to her feet. She yanked her arm out of his grip. "Your brother was an operative?"

"Kept it from us for years, the bastard. I only found out when our mother died and he was off in some God-forsaken third world country working inside a terrorist camp. I thought he was in Minnesota."

Ruby and Jax exchanged a look. Ruby turned on the charm and stuck out her hand. "It was nice to meet you, Chief Rolands. Like Jax said, call us if you need anything."

"What I need is a better excuse than you simply 'found' that gang banger in the Potter Feed & Grain when you went to take cover from the storm."

Augustus Nelson's body was at the morgue, which doubled as a doctor's clinic a mile down the road. Chicago PD had no interest in it. Neither did the Feds, from Rolands' statements. The only ones who would care about the cause of death was the CIA, and they were mute on the subject so far, leaving Nelson in the hands of the small town doctor.

Jax had little faith in the Pottersville system, whose police and medical experts had no vested interest in why or how Nelson had died.

Ruby touched the man's hand since he didn't offer to shake hers. She leaned forward, lowered her voice. "I wish we could tell you more, I really do, but you could end up dead like Mr. Nelson if we did. I don't want to be beaten to death, and I know you don't either. It's safer we keep certain things under wraps. Okay?"

She winked at Rolands and something happened. The old guy grunted and nodded, his lips softening into half a smile.

Which was when Jax realized the detective was staring at Ruby's breasts through the wet fabric of her shirt as she leaned over his desk.

I'm going to break every bone in his body.

Jax must have tensed because Ruby straightened, grabbed his arm and jerked him toward the door. "Talk soon," she called over her shoulder to Rolands as she hustled them both out of the man's office.

They blew by the cop pit where outdated computers decorated banged up wooden desks. All the beat cops were out on calls resulting from the storm. While the town's main drag had survived untouched, the outlying areas had sustained a lot of damage.

The receptionist openly stared at Jax as they exited the front door, just like she had when they'd entered.

"Pig," Ruby said under her breath once they hit the parking lot.

Jax stretched, clearing his lungs of the stale police station odor. "Give her a break. She's closing in on ninety and probably hasn't seen a good-looking guy in a long time."

Ruby swung to frown at him. "Not the secretary. Chief Rolands."

"Oh, yeah." Jax rubbed his arm, where multiple bruises had formed thanks to his vice grip on the machine leg. "He was definitely a pig. I nearly nailed him to his desk."

Ruby's hands went to her hips and she looked around. "So we have no car and no place to stay. We need clothes, wheels, and I gotta pee. Suggestions?"

Jax's phone beeped with an incoming text. He pulled it out. "Apparently Beatrice reads minds as well as everything she else she does. She says there's a bed and breakfast a half mile from here. We're to go there until a car arrives for us."

"This Beatrice gal gets shit done," Ruby said. "I like her."

Jax laughed. "She takes care of her own, and believe me when I say, she owns me."

They took off walking in the direction of the B&B. The sun was setting, turning the western sky a beautiful peach color.

"How so?" Ruby asked. "Beatrice, I mean. How does she own you?"

She was missing a shoe, having lost it in the storm. Jax wished she could wear one of his, but her feet were munchkin size. "You okay to walk like that?"

Not missing a beat, she nodded. "Tell me why Beatrice and Rock Star Security own you. What do they have on you?"

"Loyalty."

"What?"

"They don't have anything *on* me. They offered me a job after Morocco and the whole Hayden mess."

She snorted. "You had a perfectly good job with the SEALs. You were born to be a frogman. Why leave?"

He focused on the scenery as they passed the post office and library all housed in one building, then a quilt shop and lawyer's office next to it. Thinking about how he'd ended his Navy career wasn't pleasant. "I broke rank. No going back after that."

"Broke rank?"

He needed a diversion; saw nothing but dead corn fields. "When I went to the Justice Department about Hayden, my CO didn't like it. Turned my team against me."

Ruby's footsteps faltered. "What? Why?"

"I went to my CO and told him my suspicions about Hayden killing Al-Safari. He told me to keep my nose out of it. None of my business; let the CIA handle it. But you know me, I couldn't let it go. I disobeyed a direct order, left San Diego to go to Washington, and burned my career."

She was quiet for a moment. "You did what you thought was right. Your CO was an idiot. He should have respected that."

His CO wasn't an idiot. That was the thing. "I had nothing after the SEALs." *Not even you.* "Beatrice showed up and offered me a job with her group. She liked my renegade style. The fact I had medical training under my belt helped too."

"All SEALs receive combat medical training."

He gave up holding his shirt together, letting it flap in the breeze. "Mine's a little more than that."

She rolled her shoulders and grimaced, used her right hand to massage her neck. "Oh, yeah? Like what?"

He kicked a rock. A car whizzed by them on the road, sending his shirt tales flying like wings on either side of him. "I dropped out of med school one semester short of graduation. Left a highly sought-after residency to join the Navy."

Something in his tone must have alerted her to the fact he wasn't proud of that. "I'm sure you had your reasons."

"I thought being a doctor was the ultimate make-a-difference career. My mom and dad are both doctors—Dad's a surgeon, Mom's a chiropractor. I grew up on family dinner discussions about anatomy, diseases, and drug interactions. I never considered anything else."

They walked on, Ruby slowing to his pace, staying at his side as he talked. "My best friend was a SEAL. He'd been all over the world, making a real difference by shutting down terrorists and evacuating Americans caught in bad situations. I admired his dedication but I thought he was crazy."

"What happened to make you change your mind?"

"He came back from a rescue mission in Belgium missing both legs, thanks to a car bomb."

She shook her head. Another car went by and honked its horn at them, some young guys angling their heads out the car windows to hoot at Ruby. "God, I'm so sorry."

Jax wanted to hit the still-ogling kids as they raced away down the road. He flipped them the bird instead. "It sucked. I joined the Navy two days later and never looked back."

"I don't really get that," Ruby said, shooting him a look. "Your best friend gets his legs blown off and you join the Navy?"

He wasn't proud of the reason. "I wanted revenge."

"Revenge on the terrorists?"

It was a muddled mess, his emotions and stupid logic. "The group responsible for the car bomb. His team wasn't even after them. They were there on a training mission. An American diplomat whose son was part of the group invited all of them to his house for a dinner at the Embassy. The terrorist group set off a bomb outside the Embassy because of America backing some ridiculous political accord that Logan had nothing to do with."

She pulled up short. "The Moroccan 5."

"Yep, that was them. One of their many hits on Americans."

She started walking again, head down. "So you joined the Navy and worked your ass off to become a SEAL in order to hunt those men down?"

"Sounds childish, doesn't it?"

"Sounds brave to me. You gave up a lucrative career and promising future as a doctor to bring justice to your best friend."

"My parents had a cow. Twin cows. They disowned me."

"What?" She swung around in front of him and stopped. "You're joking, right?"

He shook his head, also coming to a stop. "My parents told me I was being ridiculous and not to come home until I got my shit together and appreciated the sacrifices they'd made to get me into Johns Hopkins and line me up for the best cardiac residency program in the country."

Her forehead scrunched and her eyes blazed with indignation. "Jax, that's terrible."

He shrugged. "I understood their disappointment. I tend to do my own thing for my own, selfish reasons, and it seems to always hurt other people. My CO told me as much when I disobeyed his orders and went to Washington to rat out

Hayden. He was right. I'm not dependable, and what good has it done? The Moroccan 5 were caught and killed by the Israelis, and, now, I think Hayden may be innocent."

The crease in her forehead deepened. Her lips thinned in a tight line. "The Moroccan 5..."

He waited, but she didn't say anything else, instead whirling around and walking again. He could see the B&B at the corner. "What about them?"

One finger brushed hair from her face, curling it around her ear. "There's more to the story than you know."

He grabbed her arm, stopped her again. "What are you talking about?"

She bit her bottom lip, wouldn't look at him. "It's classified. I can't share it. Forget I said anything."

He let her walk off, his feet stuck to the ground. She hopped onto the sidewalk that ran in front of the bed and breakfast, and then when she realized he wasn't with her, she stopped and cupped a hand over her face to shield her eyes from the sun. "You coming?"

His chest felt tight. She stood there, clothes sticking to her body, her feet bare and dirty from the walk. One ankle was bandaged. What did she know about the Moroccan 5 that she wasn't telling him?

"Tell me the truth, Ruby," he called.

Her hand fell. "I can't, Jax. I've already said too much."

Really? After all they'd been through, she was going to keep whatever nugget of intel she had about a subject that had changed the entire course of his life?

Fuck this.

He was done playing games. Damned tired of being dicked around.

Jax turned on his heel and headed for the road leading out of town.

CHAPTER THIRTEEN

"Jax!" Ruby flew off the sidewalk, running after him. "Wait! Where are you going?"

No response. He didn't even slow down, boots hitting the earth as if he were Godzilla, bent on destroying the city under his feet.

Running in her bare feet, she jumped over a downed tree branch and landed on a rock. The sharp edge bit into her arch, and when she tried to pull up, she managed to twist her ankle. The same one she'd twisted at the club.

She went down on all fours, skidding into some gravel. "Damn it!" she swore, ignoring the sting of pebbles embedding themselves in her palms and ripping through the knees of her jeans.

Her clumsiness had one benefit—Jax came hustling back to lift her up.

Seemed like he was doing an awful lot of that lately.

For some stupid reason, her eyes filled with tears. Everything was so beyond messed up, she didn't know how to start putting the pieces of her life—as well as Elliot's and Jax's—back together.

But she had to try.

Because everything had gone wrong for all three of them in Marrakech.

A hiccup left her mouth and she bit down on her tongue to stop herself from all-out crying. That still didn't stop her mouth from opening and a sobby-sounding "I'm sorry" spilling out.

Jax brushed rocks from her knees and then from her palms. "I can't do this anymore, Ruby."

"I know," she said, although she wasn't sure exactly what part of *this* he was talking about. Did it matter? "I can't either."

He hugged her briefly. "Right now, you and I... We only have each other. If we can't be honest with each other, even if it breaches our personal or working code of ethics, we've got nothing."

She nodded and swallowed hard. "Come back to the bed and breakfast, and after I get cleaned up, I'll tell you everything while we wait for the car."

His eyes searched her face as if he could ferret out whether she was being completely honest with him. She stared back, not flinching, even though her body ached. Hell, her entire system ached—body, mind, and soul.

Jax didn't look convinced, but he nodded and helped her to the sidewalk and up to the wide front porch of the house.

A soft, high melody came from inside when Ruby pushed the doorbell. A moment later, an elderly lady with wire-rimmed glasses and a sunflower apron opened the door. "Yes?"

They must have looked a sight, soaking wet, dirty, with ripped clothes, because the lady's eyes widened behind her glasses.

Ruby put on her best smile. "We need a room. Do you have any vacancies? We only need one for a few hours."

The woman's eagle eyes sized up Ruby, three tiny lines developing between her eyebrows when her gaze landed on Ruby's ring finger. Her soft, doughy cheeks slid down into a frown as she glanced at Jax's ring finger as well. It didn't take a genius to realize she was checking to see if they were married.

The eagle eyes narrowed as her nose went up in the air. "I'm sorry, but I don't cater to that sort of thing here, young lady."

Jax chuckled beside her. "What Ruby meant is, we got caught in the tornado and our car is damaged. Your police chief recommended we rent a room so we can clean up here while we wait for our friends to come from Chicago to pick us up."

"Oh." The woman gave him a longer look and the lines between her brows softened. "In that case, I suppose I can rent the two rooms upstairs. You'll have to share a bathroom."

"That'll be fine," Jax said. "We'd appreciate it."

Stepping back, she let them in, introducing herself as Paula and directing Jax to take off his wet, muddy boots before they both followed her upstairs.

The place was straight out of a Norman Rockwell painting

with hardwood floors, a steep staircase, and floral wallpaper. The lady chatted about the crazy storm as they followed her, Ruby trying to make appropriate noises where necessary. She was too wrung out to make small talk.

Paula gathered fresh towels, shampoo, and soap and deposited them in front of their respective rooms. "You get the Pink Kitty room," she said to Ruby, opening the door.

A pink and white comforter covered the canopy bed. Next to it was a white wicker nightstand. More wicker in the form of a dresser and desk rounded out the furniture. Everywhere Ruby's gaze landed, she saw cats. Stuffed toy cats, pictures on the walls, porcelain cat figurines on all the shelves, a cat quilt folded on top of the comforter.

She tried to find something positive about stepping into the explosion of cats. She liked cats just fine, but there had to be two hundred versions of them in that small room.

At least there aren't two hundred of the real thing running around, she consoled herself. While Paula seemed like a good candidate as a cat lady, Ruby had yet to see any signs of living specimens.

Although, at this point, she'd take a few real cats over all the fake ones.

"My daughter loved cats when she was young, but was allergic to them," Paula said, a sadness in her voice. "We improvised."

Ruby pressed her lips together so tight, she thought she might hurt herself. She didn't say a word, accepting the towels and shampoo before nodding to Paula and backing into the room.

As their hostess turned to lead Jax to his room, Jax winked at her.

Ruby raised her pointer finger to her temple and pretended to shoot herself.

Jax grinned at Ruby, then proceeded down the hall where Paula was already waiting.

"You get the duck room," she said with a look of pride on her face. "My husband was a big duck hunter."

She pointed to the interior and Jax leaned around the frame to peer in.

Fuckin' A. More wallpaper, this time in dark greens and reds. The bed was a monstrous wood thing and above the headboard was a shelf with stuffed ducks on it. A bookshelf across from it was filled with more of the taxidermy birds. Rows and rows of dead ducks, all of their beady eyes watching him.

"Great," he said, wondering which was worse, fake cats or duck zombies. "Again, we really appreciate this."

Paula nodded and wiped her hands on her apron. "I'll round up some food and drink for you."

"We don't want to put you out."

"Nonsense. I haven't had guests in a couple of months. It'll be good to talk to someone."

Good God. He had some talking to do, but it wasn't to ol' Paula here. "That would be great," he lied.

Shoot me now. Never in his life had he used the term "great" so many times in a row.

Paula left and Jax shut the door, leaning against it for a moment as the dead ducks watched him. "Fuck a duck." Could this day get any weirder?

He heard the soft patter of Ruby's bare feet in the hallway heading for the bathroom. He tossed his towel on the bed, then slid down the door and listened to the sound of the shower coming on.

His dick grew hard. What he wouldn't give to climb in that shower with her, scrub her clean and dirty her up again.

Forget it. You need to find out about the Moroccan 5, not screw Ruby silly.

Might be fun to do both, though.

His phone buzzed. Amazingly, the thing had made it through the tornado. He'd seen some damn advanced technology, but the SFI stuff still surprised him. How Emit and Beatrice got their hands on such high-tech, field-impervious shit was beyond him.

"Yo, man, what's up?" he asked Colton, who was on the other end. "You almost here?"

"The car's on its way, probably be about an hour until they get there, but Emit wants me keeping an eye on things here, so I won't be with them. I'm calling to let you know there was a report of a man lying in a cornfield not far from you. Eyewitnesses said he was injured and bleeding, but by the time the cops got to the spot he'd been seen at, he was gone."

"Yeah, so?"

"The description the eyewitnesses gave matches your friend."

"Hayden?"

"Yep. Neither of the witnesses stopped to offer him help because he was reportedly talking to himself and seemed potentially dangerous."

"Shit, I need to go look for him, but I've got no wheels. Maybe I could hotwire a car."

"Emit says you and Ruby are to sit tight. Meantime, I did more digging into this Agent Brown douchebag. Homeland's nearly impossible to breach these days, but between Beatrice, Zeb, and I, we traced that ID badge that Brown used back to its source."

"Is it legit?"

"While Chicago PD said his credentials checked out, they called the number Brown provided, rather than digging up the number on their own."

"I suppose the number Brown gave them is bogus."

"It's not Homeland, that's for sure. Whoever was on the other end of that phone that verified Brown as an employee was lying."

"So who'd you trace the ID badge back to?"

"You'll never guess."

"Come on, man, pony up."

"Rory's skills were put to the test with this one, but he traced the call to a small, off-the-grid, international CIA station."

Jax felt a spurt of adrenaline down his spine. "Where?"

"Morocco."

He nearly dropped the phone. "All of this circles back to Marrakech and Al-Safari."

"Hayden and Brown are the same person, aren't they? Hayden took Nelson to that old feed mill to interrogate him, then killed him and tried to escape before the storm caught him."

"It does look that way, but things aren't adding up," Jax said, hearing the shower in the bathroom shut off. "You think someone's setting up Hayden?"

He got up and walked over to the bed, where he plopped down and rubbed his eyes. "I think it's more than one."

"More than one person? Like a conspiracy?"

"I think it's the whole fucking CIA."

A pause as Colton digested this news. "Hell, if that's the case..."

Jax stopped hearing the rest of the words as the door to his room opened and Ruby, hair wet but shiny and smooth now, glided in, wrapped in nothing but a pink towel.

"I've got to let you go," Jax said, disconnecting Colton in mid-sentence.

"My clothes are all wet and dirty," Ruby said, leaning back against the door. "I didn't want to put them back on until I have to."

His mouth was dry. The towel barely came down below her ass and her full breasts bubbled up at the top where she clenched the towel in one hand.

"Great," he said, and mentally kicked himself, because he literally couldn't form any other coherent word. "I mean, um... Okay."

He scooted over a foot and motioned to the spot he'd vacated. "You want to sit?"

She eyed the duck zombies over his head, glanced over at the shelves of them. "Yikes. I think I like cats better."

But she strolled over to the bed and sat next to him.

Which was a good thing since it saved him from standing up and revealing the growing bulge in his jeans.

She smelled like flowers and soap. Her face was scrubbed clean for the second time that day, a mild cut along her hairline on the left side that he hadn't noticed before, probably due to the dirt. Her lips were their natural peachy-pink color, her eyes clear and somewhat wary as she met his gaze.

It was all he could do not to let his focus dip down to the luscious mounds topping the towel or the expanse of creamy skin where the towel split along her right leg.

"So, uh...," he started, fumbling to put his phone away. When he couldn't hit the pocket, he gave up and tossed it onto the bed. "Tell me what you know about the Moroccan 5."

"Don't you want to get your shower first?"

Had she really come in here to talk while her clothes dried out? The look in her eyes said no. She wanted something else. Something she'd had earlier in the day.

And goddammit, he wanted to give it to her.

But not until he had the information he needed. "What I want at this moment is for you to be honest with me."

He saw the flare of rebellion light her up. Just as quickly, she shut it down. She gnawed on her lower lip for a moment and stared at the floor. With a heavy sigh, she closed her eyes, then opened them and picked at the hem of the towel. "The Israelis didn't catch them. We did."

"We?"

"Yeah, we. As in…"

She bit that lip again and his groin went crazy.

"Come on, Ruby. Spit it out. Who's we?"

Her attention went to the mirror over the dresser. She stared at her own reflection for a moment, then met his eyes there. "As in, me and Elliot."

What the fuck? "Are you kidding me?"

She shook her head, dropped it to stare at the damn floor again. "Because of some deal Homeland had with Mossad, they were given credit for the capture and deaths of all five men, but El and I found them in Paris, lured them into a CIA safe house there and trapped them. We sent them on to the US for incarceration. All but one, apparently."

"Which one?"

"Abdel Al-Safari."

Jax ground his teeth. "Al-Safari was part of M5?"

"I only just learned that Elliot turned him into an asset to get close to Izala, I swear. As far as I know the rest of the members of M5 were sent to Guantanamo. Eighteen months ago, orders came down to release them. The CIA kept eyes on them; they all went back to their native stomping grounds in Morocco and hooked up with Izala there."

"You're fucking kidding me right now."

"I wish I was. Whoever got to the president and convinced him to let them loose wanted a bigger fish. M5 was the way to get to that fish."

"Mohammed Izala."

"That's my guess."

"Fuckin A."

"He's been on my personal radar from my first mission for the Agency. He's the big catch every agent in the field wants to haul in."

"Did the other M5 members know Al-Safari had been turned into a CIA asset?"

She shrugged. "They were separated in transport to the US and, as I understand, kept separate at Guantanamo. They probably never realized Al-Safari wasn't incarcerated with them. Obviously, I didn't."

His head spun with all the connections. "Was it possible they figured it out and were going to expose Al-Safari to Izala?"

"It's possible, but there's also the fact that Al-Safari had been loyal to Izala's cause before we nabbed him and his M5 brothers. I've been thinking about it since Elliot told me the truth. It's possible Al-Safari only went along with being an asset to save his own skin. When the Moroccans captured him, he sent up a white flag to Elliot, no doubt so we'd bail him out. I'm still not sure why he would kill himself after we rescued him, though."

"If he was in deep with Hayden and James, Hayden killed him to keep his own illicit activities under wraps."

She nodded slowly. "That, unfortunately, is also a possibility."

Jax rubbed his beard. "I fucking hate all this spy shit."

"Right now,"—Ruby leaned forward, propping her elbows on her knees and plunking her chin into her hands—"I do too."

Her hair fell over the front of her shoulders, exposing her back and shoulder blades. Jax felt the urge to plant a kiss on her spine.

Nope. *Not going there.* No touching allowed.

Except his fingers had a mind of their own. They snuck out and gently traced the small bumps of her vertebrae.

She shivered under his touch. "He did it, didn't he? Elliot killed Al-Safari and is now trying to clean up loose ends. He lied to me."

The raw pain in her voice nearly undid him. "We don't know for sure, and honestly, the deeper we get in this shit pile, the more I believe Elliot may be innocent."

Ruby straightened up and looked at him. "You don't have to say that."

He brushed a strand of hair from her face. "I'm serious, Ruby."

She leaned into his hand, letting him cup her face. "Why are you so nice to me when I've been nothing but a bitch to you?"

"Because…"

He almost said it. Almost admitted how much he needed her.

But then she uncrossed the towel, laying it open for him to see all of her luscious body.

Jax's brain went blank.

CHAPTER FOURTEEN

Mission first and always.
Her mission at this moment was to get Jax out of his clothes.
Bed.
Naked.
Time on their hands.
What else was there to do?
Don't think. Just act.
That was so wrong. They were so screwed up. One minute, his fingers were bringing her to orgasm, the next, he was walking away from her. He didn't know whether to fuck her or hate her.

Wasn't that a pickle. She didn't know whether to love him or walk away from him.

The way he was staring suggested that dropping her towel had at least made the decision easier for him.

For her too.

No predicting the future. This might be the last time she'd ever have him alone, and she was damn sure going to take advantage. She didn't want to think, analyze, or confess to any more sins.

She wanted him inside of her.

He hadn't moved though. Not a lick. No touching, no grabbing her and kissing her.

He just stared.

The rush from surviving the tornado refused to wear off. *Maybe it isn't the brush with death.*

Maybe it was the act of living she was about to do with the hero in front of her.

"Jax?" she said. "You still with me?"

His attention was focused on her lips. "Hell, yes."

Still, he didn't move. Didn't say anything else.

"You do understand why I'm sitting here naked, right?"

"Oh, I understand."

Was he still pissed about the M5 revelation? "I get the feeling you're not interested."

"I'm very interested."

"Then what's the problem?"

"Who said there was a problem?"

"You're not touching me."

"That's a problem?"

Well, duh. "Don't play dumb."

A smirk broke his serious countenance. "I'm looking."

Ruby had rarely been self-conscious of her body as an adult. Jax's intense scrutiny, however, made her edgy. She glanced down at her naked self, sucked in her belly. "Do you see anything you like?"

He moved closer, still not touching but definitely close enough to invade her personal space.

Closing her eyes, she waited for his kiss.

It didn't come.

She opened her eyes and found him staring at her lips again. "You wouldn't be teasing me, would you?" she asked, slightly breathless.

His dark eyes came up to meet hers. Satisfaction laced his voice. "Would I do that?"

Bastard. He would *so* do that.

Two could play that game.

Closing the inch of space between them, she didn't kiss him, but licked his lips with a slow sweep of her tongue. Then she turned her head and arched her neck, waiting for him to let go of his perfect control.

Her waiting drew out until, exasperated, she looked at him again.

His eyes were lit with desire, possession. "You're the most beautiful woman I've ever seen. I want to look at you. Just look for a minute."

Her nipples puckered. She blinked. Fought to hold herself completely still.

His gaze dropped, a languid glide, not missing an inch of her skin right down to her toes. That hot gaze slid back up, tracing every part of her.

She wanted to moan. It was like she could feel his touch even though he hadn't laid a finger on her.

When he met her eyes again, he smiled. His fingers came up, grazed her jawline. Taking her chin in hand, he turned her head away, exposing her neck once more.

"Is this what you want, sweetheart?" His lips touched her first, grazing the side of her neck.

A heady desire pulsed under her skin. She closed her eyes, heart hammering. "Yes."

"And this?" His tongue licked under her ear, traced its way down the side of her neck to her collarbone. His beard tickled her throat.

"Oh, yes."

One arm went around her waist, forcing her to arch back and give him access to her breast. No problem there.

As he sucked at her breast, she removed his shirt. When he switched to her other breast, she worked on his belt buckle.

Teamwork. *Fucking A.*

He was glorious. Muscled, strong, sexy as hell. She wanted him. All of him.

Between them, they got his pants off and he stood before her, heavy and thick. She slid off the bed and went to her knees, needing to taste him.

She knew his taste, knew the groan he made. He only let her have a few strokes before he pulled her back and tossed her onto the bed.

A small cry left her lips. He stalked towards her, sank his hands in her hair and tipped her head up for a kiss.

Rough, deep, needy. It stole her breath and made her weak. She fell back onto the covers and waited for him to take her.

Instead, he grabbed her hips, flipped her over, and set her on her hands and knees.

His hands kneaded her ass, slipped down her thighs, came back up to her hips. "Move for me," he murmured.

They both liked things a little rough. "Make me," she said.

Smack. The sting of his playful swat caused pleasure to whip through her. She jutted her hips up and did a slow side-to-side shake.

"That's what I like." He moved closer, his erection brushing the inside of her thigh.

She spread her knees wider, giving him the access he wanted. Reaching between them, she grabbed his heavy erection. "And this is what I like," she purred, guiding him to her entrance.

She was wet for him, her lust demanding. Her legs trembled as she pulled him to her. He reached for her breasts, his big hands tugging on them, his fingers flicking over her taut nipples.

His cock pushed against her core and a moan slipped from her lips. She shifted back, encouraging him to drive himself home.

Take me.

Hard.

Fast.

The way they both liked it.

Once again, he held back, teasing her with the end of his hardness, but not breaching the walls. Dipping in only a little and then pulling back.

"Give me what I want," she pleaded, bracing her hands against the bed.

His chuckle surrounded her, his hands coming back to lock onto her hips. "Is this what you want?"

His cock pushed between her legs, into her folds, going deep this time. He was so big, so thick, he stretched her to the max and Ruby cried out.

So good. He felt so damn good.

"Yes." She started moving against him. "More."

He thrust deeper. Faster. Fingers found her sensitive spot between her folds and rubbed a sweet rhythm. He filled her to the brim, stretching every inch of her.

The bed slammed into the wall, over and over again. A stuffed duck fell from a nearby shelf and hit the floor. He kept thrusting, her name a chant on his lips.

She thrust back, her sex clamping down on him. The sound of their bodies slapping together filled the room, keeping time with the headboard. He spanked her bottom again. "Give me what I want now, Ruby."

Pleasure rose and spiraled out of control. Her climax hit and she gripped the bed sheets, his name ripping from her throat.

His climax followed, arching his back as he exploded inside of her.

The bed stopped banging. Ruby let herself fall into the sheets, her limbs weightless.

A moment later, Jax shifted them around, crawling into the bed and cuddling her to him.

He held her tight, and she held him back.
Mission accomplished.

⌀————◆————⌀

So the day could, in fact, get even weirder.

Thank God Ruby was hidden under the covers, but holy hell, she hadn't realized they had company and her mouth was doing things to Jax that made his eyes roll up in his head.

Beatrice stood in the doorway, one eyebrow lifted. Behind her Trace Hunter stood guard, a smirk on his face as his eyes looked everywhere but at Jax.

"Um, Ruby," Jax murmured, patting the top of her head—at least he thought is was her head. "Stop."

Jesus, he didn't want her to stop. Never, ever. But getting caught by his boss during a blow job? And the person servicing him was a client?

Shit. Fuck. Damn. There weren't enough swear words, even in his extensive dictionary, to cover this moment.

The heat of Ruby's mouth left him and the comforter jiggled with her laughter. "Stop? Since when have you ever asked me to stop while I'm—"

Jax cut her off by stuffing some fabric into her pie hole and clearing his throat loudly. "*We have company.*"

Beatrice crossed her arms. "Need I remind you," she tapped a slender finger against her bicep, "Policy 6-3B states Rock Star Security agents do not sleep with clients. Care to explain…"— she waved a hand at him and the lump under the comforter— "this?"

Ruby was spitting as she threw back the covers. "What in the world?"

She now sat on top of Jax, hair mussed, lips swollen from his kisses, and looking absofuckinglutely beautiful.

And very, very naked.

Totally exposed for everyone to see.

That got Hunter's attention and the guy had to jam a fist against his mouth to keep from bursting out laughing.

Jax smiled ruefully at Ruby and adjusted the comforter to cover her as best as he could. He pointed over her shoulder to their guests in the doorway. "Ruby, meet my boss, Beatrice Reese."

As Ruby's eyes went wide, she whirled, scrambling off of him and giving a startled cry. Her usual gracefulness deserted her as she grabbed at the comforter, losing her balance and, before Jax could catch her, tumbling over the side of the bed.

Taking the whole damn comforter with her.

Well, hello there. His massive woody stood at full mast, waving at his audience.

Hunter couldn't hold back anymore. His sharp laughter echoed in the room as Beatrice quickly shifted her attention off Jax and over to Ruby who was tangled in the covers so badly, she couldn't quite get to her feet.

Jax rolled off the bed, reached down and pulled Ruby and the comforter off the floor, effectively righting Ruby and hiding his erection.

"Boss," Jax said, giving Beatrice his best *please don't kill me* grin as he squeezed Ruby's shoulders. "This is Agent Ruby McKellen."

Ruby brushed hair from her eyes and offered a fragile smile as she stuck out her hand. "Nice to meet you."

Beatrice's blue eyes scanned both of them, irritation radiating off of her.

Not good. She rarely showed anger, but her current hormonal, very pregnant self was sending off enough disappointment and displeasure, the Pope could probably feel it all the way over in Rome.

"You have five minutes to clean yourselves up and meet me downstairs," she ground out. Turning on her heel, she blew past a still-laughing Hunter.

Once Jax was sure his boss was out of earshot, he hissed at the man. "You brought Beatrice?"

"*Brought* her? Hell, no. I tried to get her to stay in DC," Hunter said. "She shouldn't be flying, and she sure as hell shouldn't be stressed out about you. But she is, and she's here, so focus on getting her back to DC before that baby comes and Callan Reese shoots us both."

"Oh, my God," Ruby murmured, still trying to get her feet untangled from the covers. "I can't believe she just walked in on us like that."

Hunter zeroed in on a mallard duck near the doorway, screwing up his face as he turned the thing so it wasn't staring at him. "She couldn't raise you on your cell," he said to Jax.

"The owner of this place told us you hadn't come out of the room since you got here, not even to eat. Beatrice was worried."

Ruby, her bare feet finally untwisted, took off for the cat room. "We're down to four minutes," she said over her shoulder to Jax as she pushed past Hunter. "Get your ass in gear."

Jax watched her go, his woody now deflated. Hunter gave him another smirk and a thumbs-up before he disappeared from the doorway. "Zeb's here, too," he called.

Jax had never gotten a shower and reeked of sex and sweat. His boss had just seen him naked and standing at full attention. "Hunter," he yelled.

After a second, Trace's face appeared once more as he leaned around the frame. "Yeah?"

"How'd Beatrice take it when she found out you were sleeping with Savanna?"

Hunter's face screwed up like it had before when he'd examined the stuffed mallard. His first assignment had been to protect the woman who'd labeled him a traitor on national television. Somehow the two of them had ended up trading bodily fluids while Hunter had been her bodyguard and now they were engaged. "Not well. I suggest you bend over and kiss your ass goodbye."

"But you're still working for her and Petit."

"I have skills, man. Skills they can't find anywhere else. You know that."

"I'm so fucked."

"Maybe not. Poison and his client are together and he still has a job."

Miles Duncan and Charlotte Carstons. Jax had helped them bring down a Romanian crime lord and a British agent who'd turned traitor a few months ago. They were also engaged. "Yeah, and Miles doesn't have superhuman skills," Jax said, feeling slightly better.

"True, but Beatrice has a soft spot for him because of what happened with his SEAL team. He reminds her of Cal."

Hunter disappeared again. Jax fisted his hands, rubbed his eyes. He might as well hand over his SFI badge right now.

"Why aren't you dressed?"

Ruby was back, her clothes mostly dry. She finger-combed her hair, pulling it into a ponytail.

"B's going to fire me." Jax found his pants on the floor and yanked them on. "I'm not in a hurry for that."

"Fire you? Don't be ridiculous. She's upset, but we'll explain things, and it will all work out."

He thought she was joking, but as he drew on his shirt, he saw she wasn't. She was serious.

"You don't know Beatrice," he said, plopping onto the bed and tugging on a boot.

Ruby made a face at him. "So that's it? One screw-up and you're done?"

Quitter.

It was right there. That ugly voice he hadn't heard in a while.

Anger fired in his chest. Everything was so fucking messed up. He needed a minute to sort it all out.

"You don't understand," he heard himself saying.

Ruby crossed her arms over her chest. "You're not even going to try to explain things to her?"

Quitter.

That word. What his dad had called him when he'd told the man he was leaving med school.

The awful burn of anger and hurt spread, engulfing his diaphragm, his back, his shoulders. He hoisted the other boot on, stood. "How do you propose we explain this?"

A shrug. A grin. "I'll tell her it was my idea. I seduced you."

That grin got him. Her nonchalance. He didn't want to lose his job with SFI, but hells bells, if he lost that, yet kept Ruby, it was worth it, wasn't it?

I'm not losing either, goddamn it. "I'll take care of the explanation. You stay quiet. Agreed?"

Her grin widened. "I'll try."

"Try hard. Please."

Ruby linked an arm through his. "You're a good guy, Jaxon Sloan. Beatrice is lucky to have you and I'm guessing she knows it."

A good guy? Nah.

But one thing he wasn't was a quitter.

CHAPTER FIFTEEN

Paula, the owner of the B&B, was nowhere in sight as Ruby took Jax's hand and they hustled down the stairs.

The man Jax referred to as Hunter stood in front of a set of double doors that led to the sitting room off the foyer. He was tall, leaner than Jax, and had an edge to him Ruby associated with an elite soldier—superb fighter, superior tactical skills. Nothing got by him. Not the slightest detail. Ready to respond to the slightest hint of danger. She remembered his laughter upstairs...it was the only thing that made him seem human.

Hunter's attention followed them as they made their way across the foyer. He stopped Jax at the door. "Beatrice requested to speak with Agent McKellen first, privately."

The nerves thrumming through Jax's body invaded her own. At Hunter's announcement, he tightened his hold on her hand and bristled even more. "What the hell for?"

"You know she doesn't share her reasons with me. All I know is that she asked that I send Agent McKellen in first, on her own."

"Bullshit."

Jax started to push past Hunter when Hunter put a hand on his bicep. "Don't, man."

The two stared at each other, and Ruby felt a spurt of fear. The last thing she needed was for Jax to pick a fight with Beatrice's bodyguard.

Not that Jax would lose, but...

Hunter was definitely no one to mess with. Someone would

get hurt, and Jax would most certainly lose his job if he jacked up Hunter.

Ruby tugged on Jax's hand, pulling him back. He was still giving Hunter a challenging stare and Ruby touched his face with her hand to bring his attention to her. "Hey. Back off, big guy. It's okay. I can handle it."

She'd had her fair share of dressing-down moments with her superiors lately. If Beatrice Reese had an issue with what had just happened upstairs, Ruby wanted to straighten things out. She didn't want Jax to be in trouble because she'd practically thrown herself at him.

His eyes finally shifted to her face and she smiled, remembering the way she'd felt on top of him. Bending him to her will, making him want her.

"It's not okay," he murmured to her. "I take responsibility for...you know."

His gaze bounced upward, referring to their activities in the bedroom.

One of the doors opened from the inside, and the very pregnant Beatrice Reese herself filled the frame. Her beautiful blue eyes bounced from Jax to Ruby and back to Jax. "The subject is non-negotiable, Jaxon. I will speak to Agent McKellen alone, and then I'll speak to you."

Okay, then.

Beatrice moved out of the doorway, apparently certain her orders would be followed. Ruby gave Jax's hand another squeeze.

He grumbled, then turned her loose. "I'm right here if you need me," he whispered in her ear before she went in.

She gave him a wink to relieve his worries. At least she hoped it did.

Beatrice was a whole other animal from her bodyguard— intellect-driven, the ultimate strategist, not a hint of humor or of Hunter's edginess. She was calm, cool, collected.

And annoyed.

"Close the door," she said as she sat in the room's window seat and stared outside.

Ruby did as asked, then made her way to stand in front of the woman, taking note that an older man with a bald head and a glint in his eyes stood at attention near the fireplace.

"Hello," Ruby said, nodding to him.

He nodded back, but didn't speak.

She turned to Beatrice. "Look, what happened upstairs wasn't Jax's…"

Beatrice cut her off. "We won't speak about what happened between you and my bodyguard upstairs ever again. I don't want to know any more than I already do." A tiny shiver of what Ruby figured was revulsion shook Beatrice's shoulders before her gaze swung to look at Ruby. "Are we clear?"

No arguing. Got it. Ruby simply nodded. She didn't want to discuss it either.

Beatrice motioned at a nearby chair. "Have a seat."

Ruby did as instructed, biting her lip to keep from blurting out something inane about the weather or the collection of antique spindles Paula had lining the fireplace mantel. The man there was no longer watching her, reading something on his phone.

She'd been trained to never volunteer information or make small talk unless it was part of her cover, but for the life of her, she wanted to say something that would break the ice between her and Jax's boss.

What exactly that would be was beyond her. Words slipped out of her mouth anyway. "Jaxon saved my life during the tornado. I'm lucky to be here, and you should commend him for his service."

One perfectly groomed brow arched at her as if asking whether Ruby really thought she should tell Beatrice what to do. "Describe Elliot Hayden and your relationship with him."

Beatrice obviously wasn't one for small talk, either. Ruby cleared her throat, shifted slightly in her seat. "He was my partner for five years. Since the CIA hired Jax to recover him, I assume they filled you in on the rest."

"I would prefer to hear your version."

"My *version*?"

"Was Mr. Hayden your handler, Agent McKellen?"

"My handler?" She felt like a myna bird, repeating everything Beatrice said. "He was my partner. I report directly to the director of operations."

"How often did you check in with him?"

"Why?"

"Please answer the question."

"Not until you tell me why."

Hard head meet hard head. Ruby expected Beatrice to lose her calm facade. She didn't.

Crossing one leg over the other, she folded her hands over her belly and looked amused. "You are my client, but so is your employer. As you can imagine, this puts me in an onerous position."

"How is that exactly? Jax is bodyguard for the Rock Stars, not a bounty hunter. Rock Star Security is a whole lot more than a bodyguard service, isn't it?"

"You've been out of the country for much of the past year, haven't you?"

"Oh, for cryin' out loud," the man at the fireplace said, running a hand down his face. "You two stop dancing around each other or we'll be here all bloody day. Beatrice and Emit run a paramilitary group behind the scenes of RSS, Agent McKellen. Trust me, they understand your situation with the Agency."

Beatrice looked slightly perturbed, but didn't miss a beat. "Jaxon is both your bodyguard at the moment—although he seems to have taken that term a bit far—and he has been hired by the CIA to hunt down your former partner. I believe it's fair for me to understand exactly what kind of danger he may be in from both of these missions. Do you not agree?"

Beatrice Reese was used to people agreeing with her. It probably happened a lot since she was obviously skilled in logical manipulation.

Ruby had experience with that as well. "You and I both know Jaxon's line of work is a dangerous one, whether it's as a bodyguard or something more, and he thrives on taking risks. It's not my intent to put him in unnecessary jeopardy, but he did come to me for help. I've done what I can to assist him and your team in finding Elliot."

"And yet, here we are, some of the brightest minds in the United States, along with the best hackers, and a highly-trained undercover operative who knew Agent Hayden quite well from my understanding, and yet, we have no idea where the man is."

"Is there a question in there somewhere?"

The slightest movement of her lips suggested she was once more amused. "When did you meet Elliot Hayden?"

What did this have to do with finding him? "We went through the Farm together. We were paired up for a couple of trial run missions, discovered we worked well together, and our teachers agreed. The Agency decided to use us as a couple for our first mission after we graduated. The mission was a success and we were kept together to continue as partners."

The man at the fireplace straightened from his spot. "The Agency doesn't normally use partners in the field. You didn't think it odd that they kept the two of you together as a team?"

True, most agents worked alone, but it wasn't written in stone. "I'm sorry, who are you?"

"You can call me Zeb."

Which explained nothing. Ruby spoke to Beatrice. "What exactly is Zeb's role here?"

Beatrice didn't miss a beat. "He contracts for me."

Doing what?

What else? He wasn't military, and Ruby doubted he was a hacker. So that left operative.

Former operative anyway. The wrinkles on his face told her he was well past his prime and the way he smiled at her suggested he knew how to kill her quietly in at least a dozen ways.

She smiled back, letting him know she could take him any day. "Elliot and I had good chemistry together and our skills complemented each other. The DO was once an operative himself and knows how to exploit his agents' skill sets. That's all."

"Well," Beatrice said, pushing herself to her feet. "I suspect your director—whose renegade reputation in the field is well-known in certain circles—selected you in particular to work with Agent Hayden."

"Who, by the way," Zeb interjected, "was on the Agency's payroll three years before he went through the Farm with you. He worked for them for two years, was recruited by National Intelligence for something we don't yet have intel on, and then magically appeared back at the Farm for new agent training at the same time you showed up."

Ruby blinked. "What are you saying?"

"The Agency lied to you," Beatrice said. "Elliot Hayden was placed into the Farm, into your world, on purpose."

Seconds passed and Ruby heard her pulse loud in her ears. "Why?"

"We don't know," Zeb said, "but we suspect all of this with Hayden, Nelson, and James, is tied back to that reason, whatever it is."

Ruby turned away, adrenaline pumping in her veins. None of

this made sense. Elliot had lied to her, more than once, it appeared, but her boss had lied to her as well?

Either that, or Zeb and Beatrice were full of shit.

She whirled back to face them. "I want to see your intel on Elliot."

Beatrice nodded, no surprise on her features. She withdrew a tablet from a black bag resting on the couch and held it out to Ruby. "You might want to sit down."

Stomach churning, Ruby hesitated. Whatever was on that tablet might change her life forever. Change who and what she trusted.

She reached for it and punched on the power button.

Thirty seconds later, it was a good thing she was standing in front of the couch. Her legs gave out and she dropped into the cushions, speechless.

Jax was losing his mind waiting for Beatrice to get done interrogating Ruby.

Because that's what it had to be, an interrogation. Why else had she insisted he stay outside? Did she not trust him to give her all the details or tell the truth about what was going on?

"What the hell are they doing in there?" he mumbled to Hunter.

The man was a statue, feet wide, hands folded in front of him. "Getting answers, I imagine."

"Answers about what? I told Emit what happened, that we followed Hayden from a GPS unit Ruby had put on the guy. What's the big, hairy deal?"

"Not about that. I believe Beatrice is trying to figure out Agent McKellen's background and her relationship to Hayden."

"Her *relationship*? They were partners. That's no secret."

"Um-hmm."

Jax stopped pacing and faced Hunter. "What does that mean?"

Hunter met his gaze. "I was agreeing with you."

"Your tone suggested you weren't. Like there was something more between Ruby and Hayden."

"Was there?"

"Fuck, no. She thinks of Hayden as a brother, that's all."

Hunter nodded. "I wasn't suggesting it was a sexual relationship."

"Then what *are* you suggesting?"

At that moment, the door opened and Zeb's ugly mug popped out. "Jaxon, get your Cro-Magnon ass in here."

"About time," Jax groused.

He and Zeb exchanged back slaps and Jax let out a relieved sigh when he saw Ruby sitting on the couch.

And then he saw how pale she was and a spurt of anger hit his blood. What had Beatrice said to her?

Clenching his fists, he marched over to where Beatrice sat in the window seat. "What's going on? Why are you harassing Ruby?"

Beatrice rose, and even though she was considerably shorter than him in her sensible, low-heeled shoes, she cut him down to size with her steely gaze. "First of all, lose the attitude, Jaxon. I'm on your side and I'm doing my best to protect you and Agent McKellen. Secondly, sit down and shut up or I'll have Hunter throw you out on your ass and turn this investigation over to Shinedown."

Hunter, now standing inside the doors, gave him a friendly wave and a grin.

Bastard loved a good fight.

So did Jax.

Unfortunately, Hunter had superior fucking everything. No one could beat the guy at hand to hand. Or anything else. Jax had already tried. Miles and Colt had too. In fact, the three of them had ganged up on Hunter and still been handed their asses.

"It's okay, Jax," Ruby said. Her voice sounded small and hollow. "Beatrice has done me a giant favor by uncovering the truth about Elliot—and my job."

"The truth?"

"Have a seat, Jax," Beatrice instructed again. "I'll let Ruby fill you in."

Ruby cleared her throat and looked back down at the tablet in her lap as Jax sat next to her on the couch. "It seems Elliot is—was—actually working for National Intelligence."

Okay, so that was interesting, but not the end of the world, so why was Ruby acting so gutted? "Doing what?"

"Intelligence collection. Military intelligence specifically."

Again, an interesting revelation, but not earth-shattering. Goddamn spies were always running undercover ops on top of undercover ops. "So Hayden went from NI to the CIA. What's the big deal?"

"That's what we're trying to hash out," Zeb said. He plopped into a recliner and put his feet up. "He didn't go from NI to the CIA. The CIA originally recruited him, then NI plucked him from the CIA ranks and gave him a job working in their bowels, possibly with direct links to Homeland. Somewhere along the line, Homeland took him from NI and inserted him back into the Agency as a new agent in Agent McKellen's class. We believe they purposely hooked him up with Agent McKellen, but we don't know the why of that either."

Beatrice shifted, as if uncomfortable, in the window seat. One hand rested on her stomach. "What we strongly suspect is that Hayden was running duel missions on the overseas operations he shared with Agent McKellen. On the surface, he was working legitimate, Agency-approved missions, but underneath that, he was secretly running a mission for NI under the direction of Homeland."

"Moroccan 5," Ruby mumbled.

Hunter moved away from the door, producing a bottle with a thick, pink substance in it. "Drink," he said to Beatrice. "You're getting dehydrated."

Had to be Beatrice's favorite—a fruit smoothie. She took the bottle, sipped. "What about M5?"

"From the moment we graduated from the Farm, that was our target—taking that group down and bringing them into custody to be interrogated. The CIA knew the M5 were front soldiers for a much larger terrorist group and the plan was to infiltrate that group and bring it down."

"Mohammed Izala's group?" Beatrice asked.

Ruby nodded. "I'm not sharing anything here that you couldn't find out on your own, and since my career with the Agency is pretty much over anyway, I'll tell you what I know. Izala grew up under Saddam Hussein's regime. He's suspected of being a distant relative, as you probably know, and saw himself as the next great leader in the Middle East. When bin Laden became a superstar, Izala saw him as competition, but there were advantages to staying in the shadows. He studied bin Laden, learned what *not* to do as well as what to do to hurt America and their allies."

"He stayed out of the limelight," Zeb said, "building a multi-layered, guerrilla army."

"M5 was quick, agile, and highly effective at staying under the radar. Instead of broadcasting executions and sermons on YouTube, and recruiting on Facebook, they did things the old fashioned way, making them much harder to track." Ruby rubbed one edge of the tablet in her lap. "They stayed on the move, hit their targets fast, got out just as fast, and disappeared."

"Like SEALs," Jax added.

"Like SEALs," she agreed. "Elliot and I spent several years tracking them, and for a long time, we believed the group kept changing, evolving, morphing. After each mission, one or two of the members would change. They'd go back to Izala's headquarters or underground and others would take their place. It was like chasing a ghost. We'd get a lead on one of them and they'd disappear."

Zeb sat forward. "Tell us about Al-Safari."

"After we'd been chasing our tails for three years, the group seemed to stabilize. We were able to trace the same five members to several attacks over a three-month period. Al-Safari was one of the men in the group. We strongly suspected he was their leader." Ruby told the story she'd shared with Jax earlier, then added. "I had no knowledge that Elliot had turned Al-Safari into an asset until the other night when El confessed that to me."

"You believed Elliot was innocent of shooting the man, correct?" Beatrice asked.

"I did." Ruby sighed. "Now, I'm not so sure."

"Did you have another assignment that went beyond stopping M5?"

Ruby paused, seeming to choose her words carefully. "I'm not sure I understand what you mean."

Beatrice sipped her smoothie. "Sure you do."

Jax's head was getting tired from the volleying back and forth. "Well, I don't."

Ruby's lips screwed up for a moment. "My end goal was always the apprehension of Mohammed Izala. Chasing M5 and shutting them down was imperative, but my ultimate assignment was Izala. My boss knew with my...looks...I could open doors Elliot never would. The other night, Keon James told me Izala was coming for him. For me, too."

A boil started in Jax's blood, just thinking about Ruby using her feminine charms to get close to a terrorist. It was the same feeling he'd had the other night at the club watching her flirt with the guard outside Nelson's private party. "Why didn't you tell me that earlier?"

"Izala is somewhere in Northern Africa, possibly in the Middle East." She looked completely unconcerned. "He's not my biggest issue at the moment."

Jax bit his tongue. She was right, and yet, the omission sat like a day-old burrito in his stomach.

Apparently, Beatrice didn't much care for the omission either, but they were dealing with a spy. Secrets came with the territory. "Did Agent Hayden know Izala was your target?"

Target? Whoa. Jax shot Ruby a look. "As in you were supposed to hunt down and kill him?"

"Not exactly." She looked a bit skittish of a the idea of sharing what was classified information. "I had verified intel the night we were in Marrakech that Izala was just outside the city in Ben Guerir. My secondary mission after we picked up Al-Safari from the Moroccans was to confirm Izala's location."

"And do what with him?" Jax said.

"Your SEAL team wasn't there to assist Agents McKellen and Hayden with Al-Safari's transport," Beatrice offered. "You were actually on standby in case Agent McKellen confirmed Izala's location. Is that correct?" she said to Ruby.

A reluctant nod. "If I found him, I was to call my boss, who would go up the chain and get the SEALs activated."

Make that a two-day-old burrito. "You spent the entire night with me, until Al-Safari blew his brains out. My team was never called in to apprehend Izala."

Ruby actually blushed, glancing at Beatrice like a kid caught with her hand in the cookie jar. "No shit, Jax."

She took a deep breath and blew it out through her lips. "I screwed up. I got carried away with you and then I couldn't…"

Her eyes filled in the rest as she looked at him. *Leave you.*

And *ah, shit,* he suddenly understood much more than he had before.

"I chose you over my mission," she finished softly.

He wanted to grab her, hug her, hold her hand, something. But she would hate that. "You're on probation for blowing off an order, not for what happened with Elliot and Al-Safari."

She acknowledged his statement with a slight incline of her head. "I've regretted that decision multiple times."

Low blow, right to his gut. The emotional burrito was

twisting his guts big time. About to blow, he stopped when Beatrice cleared her throat to get his attention. The look on her face told him to keep a lid on his emotions.

Count. One, two, three, four...four, three, two, one.

He tried to imagine the waterfall, the white room, any fucking thing that would keep him from exploding.

One, two, three...

Oh, hell.

Fisting his hands, he imagined beating up Elliot, then Al-Safari, and finally Mohammed Izala.

That calmed him down.

But his heart, stupid muscle that it was, beat too fast. It actually hurt as if Ruby had stuck her hand inside his chest and was squeezing it.

"Al-Safari was a chemical weapons expert," Beatrice said, moving on and nursing her smoothie. "For the moment, let's assume Al-Safari was a legitimate asset for the United States. National Intelligence was running Elliot on military intelligence ops from what we've concluded. What were the two of them working together to do?"

The question of the hour.

Before anyone could throw out a hypothesis, the double doors opened and Paula peeked a head in. "Sorry to interrupt, but there's someone here who needs to speak to you."

Hunter started for the doors when the second door flew open. Chief Rolands brushed by Paula and swept his eagle eyes around the room, landing on Zeb. "Your boy's been spotted along the road heading east. Thought you might want to go with me to look for him."

Zeb came to his feet and clapped his big hands together. "Hotdog. Let's go hunt down a felon, brother."

Chapter Sixteen

Ruby was up out of her chair. "You found Elliot?"

"Wait," Jax said, rising as well and glancing between Zeb and Chief Rolands. "You two are brothers?"

"Half brothers," the two men said at the same time.

Zeb clapped a hand on Chief Rolands' shoulder. "Everyone, meet Caleb. He's the chief in town."

"We met," Rolands growled, giving Jax the once over.

They were about the same height, and Ruby could see their eyes matched, but that was the extent of the similarities. "Can the family reunion wait?" she said. "We need to catch Elliot."

"No need for the attitude, little lady," Rolands chastised. "Your friend's on foot, and appears to be injured. Mike Lostrom owns a farm out that way and called it in. Said the guy had blood all over his clothes. I'd have sent a deputy to bring him on in, but everyone's on storm cleanup duty."

Was it Elliot's own blood covering his clothes or was it Augustus Nelson's? "He may not be as injured as you think, and he's quite skilled at evasion." She shot a look at Jax, then Beatrice. "We need to move. Now."

Beatrice nodded at Trace Hunter, who helped her up from her seat. "Zeb, ride with your brother. The rest of us will follow you, Chief."

Rolands tipped the brim of his cap at her. "Hope you don't mind me saying, but maybe you should stay here and take a load off."

Beatrice straightened her maternity blouse. "Pregnancy is not a disability, but I know you mean well, so I'll let it go." She motioned to the door. "Shall we? As Agent McKellen stated, the man we're after is quite adept at disappearing."

Rolands looked at Zeb and rolled his eyes. As the two went through the foyer, Ruby and Jax on their heels, she overheard him say, "Who is this guy? Jason Bourne?"

"Nah," Zeb replied, opening the front door. "That guy back there with the pregnant gal is Jason Bourne."

Rolands turned to look back at Hunter, then he sized up Jax. "Quite a group you fell in with again, Zebulon."

The old guy chuckled. "I like things interesting."

Outside, Jax hustled Ruby over to a black SUV that looked a lot like Emit Petit's. Did the company have an entire fleet in Chicago?

Paula came running out of the house. "Take this." She shoved a cloth bag at Jax. "You didn't get to eat earlier. A shame for all this to go to waste."

The bag was covered with cats. "Thank you," he said, as he accepted it from her.

She glanced over all of them. "And who's settling the bill for the rooms?"

Hunter helped Beatrice into the front seat, but when he started to pull the seatbelt out for her, she slapped his hand away. Wrestling with it herself, she cast a look at the owner of the B&B. "You'll find an envelope on the window seat that should more than cover the cost of rooms. Your discretion about our presence here today is expected. If anyone asks, we weren't here. I believe you'll find I can be quite generous in exchange for your silence."

Paula looked a tad confused for a moment. "Why do you care if people know you visited my little bed and breakfast?"

"You should be more careful who you open your door to," Beatrice said, struggling with her seatbelt. The poor strap could only reach so far. "In addition, I strongly suggest you change that egregious wallpaper throughout the house. Someone might kill you for your abhorrent taste in decor."

Jax piled into the backseat next to Ruby as Hunter shut Beatrice's door and hustled around to the driver's seat. Paula stood, wringing her hands and looking even more confused.

"You have to stop using such big words, boss," Jax said, chuckling. He leaned forward, reached around Beatrice, and grabbed the seatbelt out of her hand. "We talked about that, remember?"

She smacked his hand. "What did I say that a person of average IQ couldn't understand?"

He didn't let go of the belt, managing to snap it into place. "Abhorrent is one thing, but egregious? Come on. No one uses that word. Next time, try 'appalling' or plain ol' 'flat-ass ugly.'"

Beatrice's chest rose on a slow, deep breath, as if she were struggling to control her irritation. Her gaze focused on the cop car pulling out ahead of them. "Curse words are base and uncalled for."

Jax sat back as Hunter took off after Rolands. He winked at Ruby. "They get the point across, don't they?"

"Oh, Jaxon," Beatrice sighed, but she sounded like a tired mother rather than an aggravated boss.

The cruiser generated a lot of dust as they took a dirt road off the main one Ruby and Jax had walked to get to the B&B. "Where are we going?" Ruby asked.

Hunter shrugged. "I imagine the chief knows a short cut."

Good thinking. "What do you plan to do with Elliot once we catch him?" she asked Beatrice.

Beatrice took a pair of sunglasses from her bag but didn't put them on. "That depends on you, Agent McKellen."

"Call me Ruby, please."

The woman shot her a look over her shoulder. "What do you wish to do with Elliot Hayden?"

There was something in the steady gaze she gave Ruby over her shoulder. A question under the question. Ruby felt like Beatrice, out of any of them, might understand her predicament. "I need to know the truth."

A slight nod. "I'll make sure you have time to speak to him before we turn him over to the CIA. My only request is that Jax is present during the interview."

In other words, Jax would interrogate him. Beatrice wanted answers too. "Jax doesn't have clearance to..."

"It's Jax or me," Beatrice said. "Your choice."

Jax had his head turned, pretending to be interested in the passing landscape. Ruby could still see the grin on his face.

Ruby met Beatrice's gaze. "Who did you work for before you took this gig?"

"I suppose that does matter to you, doesn't it?"

"It does."

"Fair enough. I was NSA. Part of a specialized, top-secret group called Command & Control. I can assure you, my clearance level was beyond anything you've ever even heard of."

"But you don't work for the government anymore. Your former clearance level means jack squat."

There it was again, that flare in her eyes and the slight crook of her lips. "I like you, Agent McKellen. You're passionate but intelligent. An agent who knows when to bluff and when to be a straight shooter. But let me make this very clear to you. While you are currently a client of Rock Star Security because of Emit's insistence, I'm running this show. My main concern is for Jax's safety. Secondary to that, is the safety of Emit Petit's company. If you don't like the way I handle things, Trace will stop the vehicle and you can exit it. Meanwhile, I will find Agent Hayden and bring him in. Once again, your choice."

God, what a hardass. Beatrice made the Colonel look like an easy boss in comparison. She could only imagine what would happen if she put the two of them in a room and let them duke it out.

But down the road, Ruby could use a hardass like Beatrice to help her get her position with the Colonel's secret army back. Might be wise to keep Beatrice in her friendly column.

Besides, what real choice did she have? This little party would definitely catch up to Elliot before she did and she was out of resources.

She wiggled her bare feet, sore from walking on blacktop and gravel. "Jax it is, then," she said, twisting the Rock Star bracelet still around her wrist. Sometimes you had to play along to get what you wanted. "You're welcome to sit in on the interview as well, Ms. Reese."

A slow, knowing smile crept over Beatrice's features. "You are good, Agent McKellen. I see why Elliot wanted you as his partner."

The burn of betrayal ate like acid in her stomach. Up ahead, she saw the cruiser pull to an abrupt stop along the side of the road.

"What is it?" Jax asked, sitting forward.

"Body," Hunter replied. He drew up behind the cop car. "In the ditch."

Ruby was out of the SUV before it came to a full stop, Zeb exiting the cruiser and looking down into a clump of tall grass in the ditch.

Rocks bit into her already sore feet as she tore across the gravel, not missing the trail of blood on the dirt road. The grass was slick from the rain, causing her to slide and nearly go down on her butt.

A strong hand grabbed her from behind and hauled her back up. "Whoa there, sweetheart," Jax said. "Let Rolands take a look first."

Ruby's eyes locked on the blood trail that led to a folded down patch a few feet away. A body lay facedown, the sun, now low on the horizon, spilled soft rays across a head of blond hair. The man's clothes were streaked with dirt and blood.

He didn't appear to be breathing.

"It's him," she whispered as the Chief snapped on latex gloves.

Time seemed to freeze as Rolands leaned over and felt for a pulse.

"He's dead, isn't he?" Ruby asked.

Rolands silenced her with a glare, stayed stationary for a minute longer. Finally he drew his hand away. "Not yet," he said, carefully rolling the body over.

The sight of Elliot's face made her breath catch. He was gray, a large bruise on one cheek, blood streaming from his hairline.

Rolands shook his head as he eased him onto his back. "But he's about as close as you can get to meeting his Maker."

Trace stood next to Beatrice's open window. "Should I call 911?" he asked as they watched Jax approach Hayden's broken and battered body.

"No." She reached down next to her leg—which was no easy feat, thanks to her gigantic belly—and brought out Jax's medical bag. He'd left it in his car back in Chicago. "Let Jax stabilize him, then we'll move him to an approved medical clinic."

"*If* he can stabilize him," Trace said, taking the bag through the window. "Looks like the guy's been shot."

Jax appeared to come to the same conclusion as he lifted his head. "GSW, left thigh. He's bleeding out."

Ruby stood beside the road, body frozen, eyes locked on the scene in front of her. Her shock was palpable, and for a moment, Beatrice felt the urge to hug her and tell her everything would be all right.

The baby is making me soft.

Logically, there was no way in Hades that Elliot Hayden was going to make it out of whatever jam he'd gotten himself into. Whether he was the culprit behind all of this or simply a pawn, he had obviously ran afoul of someone very powerful.

"I'll call 911," Rolands said, hitting the mike on his shoulder to alert his dispatcher.

"Don't." Trace stepped forward so quickly, he was a blur as he reached out and stopped Rolands' hand. "There are people after this man. People who are monitoring their scanners for any type of call like this."

The Chief's face went hard. "The man needs medical treatment."

Trace raised the black bag and held it out to Jax. "And he's going to receive it."

Jax snapped his attention from the bag to Beatrice with a question on his handsome face. He gave her a tiny shake of his head. "He needs surgery and a whole lot of blood."

Beatrice was already on her phone, dialing Rory. Trace resumed his post as her bodyguard, scanning the area with his razor-sharp gaze. "You know what to do to stabilize him until we reach an appropriate facility, Jaxon," she said.

Appropriate in this case meant an SFI-approved clinic, where no one would find them or even know they'd been there.

"Beatrice..." Jax's voice was full of warning. "I'm not qualified to treat this man."

Trace kept his attention glued on the dirt road and fields around them. His voice was soft as he murmured to her. "I can help him if need be."

"Not necessary," Beatrice replied. Then she raised her voice to speak to Jax once more. "The lack of the initials MD behind your name is a moot point. You're a medic with plenty of field experience treating gunshot wounds. Stabilize Hayden and let's get out of here."

Rory picked up on the other end of the secure line and Beatrice watched Jax wrestle with his conscious a moment longer as she gave Rory their coordinates and explained their situation. "I need a facility to handle Hayden's care and recovery. Jax believes he needs surgery and a blood transfusion."

Making up his mind, Jax opened his bag and went to work.

Surprisingly, Ruby fell to her knees next to him and began handing him gloves and bandages.

As Rory searched for what they needed, Beatrice watched Jax and Ruby work to save Hayden's life. It was as if Ruby read Jax's mind, handing him supplies without him even asking.

They make a good team.

But when had she begun thinking of the woman as Ruby rather than Agent McKellen?

That was unfortunate, both the fact that Jax was sleeping with her and that Beatrice was growing soft about her. Like Hayden, Ruby was in deep, whether she realized it or not. Extracting her from the clutches of whatever government cover-up was involved would be not be easy.

Beatrice wished she could share an ounce of her intelligence with Jax and give him a clearer picture of what he was facing. Not that he wasn't smart and savvy—he wouldn't be on her team if he wasn't—but hormones inflated his little brain and cut off his big brain's IQ until his logic became completely buried.

"Jesus, you are in the boonies," Rory said. "If you needed a cornfield or a pig farm, you'd be set. A clinic like you're talking about is at least forty miles away."

With Chief Rolands running point for them, they could get there in under half an hour. "Send me the coordinates," Beatrice told him. "Make sure they're ready for us."

"Roger that," Rory said. "Before you hang up, there's someone who wants to talk to you."

Emit's voice took over. "B, what the hell are you doing?"

"Apprehending our target, who at the moment is bleeding out. What do you need?"

"You're supposed to be in DC getting ready to have a kid."

Jax was sticking an IV in Hayden's arm while Ruby held a pile of bandages on his leg. Rolands stepped forward to hold the IV bag above Hayden's body. "The baby is uncooperative and I have a job to do."

Strained silence. "I could have gone out and retrieved Jax and Agent McKellen. You didn't need to fly here and take over."

"I have experience with government cover-ups. My expertise was needed."

"You're having a goddamn baby, and a woman as far along as you is not supposed to fly. What if the baby has problems?"

"There is no evidence that flying is harmful to an unborn child or the mother if the mother is in good health. I am in good health and so is my son."

Another round of silence, full-throttle exasperation coming

through the invisible phone line. "Do you know how many ways your husband is going to kill me when he finds out you're here?"

"He already knows and I suspect he's on his way to Chicago to drag me back to DC against my will at this very moment. I'm here, so arguing is a waste of your time and mine. Let me get Elliot Hayden to a safe clinic and I'll deal with Cal when I'm done."

She hung up before Emit could say anything else.

Jax put a stethoscope to Hayden's heart, felt for a pulse. "We're losing him," he announced, straddling Hayden and starting CPR.

Ruby grabbed Hayden's hand and watched Jax pumping on the man's chest. "Please save him, Jax. You have to save him."

Jax was singing. Beatrice couldn't quite make out the tune, but it sounded familiar. "Is that *Staying Alive*, the pop song?" she asked Trace.

Her bodyguard glanced at her. "Most med students learn to sing that song, at least mentally, or *Another One Bites the Dust*, while performing the recommended one hundred chest compressions per minute. Both songs have the appropriate beat."

Why did she not know this?

"Sure you don't want me to help out?" Trace asked. "He's in great shape, but he can't keep up compressions for more than a minute or two. No one can. Except maybe, me."

Beatrice weighed the pros and cons. Zeb shot her a look over Ruby's distress. "Zeb," she called. "Watch our six. Trace, help Jax."

Trace nodded, switching places with Zeb, and then taking Jax's place over Hayden, continuing the chest compressions.

"Adrenaline, in my bag, Ruby," Jax ordered as he shook out his hands. "Can you find it?"

Ruby bit her lip, let go of Hayden, and came up with the syringe from the bag a second later. "Is this it?"

She handed it to Jax, who nodded and tore the plastic covering off. Taking his place at Hayden's head, he primed the syringe, brought it up, paused, and plunged it down, straight into Hayden's heart.

The body convulsed, Trace stopped chest compressions, and Jax slowly pushed down the head of the syringe.

Seconds ticked by. Jax removed the needle from Hayden's

heart, threw it down and leaned over to put his ear next to the man's lips.

Hayden was stone still. So was Jax. His massive body was so inanimate, Beatrice found herself holding her own breath in anticipation. Jax closed his eyes and Beatrice thought *oh no.*

They'd lost Elliot Hayden.

Now they'd never know who he'd been working with or what plan he had put in motion. They'd never know what had cost the man his life. His and Nelson's and James'.

Ruby's shoulders shook, her sobs silent. Her chin went to her chest.

"Dammit," Zeb swore, shaking his head.

And then, without warning, Jax reared back and sent a fist into Hayden's chest. "You goddamn bastard." His voice echoed across the field. He reared back and hit him again. "Don't you dare die on me."

A moment later, Elliot Hayden's body convulsed. His eyes flew open and he sucked in a sharp breath.

CHAPTER SEVENTEEN

Trace Hunter moved off Elliot and Ruby didn't know whether to throw herself at her former partner and hug the crap out of him, or slap him across the face for scaring her to death.

Slapping an injured man who'd just come back from the dead was loathsome and barbaric, so she threw herself at him instead.

"Elliot!" She cradled his face, touched his shoulders. "It's me, Ruby."

His eyes were dazed, pupils unfocused as he stared past her at the sky. His mouth moved, but no words came out.

"Ruby, back up," Jax said.

His face was tense, a muscle in his jaw jumping, brows drawn in a severe frown. Looking at the man who'd saved her partner, she nearly threw herself at him as well. "Thank you for saving him. You're amazing."

At her words, a light came into his eyes. Confidence. Pride. And then it was gone just as quickly. "We're not out of the woods yet. Hunter, we need a blanket."

From the black SUV came Beatrice's voice. "Get Mr. Hayden in the vehicle and let's go. Time is of the essence for both him and us."

"He's not stable," Jax argued. "He could go into cardiac arrest again at any moment."

Elliot's eyes stayed open, his focus landing on Ruby as his lips trembled with the effort to speak.

"Rub...sor..ry..."

"Shh," she said, stroking his battered face again. "It's okay."

From the Escalade, Beatrice's tone brokered no room for

negotiation. "I suggest you do your best to keep that from happening, Jaxon. An appropriate clinic is forty miles from here. The sooner we get Agent Hayden there, the better."

Ruby saw the struggle on Jax's face. He wasn't about to lose his patient, even if he did hate the guy. "I need five minutes."

"You have three."

He sent his boss an ugly look, but kept his mouth shut as he searched his black bag for something.

Elliot blinked and Ruby squeezed his hand. She wanted to believe he had a good reason for what he'd done. A reason she could get behind. "El, tell me what happened. Who did this to you?"

His gaze zeroed in more intently on her, his eyes sunken in his pale face. He'd lost a lot of blood, his body definitely in shock. Nothing came out of his mouth but nonsensical whispers.

Ruby leaned forward, placing her ear close to his lips in hopes of figuring out what he was saying. He grunted and she knew he was trying.

Jax took another syringe from his bag and injected it into the IV port. He tugged her out of the way so he could listen to Elliot's heart.

Ruby watched, a flood of emotion heating her chest. Jax looked rough and tough, a day's worth of beard on his face, the tats on his arms and the scar on his temple suggesting he was a fighter, not a healer. There was nothing about him that looked like a competent, skilled doctor, and yet, at that moment, Ruby was sure Elliot couldn't have been in more capable hands.

"What can I do to help?" she asked.

He glanced at her, slinging the stethoscope around his neck. "Let's get a bandage on his leg."

"Time's up," Beatrice announced. "We need to move."

"That wasn't three minutes," Jax yelled.

"Rory has informed me that we're about to have company," she replied. "They're coming in hot."

"Who?" Hunter and Jax asked at the same time.

"Their identities have not been ascertained yet. Therefore, I advise we depart without further delay."

No worry in her voice, no concern. Beatrice was calm under the most extreme situations and something about that calmed Ruby as well.

Ruby said to Jax. "I'll help you move him."

"Jax and I will move him," Hunter informed her. "You grab the bag."

They worked together, the three of them, with Chief Rolands holding the IV. Hunter grabbed a blanket from the back of the SUV and he and Jax lifted Elliot and placed him on it.

Zeb folded down the second and third row seats and the two men easily carried Elliot to the vehicle and slid him into the makeshift hospital. Elliot grunted a couple of times from the treatment, but he maintained consciousness.

Ruby made sure they left nothing behind—no bandage papers, no plastic bags from the syringes. She even took a quick moment to fluff the crumpled grass where they had walked. Unfortunately there wasn't anything to be done about the blood on the road and under the spot where Elliot had lain.

Zeb took over holding the IV bag, while Hunter hopped into the driver's seat. Beatrice instructed Chief Rolands to take off without the sirens, then she gave him the coordinates to the clinic.

Whoever was approaching was no friend, Ruby was sure of that. Were they after Elliot? Or was it a cleanup team to take out all of them? The CIA? Homeland?

Between her, Hunter, and Jax, she wasn't worried about a confrontation. Hell, even Beatrice probably knew a thing or two about guns and self-defense. But with Beatrice being pregnant and Elliot in critical condition, a stand-off with a possible wet job team was a losing battle from the get-go.

The gravel road was bumpy as hell as they flew east. The sun sank behind them, streaking the sky with amber. As Zeb balanced the IV near Elliot's head, Jax and Ruby sandwiched their patient between them and went to work re-bandaging the gunshot wound.

There was still so much blood, Ruby wasn't sure exactly where it was all coming from. She used her phone's flashlight to illuminate the area and lifted Elliot's leg when Jax instructed her to so he could wrap the thigh with gauze.

Rolands took them around a bend in the road and past an abandoned farmhouse. In the distance, shadows grew as a wooded area came into view.

No one was riding with the chief, and while Ruby heard the soft chatter of radio communications coming from the front where Hunter and Beatrice were monitoring police channels, she had a sudden spurt of uncertainty.

"You trust Chief Rolands?" Ruby called to Beatrice as he took them on another unpaved road leading toward some woods.

"Hey," Zeb complained. "That's my brother."

"Half-brother," Ruby reminded him. "Sorry, but I can't take chances."

"She doesn't trust anyone," Jax added.

Beatrice glanced back. "Rolands is our best chance at getting us where we need to go."

Not a definite yes or no. Ruby suspected Beatrice didn't fully trust many people either.

But she sure believed in Jax.

That makes two of us.

A fresh bump sent all of them bouncing. Elliot cried out and Jax swore. Elliot's hand grabbed onto Ruby's and he mumbled something.

She leaned forward, desperate to hear what he was saying and reassure him at the same time. "We're headed for a clinic where they can remove the bullet, El. Just hang in there."

"N-n-n..."

His face strained, his jaw clenched. The hand holding hers loosened.

While she was desperate for answers, she was just as desperate to keep him alive. "Don't talk. Save your energy. Once you're patched up, you can tell me everything."

Another curve. Ruby couldn't see anything through the windshield except trees, trees, and more trees. They seemed to be going downhill—she saw the flash of a creek bed to her left—but the overgrowth was blocking out the last of the sun's rays.

Elliot worked his mouth again. "N-n-night..."

Night? "Yes, it's almost night. Don't worry about what time it is. Focus on conserving your energy. We're taking care of you."

Jax finished securing the bandage. In the glow of the flashlight beam, he sent her a look that sent a chill down her spine. "Let him speak. It may be his last chance to tell us what we need."

Last chance.

Those words. Heartless, cruel...but realistic. Jax was doing everything in his power to save Elliot's life, yet he knew his chances of survival were slim.

"...coming," Elliot murmured.

"Who's coming, El?"

The man's throat worked. His lips parted, closed, parted again. A sigh escaped them, and then he looked her right in the eye. His sunken sockets looked bruised, terrified. "Ghost. Night…shade," he whispered.

"Nightshade?" she echoed. "What are you talking about?"

Before Elliot could say anything else, bullets riddled the back end of the SUV.

"Get down!" Jax shouted, pushing Ruby to the floor between the flat seats and covering her with his body.

Bullets pinged off the back window, Jax sending up a silent thank you to the heavens—as well as Emit—for the custom-designed tank of an SUV they were in that included bulletproof glass.

The road they were on was narrow and rocky. As Hunter kicked the vehicle into high gear, he nearly ran into Rolands' squad car ahead of them. Since the SFI Escalade was equipped with a push bar, Rolands might find himself going for a joy ride any minute.

"Holy fucking spitballs," Jax swore out loud as Ruby clung to him with one hand and pulled out a Glock from her waistband with the other. "Where the hell did you get that?"

"I took the backup from your medical bag," she said. "You already have one and mine was lost in the tornado."

He'd been so focused on Hayden, he hadn't seen her steal his weapon. She was good at that—stealing things. Her slight of hand was better than anyone he'd ever seen.

Might be why she'd stolen his heart somewhere along the line when he wasn't paying attention.

Hunter killed the running lights and they nearly missed a Y intersection in the road. Rolands went right, his taillights a red bulls-eye. Hunter veered left.

Either Ruby's intuition about Zeb's half-brother had been accurate, or Hunter's superhuman Spidey senses had told him something.

The sun was long gone, a sliver of moonlight rising through the trees here and there. Ruby's phone had slid into a crevice near Jax's foot. He grabbed for it, shut down the flashlight. *Time to become one with the night.*

Disappearing in these woods under normal circumstances would be a piece of cake for him and Hunter, both trained in the art of evasion. For the others, not so much. They had to stay in the SUV, complete with a wounded man and a very pregnant woman. Vehicles were much easier to track, especially when the truck hunting them had spotlights on the top that made the lights at a football stadium look like miniature flashlights. Even through the tinted windows of the Escalade, those lights about blinded him.

Perfect. Just fucking perfect.

He'd had about all he could take in one day. Pushing Ruby farther down, Jax called to Beatrice. "Return fire?" he half-asked, half-insisted.

Hunter had killed the dashboard lights along with the rest of them. Even so, Jax could see the pale glow of Beatrice's white-blond hair. "Negative. Hold your fire."

Dammit. Jax clenched his jaw and ground his teeth. He couldn't properly take care of his patient, protect Ruby, or keep the bad guys at bay hunkered down like this. He badly wanted to jump out and take each and every one of the sleezeballs in the truck behind them out, one by one. Punch their lights out and break their necks.

That was the rage inside you talking, buddy. That rage that had brewed ever since his friend had come back disabled. Ever since his parents had kicked him out.

It was always there, burning, needy, addicting. He'd tried counseling, tried a hundred different tools to manage it. Like dried out tinder, all it needed was a single spark to ignite, erupting into a fire of epic proportions that devastated everything and everyone in its path.

Including him.

Which had made him an effective soldier. He'd learned to channel his hurt and anger into something positive the only way he knew how.

He wasn't that warrior anymore. He needed to get back out into the field where he could do battle and let the rage demon have its head.

If only Beatrice wasn't determined to make him bring that demon to heel first. She insisted he had to manage his anger before she would allow him to manage a team of SFI operatives.

A light touch on his arm brought him back from the edge.

Ruby raised up, putting her face close to his. "I'm sorry," she murmured in his ear. "This is all my fault."

He touched her head, letting his fingers slide over her soft hair until he could cup the back of her skull. The fire inside him cooled, still there, but morphing into the desire to keep her safe, keep Beatrice safe.

Save the fucking day.

The Escalade swerved, Hunter going off-road. The vehicle bounced, crashing through brush and small trees, limbs whacking against the sides and windows as the push bar did its job, mowing down a path.

Without warning, Jax's stomach dropped.

And ah, shit. He knew that feeling.

He almost let out a whoop, the sensation one he adored.

Airborne. The fucking truck had left the ground and was sailing through the air.

Ruby let out a quiet yelp and clutched his arm tighter, not seeming to enjoy the drop of her stomach as much as he did. Jax clasped the back of her head tighter and drew her to him. He felt the SUV stall out under him, felt the pull of gravity bringing them back down.

They dropped like a ton of bricks, the Escalade's suspension taking them on a whiplash of a ride and knocking Jax's head into the roof. Outside the bulletproof doors, Jax heard the splash of water.

The creek. They were driving down the creek bed.

Good thing the Escalade was kitted out with off-road tires as well as everything else.

"Sorry, boss," Hunter said to Beatrice.

"I'm fine. Keep going," she replied.

Unbelievably, Zeb was humming under his breath somewhere off to Jax's left. Jax couldn't see the man, but he sounded every bit as unconcerned about their circumstances as Beatrice.

What is wrong with these people?

The thought, combined with the adrenaline in his system, made Jax laugh.

What about Elliot?

He couldn't see his patient, but the man was no longer making grunts or speaking in whispers. Jax felt for his pulse and found it. Light and thready, but there.

Alive.

Goddamn bastard. If nothing else, Jax wanted to save him so he could strangle him.

Nightshade. What did that mean?

The Escalade went down an incline, pulled a tight left, and suddenly, Hunter cut the engine.

"Positions?" Jax called to Beatrice, releasing his grip on Ruby.

"Yes," she said, as clear and concise as always.

He yanked out his weapon, spun away from Ruby and Elliot and scooted his ass over to peer out the back window. Ruby took up a position near the side window opposite Zeb. As Hunter climbed out of the truck, Jax saw the glint of moonlight on an M6 in the man's hands.

The *thudthudthud* of Hunter's boots on the top of the truck echoed in the silence as their super soldier went into action. Hunter had extrasensory skills that came in handy in these kinds of situations. No night vision goggles needed; he could see just fine in the dark, like some bloody nocturnal animal.

Made Jax a little jealous.

It also made him itch to join his friend and fellow SFI operative. "I'm going out," he told Beatrice. "Ruby, take the wheel. Anything happens to me or Hunter, drive like hell and get everyone out of here."

Ruby touched his shoulder. "Are you sure you should—?"

Beatrice interrupted her. "That isn't necessary, Jaxon."

"The hell it isn't," he growled. "I love you, boss, but this is *my* area of expertise, so stay in the car and stay quiet. Hunter and I will take care of these guys."

"Don't kill them," Ruby called softly. "I want to interrogate them. We need to know who they're working for."

Don't kill them. Right. "No guarantees, babe. They're out for blood. So am I."

Without another word, he slipped out into the night.

The sounds of insects met his ears. He sensed Hunter's presence on the roof, knew the man was watching for the men hunting them.

"Anything?" he murmured.

"Maybe," Hunter murmured back.

Well, wasn't that informative.

Jax listened, straining to hear the sounds of an approaching vehicle. In the distance, he thought he heard a siren. Rolands?

Maybe the chief had pulled a U-ey and was headed their way. He wouldn't go off-roading in the cop car though.

If he caught up to and tried to apprehend the men in the truck, he was dead.

Shit. They might have unintentionally lured Rolands into a fight he couldn't win.

But there was nothing he could do about it now.

"Three o'clock, a hundred yards," Hunter said. "Vehicle stopped."

Their pursuers weren't interested in diving off into the creek.

Taking this direction had been a good call on Hunter's part. "They coming on foot?"

"Two confirmed. The others are staying with the vehicle."

Interesting. "You want the bipeds or the sissies in the truck?"

Hunter jumped off the roof of the SUV, landing next to Jax's feet. "Tough choice."

"I'm feeling the urge to go fisticuffs myself."

"I could blow up the truck," Hunter mused.

"Ruby wants one of them alive to interrogate."

"They won't let us take them alive. Deadly force will be necessary."

"Gee, that's too bad. How do you know, man?"

"It's a mercenary squad. I've dealt with this type of problem before."

Jax didn't question him further. "I'll wait for my guys at the bottom of the steep hill we just sailed over, take them out one at a time."

"We have a plan."

The rising moon peeked through the trees, giving him a modest amount of shadowy light. He saw Hunter raise a fist and Jax bumped it with his own. "We have a plan, my brother."

"Take this," Hunter said.

A small set of night vision goggles. So maybe the super soldier still needed some help with his long-distance vision at night. Jax accepted them and started forward into the dense woods.

He hated to leave his patient and Ruby, not to mention Beatrice, but if he and Hunter didn't get rid of their trackers, no one was getting out of this alive.

I'm sorry. Ruby's words echoed in his skull. Somewhere

ahead of him, Hunter was already climbing the embankment, avoiding the two men on foot. Jax heard the sounds of footsteps in the leaves, the snapping of twigs. Not Hunter's, oh no. The mercenary squad needed to brush up on their stealth skills.

Shaking Ruby's voice out of his mind, he centered himself and went into predator mode near the far edge of the creek.

Come to Jaxon, boys.

Waiting was the most challenging of all survival skills. Patience was not his forte. Endless training had honed his abilities, though, so as long as he didn't let his brain take over, he could stay unmoving for hours.

Tonight, he wouldn't need to. Off to his right, he heard his first victim. The second wasn't far behind. A two-for-one.

My favorite.

The goggles pinpointed the movements of his prey. He might not be as quiet as Hunter, but he was still a SEAL in his blood, in the very marrow of his bones.

As Bad Guy One moved into position, Jax let the rage burning inside him have its head.

The short, beefy fellow didn't know what hit him as Jax reached out from behind a tree and hooked the guy's neck with his arm. A sharp snap to the left and the guy went down without so much as a squeak. Neck broken.

Sorry, Ruby.

The second man provided more of a fight. Dark-skinned like his partner and wearing dark fatigues, he blended into the night. He was Jax's size and almost as tough, but he wasn't carrying a gun.

He had a knife, and the bastard apparently knew how to use it.

Back and forth the blade cut through the air, making little noises with the speed at which the man sliced it. At one point, as Jax danced away, it ripped through his already destroyed shirt. Jax considered shooting him but what fun would that be?

A chance trip on a tree root sent the man off balance and gave Jax the opportunity to grab his knife-wielding wrist. A hard slam of the man's hand into the massive tree trunk, and the knife fell to the ground.

Jax's rage was hot and powerful. As he gave into it, it cleared the constant nagging voice in his head. Cleared the endless chatter. Giving into his rage was the only way he'd ever found to access that kind of peace. It blotted out his emotions. Blotted out the endless loop of negative messages his subconscious fed him day and night.

Before he knew it, he'd taken Bad Guy Two to the ground. They wrestled for several long minutes, but only because Jax toyed with him. If he was going to interrogate the man, he had to hurt him first to soften him up.

Jax finally broke one of the man's arms and pinned him to the ground. The guy didn't cry out, only half-chuckled.

"Who are you?" Jax asked. "Who are you working for?"

"Fuck you and your mother too," Bad Guy Two spit.

"Dude, you're gonna wish you hadn't said that." He tweaked the guy's broken arm, shoving his face into the mud, suffocating him. The big guy flailed around, and after a good goddamn minute, Jax allowed the man to come up for air. "Start talking, asshat. Who sent you after us? What do you want?"

"The spook, who else? We're going to kill the rest of you."

The man laughed as if this were a fun little game. The image of Ruby dying sent Jax's rage demon howling.

The man tried to flip Jax off to the side. Hit Jax with one of his booted feet and the demon inside Jax snapped.

Bad Guy Two met his Maker a moment later.

As the man's body went limp, Jax climbed off of him.

Save a life. Take two. It seemed his scale was never in balance.

And Hayden, the life he'd saved only a few minutes ago, wasn't out of the woods yet.

Wet and muddy from his tumble with the second bad guy, Jax brushed dead leaves from his pants and started back for the Escalade. Behind him, a sudden explosion rocked the night.

Damn right. SFI, one. Bad Guys, zero.

CHAPTER EIGHTEEN

Ruby paced inside the clinic, feeling slightly claustrophobic. The place wasn't small, but she didn't do well without windows. Thanks to one of her first assignments in the smuggling tunnels of the Gaza Strip where she'd almost died during an explosion, she had an aversion to being underground. Elliot had been in surgery for nearly two hours. Jax was in there assisting Dr. Maria Oswalo, a woman with a beautiful, flowing South African accent and a placid demeanor that Ruby was sure hid a very clever intellect. Dr. Oswalo and Beatrice had exchanged nothing but a few murmured words before the doctor and two nurses whisked Elliot and Jax away to the operating room.

Beatrice had suggested Ruby shower in the clinic's locker room. Locker room was an overstatement. The place was barely bigger than a supply closet with a tiny shower head poking out of a cement wall. The overhead fluorescent light had made her look like a zombie in the oval mirror hanging from a wire.

She opted to wash her face in the sink, and had borrowed some scrubs to replace her clothes that were covered with Elliot's blood.

What Jax had done to save him was incredible. She'd known of his medical background even before he'd told her about his parents—she *had* run a background check on him—but she hadn't realized how talented he was. A part of her could now understand his parents' disappointment over him abandoning a career in the medical field in order to join the US Navy.

What they'd done to him wasn't right, and she hoped somehow, some way, they might work it out as a family down the road. She'd always been close to her family, and even though they thought she was a filing clerk at the CIA and knew nothing of her overseas exploits, she loved them dearly and couldn't imagine being estranged from them.

For years, she'd wrestled with lying to them, but it was for their own safety as much as hers. When she'd ended up in Chicago on probation, she'd told them the CIA had sent her there for training on a new filing system. She'd gone for Sunday dinner and enjoyed the quiet of normal life for an afternoon. Hopefully, she'd be done here by the end of the week and back in Virginia before the next Sunday dinner rolled around.

Although, she would miss her mom's homemade cherry pie.

Ruby hit the end of the hallway and turned on her heel to pace to the opposite end. Zeb was walking toward her with a cup of coffee in his hands.

They met in the middle. "Thought you might need a pick-me-up," he said.

She accepted the coffee and the warmth of the Styrofoam cup shocked her. Her hands were freezing. "Any word?"

He shook his head. "Sorry, no."

"Seems like an awful long time, doesn't it?"

His gaze went past her, over her shoulder. "Nah. Digging out a bullet can be tricky. It hit close to his femoral. The artery might even have been nicked, which explains the hefty amount of blood he lost. Keeping him stable and performing surgery is a balancing act. I wouldn't worry yet, girlie."

Girlie. Rolands had called her the same thing. "Your brother okay?"

Trace Hunter had told them that the men in the truck had run Chief Rolands off the road. He'd hit a tree, his airbag going off, and was about to be on the wrong end of a gun when Hunter had intervened.

"Yep. The ambulance arrived shortly after we left. He's at the hospital. I checked on him a little while ago. He's got some bruises and a whole lot of pissed-off-ed-ness, but he'll live."

"I'm sorry for all the trouble Elliot and I have caused."

Zeb's focus came back to her. "Are you kidding? I live for this shit. What's an old field operative like me gonna do anyway?"

Jax had told all of them that the last man he'd killed had said he was after Elliot, that the rest of them were going to die. But who was after El and why?

Zeb and Ruby started walking back to the others. "Do you miss it?" Ruby asked. "Fieldwork?"

"Hell, yeah. Best days of my life."

"And now you work for Beatrice?"

He half-nodded. "I subcontract on occasion."

As they approached the room where everyone was waiting, Ruby heard a familiar voice. *Jax.*

Her feet picked up speed.

Sure enough, he was in the room, his scrubs covered with blood, a weary look on his face.

Ruby's heart sank to her feet. "Is he...?"

Seemed like she was asking that a lot in the past twenty-four hours.

Jax shook his head. "We got the bullet out and Dr. Oswalo sewed him up. He lost a lot of blood, needed a few stitches, and has a couple of bruised ribs. It's going to take a while for him to recover."

"Did he say anything else?" Beatrice asked. She was sitting on the couch with her feet up. Hunter stood next to her, quiet and still as a mannequin.

"Not a word." Jax crossed his arms and leaned a shoulder against the door frame. "Any idea what nightshade is?"

"Not a what," she said. "A who."

"Nightshade was a senior military intelligence commander who once ran a secret branch of counterintelligence," Zeb said. "His real name is Christian Pierce."

Beatrice sipped from a Styrofoam cup with a teabag in it. The clinic didn't have fruit smoothies apparently. "He disappeared in Northern Africa in 2008 after a raid on a private camp there. The US believed Mohammed Izala kidnapped him, but they never found any evidence to confirm it. No body was ever found, dead or alive. It's possible he was interrogated and killed."

Zeb plopped down in a chair. "Or he may still be a prisoner. Either way, the US believes he gave up intel on military operations that has crippled us multiple times in the Middle East and Northern Africa."

"The Moroccan 5," Ruby murmured. "We always thought they had insider information about the US targets they picked in foreign countries."

"What was a senior commander doing in a private camp in Northern Africa?" Jax asked. "Surely not on vacation."

"And what does he have to do with Elliot, James, and Nelson?" Ruby added.

"We don't know why Commander Pierce was at that camp," Beatrice said. "My guess is, he was making a deal with someone high up in one of the political groups who wanted to overthrow a local government."

"A political coup?" Ruby asked.

Beatrice nodded. "As you know, at times when the US wants someone out of power, and needs to make a deal, they send in a high-ranking, discreet military commander to do the job. As to what that has to do with Agent Hayden and the others, well, if Commander Pierce is alive and missing in action, it's possible Homeland is using CIA and NI operatives to try to locate him. Agent Hayden may have received that assignment and availed Keon James and Abdel Al-Safari to help him locate Commander Pierce."

Jax ran a thumb along his jawline. "Once Hayden found the commander's location, the US could call in the SEALs to rescue him."

"And Augustus Nelson?" Ruby asked. "What is his connection?"

Beatrice shifted in her seat. "Either Keon James shared information with his almost-brother that got him killed, or Agent Hayden and James were using some of Nelson's underworld contacts in Northern Africa to try to locate Commander Pierce."

Ruby rubbed the back of her neck. She ached all over and could barely keep her eyes open. Beatrice and the others were now saying Elliot *wasn't* a traitor. Her heart loved that idea, but it all made her head spin. "So who killed James and Nelson and nearly killed Elliot? Who sent those men after us?"

"At this point," Zeb interjected, "*why* may be the better question to ask. If we figure out the motivation behind all of this, it will lead us to the murderer."

Ruby had a better idea. She shifted her tired gaze to Jax. Her eyes felt like they had sand in them. "How long before Elliot wakes up and can answer our questions?"

The lines around Jax's mouth tightened. He shook his head. "The man underwent major surgery, Ruby. It's going to be a while."

Damn. She needed answers now. Surely there was some way for Jax and Dr. Oswalo to wake him up sooner.

The thought pulled her up short. Elliot had actually died by her estimation—for a few seconds, anyway, until Jax had resurrected him—and here she'd been mentally whining because he was still out cold from surgery. What was wrong with her?

All during her time with the Agency, they'd drilled it into her: *Mission first and always.* Above her own wants and needs. Above the well-being of the people involved.

As she looked around at the men and one woman in that room with her, she knew that the mantra she'd always used to keep her focused was bogus. Total bullshit. Regardless of what the Agency wanted from its operatives, people mattered more than the mission.

Still, frustration burned inside her, mixing with her exhaustion. "If you guys hadn't killed all four of those men who came after us, we could have interrogated one of them and found out who sent them."

Trace Hunter and Jax shared a look. One that said they didn't like being second-guessed.

Beatrice didn't seem to like it either. "Those men wouldn't have given up anything, Agent McKellen, and we didn't exactly have time to grill them. As you'll recall, it was imperative we get Agent Hayden to this clinic."

"The Escalade is big, but it ain't that big, girlie," Zeb added. "We were at maximum capacity as it was."

Everywhere she looked, she was met was hostile glares. Each and every person in the room was as tired as she was, and they'd gone beyond what most people would have done to help her.

Time for a little gratitude. "I'm sorry. I didn't mean that to come out as ungrateful. I've gone from believing my partner was innocent, to wondering if he was guilty, to coming full circle and believing he's innocent again. The Agency lied to me. Elliot lied to me. I've burned my career. It's been one long, shitty day."

"No need for apologies," Beatrice said. "We've all been in your shoes."

Had they? Probably so. Beatrice was evasive and manipulative when she wanted to be, but spoke the truth. Ruby toyed with the Rock Star bracelet. "No, I do owe you an apology. You've been nothing but helpful. Elliot's alive because of you. All of you."

The glares receded. The heavy air in the room lifted.

"The thing is," Ruby continued. "I don't like unanswered questions, and our lives are all still in danger until we get those answers. I need to know if Elliot has been actually trying to find this Commander Pierce while acting as my partner and I need to know who took out the only two leads I had to prove Elliot is innocent of killing Al-Safari. Obviously, James and Nelson knew something that got them killed. I need to know what that was and if Keon James was right...that there's a cover-up going on and someone double-crossed him."

Beatrice's cell rang and she fished it out of her pocket. "Yes, Rory."

She was silent for a long moment, her face expressionless. "Please get confirmation on that, asap. Yes, I understand."

She hung up, and after inserting the phone back into her pocket, she looked up with consternation etched on her face.

"What is it?" Jax asked.

"I believe I may know who is after Elliot," she said.

"Who?" everyone asked at the same time.

Her brows knitted. She rubbed her oversized belly. "Rory has been doing an exhaustive facial recognition search on everyone at the club the other night when Keon James was killed."

"And?" Zeb asked.

Her face showed a touch of disbelief. "Facial recognition has identified a man whom we know to be involved in all of this."

Ruby felt goose bumps rise on her arms. "Who?"

Beatrice stared at the floor for a moment, then raised her piercing blue gaze to Jax. "It seems that known terrorist and member of the M5 jihad group, Abdel Al-Safari, is currently in Chicago."

Fucking A, his ears had to be deceiving him. Either that, or Beatrice Reese was pulling one horrible joke on him.

"Al-Safari is dead," Jax said, tired, confused, and a little pissed off. This was no joking matter.

It occurred to him that Beatrice wasn't one to joke. She

didn't kid around, found sarcasm childish, and never teased anyone, not even her husband, that Jax had ever heard. And yet this had to be a jest, a prank. Beatrice was punking him.

Hard.

Her unwavering gaze said differently. "Rory got a match from TracRec."

Ruby had the same half incredulous, half irate look on her face, as if she wanted to shake some sense into Jax's boss. "Rory is wrong. It must be someone else."

A crease laced across Beatrice's forehead. "While Rory is, on occasion, incorrect, TracRec never acts erroneously. It labeled a man outside the club after the mass evacuation as Abdel Al-Safari. The footage came from a compilation of cell phone videos Rory was scanning. Rory checked the club's video footage and caught what he believes to be the man inside before the gunshots, but Al-Safari kept away from the cameras so he can't confirm."

"Maybe you're not hearing me." Jax pushed off from the wall that had been holding him up. His legs protested, the day from hell taking its toll on his body. "Abdel Al-Safari is dead, boss. I was there when it happened. Hell, I tried to resuscitate the guy. He—or Elliot—blew his brains out. Whoever TracRec picked up on, it's not Al-Safari."

Beatrice's eyes hardened. "I'm inclined to disagree. The TracRec facial recognition software is the foremost technologically advanced system there is. If it registers that the man known worldwide as Abdel Al-Safari was in Chicago last night, then I have no doubt he was."

Hunter, who'd been silent like usual, rubbed his thumb over his chin. "Which means the man in Marrakech whom you thought was Al-Safari," he said to Jax, "was really someone else."

Ruby moved so she was standing next to Jax, as if physically adding her support to him as well as to his argument. "I don't believe that. Elliot and I were following Al-Safari and the Moroccan 5 for years before we caught up with them. I saw Al-Safari's face on several occasions. The man we took into custody in Morocco was the same man in the Moroccan 5."

"Who confirmed the man's identity to begin with?" Hunter asked.

Ruby started to speak, halted. "Shit," she whispered and looked at Jax. Disheartenment showed in her eyes.

"Who was it?" he asked her gently. "Elliot?"

She closed her eyes for a second, then opened them and nodded curtly.

Shit was right. Elliot had mislead her in more ways than one.

But it didn't confirm or repudiate the guy's innocence.

Repudiate. What a fucking Beatrice-like word.

Jax rubbed his eyes. He needed food and sleep, and for this goatfuck of an assignment to be over. Except then, his time with Ruby might be over too.

Good thing he hadn't eaten in a while because his empty-as-hell stomach revolted. "So who the hell was the guy in Morocco?" he ground out.

"Wait," Ruby said, brightening. "Homeland confirmed Al-Safari's identity after his death."

When everyone—including Jax—gave her a *hello, think about it* stare, her countenance dimmed again. "Right. Duh. Elliot, and/or his handler at Homeland, fudged the confirmation, didn't they? But why?"

"But why, is right." Zeb was stuck on the reasons behind all the fallacies and illusions the Department of Homeland had orchestrated. "That's what I'm saying. We need to know the why before we can nail the who."

"Does Al-Safari have any known brothers?" Beatrice seemed to be on her own mental train of thought. "Any close male relatives?"

Ruby brightened again, apparently following the train. "You think the man at the club is Al-Safari's brother? Like a twin?"

"Not at the club," Beatrice said. "The man who died in Morocco. The man you were led to believe was Abdel Al-Safari. It's possible the real Al-Safari had a look-alike and he sent that man to act in his place when it came to dealing with Elliot, knowing that at some point, Elliot might renege on their deal and take him back into custody or kill him."

"A look-alike?" Jax asked. "You mean like the men Saddam Husain had who stood in for him in public?"

"It's believed bin Laden had several as well," Zeb added. "Many leaders have used them over the years to protect themselves. I wouldn't be surprised if Mohammed Izala has a few himself."

Beatrice sent a glance at Hunter, then Zeb. "What are your thoughts?"

Hunter conceded the floor to Zeb with a nod. Zeb said, "Agent Hayden and Keon James were trading secrets to Al-Safari's look-alike in an attempt to get proof of life or death on Commander Pierce. Abdel, himself, was probably completely out of it. If Pierce was indeed alive, the US was willing to trade some big ass secrets to get him back, so Homeland fed Agent Hayden, who in turn fed them to Keon James, in hopes of rescuing a man with far more military intelligence in his little finger than we can imagine. What they were feeding Izala was probably nothing in comparison, but Izala didn't know that."

"Or he did," Jax said, "which is why they never got anywhere. Izala was getting military info from both Hayden and Pierce. Fucker."

Ruby rubbed her temples and blew out a tight sigh. "My brain is cramping. I need a white board or something to write all of this down on so I can visually see the connections."

The crease in Beatrice's forehead eased. "That's an excellent idea, Agent McKellen. I'm sure Dr. Oswalo has one of those around here somewhere. Trace, please go find it for us."

As Trace left the room, she gave Jax a pointed look while speaking to Ruby. "I think my operative could use a shower and some coffee. Why don't you two freshen up and see if any further ideas come to you. We'll reconvene in an hour and write all of this out on the whiteboard."

Jax started to argue, but Beatrice shut him down with a lift of her hand and a glare. "You're dead on your feet, both of you, and I'll admit, I'm tired as well. Let's all take a break. You're no good to me if you can't think straight or function at full capacity should we encounter other hostile forces."

She had a point. While he'd prefer another round of sex with Ruby to rev him up, he wasn't going to look a gift horse in the mouth. Ruby needed a power nap, and it wouldn't hurt him to catch a few winks himself.

Besides, his boss had just admitted she was tired. He walked over, checked her pulse.

Steady, normal.

"What are you doing?" she said.

"I'm worried about you. How's your lower back? Any cramping or contractions you're keeping from us?"

She pulled her wrist away from his fingers, but a small smile curved her lips. "I'm fine, thank you. A nap would be nice, though."

"A nap, right. Whatever you say, boss. We'll be back in a few." He grabbed Ruby by the hand and hauled her out of the room.

"What was that all about?" she said as they walked down a long hallway, Jax poking his head in a room.

"Power struggle. We have them all the time," he said. "She's just as tired as I am, but she believes she's invincible. On the other hand, she's right. I haven't slept in nearly three days and I just helped perform major surgery on a guy. As a SEAL, I was trained to handle shit like this on an ongoing basis, but I must be getting soft. I'm beat, and Beatrice knows it."

"Need I remind you, you survived a shooting at the club, a tornado, and a few rounds of sex with me at the B&B. The sex with me alone would be enough to make any man tired."

Even though she was barely putting one foot in front of the other, she gave him a wicked wink. One that caused a surge of *hell, yeah* in his worn out system.

"Funny, that always seems to have the opposite effect," he snickered, finding the entrance to a small locker room. "I can never get enough sex with you."

He dragged her into the room, found the three-man shower stall and turned on the water under two of them. As it heated, he shucked his scrubs, enjoying the way Ruby's eyes scanned his now naked body. Strutting forward and letting her see how ready he was for her, he reached for the hem of her scrub shirt and pulled her close.

Peeling the shirt up slowly, he locked his eyes on hers. She lifted her arms, allowing him to slip the fabric up over her breasts, his fingers taking advantage of her bare skin and brushing against her stomach, her ribs.

She shivered under his light touch, her gaze breaking contact with his only when the fabric slipped up over her arms. Even then, he could see her eyes through the thin cotton, watching, waiting, wanting more.

Jax continued his slow undressing, allowing the soft material to glide and tease the sensitive skin under her arms, her elbows, her wrists.

He bunched the shirt around her wrists, drawing the material together in one hand and binding her wrists above her. Backing her up against the flat side of the row of lockers, he enjoyed her gasp as her naked skin touched the cool metal. She arched, her breasts rising. Lowering his head, he licked one of the rose colored nipples, teasing it into a hard pucker. He took it between his teeth, gently nipping.

Steam rose in the room mixing with her whimpers. Another arch toward his eager mouth and he caught her breast more fully, sucking at her, drawing her whimper into a cry of pleasure.

With his other hand, he untied the drawstring of her pants, slipping his fingers inside. Oh, yeah. She was ready for him too, her folds slick with moisture. Kissing her deeply, he allowed his fingers to mimic his tongue, diving in, drawing back, diving in again.

She bucked her hips, driving her pelvis into his hand, more sounds coming from her throat, encouraging him. A few more skilled movements and she was close to climax, her body demanding he speed up his tempo and give her what she craved.

Like always, his own body demanded the same, a quick, hard coupling that would leave them both gasping for air. In the back of his mind, the niggling thought that this could be their last time made him slow down. When Hayden woke, they'd have their answers to the questions boggling all of them. They'd have a solution.

He'd done his job; captured the fugitive. Whatever the outcome—whether Elliot Hayden was guilty or innocent—the mission was over.

Which meant Ruby would most likely go back to the CIA, regardless of her renegade behavior. Her boss liked operatives who got the job done, and Ruby did that. She might get another reprimand and a few more months of probation, but she'd go back to being a spy because she loved the work and the Agency needed her. She'd throw on a wig and change her appearance and all would be well.

And that, right there, friends, would leave him in the dust of her wheels as she beelined out of his life once again.

So he slowed it down—his fingers, his tongue, his mind. Taking his time and soaking her up. Memorizing every sound she made, every brush of her body against his as she rocked her way toward an orgasm. He wanted to remember everything. The way she smelled, the way her eyelashes lay against her skin, the way her tongue danced with his.

"Please," she murmured into his mouth. "Jax...*please.*"

Ah, yes. He loved to hear her beg. Loved the feeling of making her so crazy with need that she would lose her cocky, over-confident self long enough to plead—instead of demanding—that he get her off.

Under his breastbone, a new feeling broke open. Warmth spread inside his chest as if all his blood had suddenly turned to syrup, gliding over his battered heart, his always tight ribcage.

Fuckin' A. He wanted that feeling to continue.

The only way for that to happen was to keep this woman in his life. Here, now, always.

"Tell me what you want," he murmured, teasing her lips with tiny nips of his teeth. "Tell me, Ruby McKellen, what you really want from me."

"Everything," she whispered without hesitation. "I want it all."

Another wave of release and joy spread through his system. Jerking the shirt off her wrists, he freed her, letting the fabric fall to the floor as he went to work on the pants. Once he had her fully naked, he lifted her from the floor, her legs going around his waist, as he carried her into the showers.

CHAPTER NINETEEN

Ruby dreamed about Jax. Wind swirled around both of them and she was struggling to hear something he was saying—reading lips had never been her strong point and the damn wind was too loud, too strong. She cried out as it ripped him away from her—screaming his name as she flung her arms out to try to catch him, and…

The door to the hospital room banged open, wrenching her from the dream. She sat up before her eyes were fully open, realizing she was still naked under the sheet and Jax, lying next to her, was naked as well.

"Sorry to disturb you," a nurse named Molly said, "but your friend is lucid. He's fading in and out so you better come quick if you want to talk to him."

Jax threw his legs over the edge of the bed, kissed Ruby on the nose. He snatched up the fresh scrubs he'd grabbed from the locker room as Molly disappeared, letting the door close behind her.

His voice was rough as he spoke. "Shit, what time is it?"

They'd fallen into a deep sleep after their love-making—which was the only way to describe what Jax had done to her. He'd made love to her until the water in the locker room shower ran cold. Then he'd carried her—because she hadn't been able to walk, her legs were so weak—into this room where he'd made love to her again. Slowly, skillfully, masterfully. For hours, she'd left the rest of the world behind and surrendered herself to him and his amazing hands and lips.

As she scrambled for her clothes, she felt happier than she had in months. She and Jax had reconnected in a way that was even more than she could have hoped for. She wasn't sure at this point what the future held for her job-wise, but she'd figure it out. Troubleshooting was a strong point. She'd free Elliot and figure out where this thing with Jax was going. The future seemed full of possibilities.

She squinted at the clock on the wall across the room. "0100 hours," she told him.

His morning hard-on was big and she wished they had time for her to help him with that. He made a painful face as he forced it under the waistband of the scrubs, then gave her an evil grin as he saw her watching him. "Later," he said, as if reading her mind.

Later, right. They had to get to Elliot while he was awake.

"I'll hold you to it," she said, hurriedly yanking up her own scrubs.

The hallway was too bright compared to the room, forcing Ruby to blink a few times for her eyes to adjust. Jax's long legs ate up the linoleum and she had to double time it to keep up. They turned a corner into a separate wing and found Trace and Beatrice coming from the other end.

They met in front of the door that Elliot was behind. Jax didn't slow, yanking open the wooden door and holding it for the others. "Let Ruby do the talking," he told Beatrice, and it sounded like a warning to Ruby's ears.

A surge of pride went through her system. Silly, but true. She *should* be the one to talk to Elliot—he trusted her and he didn't know Beatrice or Trace. His feelings for Jax weren't exactly great, either.

So while it was a solid tactical move on Jax's part, it felt like something more. Especially as Ruby met his eyes and he gave her a quick nod. A nod and a look that said *you got this.*

She strode into the room feeling ten feet tall.

The nurse, Molly, was checking Elliot's vitals. He was pale as a hospital sheet. Not the one he lay under—the clinic's bedding was a soft blue. But if he'd been in a normal hospital, he would have won in the white category.

His eyes were closed, his mouth slack. Molly released his wrist and scurried out as the four of them surrounded the bed.

"El," Ruby said quietly, reaching down and taking the hand Molly had placed on top of his stomach. "It's me, Ruby."

His mouth worked a moment and his eyelids fluttered. "Ru...Ru..."

"Yep, it's me. You were shot. Jax saved your life and we brought you here to recover. The bullet's out and you're going to be fine. Do you remember what happened? Who did this to you?"

His eyelids opened a crack, blinked closed, opened more fully. His pupils were unfocused, though, as he met her gaze. "Ruby?"

She combed back a hunk of bangs from his forehead. "Yes, El. I'm here. You've had surgery and are groggy, but you're going to be okay thanks to Jaxon."

Elliot swatted at the oxygen tube in his nose. "Jax...?"

She drew his hand away from the tubing. "He saved your life."

Beatrice shuffled her weight from one foot to another. Ruby understood her impatience but there was no hurrying this process.

"Elliot, you need to rest, but before I leave you, can you answer a couple of questions for me?"

A light squeeze of her hand.

She'd take that as a yes. "Tell me who shot you."

Elliot shook his head, slowly rolling it from side to side. He seemed to notice the others circling the bed, his gaze landing on Jax and staying there. "I...can't..."

Ruby felt her confidence draining away. "El, we know about Nightshade, about Commander Pierce. Were you looking for him?"

Elliot's gaze meandered back to hers. "Pierce?"

"Were you and Keon James searching for him in Marrakech?"

"He's...a...alive."

Sounded like a statement. She'd take it as such. "And Al-Safari was helping you find him, wasn't he?"

At the mention of Al-Safari's name, Elliot stiffened. "Stay...away."

"We know about Al-Safari, too," Ruby said, rubbing his hand to calm him. "The man who died in Morocco wasn't Abdul Al-Safari, was he? The real Abdul Al-Safari is still alive. Facial recognition confirms he was at the club the other night. Did he kill Keon James?"

The pressure on her hand increased. "Can't...go there."

"We're nowhere near the club, El. Do you remember going to the police station and posing as a Homeland agent to get

Little Gus out of questioning after the shooting at the club? You drove him out of Chicago to a small town called Pottersville. To an abandoned feed mill. We found him there, dead, along with the go-bag I gave you. Did you kill him or did someone else?"

A bob of his head that might have been a nod yes. But yes to which part of her question?

Elliot worked his mouth again, his tongue snaking out to wet his lips. "Tried...to save...him."

"Here," Jax handed Ruby a cup of water from a nearby cart.

Of course, the man's mouth was dry, making his attempts to communicate harder than they had to be. Duh, why hadn't she thought of that?

So much for my interrogation technique. Ruby held the cup, complete with a straw, so Elliot could drink. A long sip later, he laid his head back and licked his lips once more. "Better," he whispered.

"Who did you try to save? Little Gus?"

She handed the drink back to Jax and started to launch in again, but Elliot held up a shaky finger and closed his eyes.

Damn, was he going to fall back asleep already? She hadn't gotten anything substantial from him.

She was about to shake him when he started talking. "The Moroccan 5...had Nightshade. Needed to find him. Caught the 5, but they had turned Pierce over to Iz...Iz..."

"Izala," Ruby finished for him. "Al-Safari knew where Pierce was, didn't he? He offered to get the location in exchange for his freedom."

Another bob of Elliot's head. "Izala kept moving him...or so we thought."

"Al-Safari was dicking you around, wasn't he?" Jax interjected. "He'd ask for military intel to feed to a source who claimed to have a lead on Pierce, then the lead would turn out to be nothing. So you kept feeding him intel, and he kept you chasing your tails."

"Brought him in, faked the capture by Moroc...Moroccan intelligence."

"But it wasn't him," Ruby said. "He knew you were onto him. Knew he was going to end up in prison or worse, so he sent a double to take his place. You were instructed to kill him and make it look like a suicide. Is that it?"

Elliot's eyes cracked open. He stared at his hand where

Ruby's was interlinked with it. "I thought it was him, but..."

"It wasn't."

"No." He motioned for another drink. Jax gave it to him this time.

After another long sip, Elliot released the straw and offered up a long-winded sigh. "After you," he said, looking directly at Ruby.

Her confidence was back, but a cold drop of fear fell into the pit of her stomach. "After me? You mean, Al-Safari was after me? Why?"

"Izala wants you."

The drop of fear morphed into a snowball. "Why would Mohammed Izala want me?"

Elliot dropped his gaze to the blue sheet and their hands, his lips drawing tight.

Zeb made an entrance, interrupting them, and all eyes, with the exception of Elliot's, turned to him.

"We have company," the old guy said, fiddling with his cell phone. For the first time since Ruby had met him, Zeb seemed nervous. He gave Beatrice a pointed look. "I think you're going to want to take this one personally, B."

Jax was torn. He needed to stay with Ruby and find out more about the bombshell Hayden had just laid on them, but he also needed to see who the "company" was that Beatrice was heading out of the room to deal with.

As if reading his mind, Ruby touched the top of his hand and cocked her chin at the backs of Hunter and Beatrice, filing out the door. "Go. I'll stay here with El."

And see what else I can find out... the words hung unsaid in the air between them.

He gripped her hand, and thought of the weird triangle the three of them—her, Elliot, and him—were still forming all these months after Marrakech. "You sure?"

She nodded. "I'm sure, now go."

His gut cramped but he let go of her and headed out the door.

He jogged to catch up to the others, Beatrice's belly not slowing her down much. If he had to guess, the mystery guest wasn't the enemy or they'd be knee-deep in gunfire already, trying to protect the doctor and staff as well as Hayden.

No, if he were a betting man, he'd say their mystery guest was a noncombatant, but one who could turn pretty downright violent if he wanted to.

And he might just want to, considering his pregnant wife was in the field being shot at by an unknown source.

Jax just prayed their visitor didn't decide to take out his frustration and anger on him.

Turning the corner, he pulled up short, because, *yesiree*, there was one angry former SEAL with his feet planted and his arms crossed looking like six kinds of angry.

But, hoo-wee, that look morphed into relief and unconditional love the moment Callan Reese saw his wife.

Without a word, Beatrice went to him, and he opened his arms and took her into an embrace. She murmured something soft and low in his ear and Reese closed his eyes and hugged her tight, nearly lifting her and the child still in her stomach off the floor.

It sounded like he said, "Why do you do this to me?" against Beatrice's hair, and she chuckled.

And then over her head, Reese shot Hunter a look that said the man's time on this earth might be about to come to an end. "You were supposed to keep her off her feet and relaxed."

Jax had to give Hunter credit. He didn't flinch at the menacing glare on Reese's face, nor did he argue with the man about the stubbornness of his charge. "She's in good hands at this moment with Sloan and Dr. Oswalo. They've kept a close eye on her."

Jax had checked on Beatrice before midnight, slipping out from a sleeping Ruby to make sure his boss's blood pressure and other vitals were normal. They had been, and Beatrice had assured him she was eating fine and felt good. Dr. Oswalo and Hunter had seconded the fact that for a pregnant woman several days past her due date, Beatrice was the epitome of health.

A petite woman with dark hair and numerous wrinkles stepped out from the shadows. "That will be for me to decide."

Reese had brought the midwife. Smart dude.

"You're fired," Callan said to Hunter, and Beatrice smacked his arm.

"He is not," she countered and then spoke to Jax. "Get back

to Ruby and Elliot. We need to know as much as possible about who's hunting Agent Hayden. Our lead suspect at this point is Abdel Al-Safari. Do you agree?"

Jax could only nod. He did agree, but the possibilities were endless with Homeland and the CIA involved. They still didn't have the full story, and even though his gut said Hayden was nothing more than a pawn in that story, Jax wasn't about to let down his guard with the man. Hayden was a skilled operative who'd apparently lied to and fooled Ruby and a whole lot of other people. "I'll find out everything I can, but I want outside verification of anything Hayden tells us."

Beatrice nodded. "Agreed. Anything that comes out of his mouth is circumspect, but at this point, we don't have enough information to confirm or deny what he's told us so far."

"Do you want me to go with you?" Hunter asked. "I know a few interrogation techniques that might come in handy."

Techniques. A nice word for torture. "Let's give him a chance to fess up," Jax said. "And a few more hours to stabilize from the surgery. If we haven't got anything worth its salt by then, he's all yours."

The two of them shared a fist bump and Jax left Beatrice and the others to deal with Cal and the midwife.

Izala wants you. Hayden's words to Ruby rang in Jax's head as he made his way back to the recovery room. Was Hayden telling the truth or making shit up again? If it was true, how had Izala found out about Ruby? Had he learned that she was hunting him for the CIA?

Worse, what had he intended to do with her if he caught her?

Uncomfortable images swam through Jax's mind, nauseating him. What did any psychopath want with a beautiful woman?

What had the man in the woods said? Him and his buddies were after the spook.

Not Elliot Hayden.

Ruby.

Al-Safari was in Chicago. He'd been looking for Ruby. The torn up apartment, the mercenaries.

All after her.

Jax picked up his pace, needing to put eyes on the woman who'd upended his world. No one was laying a hand on her, and by God, if Al-Safari came after her, Jax would kill him without a second's hesitation.

The door loomed on his left and he was mere steps from it when it flung open and Ruby came barreling out. She turned to her left, not seeing him, her feet breaking into a run as she headed for the far end of the hallway.

Her hands were up, palms on her cheeks, and Jax had the faint inclination she was hyperventilating as she hustled away, heading toward a door with a standard Exit sign above it.

"Ruby," he called, running to catch up to her. "Ruby, stop!"

She didn't seem to hear him, her hands flying out to hit the bar on the door before she shoved it open. Somewhere behind him, Jax heard an alarm blare.

A few strides and he hit the door as well, heaving it open and taking the stairs that led topside two at a time. "Ruby! Stop. Where are you going?"

He caught her as she stepped outside, but he didn't yank her back when he saw the panic on her face.

"I'm okay," she insisted around gasps. The door banged closed behind them. "Just a little claustrophobic."

He pulled her in close, snugging her body against his as he stared out at the indigo night. "Since when are you claustrophobic?"

She tried to laugh. The sound she made was more of a wheeze. "Since Palestine. Long story. I'll tell you some day."

He planned to hold her to it. They were close to the Wisconsin border, nothing but bluffs on one side, wide open prairie on the other. The secret clinic burrowed into and under one of the bluffs, providing a very secure fortress, completely obscured to the human eye.

They were safe here, hidden away. Still, hyperawareness of his surroundings had been embedded in his psyche from SEAL training. He quickly scanned the area, seeing nothing but the quarter moon and a blanket of stars over their heads.

Somewhere in the distance, a brook hiccupped and chirped. A chorus of night insects and frogs filled the humid air with comforting sounds.

Ruby gulped air, her hands delving into this shirt and gripping it tightly. He glanced down and saw the taut strain on her face.

Definitely hyperventilating even though she wasn't underground anymore. "Breathe," he told her. "Inhale. One…two…three. Now exhale twice as long. One…pause…two…pause…three. Do it again."

Beatrice and Hunter's little mind trick worked. Ruby's

breathing stabilized, her eyelids fluttered open, and her face relaxed. But she didn't let go of his shirt.

He rubbed her back, scanning her face as if he could figure out what had caused this sudden panic attack. She stared back, her eyes giving nothing away.

Easing her around so she could see the prairie before them, he encircled her in his arms and held her back close to his front. It wasn't a white room, but it would do.

He dropped a kiss onto the top of her head. "Nothing but wide, open space out here. Nothing closing in around you except my arms, sweetheart."

They stayed like that for long moments, her head resting against his collarbone.

It wasn't that he didn't believe her about Palestine but he suspected her panic attack had been more about something else. Perhaps the news that Izala was hunting her.

She surprised him when she spun inside his arms, then went up on her tiptoes and laid a kiss on him. Though completely unexpected, he wasn't about to look a gift horse in the mouth. Parting her lips with his, he poured what he was feeling for her into the simple act of kissing her back.

They stayed that way for long moments, Ruby's breathing becoming heavier, more rapid again. This kind of rapid breathing had nothing to do with panic, however. She slipped her tongue inside his mouth and, *bam*, just like always, his body felt that zip of electricity pass between them that happened every time they touched.

How long they stayed that way, he didn't know. Someone came out the door, saw them making out, and went back in, assured that the security breach was nothing more than a pair of lovers looking for some privacy.

Beatrice would still have his hide for standing outside in the open, even though there was no threat of them being seen unless the dead guys were zombies and had somehow managed to follow them.

When Ruby finally stopped molesting him, he was a bit disappointed, but he needed to know what else Hayden had said and why that had sent her sprinting for the exit. If he hadn't been there to stop her, how far would she have gone?

She licked her lips and looked down as he slipped a piece of her hair behind her ear. "What happened, Ruby? Why did you freak out and run?"

Turning away, she glanced out over the prairie and bit her bottom lip. "That was unprofessional, huh? Having a panic attack like that. It's just..."

"Just what? Did Hayden say something?"

"He did indeed," she said on a chuckle. There was no humor in it though. "He told me why he killed the man we believed was Al-Safari and why Al-Safari is now here, in America, coming after him."

Her tone left no doubt in Jax's mind that he wasn't going to like what he was about to hear. Sliding a hand into hers, he interlaced their fingers, hoping to let her know that no matter what it was, he was there for her. He wouldn't let her down. "Why?"

"Izala found out Elliot and Keon James were searching for Commander Pierce. He offered them a deal that El refused to take."

"What kind of deal?"

"He would give them Commander Pierce in exchange for someone of equal value."

Jax's stomach dropped. "You."

She nodded. "Al-Safari—the real one—somehow found out about me, about my assignment to hunt down Izala. I guess Izala saw me at some point while he was keeping tabs on Elliot. He likes experts—he...*collects* them, you might say. He figured adding a top CIA operative to his collection would give him even more power to bring down the US."

Jax's jaw went wild as he sheered enamel off his teeth. "He wanted to do more than that, I'm sure."

"I suppose he did. He offered El a deal. When Elliot refused, Al-Safari let his double be caught so he could lay a trap."

Her dark eyes lifted to meet his. "Elliot did, in fact, kill that man we believed was Al-Safari, Jax. He killed him because the man was going to kidnap me and take me to Izala."

CHAPTER TWENTY

Beatrice suffered silently through her third checkup in less than twelve hours as her midwife, Maria, chastised her. Not for flying this late in her pregnancy, but for flying off to Chicago without her. Apparently Maria loved the Windy City—at least from what she'd seen on her favorite TV shows—and wanted to visit.

Cal, on the other hand, was not so open minded about the whole thing. He stood, arms crossed, glaring down at Beatrice as she lay on the couch with her feet propped up at one end while Maria went on and on about her favorite episodes of some show about Chicago firemen.

Beatrice waited for Cal to cut off Maria's litany, but he didn't, his SEAL training evident in his considerable patience. Behind his hard eyes, Beatrice saw the vexation and displeasure he held in check. His mouth was a hard line; his stance one of controlled outrage.

Arguing with her would only lead him to more irritation and frustration; he knew it and so did she. Her logic was hard to beat in most instances, and sometimes, during their arguments, she gave in out of love for him. She didn't need to always win, especially since she knew she was always right.

This time, she might not give in. She hadn't decided. She and the baby were healthy. Jax and Ruby had needed help—and yes, some of the others could have helped them, but Beatrice had first-hand knowledge of the people and experience in the situations the two of them were facing. Direct knowledge and experience that not everyone on the SFI team possessed. She'd felt it imperative to join them in the field and make sure her operative and his charge didn't end up in some secret, off-the-books, government prison...or worse.

"She's doing great," Maria announced to Cal. "I do need to check to see how far dilated she is, but everything else is copacetic."

"Later," Cal said, ushering the woman toward the door. "B and I need to talk and then she needs some sleep. We'll head back to Chicago at first light and take the plane home. Sound good?"

He didn't wait for her reply, shoving her out of the room and closing the door behind her.

"You could at least help her find a room so she can catch some sleep too," Beatrice said, feeling sluggish, even after her nap. While she'd actually enjoyed the excitement with Jax, Ruby, Zeb, and Trace, it had been a long day—and night.

The edge of the couch dipped under Cal's weight as he sat next to her and took one of her hands. "What am I going to do with you, woman?"

"Keep loving me and don't have a hemorrhage over this trip. I'm fine to fly and I needed to make sure Jax didn't end up dead. He and Agent McKellen are in deeper than they realize."

Cal started to say something—no doubt to argue—but stopped himself. "Tell me what's going on."

She gave him a brief update, loving him for understanding her need to be in the middle of this. That's what strong, decent husbands like Cal did. They looked at it from a logical, non-emotional angle, saw the validity in it, and put aside their frivolous emotional turmoil. Which was all this was. As Maria, Jax, and Dr. Oswalo had all insisted, she was healthy as a horse and the baby was still MIA.

Speaking of, the baby moved every time he heard Cal's voice. Beatrice moved Cal's hand to her stomach as he spoke next. "Your expertise in these things is superior to everyone, B, but...whoa."

His face lit up as he felt the baby kick. "She's giving you hell, isn't she?" he said, grinning.

"*He* is happy you're here."

Their ongoing argument over the sex of the child didn't stop Cal from continuing to scold her. "Couldn't you have simply called Jax and given him the lowdown? Did you really think it necessary to fly all the way here and hunt him down?"

At a particularly sharp kick, she laid her hand next to his. "I know you think I'm taking a risk here, but I'm not. I would never put our child in danger."

"And yet, Zeb told me you took gunfire from pursuers before you arrived here at the clinic."

Damn man. "I—we,"—she rubbed her stomach around his hand—"we were all behind bulletproof material with Trace at the wheel. The baby and I couldn't have been safer."

The corners of his mouth tipped down, but no argument ensued. Trace was the ultimate bodyguard, which was why Cal had assigned him to her. With his superior skills and capabilities, nothing and no one would get through him. Zeb and Jax weren't bad to have on her side either, and Cal knew it.

Leaning over, he kissed her and Beatrice smiled against his lips. "I love you," he said. "But we need to go home. Even if you're right as rain, I'm about to have a coronary."

"I know." She understood where he was coming from. "This is a lot to ask of you."

"Damn straight."

Cal was going in for another kiss when a soft knock sounded on the door. "We're busy," he called.

"It's Jax and Agent McKellen," Beatrice said, gently shoving him back. She raised her voice. "Come in."

The door cracked open and Jax peeked around it. Cal raised an eyebrow at Beatrice, suggesting he wanted to know when she'd acquired ESP. Silly man. She knew Jax's knock just like she knew Cal's and Trace's and everyone else's who frequented her office.

"What did you find out?" she asked Jax as she swung her feet around.

Cal helped her to a sitting position as Jax and Agent McKellen stepped inside. They stayed near the door, both looking a bit sheepish at Cal.

"She needs to sleep, so make it quick," Cal growled.

Jax nodded. He looked fierce and determined, the tired haze from earlier gone. "CliffsNotes, Izala found out about Hayden and James looking for Commander Pierce, probably from Al-Safari, who was playing both sides of the fence. Izala decided Pierce had given up all the intel he was going to and he wanted to make a trade."

"For me," Agent McKellen added. "Abdel told him I was an elite CIA operative and beautiful. He wanted me."

Beatrice tapped a finger against her belly. "And your partner refused to give you up, so Izala used Al-Safari and his double to try to get to you."

"Correct. When Jax, Elliot, and I were bringing the man we thought was Abdel Al-Safari back to the States, it was actually a trap for that man to capture me and kill Elliot. Elliot killed him instead, but because of the secrecy surrounding his mission to locate Commander Pierce, Elliot wasn't at liberty to defend the charges brought against him. Homeland was supposed to back him up, but they didn't. My boss at the CIA doesn't know, according to Elliot, that any of this was going down, and most likely, neither organization is aware that Al-Safari is still alive. It's taken some time, but the real Abdel Al-Safari has managed to make his way to America because he's still after me for Izala. Elliot believes there is someone inside Homeland who may have aided him to get him into America."

"Because they're still looking for Commander Pierce," Beatrice supplied. "They'll do whatever it takes to find him, including give you up."

"Nice," Cal added. "What a fucked up government we work for."

"Used to work for," Jax amended.

Beatrice waited for Jax to volunteer his idea on how to find Al-Safari, but her operative stayed silent. "So what is your plan, Agent McKellen?"

Ruby lifted her brows. "My plan?"

"I assume you have one."

She grinned and glanced at Jax next to her. "Actually, *we* have a plan," she said, fiddling with the bracelet on her arm. "If you're willing to keep me on as a client."

Sitting back and knowing Cal wasn't going to let her direct this operation, whatever it was, Beatrice sighed quietly. "I'm listening," she said, and prayed that somehow, some way, Jaxon Sloan could keep Agent McKellen alive.

TWENTY-FOUR HOURS LATER

Ruby sat at the desk in her living room, pretending to be

working on her computer. The first part of her plan to draw out Abdel Al-Safari was in motion. The second half of her plan—the half no one else knew about, not even Jax—still had some details to work out.

The thrill of running undercover ops never got old; the adrenaline rushing through her veins, the anticipation of putting her acting skills to the test made her happy. Lying was easy for her, maybe too easy, but it was a skill like any other. There was a place and time for it, and lines sometimes blurred between right and wrong.

Like what she was going to do once they'd captured Abdel Al-Safari.

Elliot was still at the secret clinic, his recovery going well. Beatrice, her husband, and the midwife had returned to Chicago along with the rest of them, Beatrice insisting they stay until one of two things happened: Jax and Ruby caught Al-Safari or the baby decided to come.

At which point, if the baby showed up, Ruby was pretty sure Cal Reese would kill her.

Beatrice was a unique woman, that was for sure, and Ruby admired her guts and her ability to motivate the men around her with nothing more than simple logic and straight-out facts.

For now, Ruby hoped that between her, Beatrice, Jax, Zeb, and the others, they could capture Al-Safari alive. *No killing him*, Ruby had demanded. *We need answers.*

Elliot had given her the last known coordinates where he suspected Commander Pierce to be located. Beatrice had asked Jax to put together a commando team to go after him, but Jax had refused.

That hadn't gone over well—Ruby had seen the annoyance in Beatrice's eyes. She'd gone behind closed doors with Emit and Cal and a while later, Emit had disappeared. So while Rory was on the other end of the comm in Ruby's ear, and she knew he was monitoring the sound and video coming from her apartment as she played bait for Abdel, she suspected he was also monitoring a certain group of Emit's Rock Stars who were on a mission to bring Pierce home.

Damn, if she wouldn't give her right pinky finger to be part of that mission.

It had killed Jax, too, to let someone else go after Pierce, but he'd said it flat out—no way was he leaving Ruby. *I take my bodyguard-ing fucking seriously*, he'd said, making Ruby laugh.

She just wished she wasn't going to have to leave him behind once they had Al-Safari.

But she *would* have to.

Because this wasn't over until Mohammed Izala was also in custody.

The mastermind terrorist leader wouldn't stop coming for her. Especially not after she took down his lieutenant, which she figured Al-Safari had to be. Abdel had played the ultimate double cross, saving his own ass a dozen times over while manipulating Elliot, Keon James, and who knew how many others. He'd dangled the carrot of Commander Pierce enough times, leading Elliot on a wild goose chase that had lasted years, to get twice the priceless, top-secret information Izala had wanted. Yep, two for the price of one. Pierce gave up military secrets under torture and the CIA and Homeland fed Izala even more in an effort to get Pierce back.

What a deal.

Izala had to be stopped, one way or another, and Ruby was going to be the one to bring him down.

"Activity?" she murmured to Jax, who was stationed outside the apartment with Shinedown. She'd heard his real name used enough that she knew it was no longer forbidden for her to use it, but somehow, Shinedown stuck with her. He and Jax were hidden in a willow tree across the road with goggles and high-powered rifles.

Jax's voice was soft and deep in her ear. "None. Not even your pot-smoking neighbor and his dog."

His reassuring voice only made her resolve to leave him out of the hunt for Izala stronger. He was a good man, one who deserved an easier life than the one he'd had so far. Maybe once she put Izala away, she could enjoy that life with him—one with less drama and danger.

Probably not. That wasn't either of them. They both lived for danger; she couldn't imagine the two of them settling for an easy life.

A dangerous life with Jax was still better than a life without him at all, though. She hoped after this was all over, he might forgive her and float her a second—or would it be third?—chance.

Going after Izala was extremely dangerous, and totally unsanctioned. No way the CIA or Homeland or anyone would give her the okay for it.

Especially not if Homeland was willing to trade her for Commander Pierce.

Fuckheads.

But Izala wanted her. That was part of the reason Al-Safari was here. Sure, he'd silenced James and Nelson, and nearly killed Elliot, but he was here for *her*. She could feel it in her bones.

Beatrice would probably laugh at that, although when Ruby had spoken to her in private, they'd agreed that Izala wouldn't stop until he had what he wanted. What he wanted was her.

Al-Safari wanted her. Izala wanted her.

I haven't been this popular since high school.

Not.

She'd been a big, dopey outsider in high school with braces and a fondness for black nail polish, full moon rituals, and hemp bracelets. One of her friends had been a Wiccan, a couple others had been Goth, another considered herself a reincarnated hippie.

Ruby still wasn't sure how she'd made it through those formative years without being anything more than a cafeteria Catholic—her family picked from religious customs and beliefs—but here she was. She knew the lines of love spells as well as she knew the Kyrie Eleison. She could belly dance as easily as she could genuflect. She still appreciated the magnetic pull of a full moon and her personal smorgasbord of experiences and skills had made her a pretty damn good operative.

While being popular with terrorists had never been a goal, it seemed fitting that she would break the norm here too. Having two of them hunting her—and leaving a wake of bodies in their path—was unnerving to say the least. Exactly why she had to turn the tables. She'd never been one to play the victim or sit by and let herself be preyed upon and she sure as shit wasn't about to start.

So first, Abdel.

Then Mohammed.

With the two of them out of the way, and Commander Pierce hopefully safe in the States once more, she'd be free to start a relationship with Jax.

If he still wanted her.

There was a strong possibility he wouldn't. She wasn't exactly easy to get along with. Between her and Elliot, they'd caused him a boatload of trouble.

"I know he's out there," she said.

"I believe you." Jax wasn't one to rain on her parade, whether he believed in her gut instincts or not. Most likely, his own were giving him the same message.

Of course the facts were the facts. Elliot had told her everything. First and foremost, that Mohammed Izala was still on the hunt for her. His Homeland contact, the one running the show, had visited him in prison and told him. That was the real reason her partner had escaped from prison. To protect her.

When she wouldn't run away with him, he'd known he had to change tactics and try to draw out whoever Izala sent to him.

Except Izala's man had been Abdel Al-Safari, and Al-Safari had an axe to grind with Elliot over Elliot killing his double and screwing up his attempt to kidnap Ruby.

From what she could piece together, Abdel had followed her to the club the other night. He probably would have grabbed her if Keon James hadn't pulled a gun when he saw him and started shooting. Al-Safari hadn't been able to get her then, thanks to Jax—and the police—but he'd killed Keon James so the man couldn't alert her. She'd ended up in the med unit, and while there, he'd sent someone to raid her apartment. The reason wasn't entirely clear, but most likely he'd learned by then that Elliot had busted out of jail and Al-Safari wanted him just as badly as Izala wanted her.

Abdel or one of his men had been watching the station when Elliot posed as Agent Brown and took Augustus Nelson away, trying to save the man. Elliot had told her that Little Gus had claimed he'd seen Al-Safari that night at the club, but blew it off since Keon had told him the man was dead. He'd never worked face-to-face with Abdel, so he couldn't be sure of his identity.

Abdel believed Nelson was on to him and wanted to silence him and kill Elliot, so he followed them to Pottersville, killed Nelson, and tried to kill El.

He believed Elliot was dead; the last thing on his list was to kidnap her.

"Well I wish he'd get a move on," Zeb's gruff voice came over the comm. The former operative was next door in an empty apartment, ready to help once Jax and Shinedown cornered him. "I'd like to know how he thinks he's going to get you out of the country."

Human trafficking wasn't that difficult, especially getting *out* of the US. Most agencies were far more concerned with those being brought in.

Jax's voice was hard. "He's not going to get the chance."

A knock sounded on Ruby's door, startling her. "Company," she murmured. "At the door."

"Be careful," Jax said.

She put a bit of teasing into her tone. "Abdel couldn't have gotten past you guys, could he?"

Jax obviously didn't appreciate his skills being called into question. "No one has entered or left the building in the past hour that we've been here."

Abdel wouldn't show up and knock politely on the door, anyway.

Or would he?

Beatrice had put out the word to the CIA that Elliot had died in Pottersville. Only Ruby's boss at the CIA knew that El was actually recovering in the underground clinic near the Wisconsin border.

The knock sounded again. "All clear?" she asked Rory, even though she saw through the peep hole in the door that it was only Dan.

"Clear," Rory said. "If you consider dweeb-boy harmless."

"Weed-boy is more like it," Jax chimed in.

"All right, you two, can it." Dan was perfectly harmless and she felt kind of sorry for him. The poor guy had a crush on her and was overly nosy, but he meant well.

She opened the door and gave him a smile. Not too sexy—no point in leading the guy on—but friendly. "Hey, Dan. What's up?"

His eyes behind the glasses were bloodshot, his hair its normal stringy mess. "Hey, Ruby. Glad to see you're back home. Woodstock and I missed you."

"Work has been crazy." It wasn't a lie. The same one she'd been using on her family. "I've been crashing at the office."

Dan stared at her for a moment before his eyes darted down the hall. "That big guy that was here, he said your apartment was broken into the other night, and then when you didn't come home the last few nights, I got worried."

"That's sweet, but everything is okay."

Another nervous scan of the hall. "Yeah, well, if you need me…" He chucked a thumb over his shoulder toward his apartment. "You know where to find me."

"Oh, good God," Jax said in her ear. "I almost feel sorry for his skinny ass."

Ruby amped up her smile and nodded. "Thanks. I'll keep that in mind."

She was about to ease the door closed when Dan's gaze came up to meet hers head on. "I mean, we could...you know...hang out, if you want."

If she didn't know better, she'd swear there was a layer of panic in his voice. On his face, too, now that he was looking straight at her.

Jax's insolent voice piped up. "Sad. Just sad. Get rid of him, Ruby. We have work to do."

But there was something in Dan's face, in his voice, that made Ruby's internal radar ping around like a pinball machine. "Sure, Dan. We'll get together soon."

"If you could come right now, that would be great. Woodstock would love it."

Hmm. "Okay, I'll come over in a few minutes."

"Now," he said, and his voice came out flat, blunt. "Please come now. I need to show you something. It's..."

"What the hell?" Jax said.

Zeb joined in. "This dude needs lessons on picking up women."

"...Woodstock," Dan continued, oblivious to the chatter in her ear. "She's not feeling well. I wondered if you could take a look at her. Maybe you can figure out what's wrong."

"Bullshit." Jax again. "What is he up to?"

She wondered the same. Was he just trying to get her in his apartment to seduce her or was something else going on?

Regardless of Dan's awkwardness, the way he rubbed a hand over his mouth and the look in his eyes told her it had nothing to do with seduction. Something was wrong.

"I really need to insist you come with me," Dan said. "I mean, yeah, I'm sorry, but it's important...and..."

In her ear, several people spoke, all echoing the one voice that overrode them all. Jax's. "Ruby? Ruby, whatever you do, don't..."

Too late. Ruby put a finger to her mouth, signaling Dan to stop talking as she pulled her gun from the back of her waistband. His eyes went saucer-wide and she motioned him to lead the way back to his place, shutting her apartment door behind her.

CHAPTER TWENTY-ONE

Dan's head was down as he opened the door to his apartment. "I'm really sorry," he muttered. "But if I didn't do what he said…"

Ruby swept in, gun drawn, noticing peripherally that Dan's apartment mirrored hers. The entryway was nonexistent, the door opening directly into the living room. An open doorway on one side lead to the kitchen, the bed and bath connected to the living room on the other end.

Shabby furniture, dark curtains, a poster of Bob Marley over an old-school TV.

"He, who?" Ruby asked, furiously searching for whoever was in the apartment. "Who said?"

In the corner farthest away from the door, an upholstered rocking chair that once had been green but over time had become gray, faced away from her. A thumping sound came from it as it slowly began to turn.

The thumping increased as Woodstock saw Ruby. The dog sat in the lap of a man who held her by her fat neck with one hand and aimed a black gun at Ruby with the other.

Oh, crap. Her fingers flexing on the trigger of her gun.

Abdel Al-Safari was dressed like a businessman, his hair trimmed and neat, his dark suit displaying the short blond hairs of Woodstock's shedding. He tightened his choke hold on the dog, Woodstock's already strained breathing becoming more labored, even as she wagged harder at Ruby. "Welcome, Agent Ruby McKellen," Abdel said. "Put down the gun."

She'd set a trap, then walked right into his.

Little did he know how happy that made her. He was within reach, the man who'd screwed up everything—her career, her partner, her very future. Not to mention the people who had died in his wake.

He was going to pay and pay dearly.

In her ear bud, furious commentary with plenty of curse words flew at her. She ignored all of it, keeping her gun pointed at the man's head.

A slow turn of his wrist and his gun pointed at Woodstock.

Dan, behind her, made a whimpering noise in his throat. "Please don't let him kill my dog."

Mission first and always.

She kept her gun on him, hoping, praying he wouldn't shoot the damn dog.

"I'm told my American English is excellent," Abdel said, his schooling in a top Swiss engineering university evident in every syllable. "But perhaps you misunderstood my previous statement. Put the gun down or the dog dies."

The bastard wouldn't stop with Woodstock. Ruby knew he was going to kill Dan too.

All because of her.

She'd led him here, thinking he would come for her and her alone. Now he was threatening her innocent neighbor and a dog, for God's sake.

Not happening, jackass. "Perhaps you misunderstand the purpose of me pointing this gun at your head." She smiled. "I'm an expert marksman. Try me. You'll be dead before you can flex your finger on that trigger."

"Jesus fucking Christ!" Jax yelled in her ear. "Stop taunting him. We're on our way!"

"Stand down," she ordered. This was her gig and no one had a better shot at Al-Safari than she did.

Woodstock was not going to die. Neither was Dan. No one was going to die today.

Luckily, Abdel thought her command was directed at him. "You are as cocky as your partner. Mohammed will be pleased to beat that out of you."

Ruby laughed, the dry sound echoing in the small apartment. Woodstock panted and wagged with even more gusto. "Mohammed and I are going to have a serious come-to-Jesus meeting after I'm done with you, but he won't be beating anything out of me, I assure you."

"I'm outside the door," Zeb said softly in her comm. "Give me the signal and I'll cover Dan."

All she had to do was get Abdel to release the dog and get to his feet. He wasn't walking out of here a free man, and she needed him alive for questioning because she was going to clear Elliot of everything and take down that asshole Izala, so help her God.

"Your partner is dead," Abdel said. "You know this, yes? You have no one to help you, unless you still have your Marine friend tagging along. Where is he, by the way?"

"Marine?" Jax yelled in her ear.

"He was a SEAL, asshole." She wondered if he were purposely taunting her to get a rise out of her one way or the other.

"Oh, that's right. The big, bad SEAL who got tossed out of the Navy. He was recently your bodyguard, wasn't he?"

"He was ordered to bring Elliot in. Elliot's dead, so he's returned to Washington, DC."

"He abandoned you?" Abdel tsked. "You should be more careful about who you trust."

On the side table next to the rocking chair, a cell phone lit up. Without taking his eyes from her, Abdel answered it. "Very good," he said into the phone after a brief pause. "Stream the live feed to me."

Ruby frowned as he turned the phone for her to see the screen. "I suggest you accept your fate, or these people will pay the price."

"We're on the stairs," Jax said to her. "Give us the signal and we'll bust in."

A ticking started in her ears, became a flood of white noise as the video on the screen came into focus.

A building. One in downtown Chicago. Someone was on the roof across from it, taking a video through a high-powered camera lens of...

The conference room at the new Rock Star Security headquarters.

Where Emit, Cal, Rory, and Beatrice were gathered around the table.

Shit. Shit. *Shit.*

They hadn't finished switching out the windows for those with reflective coating and bulletproof glass.

"Two of my men are across from this building. As you can see from the video, they are in position to, shall we say, cause trouble for the people gathered in that room. If the people in that room try to leave…"

He zoomed out and she saw a car sitting on the side street next to RSS headquarters. "Boom," he said.

A car bomb. Her mental curses rivaled those Jax was using in her ear.

He was the mastermind behind the bomb, this she knew. Although his expertise was in chemical warfare, chemicals needed a way to be dispersed. Bombs were the easiest and quickest way to disperse anything he liked.

A new thought registered. Abdel was probably the man who'd created the bomb that had taken the legs of Jax's friend.

No one could see what she was seeing, yet she hoped from Abdel's description, they understood there was a bomb. And snipers.

Her repertoire of curse words was pretty extensive, but she kept coming back to *shit*. Because heaven help her, she was knee deep in the stuff.

"I'll tell you what," she said, lowering the gun. "I'll cut you a deal."

"Ruby" Jax snarled. "What's going on?"

Abdel stared at her, nonplussed. "I believe this will be entertaining. Please, go ahead. Tell me about this deal."

So smug. She wanted to wring that out of him.

But not yet. First, she needed to save the dog and the people inside Rock Star Security.

She attempted to put more sincerity into her smile. Her lips didn't want to cooperate. "I'll come with you willingly if you leave my friends alone. No fuss, no fight."

"Oh, well, of course." Abdel rocked in the chair. He didn't seem moved by her act or the fact she'd lowered the gun from his head. "That seems so reasonable, especially since you have no options."

The mockery in his voice made her see red. She had to control that reaction since that's exactly what he wanted. For her to lose control and give him a reason to shoot the damned dog and take out everyone at RSS.

You're good but I'm better, she mentally taunted him.

It wasn't bluster. She *knew* she was better than Abdel Al-Safari any day. He may have fooled her once, but he didn't have that upper hand anymore. She knew him for what he really was now, and her gloves were coming off.

But not until Beatrice and the others were out of the line of fire.

She needed a bluff. A solid one. "I'm serious, Abdel. I'll put down my gun and let you handcuff me. We'll walk out together. No one gets hurt."

Except you, jackass, when I rip your evil heart out.

In an effort to convince him, she laid her gun on the floor.

God, did that kill her—to be unarmed and at his mercy, even if it was only for a few moments. It would have been easier to put a bullet in his head and end this right now.

As if he'd read her mind, he added some insurance to his threat. "If anything happens to me, my men are instructed to shoot to kill."

Of course they were. She hoped Rory or Zeb or Jax was picking up on this and understanding there was another layer of danger here.

"What's he talking about?" Rory said in her ear. "The men he's referring to, the 'boom' he mentioned. We're under surveillance here, aren't we? There are guns on us? A bomb?"

Bless him. "You've covered all your bases, haven't you, Abdel?" she said. "Threatening innocent people here in my apartment as well as those in the Rock Star Security office."

"Holy shit," she heard Jax say, his exclamation followed by those of Zeb and Rory.

They knew, and the specifics of what they didn't, they'd figure out in short order. In the meantime, she had to play along until someone got Beatrice and the crew to safety.

The man in the thousand dollar suit appeared pleased with himself. "Mohammed and I are not your everyday terrorists, Agent McKellen. We are businessmen. We play into your stereotype of Middle Eastern terrorists because that's what you want and that gets us what we want. You believe we are short-sighted and only focused on wiping out the infidels, while in reality, we want so much more."

She needed to keep him talking in order to give the others time. "And what is that?"

"The world." He sounded as if he were disappointed at her obtuseness. "We have been infiltrating every major military and spy group in the world for years. From Mossad to M5 to your own Department of Homeland Security. When your partner offered me a deal to be an asset inside Mohammed's camp, I nearly laughed. It was so easy saying yes while I planned an extensive strategy to lead the US into giving Mohammed whatever he needed to expand our military knowledge of your endeavors. You are not dealing with a small-time organization. We are superiorly educated, well-funded, and shrewd. As you can see by the fact that I am here soliciting your cooperation."

What a nice way of putting it. He was blackmailing her as he'd done with Elliot. Only with Elliot, he'd dangled a carrot. With her, he was threatening to kill people. "I'll do whatever you say, Abdel. Just don't hurt anyone, okay?"

"Kick the gun over to me." Smugness coated his words and brightened his face even more. "Get on your knees."

Forcing her to her knees was smart, making her less dangerous.

At least that's what he thought.

Ruby kicked her gun toward him, the butt end coming to a stop under his loafered foot. "Let the dog go," she said. She needed something in exchange for her bowing to him. "Then I'll get down on my knees."

He eyed her as if she were a toddler throwing a temper tantrum. "You'll get on your knees, Ruby McKellen, or the dog will die. The humans as well."

Dan let go another whimper. Rory was talking in her ear, saying they'd found the snipers' positions but didn't want to alert them, so they had to sit tight for now.

So they knew about the snipers, but did they grasp there was a car bomb?

Jax spit commands at her...what she should say, what she should do. Near her, Dan continued to whimper.

Concentrate! Tune them out.

This was on her. She needed to look at this awful situation from every angle, fast. Was there any way to alert Jax to the car bomb?

Was there a way to keep Jax from plowing into this apartment at any moment and taking Al-Safari out?

Doing that would result in the worst of outcomes. If none of the others realized there was a bomb, Jax taking out Abdel would end in massive bloodshed, and it would all be on Jax's conscious.

And hers.

"You're going to ruin that perfect suit of yours by shooting the dog?" She shook her head at Abdel. "For all of your education and shrewdness, that doesn't seem like your style.

That thing probably cost more than my boss at the CIA makes in a year. I have a hard time believing you're going to ruin it with dog brains."

Dan's whimper turned to a cry. The man was sobbing.

Maybe she had been a little graphic with that one, but she couldn't give into him too easily or Abdel might get suspicious.

"And unless you have a spare suit in Dan's bedroom, you're going to have a tough time getting me out of the country if you look like you just murdered someone."

For a long moment, Abdel held her stare, his eyes calculating, cold. Maybe he did have a fresh suit waiting for him.

Begrudgingly, she folded herself down until she was on her knees, holding her hands up in surrender. "There. Satisfied? Now let the damn dog go."

The corner of his right eye twitched. The slightest of movements, but it conveyed his delight in her surrender. He gripped Woodstock by the neck and dumped the dog onto the floor, the Pug hitting like a cement brick, going down on her side, but recovering as she rolled to her feet, all black tongue and wagging body.

She ran to Ruby, jumping up on her and trying to kiss her. The dog was small, but solid, and nearly knocked her over. Dan, suddenly mobilized, lunged for her, picking the mass of dog up and burying his face in the dog's short hair.

"Get out," Abdel ordered Dan, standing up and brushing dog hair from his lap. "Before I change my mind."

Really? Abdel was going to let Dan go?

No way. He probably intended to shoot the poor guy in the back.

Ruby needn't have worried. Dan sidled next to her, no longer crying, his arms still full of Woodstock. "I'm not leaving Ruby."

Oh, jeez. Now of all times, the man had suddenly grown a backbone.

Maybe it was for the best. At least he wasn't going to get shot in the back.

The front was still an option.

"What the fuck is wrong with this guy?" Jax demanded. "Get him out of there!"

"It's okay," Ruby told both Jax and Dan. "Do what the man says, Dan. I'll be all right."

"He's the jerk that broke into your apartment the other night, isn't he?" Dan shifted from one foot to another. His body was shaking with fear. "What does he want with you?"

In a split-second, Abdel's black gun veered from Ruby to Dan, aiming at Dan's chest. "I gave you a chance, now I have changed my mind."

"Get out!" Ruby shouted at Dan, shoving him away.

But it was too late.

Abdel's gun went off.

BOOM!

Jax's heart seized, beelining from his chest straight into the floor.

Get to her!

Bounding up the final few stairs to the third floor, he heard his own breathing in his ears. Recriminations screamed through his brain. He should have never left Ruby alone. He should have put a camera on her. He shouldn't have been so damn far away.

Setting up shop across the street had given him an advantage, assuming like they all had that Al-Safari would be coming for Ruby after she was home. They'd stayed well back and out of sight in case the bastard was watching the place.

The damn terrorist had already been inside.

He'd outsmarted them.

Jax hated being duped. He'd always been skeptical, cynical. Yet, here he was being outmaneuvered and outplayed by a goddamn terrorist.

Again.

The sound of the gunshot had erupted in stereo, making it all the worse. He'd heard the boom in his ear bud as well as from inside the room itself as he'd hauled ass down the hall.

They couldn't take the chance that Al-Safari was working alone, especially since he had men stationed at the new headquarters. He might have a few with him here, too. It only made sense.

Rory had told Jax and Colton to wait—give him a minute to scan the area for other mercenaries—before they rode to Ruby's rescue.

And now she might be dead.

Because he'd listened to logic instead of his gut.

Standing just outside the door of Dan's apartment, Zeb across from him and Colton behind him, Jax forced his heart to stop throwing itself against his ribs like a trapped gorilla wanting out. He nodded at Zeb and prepared to kick in the door.

Rory shouted in his ear, "Stand down! Stand down! I've detected a car bomb outside our building. Kill Al-Safari and we're all going up in a ball of flames here!"

And shit to the tenth, what the hell did he do now?

A car bomb? A fucking car bomb outside SFI headquarters?

The place would never stand up to a car bomb. Not in the middle of the remodeling when only half of the security measures were in place. Emit, Cal, Beatrice, Rory…all of them would die.

Pressing his ear to the door, he listened, trying to gauge what was going on inside. He heard the sound of scuffling and…

"You fucking bastard. You didn't have to shoot him."

Ruby?

A flush of short-lived relief rushed over him. Her comm must have come off because her voice was floating through the door, not in his ear, but it was her. She was swearing and…

Pleading?

"Don't, please, just don't. He never did anything to you. He shouldn't die simply because he's my neighbor. Let me stop the bleeding. Someone will have heard the gunshot. They'll call the police. We should go."

He wanted to say her name, to burst inside and make sure she wasn't injured.

But hell, he couldn't do it. Not with the others trapped in the SFI office.

She was alive and begging for Dan's life. He needed to believe in her, in her training. She wasn't the Agency's top operative for nothing.

Had been the Agency's top operative. He'd screwed that up royally for her, hadn't he?

No time to worry about that now.

"Take me," he heard Ruby say. "Let's go before the cops get here."

"Fall back," Rory said to Jax and his crew over their comms.

"Now, before you get caught and Al-Safari blows us sky high."

Goddamn it. Their only chance of getting Beatrice and her baby, Cal, and Emit out of this alive was to let the bastard go.

With Ruby.

Not going to happen.

Jax motioned at Colton to fall back. Zeb faded into the shadows, disappearing into the vacant apartment he'd been hiding in before. Colton went back down the stairs. Jax made haste to get into Ruby's apartment.

He was slipping inside when the door to Dan's apartment flew open and Ruby came tripping out, her hands zip-tied in front of her. For a brief second, as she slammed into the far wall with her shoulder, her eyes met his.

Deep concern etched her forehead, but controlled confidence shone in her gaze. It only took that split-second for him to know she had this. She knew what she was doing and knew that he was going to back her up.

He gave her a nod, putting all the silent encouragement he could into it, letting her know she was right—he wasn't letting her down. He had her back and he would damn sure not let Al-Safari hurt her.

He may have put a little something extra into his look as well. Something that he hoped conveyed how he felt about her. How much he...

Oh, hell. *I love you.*

As if she read his mind, her face softened a bit. A tiny twitch at the corner of her mouth told him she got his message.

The dog, Woodstock, was barking like crazy and Al-Safari was swearing in his native language. Ruby's gaze cut right, signaling Jax that the terrorist was about to emerge.

Jax raised his gun.

One shot and he could take the bastard out, Ruby's orders about leaving the man alive be damned.

But he saw her shaking her head, tiny movements so she didn't call Al-Safari's attention to her, but letting Jax know that she didn't want him to intervene. Not yet.

She had a plan.

And she wasn't putting Beatrice and the others in any more danger than they already were.

Both frustration and pride bloomed in his chest. Ruby was the consummate spy, no matter what was on the line. She knew taking out Al-Safari wouldn't only kill any chance she had at finding out all the facts about his and Izala's intricate plans, but it might also seal the fate of those back at SFI headquarters.

He lowered his weapon and pulled back, a second before Al-Safari emerged.

He closed the door to Ruby's apartment, mentally cursing every bone in his body. As a SEAL, he'd been trained to never believe in a no-win situation. There was always a way around, under, or through any circumstance, he simply needed to figure it out.

The familiar burn of anger turned his stomach to acid. He hated Al-Safari, hated himself for letting this low-life, scum-sucking SOB get the drop on him.

The thin door muffled the shuffle of footsteps in the hallway. "I need clothes, toiletries," Ruby said. Her voice was strong and the violent red haze in front of Jax's eyes cleared a bit. "Let me stop at my place and grab a few things."

The terrorist laughed, a sharp sound that pierced the air. "You still consider me easily duped. You'll touch nothing in your apartment, Agent McKellen."

"You're kidding, right?" Jax heard Ruby stop outside the door and his intuition wavered between hiding just in case she got Al-Safari to go along with her, and needing to be this close to her, hear what she was saying. "I'm not going to try anything. You've proven you're a worthy adversary and I agreed to go along peacefully, but I need my things."

"You won't be needing your things where I am taking you."

"You don't understand." Her voice was thick with earnestness. "I'm..."

"We do not have time for this. The jet is waiting. Move."

A jet. He was going to fly her out of the country on a private plane.

In Jax's ear, Rory spoke up. "Contacting O'Hare and Midway now for flight plans filed by private aircraft."

Jax heard a slight struggle, as if Al-Safari had grabbed Ruby and she was resisting.

Every cell in Jax's body reacted, urging him to throw open the door and riddle the terrorist with bullets.

Ruby's voice rose. "I'm having my period, you idiot. I need my goddamn tampons."

A heavy silence fell. No struggle, no arguing, as if the two had squared off against each other just outside the door.

Jax almost snickered.

Al-Safari no doubt didn't one hundred percent believe her. On the other hand, if she were telling the truth...

"Unless, of course," Ruby continued, "you want me to bleed all over your fancy leather seats in the jet."

One, two, three heartbeats of dead quiet passed. Al-Safari, like any male, didn't want to talk menstruation, but had to analyze the risk of going without tampons.

Nothing changed, but Jax took one step back from the door, then two. He'd swear on a Bible, the terrorist was about to give in.

Once again amazed at Ruby's resourcefulness, he slipped silently into her bedroom, past the bed, and into the bathroom. Prayed.

The click of the apartment door was loud as Ruby burst in.

She'd won the skirmish. Al-Safari had given in.

All Jax had to do was stay concealed until Ruby was ready to take the bastard down.

He slid behind the bathroom door, concealing himself.

Chapter Twenty-two

Ruby moved through the apartment quickly, Al-Safari on her heels. Where was Jax? There weren't a lot of places to hide, especially for someone his size.

Dan was still alive; someone, hopefully Zeb, had called an ambulance and was sneaking into Dan's apartment to administer first aid.

She stopped outside her bedroom and held up her bound wrists. "Untie me. I'll just be a moment."

"The ties stay on and you will stay in my sight."

She gave him an indignant look. "You can't be serious. I have to go to the bathroom and *change my tampon*. I can't do that with my hands cuffed and you watching me, you perv."

His right eye twitched. At her detailed description or at the derogatory label? She could get more descriptive if necessary, dig a little deeper into the uncomfortable zone. No man alive liked to have anything to do with a menstruating woman, and certainly no Middle Eastern male she'd ever met.

"I know what you are trying to do and I will not play your game."

"Is that what this is?" She moved closer, invading his personal space, even though his gun was pointed at her. "You think I would jeopardize my friends' lives to save my own life? How many men do you have watching them? Two? Three? A hundred? How many men do you have here, helping you? One, I'm guessing. He's downstairs with the car running, isn't he? So you know what I think? I think you're scared that this washed-up CIA operative is going to get the jump on you and kick your ass. That's why you won't let me go to the bathroom by myself."

His free hand reached into his pocket, flipped out a small knife, and sliced through the ties in one easy movement. "If you go for a weapon, I will kill you."

The plastic zip tie fell to the floor. "And my friends. I get it. Like I said, I would never jeopardize their lives to save my own. You have nothing to worry about."

If anyone at Rock Star Security downtown was still paying attention, they'd see her and Al-Safari on the cameras and notify someone—probably not Homeland, since they didn't know who to trust, but possibly the local SWAT team or FBI office. Someone would come. Someone, along with Jax and his crew here at the apartment, would stop Abdel.

If she could drag this out, they'd have a chance at saving Beatrice, Cal, Emit, and the others, and keeping the terrorist from leaving the country.

With her onboard.

"You will not leave my sight," Abdel repeated.

There was no way she was flying out of the States with him. Once he had her in the air, she would be much harder to track. She'd be without resources, without any partner or backup. Her chances of survival as anything more than Mohammad Izala's prisoner plummeted to zero.

She'd kill herself before she let that happen. "Fine. You wanna watch me change my tampon? Come on in."

Swinging around, she started into the bathroom. In her peripheral vision, she caught sight of the mirror over the sink. Reflected in the glass was a hulking body she knew all too well. *Shit!*

Whirling back and blocking her captor's view, she put her hands on either side of the doorframe. "I'll be sure to let your boss know what a perv you are. How you liked watching me while I—"

"Stop!" Abdel demanded, his lips firming in a thin line. "You have one minute. Leave the door cracked open. Try anything and your friends will indeed die."

All she needed was that tampon box. Every plastic "tampon" case held a weapon. Some held syringes filled with drugs that would immobilize a man, put him to sleep, or even kill. A couple held extra bullets for her gun. A few more held tracking devices. Her favorite weapon was a steel projectile that resembled an old fashioned car antenna. It retracted down to a two-inch long pen of sorts, easily hidden in a purse, a pocket, even her hand. Once activated, it extended up to a foot with a razor-sharp end, perfect for poking an eye out, driving up the nose of the enemy, or into the ear of an attacker.

If she could just get her hands on that...

First, she had to figure out what to do with the ex-SEAL trying—and failing—to hide himself behind the bathroom door.

Abdel was still staring her down and she could tell his resolve to allow her this whopping minute of time was wavering. She'd pushed him as far as he would go. Time to get down to business and get that damn tampon box.

She was about to nod agreement to his terms when she felt the weight of Jax's stare on the back of her head. It wasn't hard to read his mind. She'd seen it in his face in the hallway, his hate of the man. His rage over this situation.

Jaxon Sloan had the overwhelming desire to pull the trigger of the gun she knew he had pointed at the door, right where Abdel stood on the other side. One wrong move on Jax's part and Al-Safari would see him. The gig would be up.

And they'd be burying bodies.

Be still, she mentally ordered Jax. *I've got this.*

To Abdel, she said. "Turn your back. Give me at least that much privacy."

Abdel raised the gun, pointed it at her forehead. "Get this done. Now!"

But as she raised her hands and backed into the bathroom, he turned sideways.

Sideways was not the best, but it was workable. Especially since he faced away from the mirror.

"Thank you," she said, the thrum of relief making her voice go soft.

Ignoring eye contact with Jax in the mirror, she went to the closet and knelt down. The tampons were on the lowest shelf and she made a big deal of rummaging around for them.

Jax could see her, Al-Safari couldn't. She raised her gaze to her bodyguard and showed him a yellow encased tampon. He watched as she ripped the plastic off and withdrew the tiny, but effective syringe.

One of his brows cocked but he grinned. Ruby slid the syringe into her pocket.

By weight and color of the plastic they were wrapped in, she counted her collection of various weapons. Then she went to the toilet, in case Al-Safari was listening or happened to peek in.

She didn't need a real tampon, so she faked it, made a lot of noise with unrolling tissue paper and flushing. When she glanced up, Jax was holding up a small square of toilet paper he must have snagged before she'd entered. On the square were five hastily scribbled words.

With you all the way.

She wasn't in this alone. She had a partner she could count on. Locking eyes with him briefly, she blew him a kiss and winked.

At the sink, she washed her hands, smiled at him in the mirror.

"Finish," Abdel demanded. "We leave now."

From his end of the counter, Jax slid the square of toilet paper her way. She touched his fingers with hers, then snatched up the message and hid it in her bra. As she gathered the tampon box and jammed it into a cosmetic bag with a few makeup items, she said to the terrorist, "Coming. I have everything I need."

She did, too. She had weapons, her craft, her cunning.

She had Jax.

Tearing her gaze from Jax's, she took her cosmetic bag and left the bathroom. Abdel took the bag, pushed the gun into her shoulder and hustled her toward the door. "Keep your hands where I can see them," he ordered.

Putting her hands behind her back, she laid out her mental plan of attack as they walked out of the apartment.

Mission first and always.

Al-Safari's driver was waiting downstairs in a long, black limo. The kid barely looked legal and must have been hiding around the corner. He came driving up as Ruby and the terrorist hit the bottom of the inside stairs and emerged into daylight.

Dan was in good hands with Zeb. Colton hid inside Jax's car, ready to pick him up and follow the limo. Jax, having taken the fire escape and beat Ruby and her kidnapper to the ground, was peeking out from around the corner of the building.

Overhead, the skies were gray, cumulus clouds gathering for a storm. Rain already fell sparsely, a few drops hitting Jax in the face, mixing with his sweat.

For all of Al-Safari's cunning, he hadn't searched her. Ruby had her earbud in once again—he'd have to ask her how she'd managed that—and her comm was switched on. She had some kind of syringe filled with a drug in her pocket. More in her little striped bag.

Most importantly, he wasn't going to lose her.

The driver opened the back door of the limo for his boss. Al-Safari holstered his gun and tied Ruby's hands with a fresh zip tie before shoving her into the backseat. He said something to the driver, pulled his gun back out, and glanced over his shoulder.

Jax was sure the terrorist couldn't see him, but only released the lock on his lungs when Al-Safari climbed into the backseat.

Zeb chimed in his ear. "Dan is stabilized. Ambulance is on its way."

The limo's brake lights flashed as the driver pulled out of the parking lot. Static came from Ruby's comm. The limo probably had a signal jammer for security purposes. Either that, or Al-Safari had finally discovered it.

Out of the blue, Rory spoke. He'd been silent for so long, hearing his voice both startled Jax and spiked some relief. "Roger that. We are covered here. I repeat, Nickleback and Halestorm have found and neutralized Al-Safari's snipers."

Another surge of relief hit Jax in his solar plexus. Two of the new Rock Stars had come through for them.

He hauled ass across the backside of the parking lot as Colton jetted forward in the Jeep to pick him up. "What about the car bomb?" Jax asked, jamming himself and his weapon into the front seat.

Rory's voice was replaced with a female one, a voice Jax was afraid he might never hear again. "A private bomb squad of my choosing is going over the car now. We have alerted the proper authorities to begin a controlled evacuation of the surrounding area, and they are sending in their SWAT team. Mine will have the bomb neutralized before they get here. Our biggest concern, due to the fact Abdel Al-Safari is involved, is the possibility of a chemical dissemination."

Beatrice. Always one step ahead of everyone else. Except, in this case, a man who was supposed to be dead.

"Are you safe?" Jax asked her as he and Colton zoomed out of the parking lot. Jax's hands itched to be on the wheel—his whole body itched to be in control, not relying on Colt to drive—but he focused his attention on the limo ahead of them.

"As safe as I'll ever be," Beatrice assured him. "We're in a safe room below ground level. Well, at least I am. Cal, Emit, and Rory are still in the conference room, refusing to leave until Agent McKellen is returned to us safely."

Jax almost laughed. "A safe room? You have a fucking safe room at HQ and you didn't say anything?"

"Keep your britches on," Rory griped. "We discovered it on the blueprints I pulled up from the county courthouse five minutes ago. There's a tunnel under the building—"

"One of the reasons I chose this particular building," Beatrice interrupted.

"But we only just found the panic room," Rory continued.

Even when Beatrice didn't have all the facts, she chose wisely. Jax hoped she'd chosen wisely with him. "I am in pursuit of Al-Safari and Ruby."

Rory gave him a status update. "Airports have been alerted, but none have confirmed any private jet with flight plans using an ultimate destination to or from Northern Africa or the Middle East. If they are flying international, they would use O'Hare. No planes registered, obviously, under Al-Safari or Izala's names."

The limo merged with traffic on Interstate 290. "We're definitely headed west," Jax told them. "Could they be using a smaller airport to get to Canada first?"

"We'll alert Homeland." Beatrice sounded disappointed that she couldn't pull a Hail Mary on this one. "That's the only way to stop them."

"*I* will stop them," Jax told her. "Homeland will only fuck it up, and we don't know who we can trust. Remember what Al-Safari told Ruby? He and Izala have infiltrated everybody from Mossad to Homeland. If we call in the wrong person on this, Ruby could die. A lot of people could die."

A brief silence ensued. In his mind, Jax saw Beatrice screwing up her face the way she did when she was calculating odds.

Impatience made him want to argue with her even when she hadn't said a word. He gripped the armrest with one hand and his gun with the other so tightly, Colton shot him a questioning look.

Jax cut his comm so no one else could hear him. Colt did the same to his. When Jax was sure the comms were muted, he tried to explain. "Ripping the armrest off is better than yelling at Beatrice."

"Agreed," his wing man said after a pause. "She's just trying to do the right thing."

Jax knew that. But sometimes doing the right thing fucked you over. He should know.

"All right." Beatrice cut off their conversation. "Take all of that rage and frustration you've been subduing for months, Megadeth, and go do your worst to this bastard. Once you get the all-clear from Rory about the bomb, I want you to bring our client home."

She didn't need to say anything else. Jax hit his comm, opening communication again. "Roger that, boss." The he looked at Colton and grinned. "Floor it."

Tailing someone in Chicago traffic was challenging. The only benefit was the fact they were tailing a limo. What terrorist used a limousine to kidnap a CIA operative? Jax could not figure Al-Safari out.

Colt knew his stuff when it came to following a perp without being seen. Tough to do with only one vehicle to keep an eye on it though. Tailing always worked better if you had two or three cars to tag off so the driver didn't get suspicious.

Hopefully, the kid wasn't experienced enough to keep watch over his own six, and Chicago drivers, who, Jax had learned in past few days, should audition for the *Fast and Furious* movies. They drove like Indy car drivers, hammering in and out of the multi-lane highways with a speed and precision he admired.

Rory was keeping tabs on them via the GPS signals in their SFI watches and phones. "You're headed north again. Available airports are O'Hare and a small, professional executive airport in Wheeling. Seems unlikely Al-Safari is headed there."

We're businessmen. Al-Safari's statement rang in Jax's ears. "That's it," he said, both to Rory and to Colton. "That's exactly where he's going."

Jax heard Zeb in his ear. "Why would Al-Safari be going to that little airport?"

"He told Ruby that he and Izala were businessmen. They're running a business. Do they have their own company? Do they have their own private jet? He's not planning on taking her to the Middle East. He's taking her somewhere closer, I'd bet on it."

"But Izala's in North Africa." This from Rory.

"Is he?" Jax asked. "If Al-Safari made it to America, what's to say Izala didn't come with him?"

Traffic thinned and the rain picked up. The windshield wipers worked furiously to keep the water at bay.

"He's picking up speed," Colt announced.

Jax wanted to punch the dash. "We've been made."

Which meant the bastard would be checking in with his men, realizing they were out of commission. What would he do to Ruby?

As if Beatrice read his mind, she said, "Ruby will be fine. He won't harm her and she knows it."

Because Izala wanted her. The thought made Jax's stomach cramp.

They flew through traffic, minutes ticking by with every sweep of the wipers. The limo wasn't a race car, but the young driver seemed to know how to handle it well. Jax realized it was outfitted with special tires, probably bulletproof glass and panels. It was a souped-up, all-terrain vehicle in sheep's clothing.

Colt swore as he sped around a BMW and the tires hydroplaned slightly. "There's no way this kid is outmaneuvering me."

They ate up more miles, horns honking at them as they did their own version of an Indy race. At one point, the limo became squeezed behind two semis riding side by side, and the third lane blocked by a string of cars all trying to pass them. It swung a hard right and used the shoulder to go around.

As soon as Colton could, he did the same. They were under a viaduct, the rain letting up for a split second, a sudden quiet filling the car. Jax's teeth ground so hard, his temples set up a steady pounding that radiated into the back of his head and down his shoulders.

Get to Ruby.

Ahead of them, the limo jerked back into the stream of traffic. Shooting out from under the viaduct, a deluge of rain hit their windshield again, blanking out Jax's view for a heartbeat before the wipers caught up.

Suddenly, Colton slammed on the brakes. "Fuckin' A."

The back end fishtailed, Jax grabbing the dash as his seatbelt locked up. The car's back end started to swing around, and he gaped at the scene in front of him.

Upon reentering the flow of traffic, the limo had clipped a car's front bumper, knocking the car into the traffic to its left. *Bam, bam, bam,* car after car lost control as they rammed into each other at high speeds. Some smashed into others. Some spun in 360s. Drivers in all lanes trying to avoid the pileup even as they were sucked into it.

The semis didn't help things.

Colt did his damnedest to control the vehicle and keep them from ending up in the pileup of cars. Once, twice, three times they spun in a circle, hitting the shoulder, their back tires dropping off the edge and sending them backward down an incline. They stopped with a jarring thud, and before Jax could let go of a string of curses, Colton was spinning the wheel.

"Hold on, brother." He hit the gas.

One of the back wheels whirled, flipping mud up and over the truck. More cursing from both of them, then Jax released his seatbelt. "I got it."

Jumping out, his feet landed in mud. Rain soaked through his shirt and pants, coated his face.

Get to Ruby.

Ignoring the rain and the mud, he grabbed the right back bumper and whistled for Colt to floor it. The rental Jeep was 4-wheel drive, but it was old and the tires were bare.

The wheel spun anew. Mud flew.

He would not let her down. Would not let that bastard Al-Safari get her on that plane.

Every muscle in his back straining, Jax dug his feet into the incline, his boots sinking up to his ankles. Colton hit the gas again and Jax heaved with all his might.

The backend of the car rocked, bounced, the other tire starting to dig a groove as well. If both tires ended up stuck, there was no way Jax would be able to get them out of this ditch.

And maybe it wouldn't matter anyway. He couldn't see the final results of the pileup on the road, but he had the feeling the entire three lanes of traffic were completely blocked.

One problem at a time. He took a huge breath in, all the anger he'd built over a lifetime rising to the surface. His best friend coming back without his legs, his parents' rejection, the SEAL brothers he'd lost in the field.

Ruby.

I will not lose her.

On the exhale, he yelled at the top of his lungs, letting all of it go as he jerked and yanked on the Jeep's bumper with every last reserve of energy he had.

Colton floored it, and finally, the tires found purchase. Jax heaved and pushed the Jeep to higher ground.

As Colt brought the car to a halt up on the shoulder, Jax sank to his knees. Covered in mud and soaked to the bone, his muscles trembled, his pulse rapped in his ears.

But his mind felt much clearer.

As if the past had been wiped clean, the future as well. While his large body was weighed down by exhaustion and overexertion, his mind was free. No worries, no fear. Not even an ounce of anger.

It was like nothing he'd ever felt before, sort of like how Hunter described meditation and connecting with his higher self.

Whatever the hell *that* was.

Jax found himself laughing—at the sensation of detachment, of emptiness, at himself. At the goddamn rain and the mud and whatever had just happened here.

Freedom, release, higher self.

Yeah right.

Fuck this shit. Move.

Slogging through the mud, he hauled ass to the car and slid his not-so-higher self into it..

CHAPTER TWENTY-THREE

Ruby lipped off again and Abdel Al-Safari slapped her.

Her head snapped sideways and her earbud fell out.

She'd been trying to get more information out of him about where they were headed. Anything to give Jax her whereabouts as they sped through traffic.

Abdel had stripped off all her jewelry, including the bracelet Jax had put on her arm with the hidden GPS tracker in it. That had all gone out the window. She had no cell phone, no gun, and now the earbud—her last link to the outside world was lying on the seat next to her leg.

Before it fell out, she hadn't heard anything more from Jax or the team, possibly because her comm had malfunctioned or the limo had special equipment to block listening devices.

Either way, she'd kept hoping that at least her voice was getting through.

Curling her body over to the right as if nursing her injury, she blocked the ear bud from Abdel's view.

Acting once more, she cried into her hands as she coiled tight into a ball against the seat. Using her hair as cover, she managed to shove the tiny earbud back into her ear.

Dead air was all she heard.

Her fake crying almost became real. Not because of the pain, but because of the all-consuming belief she would never see Jax again.

Mission failure.

The driver had alerted Al-Safari that they had a tail moments ago, the terrorist becoming absorbed in the race, yelling instructions to the him as they wove in and out of traffic. He tried to raise his men on his cell phone, but couldn't get through at first. He punched at the screen again and Ruby heard a ringing on the other end.

She couldn't see much out the back window when she raised her head, the rain falling hard and visibility low. They'd left the accident scene far behind and Jax's blue Jeep was no longer in sight.

Abdel's phone connected and her stomach dropped even farther. He put it on speaker, an evil gleam in his eyes as he answered.

Beatrice was dead. Her baby too. As soon as Abdel told his men that someone was following them, they'd blow the Rock Star staff sky-high.

She lunged at him, but he kicked her away, a solid shot to her knee. Ignoring the crunching noise it made and fierce pain she felt, she started to lunge again when she heard a very familiar voice.

"Mr. Al-Safari, your friends here at the Rock Star Security Chicago division are no longer able to answer this phone. In fact, they won't be answering any calls from you ever again."

Beatrice!

"Who is this?" Abdel demanded.

"You don't know me, but you will. Any man who threatens my and Callan Reese's child is going to find out exactly who he's dealing with, and not in a pleasant way. Regardless of that fact, let me inform you that your bomb was well done, very difficult to disarm, but it *has* been disarmed. You no longer hold any cards, Mr. Al-Safari. I suggest you stop your getaway car and turn yourself in."

His glittering black eyes rose to Ruby's. She grinned.

Half coming out of his seat, he shot a hand out and slapped her again.

The hit was so hard, it knocked her head sideways and she cried out.

"Did you hear that, whore of Callan Reese? That is my card and I still very much hold it."

He hung up.

Seething, Ruby reached for the syringe to get it out of her front pocket and inject it into Abdel's neck. The limo veered right and she lost her balance.

Everything happened so fast. Abdel was yelling at the driver and looking over his shoulder out the back window and then the next, they jerked left again.

The impact swayed the limo's backend, keeping her off balance as it also did Abdel. He fell into her, pinning her against the door, the sound of car horns and screeching tires trailing behind them.

She drove a knee into Abdel's stomach and brought her elbows down on his back. He grunted, but his reactions were quicker then she anticipated. Her injuries were slowing her down as well. He caught her by both knees and jerked her off the seat, sending her to her back on the floor.

He dropped his own knee into her belly, knocking the wind out of her. Wrists still bound, she swung her fists together like a sledgehammer, catching him in the nose.

A crack sounded, cartilage busting. Abdel didn't howl in pain, however. He simply glared down at her, wiping a trickle of blood from his nose. "You have my gratitude, Agent McKellen."

"For what?"

"I have been waiting for a reason to hurt you."

She aimed for his groin, but in the tight quarters, his legs were too close together for her good knee to do any good. The impact, however, sent him sideways.

Using his momentum against him, she fought to get out from under his weight, kicking and hammering at him as best she could.

She gained some freedom, squirming away, but the car swerved taking an off ramp and the motion sent her down on top of the man.

The air harrumphed out of his chest and he managed to backhand her across her ear. The strike knocked her sideways and a ringing set up shop inside her head.

Heat and pain rifled through her temple, down behind her ear. She blinked away hot tears and struggled to regain some sort of balance.

Next thing she knew, Abdel had her by the back of the neck, fingernails clawing into her skin. With the car rocking and her ear ringing, equilibrium deserted her. Her body went slack and Abdel slammed her head into the window.

A cry left her lips, white-hot pinpricks dancing in front of her eyes. Her hands went out to stop her fall, but only managed to skim off the edge of the seat.

She went down to the floor again, face first. A heavy loafer came down on the back of her neck, the heel jamming into her cerebral spine.

"Stay down, bitch, unless you want more."

The overly nasal sound of Abdel's voice told her she'd definitely done damage to his nose. Turning her head slightly, she peered up at him and saw blood still running from it.

Small satisfaction, but she'd take what she could get.

Breathing in the stale smell of the limo's carpeting, she tried to regulate her pulse, blink away the pain. The edges of her vision blurred, her body feeling too heavy, her head too full.

She still had the syringe. A whole box full of tiny weapons. One way or another, she would find a way to use one.

Or all of them.

Keeping Abdel alive for questioning had been a noble goal, a smart one. She wasn't feeling particularly noble or smart at the moment. If—*when*—she got the chance, she was taking the bastard out.

Every tired, pain-filled cell in her body sent up a little cheer at the thought.

Time seemed to fold in on itself, perhaps because she kept losing consciousness, shaking herself awake more than once. The limo straightened and slowed. Eventually, they came to a stop.

As Abdel lifted her roughly from the floor and dragged her from the car, lightning cracked overhead in the darkening sky. They were at an airport, the limo inside a private hangar and a slick little jet warming its engines out on the tarmac. Across the side of the plane were the words *Avathaar Shiva*.

Sanskrit. Ruby racked her brain. She's seen those words somewhere else. Somewhere...

Marrakech. The tiny bar where she'd first danced for Jax. There had been Sanskrit symbols painted on the walls, hanging over the bar.

Brahma, the creator. Vishnu, the preserver. Shiva, the god of destruction. The bartender had told her the place belonged to Avathaar Shiva.

Avathaar. If her memory was correct, that term meant the incarnation of God taking a form that would do the most good during the age the incarnation occurred.

Avathaar Shiva. The incarnation of God as Shiva the Destroyer.

Realization hit, even through the fog in her brain. Izala saw himself as God's vessel to uplift humanity by destroying anyone and anything that got in his way.

As the limo driver delivered a bag to the plane, a man in coveralls and a hardhat came toward them. He wore an ID badge around his neck and carried a clipboard.

His large, dark eyes barely glanced at her, rain running down his brown cheeks. He and Abdel exchanged words in an Afroasiatic language that combined Arabic and Berber. *Morocco. A common dialect there.*

Abdel said something more to the man and hitched his thumb at her as he withdrew his hanky and dabbed at his nose. The man's gaze landed on her, distant, unemotional. She took a step back and pivoted, ready to run.

The sound of guns being cocked echoed in the hangar. Everywhere her gaze landed, more men with dark skin and hard eyes stared back.

A hand clamped in her hair, pulling her head back. She couldn't hear well out of her left ear. Her pulse throbbed thick and slow in her temples.

The man in the coveralls used her hair to drag her toward the plane, a gun now replacing his clipboard and boring into her ribs as she stumbled across the rain-slicked runway.

Better to die here than live as a slave in Morocco.

She dug her heels in, took a swing at him with her bound fists.

He didn't take kindly to the revolt and swiftly struck her across the back of her head with his gun.

The tarmac came up to meet her, her knees hitting the ground. She groaned and fell forward, flat on her belly. The man didn't break stride, grabbing her bound wrists and dragging her over the rough ground to the plane.

Rain fell into her eyes. Her head pounded. The rest of her body felt numb. The dead weight of her head increased, her poor neck no longer able to keep it up.

Her head lolled from side to side. She dug deeper, trying to find any kind of fortitude, power, anything. If she could just roll over. Or pull her legs under her, or...

At the steps to the jet, another man grabbed her feet. Together, her captors carried her up the steps, into the plane, throwing her at a man's sandaled feet.

"Welcome, Ruby McKellen," Mohammed Izala said to her. He was smoking a cigarette, his dark head shaved and gleaming under the overhead lights of the plush cabin. "I've been waiting for you."

At least she thought it was Izala. She'd never seen him without long hair and a beard. The man in front of her was slick and polished. His suit, like Abdel's, was high quality. His nails manicured. With the exception of his sandals, he looked as if he worked in one of the downtown Chicago banks or attorney offices.

Her throat was dry, but she managed to work up enough saliva to spit at his feet.

An unseen hand grabbed her hair and drew her off the ground into a kneeling position. Her damaged knees screamed in protest. She felt the trickle of blood down the back of her neck.

"She is as anticipated," Abdel said with a hint of resignation in his voice. "She will be an interesting one to break."

Mohammed stared at her, seemingly unconcerned about her defiance and the saliva coating a couple of his toes. "And her bodyguard? Where is he?"

"We picked up a tail—probably him—but we lost it on the interstate. He won't be an issue today."

Mohammed leaned forward, one hand rubbing his shaved cheeks as he put his face close to hers. "But he will follow you, won't he, my little *bulbul?* He'll follow you all the way back to Marrakech, where we will all be reunited."

Bulbul. Arabic for peacock. Ruby's mind raced. Reunited? What did he mean by that? "How did you get into this country?"

A flat smile. "I have friends here. Diplomatic friends. Those who have strong connections with certain men in your Department of Homeland Security. Besides, no one pays attention to prestigious businessmen, do they?"

His English was as good as Abdel's. His insolence just as infuriating.

"I hear your bodyguard is quite the expert on reconnaissance and extractions," Mohammed went on. "Also a fair medicine man. I've lost too many soldiers—valuable ones—lately. I'm in need of a warrior who can rescue those who are lost and mend those who are broken."

Expert. Oh, crap. Mohammed Izala hadn't been just after her for her CIA secrets. He was after Jax. A former SEAL very familiar with military operations in Northern Africa.

She kept her gaze steady on his, refusing to be intimidated. "Jax won't come for me. He hates me. Blames me for everything that happened with my partner in Marrakech. It ruined his career, you know. That's why he's nothing more than a bodyguard these days."

Mohammed's liquid brown eyes studied hers. She kept her face impassive, her body language resigned. Inside her chest, her heart beat with a manic rhythm against her rib cage.

Her earbud was silent, dead. She prayed that her comm worked anyway, transmitting everything Mohammed was saying. Beatrice would keep Jax from risking his life for her.

"I don't believe you." The terrorist who fancied himself a god reached out and fingered a lock of her hair. "He will come for you, and then you'll both be mine."

Abdel pulled her to her feet, dragging her down the aisle to a seat in the back near the kitchen and restrooms. Despite her resistance, he and one of the other men overpowered her, fastening each wrist to an armrest of the leather chair and tying her ankles to the seat's legs, bolted into the floor. Next, Abdel wrapped a webbed belt across her chest and tightened it in the back, making her ribs cry in protest.

A moment later, the plane's engines revved. They began to move. Wet, bleeding, and pissed off, Ruby stared out the window, trying to clear the thudding pain in her head so she could form a new plan.

The pilot's voice came over the speaker system, alerting Mohammed that they were ready for take off. Mohammed responded; Abdel belted himself into a seat facing Ruby.

The plane started down the runway a minute later, inertia pushing her deep into the soft leather as the plane accelerated.

She'd blown it. From beginning to end. She'd been duped by Izala, Al-Safari, Elliot. Every one of them had used her and now here she was, about to be used again as bait to draw Jax to Marrakech.

Closing her eyes, she blocked the depressing thoughts. She needed to preserve her strength, watch and wait for the right time to take out Izala, Al-Safari, and anyone else who got in her way.

Because it would come. Her training had taught her that there would always be an opening for her to breach the enemy's defenses.

And then Izala and Al-Safari would see the living incarnation of Shiva the Destroyer.

Lost in thought, she didn't notice at first that the plane had slowed. The pilot come over the loudspeaker again.

His frantic voice cut through her dulled hearing and Ruby snapped her eyes open. Abdel had left his seat and was leaning over her, looking out her window, and rattling off a string of curses in at least three different dialects.

Ruby ducked her head so she could see past his arm where it propped against the window.

There, approaching the plane from the end of the tarmac, was a very muddy, blue Jeep.

The plane was taking off.

No way in fucking hell was he allowing that to happen.

Colt had the pedal to the metal, bearing down on the plane, but the fucker wasn't stopping.

It seemed to slow for a moment, but then the engines kicked in full thrust again, and the plane headed right for them.

Playing chicken with a Gulfstream didn't seem like the wisest thing to do, but hell, they'd already done their fast and furious gig back on the interstate and had just now busted through the airport's security fence, which had knocked out their windshield. The plane was seconds away from leaving the ground. If they didn't stop it...

Not going to happen.

Lightning flashed, thunder boomed. Wind roared through the open windshield, driving rain into his face.

Weather sirens were going off in the distance, blaring out a severe thunderstorm warning. Seemed fitting that he would be facing down an act of Mother Nature at the same time he was facing down his arch nemesis.

If he were a religious man, he'd think God was trying to tell him something.

The silver jet was the only plane on the runway, most of the small airport deserted. Of course, even diehard businessmen wouldn't fly when storm sirens were going off.

Abdel Al-Safari might have been a cunning terrorist, but he wasn't that smart if he thought he could outfox Mother Nature.

"They're picking up speed again," Colton yelled over the thunder and wind. "What do you want to do?"

As far as wingmen went, the guy had been one hundred percent solid. Jax couldn't have asked for more. "You gotta get me as close as possible."

He floored the gas, snapping Jax's head back. "You got it, boss!"

Boss. The term made him feel old.

The pain in his body and the heaviness in his heart justified that feeling. After all he'd lived through, his body, heart, and mind were tired.

Old man, here I come.

But that was bullshit. He'd driven his body and his psychological state to the brink many times. This time was no different. He had a job to do. Someone to save.

This time is different, his internal voice insisted. *This time, it's Ruby.*

The Jeep ate up the tarmac; the plane's nose grew bigger as it accelerated. What exactly was he going to do to stop it? He had one handgun and his rifle. The rifle was a better weapon, but he didn't have time to set it up and skillfully take out the pilot. Doing so could endanger everyone on board, anyway. He cared little for Al-Safari, but how was he going to stop the plane without hurting Ruby?

Jax had lost his comm in the mud, Colt's was still working and he'd given it to Jax. Beatrice and Rory were relaying a constant stream of information he didn't necessarily need to hear. "Feds and locals are on the way," Rory said, his voice cutting in and out, "but they'll never reach you in time."

"It's us or nothing," Jax told Colton.

The kid nodded. "The Gulfstream 450 needs at least 5000 feet to take off. They're going to run right into us."

Was it too much to ask for Mother Nature to do him a solid and strike the plane with lightning?

More likely, God would hit *him* with a bolt just to laugh at his fucking ass.

Jax checked the cartridge and chamber of his Desert Eagle .45. It was ready. "Know anything about the location of the fuel tanks"

Colton shot him a look. "You hit the fuel tanks, the whole plane will blow."

"Exactly. I don't want to hit it."

The kid knew a lot about planes. Hands clenched on the steering wheel, he gave Jax the lowdown on the Gulfstream and where to aim in under five seconds.

"Stop here," Jax called over the driving rain.

"You sure?"

He nodded, and Colt jerked the wheel, sliding the car into a vertical barricade in front of the oncoming jet.

Throwing open the Jeep's door, Jax unfolded his body and climbed out.

The plane was still coming. It was close enough to hear its engines roaring over the storm's noise. He could see the pilot and co-pilot in the cockpit.

Now or never.

In his head, he heard Beatrice reciting different scenarios. If he shot the pilot, X would happen. If he shot out the tires, X and Y would happen. If he put a hole in the cabin, X, Y, and Z would happen.

All of them resulted in a dysfunctional plane and potential death for those inside.

He raised his gun. Put his finger on the trigger.

Looked down the site.

I'm sorry, Ruby.

It was a nightmare. The jet looming over him, the rain and wind lashing against him. For a moment, it seemed like he disconnected from this body, floating away because he couldn't bear the pain of knowing he might be sending Ruby to her death.

He'd never be able to live with himself if he let her go, and yet…he was seriously contemplating it.

His finger fell off the trigger. *I'm sorry, Ruby,* ran through his brain again.

He couldn't do it.

Her voice came out of nowhere, snapping him out of his reverie. "What are you doing, Jaxon? Shoot the goddamn plane!"

Was he hallucinating?

"Jaxon, if you can hear me, shoot the plane!"

Ruby! Her comm was working.

Over the wind and rain, he heard the sounds of commotion, Ruby's voice, Rory's voice, Beatrice's voice. They all ran together, a steady song in the back of his head.

The plane was nearly on top of him. He had to make up his mind.

I love you, Ruby. Why hadn't he told her that? Realigning the Eagle's site, he put his finger on the trigger.

As the plane's wheels began to leave the ground, Jax ignored his body's urge to duck, following the underbelly of the plane with his gun.

In his ear, he thought he heard Ruby's voice again, almost drowned out by the engine noise and storm. "Come on, Jax. Get me the hell out of here. Shoot already!"

The plane's shadow falling on him, Jax raised the gun a millimeter more to line it up just where he wanted it, and...

Bam, bam, bam.

He kept firing all the way down the belly. He hit an engine, saw it falter.

The landing gear, still down, nearly winged him as he fell onto his back, continuing to unload his clip into the plane.

Bam, bam, bam. Direct hit. Engine number two faltered as well.

I love you, Ruby.

The mantra played over and over again in his head with every kickback of the Eagle. As the plane rose farther into the air, smoke billowed from several places. In the span of the next few seconds, he heard the engines catch, cut out, fire again. The plane listed to the side.

Colton stood next to the Jeep, watching the plane as it continued to climb higher.

And then the engines cut out once more and didn't restart.

The plane slowed, suspended in the air for a long, horrible moment. Colt glanced back at Jax, a look of *oh shit* on his face.

Jax hauled his sore, exhausted body from the runway and started running.

Because in the next second, the plane lost its fight with gravity and crashed to the ground.

CHAPTER TWENTY-FOUR

The plane crashed onto one side, a chunk of the fuselage tearing away as it skidded and buckled. The impact rattled her teeth, a sickening, screeching noise filled her ears as Ruby kept her eyes closed and prayed.

When they finally came to a stop, she was upright once more and could see the barren field near the end of the runway through the hole in the cabin's side.

Craning her neck, she saw Jax running all out, his face filled with fear.

Shinedown was running toward the plane, too, but Jax passed him, and it looked like he was reloading his gun as he ran.

Damn SEAL. She would have chuckled if she could have drawn enough air.

Quiet reigned inside the cabin. Al-Safari lay on the floor, knocked out or shot, Ruby couldn't be sure. He'd thrown himself over Izala when Jax had started shooting, a loyal psycho to the end.

Ruby couldn't see Izala, but the pilot and co-pilot were totally silent. If they weren't crushed and lying dead, they were probably severely injured as well. The other two men who'd been inside the plane were gone, along with their seats, which had been ripped away upon landing.

Glass lay all around her, metal fragments too. Rain and wind whipped into the destroyed plane as the storm raged around it.

One of the ties around her wrist had half-broken when her

body had been tossed around in her seat. She fiddled with it, bending her hand back and tugging. The angle of her bound wrist only allowed for shallow leverage, though, and she got nowhere with it.

A moan rang out. A series of fatigued curses in Arabic.

Izala, two seats ahead of hers, was still alive.

Only the webbed belt encircled her upper body and it had loosened in the crash as well. She leaned forward, rocked hard, leaned again. Stretching, stretching, stretching, forcing the belt to give until her teeth landed on the broken zip tie. She latched on and jerked, her sore neck and pounding head raising hell with her at the sharp motion.

Another moan, the sounds of shuffling. Part of the cabin's wall a few feet in front of Izala's seat had been smashed in from the fall. She heard him shifting through debris, un-belting himself, calling for Abdel.

She stretched more, jerking on the broken tie again. More wiggling with her hand and jerking with her teeth and she felt it loosen another tiny bit.

And then she saw Izala rising from his seat.

His suit was still pristine, except for a rip in one sleeve. He wasn't even wet. He wiped a hand over his face, shuffled toward the emergency exit—what was left of it—and unlocked the metal bar.

He paused as if he felt her staring, his gaze zooming back to her.

Ruby looked down and went back to work on her wrists.

Drag, thump. Drag, thump.

Click.

Her head snapped up and she found Izala shuffling toward her, a small gun in his hand, cocked and ready.

Heart pounding, she tugged desperately against the tie at her wrist.

Drag, thump.

He was nearly on top of her now and a scream rose from her throat, her whole body lunging back and forth, trying to loosen all the ties.

Where was Jax?

The weight and friction worked, her one wrist popping free along with the belt around her chest. She dove forward just as Izala fired.

Bam, bam.

A hot poker of pain tore through her upper left shoulder, near her clavicle. Ruby buried her head between her knees and covered her ears as best as she could with one wrist still tied, slamming her eyelids shut.

Warm blood ran down her side, her leg, pooling on the floor. Her brain scrambled for an option, anything. She worked at the other wrist with her free hand, but it wouldn't give and she had no weapon. She couldn't move. Her shoulder, her neck, screamed in pain.

Drag, thump.

Her gaze flew up—she couldn't help it. Looming over her, Izala sneered a satisfied smile as he held on to the still intact chair in front of her. Gun in hand, he centered it on her face.

"Put down the weapon!"

Jax. *Oh dear God.* He was in the plane. True to his word, he had stayed with her somehow, through all of this.

But there was nothing he could do for her now as she stared down the black barrel of Izala's gun.

The terrorist didn't even acknowledge Jax as he stared at Ruby, the sneering smile growing. "Do not worry, *bulbul.* I will take good care of your bodyguard."

Izala is going to kill me and then Jax...

"Get back!" she yelled at Jax.

She saw Izala's finger move, slammed her eyes shut. The crack of the gun rang out and she flinched, waiting for the pain. Waiting for death.

But all she felt was the throbbing in her head, the searing burn in her shoulder, the blood coursing down her chest, her ribs.

A wave of lightheadedness hit, her head falling back against the padded headrest. She wanted to shout another warning to Jax, but her tongue and lips wouldn't work. Her mouth was so dry, her head so heavy...

Next thing she knew, gentle hands were on her face, her neck, stroking her hair. "Ruby?"

Her head wobbled as she lifted it, her eyes filling with tears as she forced them open. Jax knelt beside her, his face lighting up as she met his gaze.

"Jax." She sort of fell forward and threw her arms around his neck, the restraints around her ankles and one wrist keeping her from throwing her entire self at him. "Is Izala...?"

"Dead? Yeah." He hugged her tight. "Sorry about that, but I had to kill him, Ruby. I just…"

"I know. If you hadn't, I would have."

A slight chuckle from his chest radiated into hers. His voice was calm, his hands gentle as he drew back to look her over.

"You're shot."

"I'm good," she said sarcastically. Her lungs felt sore and couldn't quite seem to take in enough air. *But I'm alive. Jax is alive.* "Really," she said. "Never better."

Wind blew into the open cabin, bringing more rain with it. It became apparent in Jax's face as he checked her pulse, pulled the shirt away from her bullet wound, and ran a hand down her side, that something wasn't right. He grabbed a couple of bar towels from the galley behind them and pressed one to her neck, the other to her shoulder. "We need to get you to a hospital. This is going to hurt when I lift you. You've got a cracked rib or two."

Jesus, maybe that was why she couldn't breathe. Her chest felt like a marble was rolling around in it. "It doesn't hurt, but I can't catch my breath. My head hurts, and my shoulder hurts, but not my ribs."

"You're in shock, Ruby. You've lost a lot of blood. Can you feel your fingers and toes?"

Ruby looked down as he cut through the ties. She wiggled her fingers and toes. At least, she tried to. A couple of her fingers were doing their own thing, sticking straight out, while others curled into her palms. She couldn't move her toes at all. Couldn't move her feet or ankles either.

"The restraints cut off my circulation, I guess. I'll be fine in a minute."

Contrary to her words, she suddenly felt woozy. Jax said something, but it sounded like he was inside a vacuum. Her head fell back, her limbs went slack. Everything seemed to recede as her vision dimmed.

"Ruby." Jax was patting her face, shaking her.

She looked at him, the face of the man she loved, and tried to get her lips to tell him how much he meant to her. How much this—his coming after her—meant. She wanted to ask him to take care of Elliot for her. But she had no voice, her pulse slowing to a dull throb under her skin. Her neck and shoulder continued to burn with a fierceness she could hardly stand.

Her heavy eyelids fell, even as she heard Jax yell her name

again. She tried to tell him it was okay, she knew he'd take good care of her, but next thing she knew, death finally came.

⌁

Ah shit.

Shit, shit, shit.

Ruby had passed out on him.

She was bleeding heavily from the bullets that had grazed her neck and hit her shoulder. A few centimeters to the right with either one of them, and she'd be dead right now.

If Jax didn't get her to the hospital, she might die on him yet.

Her body was in shock, she most likely had a concussion, and from the sounds of her labored breathing, she had a broken rib or two.

Moving her was not recommended. He needed a goddamn ambulance and he needed it right fucking now.

Colton came running down the aisle from the cockpit. "Both of them are dead," he announced, referring to the pilot and co-pilot.

In Jax's ear, he heard Beatrice. "The local authorities are on their way, but the storm knocked down a tree on a nearby church where they were having vacation bible school. A bunch of kids are injured. There are no ambulances available at this time."

Well, wasn't that fucking nice. "You've got to get me some help, dammit," he said to her. "Ruby's in critical condition."

"The first responders are up to their eyeballs, Jax." This from Rory.

"You must treat her yourself," Beatrice added.

Jax raked a hand down his face, water, sweat, and mud flaking off. "Fuck me with a spade. How am I supposed to do that? I've got nothing for equipment or meds."

"Your bag's in the car," Colt offered. "That black doctor's bag?"

The original one he'd come to Ruby's with. The one with his fake credentials and a few first aid supplies. Except, he'd used most of those supplies on Hayden.

Why didn't I restock it at the clinic?

Colt stepped past him and tapped the wall between Ruby's

seat and the galley. "This Gulfstream has a first aid center. There's a back board, a first aid kit, and an AED."

AED—an automated external defibrillator. Would have been handy to have had when Elliot had flatlined, but God, he hoped he wouldn't need it with Ruby.

Jax grabbed the ends of his hair with both hands and pulled. He needed to work fast, but he needed more than a few Band-Aids to get him out of this mess.

"Grab my bag," he told Colton, because what other choice did he have? "I'll get the stretcher. We need to keep her as immobile as possible."

The kid took off, using the inflatable ramp that had opened up when Izala had tried to go out the emergency door. Jax started reassessing what to do with the injured woman in front of him.

"How far away is the hospital?" he asked Beatrice and Rory. "Please tell me it's close."

"Under ten miles," Rory said.

Ten miles. Might as well be ten thousand if he couldn't stabilize Ruby and stop her bleeding.

She'd already soaked the white towel he'd applied to her neck. The bullet had missed the carotid, but there were plenty of blood vessels it *had* hit. Her shoulder was damaged too. She'd mentioned her head hurt so he had to assume concussion, which in and of itself could be fatal. Oh, and if he moved her incorrectly, her ribs might puncture her lungs.

Great, just fucking great.

He grabbed all of the onboard first aid stuff, and shuffled debris out of the way so he could lay the folded stretcher out flat.

Colt returned with his black bag as Jax was opening the first aid kit and removing gauze. The kid looked like a wet, muddy dog. "We've got a fuel leak."

Of all the…

Jax raised his head and looked up at the ceiling. While the side of the plane had ripped open, the top was still intact. He yelled at the heavens anyway. "Is that it or you gonna throw something else at me, because honest to"—he almost said God, then decided not to push his luck—"fucking Betsy, I'm going to come up there and kick someone's ass if you don't cut me some slack here! I'm trying to save this woman's life. Help me out, for cryin' out loud!"

So much for not pushing his luck. If only there were someone whose ass he could kick. Colton took a step back and Jax didn't blame him. The chances of him getting struck by lightning were pretty fucking high at the moment.

For several seconds, the only sound was the rain hitting the metal overhead. Jax shook his head, ignored Colton's shuffling feet, and without thinking, began barking orders.

First up, they had to stop the bleeding and fast. The jet fuel could catch fire, even in the rain, with the slightest provocation, but there was way too much blood pouring out of Ruby for Jax's comfort.

He padded her wounds with squares of gauze and wrapped them with long strips of the same stuff. As soon as he finished, he and Colton carefully lifted her from the seat and shifted her to the stretcher.

A moan escaped her lips and Jax patted her arm. He and Colt worked quickly to strap her in. "I've got you, Ruby. Hang on."

Straps secured, Jax noted sirens in the distance. "On three," he said. "One...two..."

They lifted her, then fought through the debris on the floor, stepping over Izala and Al-Safari, with careful steps to the inflatable ramp.

"I'll go down first," Jax told Colton. "Then you send her and the equipment down."

Colt nodded as they lowered the stretcher to the lip of the ramp.

Jax jumped and slid, rain lashing at him. All around him, lightning cracked and popped. Poised on the ground, he waved at his wingman. Ruby, strapped tightly to the stretcher, glided down the ramp.

She barely weighed anything, Jax realized as he shifted her out of the way. Colton tossed down Jax's bag, the first aid kit, the defibrillator. Jax caught each of them, then yelled, "Come on." A pool of ugly blue-black fuel was gathering a few feet away.

All it would take was for one of those lightning strikes to hit the plane and *boom*. They'd all go up. Crispy critters.

The way his luck was running today, the probability was too high for his liking.

Colt's boots hit the ground and he started to gather Jax's black bag and the first aid kit.

"Leave it," Jax yelled over a crash of thunder. "We need to get away from here."

But Colton, the stupid kid, piled the black bag and defibrillator between Ruby's legs. He grabbed his end of the stretcher. "Ready!"

The Jeep was fifty feet away. Through the wind and the rain, they kept their heads down and ran as quickly as possible without putting too much stress on their patient. They were closing in on the muddy Jeep when lightning flashed so brightly, they both flinched and nearly lost their hold on the stretcher.

A sharp crack of thunder followed, making Jax duck instinctively. Silly, but muscle memory of bombs and other violent bangs from his days in the military still made him hunker down.

He and Colt and their precious cargo had only taken another step when the plane erupted behind them in a vicious explosion. Colt went to his knees; Jax's knees nearly gave out too.

Yep, just as he'd suspected. God or Mother Nature or some weird, fucked up karma, was after him.

The first aid supplies rolled off, but Ruby stayed on. Colt jumped up, hollered, then laughed up at the heavens as the jet burned. Jax knew it was a reaction to the adrenaline, the stress. He'd seen it plenty of times in the field when fellow soldiers had barely escaped death.

"Is everything all right?" Beatrice asked in Jax's ear. "Was that an explosion I just heard?"

Jax suddenly felt like James Bond, M asking ridiculous questions in his comm. "Everything is peachy. Also, tell Hunter I need to cleanse my aura or my karma or whatever the fuck he calls it, because I have somehow pissed off God in one big motherfucker of a way."

Colt tossed the black bag, AED, and first aid kit onto the stretcher.

"I'm sure Trace will help you with that," Beatrice said. "Although I doubt it's your past that's the problem. How's our client?"

"Unconscious."

"Then you should get back to work."

Easy for Beatrice to say. Jax pinned his end of the stretcher against the Jeep and flung open the back door. "Help me slide her in."

"Don't you want to put the backseat down?" Colt asked.

"No time." The stupid thing was stuck anyway.

It took a bit of work, but they wedged Ruby into the backseat.

The sirens drew closer. "Let's boogie," Jax said.

"Where am I going?" Colt asked as he started the car.

Jax handed the earbud to him. "Rory will give you directions."

With the jet burning behind them, and fire trucks and police cruisers heading in their direction, Colt elected to take the route they'd entered, going back through the hole in the fence at the far end of the runway.

That route involved less confrontation, but was bumpier. Jax straddled Ruby, checked her pulse. *Too slow. Too erratic.*

Her chest rose and fell in jerky gasps. Had they caused further damage to her ribs? Had she inhaled rain as they'd carried her across the tarmac?

Something niggled at Jax's brain. Her skin had a gray cast to it, her lips, blue-tinged. As he checked her pulse again, he found it was now racing as if she'd run a mile.

If he didn't know better, he'd think she had internal organ damage. Something was shutting down.

From the crash? The shock? The blood loss?

Palpating her stomach, he found it rigid and hard.

Scanning her body again, willing the problem to surface under his hands or his eyes, his gaze zeroed in on a small bulge in her front pants pocket.

The syringe. She'd shown him the tiny thing in her bathroom before she'd stuck into her pocket.

Wiggling his fingers into the pocket, he carefully drew it out.

The cap had come off the needle. A little more than half of the liquid was gone. Throwing the syringe down, he unzipped her pants and inspected the smooth skin over her hipbone, her upper thigh. Places he'd only recently kissed and sucked on.

The pinprick was minute; he almost missed it in his hurry.

But it was there. The telltale sign.

In her attempts to get loose or possibly when they'd moved her, the syringe had penetrated her skin, sending whatever was in it into her system.

And he had no idea what the drug was, or how much—or how little—could kill her.

"Drive faster!" he yelled.

The kid was already going well over the speed limit, flying around cars that had slowed because of the severity of the storm. It was nearly a replay of their earlier drive as Colton did his best Indy 500 imitation.

Yet, they were still miles from the hospital.

Ruby didn't have miles.

There were few times in Jax's life when he'd felt utterly defeated. He hated the feeling, did anything he could to avoid it, and he'd learned to suffocate it, kill it, when it did raise its ugly head.

At this moment, he couldn't find the resolution to do any of those things.

"She's been poisoned," he said to no one in particular. He knew it in his bones, regardless of the fact he didn't know what was in the syringe. "She's dying and I don't know how to help her."

"What?" Colt yelled. With the windshield gone, he was taking a pounding from the storm. "I can't hear you."

Jax reached out and took Ruby's hand. Her fingers were cold, lifeless. He'd seen plenty of death in his years, but nothing left him feeling like this.

Empty. Gutted.

He sank his back against the door, chin down as he watched her chest rise and fall in small, uneven bursts. The rhythm, already slow and unstable, seemed to slow even more.

"Beatrice wants to know what's going on," Colton yelled. He tossed the earbud over his shoulder. It landed on Ruby's stomach.

Jax stared at it, unmoving for a moment. Then he picked it up and spoke over the wind into it. "Ruby had a syringe in her pocket, Beatrice. I don't know what was in it, but half the drug is now in her system and her body is shutting down."

"So do something." Beatrice's voice sounded distant since he didn't have the ear bud in. "You can't just let her die."

Let her die? *Let* her die? White-hot rage ripped through him like the strong surge of wind blowing around him. "What the fuck do you want me to do? I don't have an antidote. I don't even have a goddamn IV because I used it on fucking Elliot!"

Ruby's body seized. Everything went rigid. If the straps hadn't been holding her down, she would have come right off the stretcher.

The earbud fell from his fingers and he grabbed her arms and held her. "I've got you," he said.

And then her heart stopped.

He knew it the minute her body went lax. "Ruby," he said, feeling for the pulse in her neck. "Ruby!"

Bending over, he listened at her heart, heard nothing— either because it had truly stopped or because the cacophony of noise around his head—as well as inside it—was too great. Fumbling in his black bag, he grabbed his stethoscope.

He listened. Hard. Held his breath.

Nothing.

He glanced at the AED. In cases of sudden cardiac arrest, the portable devices checked the patient's heart rhythm and could send an electric shock to the heart to try to restore it to normal.

From his cardiac training in school, there were two things Jax remembered clearly.

Ninety-five percent of sudden cardiac arrest patients died.

CPR might be as effective as shocking the heart, but would only keep the blood flowing until they reached the hospital and figured out what caused the heart to stop in the first place.

Unfortunately, the defibrillator needed a dry environment.

Something else he didn't have.

Plus, Ruby had rib damage. The shock from the AED could cause further injury.

His brain cramped, going back and forth. He began chest compressions, humming under his breath.

Stayin' alive, stayin' alive.

Two minutes. He needed to do two minutes of CPR before hooking up the AED and checking for a rhythm.

He'd gone about one when he couldn't take it anymore. Ruby looked horrible. She looked…dead.

He couldn't hear her heartbeat. When he checked her pulse, he thought he felt a kick, but with the weather and the rough ride—and the fact he was losing his shit—he wasn't one hundred percent sure.

He sat back, wiped his face.

Quitter.

The old, nagging voice grabbed him by the balls.

Fuck off, he told it.

Ripping open her shirt, he fumbled to remove her bra. No

metal could be around the AED when he set it off, not even the thin support of an underwire.

He threw open the AED box, keeping it away from the windows and blocking the rain coming in from the broken windshield with his body.

Her chest was damp with rain and blood and he used gauze to wipe it dry. Next, he tore open the packaging on the sticky pads with the electrodes. He positioned one on the right center of her chest above the nipple, the other under her left breast toward the ribcage.

"Fight for me, Ruby," he said, making sure he wasn't touching her anywhere before he hit the machine's 'analyze' button.

The machine was fast, the AED confirming the worst. Her heart needed to be shocked into normal rhythm.

Now.

Jax hit the 'shock' button.

CHAPTER TWENTY-FIVE

Two doctors, several nurses, and a man in a suit met them at the ER doors.

Jax was back to doing CPR. Ruby's heart was beating again, but it was struggling. It would speed up, slow to a trickle, speed up again.

His wrists, arms, and shoulders burned with the effort to keep her alive. All the while, as sweat dripped from his forehead and his brain refused to let his worn-out body stop, he sung the lyrics to *Stayin' Alive.*

"We'll take it from here, son," one of the doctor's said as he leaned into the backseat and stuck a stethoscope on Ruby's chest. "You did good."

The ER team whisked her onto a gurney in seconds as her vitals were checked and orders were called out. Jax practically fell out of the Jeep and onto the sidewalk as he tried to follow the team through the whooshing doors and into the bowels of the trauma center.

His goddamn legs wouldn't carry him. He ended up with his ass on the ground, the man in the suit watching with his hands behind his back.

Colt put an arm under one of Jax's shoulders and helped him stand. The man in the suit gave them both a nod. He had the air of a proper English butler. "Mr. Megadeth. Mr. Shinedown. Beatrice sent me."

Yeah, whatever. The man assumed that said it all, and it pretty much did. "Follow Ruby," Jax told Colton. "I need to tell the doctors about the poison, and her heart, and the bullet wounds."

"They know," Mr. Suit said. He hit the auto button on the wall next to him and the glass ER doors slid open. He held out a hand, motioning Jax and Colton in. "Looks like you two could use some medical attention yourselves."

"I'm fine," Jax ground out, letting go of Colt as he hobbled across the threshold.

Colton, fine ex-SEAL that he was, seconded the pronouncement.

"Very well, then." The man edged around Jax and turned right, heading down a hallway. "Your client will be in surgery for a bit. I suggest we get you cleaned up and into some dry clothes. Perhaps I could get you a cup of coffee or some sandwiches?"

Jax was torn between following the man and heading the opposite direction where he'd seen Ruby disappear. A couple heading past him screwed up their noses and gave him a disparaging look.

Even in a hospital where plenty of people came in bruised, bloody, and dirty, he was a sight. Clean clothes would be good. Coffee too. But no way he wanted to be on the other side of the hospital while Ruby was in surgery.

"Can you get me into the surgical room?" he asked, limping behind.

Mr. Suit was Beatrice's man after all, and Jax was due for a miracle.

The man looked him over. "Perhaps after you shower, sir."

Good answer. "What did you say your name was?"

"I didn't. You may call me James."

"All right, James. Where's this shower?"

James led Jax and Colt to an office in the far wing of the hospital. The nameplate on the door read "Doctor Null."

James unlocked the door and showed them in, leading them through a fancy, contemporary office and into a private bathroom, complete with a shower. "You may clean up here," he said to Jax. "Mr. Shinedown will be across the hall doing the same. Clean clothes are on the back of the door."

Colt gave Jax a *what the fuck* look, then followed James out. Jax shed his clothes and went to work on cleaning off the mud, caked on blood, and sweat.

As he watched the blood—Ruby's blood—swirl at his feet and drain away, he felt gutted again. As if it were his own blood washing down the drain. She was his everything and he hadn't told her.

Her body had seduced him. Her brains had challenged him. Her incredible strength of character and charming charisma had made him fall in love with her.

The thought of losing her once again hit him in the solar plexus so hard, he had to bend over and prop his hands on the shower stall wall.

He'd cried for the first time in years today. The rain had kept him from acknowledging the wetness coming from his eyes during the drive, but now he realized he was crying again. Big, tough, SEAL, acting like a pansy. The heat that had filled his stomach so many times from anger, now rose up to his chest cavity.

This heat was different, though. It wasn't rage. It didn't burn like a motherfucker. The waves of heat were warm and soothing, like the sun shining on his skin. It was...

Satisfying.

He let the sensation course through his system, Ruby's face all he could see. He heard her voice in his ears. Remembered the little O her mouth made when she was coming for him.

He loved her. Her love gave him something. Filled something. Soothed the angry demons.

He felt whole.

Healed.

The last of the blood swirled past his toes and down the drain. Jax straightened. Ruby had healed his broken heart. He hadn't even realized how his parents' rejection had split him in two. How his being kicked out of the SEALs had felt like the slap of abandonment. The people and institutions that should have offered him a family had both spurned him.

Until Beatrice and the Shadow Force team had taken him under their wing and made him believe in himself again.

Ruby had taken things a step farther. She'd repaired the cracks in his heart.

He had to tell her, had to let her know.

The clothes on the back of the door were nothing but a set of scrubs, but Jax didn't care. They covered what needed to be covered. He had to get to the surgical unit and be by Ruby's side.

James was waiting in the hallway. "Very good," he said, seeing Jax's improved state. He handed him a mug with the hospital's logo on it, steam rising from the coffee it contained. "Shall we visit the operating suite?"

"Lead the way," Jax said, accepting the coffee. "And hurry."

"Yes, sir."

A few minutes later, Jax was in the glassed-in, overhead gallery, looking down on the doctors working on Ruby.

Not exactly what he'd envisioned, but James had assured him that Beatrice had pulled all the favors she could to get him into the authorized personnel-only area. Entering the surgical room itself was out of the question.

Several video monitors gave him close-ups of the work being performed. The operating table sat in the center of the room, a host of wires, electrodes, and tubes to and from Ruby. Large lights overhead shone on her body and the anesthesia cart sat at the head of the table.

Machines to measure her blood pressure, her pulse, and her heart rate surrounded the surgeons and nurses. A cardiac catheterization machine was also nearby.

Jax's coffee grew cold as he sat and watched. James disappeared. Colton joined him, sliding into the seat next to him without a word. Just a slap on the back for support.

Over the next few hours, more people arrived. Zeb, Emit, Rory, with his cane. Hunter showed up too. They sat around Jax, not asking questions, simply lending silent support as Ruby's system was flushed of poison, her neck stitched, the bullet fragments in her shoulder removed, and her ribs reset.

At one point, several hours in, Jax felt a hand on his. He glanced up to find Beatrice had taken up residence in a chair next to him. Cal, looking fit to be tied, was on the other side of her.

"What are you doing here?" Jax asked, his voice raw.

"You're family, Jaxon." Beatrice smiled. "Where else would I be?"

Those bloody hot tears filled his eyes again and he looked away from her knowing face. "You should be headed back to DC. That baby's bound to come soon."

"I'm in an award-winning hospital sitting next to a doctor who saved two people in the same number of days. If this baby comes, he comes. So be it. We're both in good hands."

"She," Cal corrected. "We're having a girl."

Jax wiped his eyes with the palm of his hand. "I'm not delivering your baby, boss. And with Ruby, as well as Elliot, I may have violated the Hippocratic Oath."

"What part would that be?" she said watching the closest

screen as the men and women in blue scrubs circled around their patient. "It is a common misconception that the oath states 'first, do no harm'," she continued. "although I believe that to be construed in all versions, from the original to the modern ones used in US medical schools today. However, correct me if I'm wrong—and I'm not—most oaths contain this statement: *I will remember that there is art to medicine as well as science, and that warmth, sympathy, and understanding may outweigh the surgeon's knife or the chemist's drug.* You certainly have shown sympathy and understanding when it has come to the care given Agents Hayden and McKellen. The CIA, and Shadow Force International, owe you a great debt."

He'd never actually taken the oath, but of course, Beatrice knew it by heart.

Somewhere deep within Jax, a little voice told him he should go back, finish his residency, and take that oath. He'd always wanted to be a doctor. A part of him still did.

But Beatrice was wrong. Sympathy and understanding weren't going to save anyone's life. "I screwed up big time. I nearly got our client killed, and you along with her."

This time it was Cal who spoke up, leaning around Beatrice to look at Jax. "Bullshit," he said in a low voice. "You did exactly what any of us would have done. We're the best damn operatives in the business, but once in awhile, some asshole can still trick us or outmaneuver us. No one in the CIA, NSA, or the Department of Defense had a clue that Al-Safari faked his own death. What makes you think you should have figured it out?"

Because I was there when we picked him up. He'd taken Hayden's word for it, the damn Moroccan intelligence group's word for it, that the man they had arrested was Abdel Al-Safari.

"Even I didn't see that one coming," Hunter agreed behind Jax's right shoulder.

Beatrice looked at Jax as if that confirmed it.

Maybe it did.

Cal was right. The SFI team was the best in the business. Beatrice was a genius. Hunter, a superhuman soldier. Emit, the man who supplied them with every high tech gadget he could create, including his own software programs the military and intelligence services around the world would kill to have. The men who worked for SFI, like Cal, were all former SEALs. The best of the best.

The kind of experts that Mohammed Izala liked to collect.

Only all of the SFI team members worked together because they wanted to, not because some asshole held them prisoner and tortured them.

Jax glanced over his shoulder at Emit, who sat behind him. "You still want me on board, even after I turned this assignment into a goatfuck?"

Emit chewed on a Twizzler, seemed to consider the question carefully, and for a second, Jax's gut went south.

Then Beatrice gave Emit a look that made the man stop chewing and sit up straighter.

"You apprehended Elliot Hayden and cleared him of wrongdoing." Bite, chew. "You saved Agent McKellen's life, and stopped two major terrorists who found a way into our country from kidnapping her. The CIA is turning cartwheels, and her boss told Beatrice he plans to take Ruby back into Langley's folds and prime her for an officer's job."

Another bite and a chew. "She'll be running her own squad of operatives when she goes back into the field is my guess, and I just received a message from my contact at Justice—they're reopening Elliot's case, by the way, and he'll probably be cleared of all charges. My contact's been in a meeting with the president along with the heads of the Agency, the Bureau, and Homeland for the past hour, and guess what? The president reamed them all a new one for failing so badly at finding Commander Pierce and keeping scum like Al-Safari and Izala out of America. There's an investigation into Homeland already—Elliot will need to help them root out the traitor—and, oh yeah, the president is awarding you a Medal of Honor for extraordinary heroism."

"What?" Jax had to grab onto the arm rests. "I'm not even in the Navy anymore."

As if that was the real reason for his argument. They all shot him confused looks.

"I mean, that's ridiculous," he continued. Ruby still wasn't out of the woods and he'd created a mess at the airport, then fled the scene. "I'm no hero."

Hunter snickered. "The president can do whatever he wants. Trust me, I know from past experience with the previous guy who sat in the Oval."

"Jaxon." Beatrice rarely showed irritation, but it was obvious in her voice and the look she gave him. "I only hire heroes. The cream of the crop. You know that."

He started to argue—this was all surreal—but she shut him down with an arched brow and a feisty light in her eyes. "You will report for duty as usual tomorrow morning. Don't even think about not coming back to SFI."

He knew when he was beaten. There was a lot for them to talk about, but maybe right here, right now wasn't the place. "I'm still not delivering your baby," he said, only half teasing.

"Fine," she said, and he heard a note in her voice that told him she was really thinking, *we'll see about that.*

"And I'm going to need a day or two off to recoup," he added.

She narrowed her eyes, understanding that what he was really saying was, *I need to stay with Ruby until she's okay.* "I suppose you've earned a few days off after this latest mission."

"Thanks." He had to swallow hard around the lump in his throat. "Thanks also for everything you've done for me. Ruby, too."

Her only response was to squeeze his hand.

The door to the viewing balcony opened and James stepped inside. In a lowered voice, he said to Beatrice, "Ms. McKellen's parents are here."

"Thank you, James." She started to rise, and Jax grabbed her hand.

"I can talk to them if you need me too."

Emit jumped up, putting a hand on Beatrice's shoulder to keep her in her seat. "I'll handle this. You two stay put."

Beatrice nodded. "Agent McKellen's boss at the CIA has already explained most of what happened to them. It came as a shock of course, since they didn't realize she was an undercover agent."

"No problem," Emit said, following after James. "I've got this."

Jax sat back and rubbed his tired eyes. "Do I still need to talk to the authorities about what went down at the airport?"

"Yes," Beatrice said. "I've given them the details about your hunt for Agent Hayden and then for Al-Safari, but they'll want full accounts from you and Agent McKellen, once she's able."

The next few days were going to be long and tedious, but Jax didn't care as long as Ruby came out of this all right. "SFI could use a doctor on staff, don't you think?"

He was staring through the glass, looking down on the surgeons who appeared to be wrapping things up. The heart monitor beat a solid, steady rhythm. The anesthesiologist was backing off the sedation into Ruby's IV. One of the nurses turned and gave Jax a thumbs-up signal.

The tightness that had wrapped itself around his chest for the past several hours loosened. He waited for Beatrice's response.

He glanced at her faint reflection in the glass, saw one side of her mouth quirked up in a smile she was trying hard to suppress. About Ruby or about his subtle hint?

"Actually, I was thinking the same thing myself," she said quietly, and the suppressed smile broke free.

Chapter Twenty-six

Ruby woke with the lyrics to *Stayin' Alive* by the Bee Gees running through her muddled brain. A muted beeping came from her right, keeping time with the beat.

Stayin' Alive. Really?

Her body seemed too light, too *not there.* For a moment, she wondered if she'd died and gone straight to some sort of disco hell where 70's music repeated in a never-ending track. Scared to open her eyes and find herself with a flashing neon ball spinning over her head, she tried moving her fingers instead.

Softness met the tips of her fingers, the sensation familiar. Stretching a bit farther, she probed. Yep, if this was disco hell, Jax was here with her. She'd know the feel of his short, silky hair anywhere.

As always, the thought of him increased her pulse, the beeping noise accelerating. With the escalation of her pulse, a flood of images entered her mind. Most made no sense.

At least not to her brain. Her body, though, responded. Sensation returned to her limbs in a rush. Her pulse jumped again, sending the monitor nearby dancing even faster.

With the return of sensation, she realized one leg felt extraordinarily heavy. Cracking her eyelids open, she saw a blanket over her chest, an IV line in one arm.

Jax's head on her thigh.

His deep slumber reassured her and she glanced around at the foreign room. She was in a hospital bed, the blinds drawn, a couch nearby.

No Al-Safari. No plane.

Just Jax. He'd fallen asleep on her leg, one hand on her stomach, the other across her thigh.

She tried to remember what had happened, sorting through the fuzziness and chaos in her mind. Snatches of a car ride came back to her. Al-Safari, a plane...

Combing through the mess made her head throb. Her stomach lurched at the sudden gut memory of falling from the sky. A crash.

Izala.

Her breath caught at the memory of his cruel smile. The black end of his gun barrel.

He wants Jax.

She blinked her eyes, took a faulty breath. Her ribs rebelled, but they seemed to be confined.

Keeping one hand on Jax, she used the free one to lift the covers from her chest. Her shoulder injury fired at the movement, a trickle of pain, a lack of mobility. Under the hospital gown, she could see a ridge around her ribs where a bandage supported them.

She glanced over at her shoulder. Lifting her free hand, she probed the side of her neck, found another bandage there.

Shit, I'm a mess.

Her neck, her shoulder, her ribs. As she concentrated on breathing, the images flipping through her brain slowed somewhat, untangled.

She clung to the two most important ones.

Jax has saved her.

Izala was dead.

Her mouth was dry and her throat sore. Probably from the drugs they were pumping into her system to keep the worst of the pain at bay. "Ja...Ja..."

The x's at the end of his name were lost. Her tongue would not form the necessary *sss* sound.

His breathing didn't alter. Finally she pulled a strand of his hair.

"Ow!" He jerked awake, sitting straight up and swearing. "What the...?"

The curse died on his lips as he saw her smiling at him.

"Hello, beautiful," he said, grabbing her hand and kissing her knuckles. "How you feelin'?"

"Weird," she croaked.

He released her hand and grabbed a cup of water off the tray nearby. "Drink this. It'll help."

She did and it was the best damn water she'd ever had. A few more sips and her tongue worked again. "My head's in a fog and my body is really stiff."

"Not surprising after you survived a plane crash, poisoning, and two bullet wounds."

"Poisoning?"

"Yep." He grinned as he took her empty cup. "You poisoned yourself with that syringe in your pocket, sweetheart."

"Oh, jeez," she said and they both laughed. His was loose, hers was short, the bandage keeping her in check.

"Only you," he said and his laughter grew.

She knew it was part relief. Her chuckle grew a little bigger too. Jax laughing so unrestrained was rare and she enjoyed the moment. "You're never going to let me live that down, are you?"

"Nope."

She laughed harder, her ribs protesting, but it felt good. Cathartic. Tears ran out of the corners of her eyes. When she could finally breathe again, she asked, "How did you save me from that?"

"The doctors did that," he said, wiping a few tears from his own eyes. "I just got you here."

She had the feeling there was more to it than that. "I scared the living hell out of you, didn't I?"

His face sobered. He squeezed her hand. "You ever do that to me again, and I'll..."

"Kill me?" She grinned.

He grinned back. "Something like that."

They stared at each other for a moment, so many things passing between them.

Jax pulled back. "I better get the nurse."

"Wait." She held onto him.

"Your parents are here. They're anxious to see you."

Her parents. That was good and bad. She'd be happy to see them, but not to explain what had happened.

She still wasn't sure exactly what *had* happened. "Not yet. Just...wait."

He sat back down in the chair he'd fallen asleep in. "Your prognosis is good. You'll be back in the field in no time."

She didn't even want to think about going back in the field. "Izala's dead, right?"

"I sort of blew him up. Or God did. Depends on your perspective."

More to that part of the story as well. "I'm good either way, as long as he can never hurt anyone else. He wanted to add you to his collection. Just like me. I was a trap to get to you. He said he had diplomatic friends who helped get him into the country, a tie to Homeland as well. We should get my boss on it."

"Always the spy." Jax shook his head. "After all you've just been through, that's what you want to talk about?"

"Did they find Commander Pierce?"

He rolled his eyes, but answered her. "Izala's men are scrambling without him and Al-Safari. It's rumored one of the other Moroccan 5 is trying to take over, but our team found a deserter and he's talking. They've pinpointed the Commander's whereabouts. He should be home by 0800 tomorrow."

What a relief. "And Beatrice and the others? They're okay, too? Elliot?"

"They're all fine. Elliot's recovering well at the clinic, Dan's expected to get out of the hospital tomorrow and Zeb's taking care of Woodstock. Elliot's being cleared of the traitor charges as we speak. Beatrice and Cal are on their way back to DC. Her midwife mentioned she knew a way to stimulate labor by pressing a spot on the bottom of Beatrice's foot. Sounds wacko to me, but Beatrice was all over that."

"Wow. Is that possible?"

"Hunter said he'd heard about the technique, so who knows? He's going back with her and Cal. Can't hurt to try some nontraditional medicine at this point, I guess."

"You're a good doctor, Jaxon Sloan."

"I will be." He let out a deep sigh. "Possibly. In the future."

She lifted a brow. "You're going back into medicine?"

He shrugged. "Depends."

"On what?"

"You."

"Me?"

"Yep." He nodded. "If you're going back into the spy business, then I'm signing up to be your bodyguard. Permanently. You know, if you'll have me. With Hayden out of commission, you can't go tromping off all over the world without someone to save your ass."

"Hey, I'll have you know I did a fine job of taking care of myself..."

He held up a hand. "You poisoned yourself on this last go around, hotshot, after you were taken hostage by a known terrorist."

He had her there.

"You may be the Agency's top spy, but that's because you take too many risks. Your luck was bound to run out. You go back to it, fine, but I'm going with you, one way or another. I'll have Beatrice contract me out."

She was far from the CIA's top agent anymore. Maybe Timms and the FBI would find a spot for her working counterterrorism.

The thought of working for Timms sent a shudder through her.

Maybe she'd tackle something new. She had plenty of field experience, she could train operatives, or even recruit new ones to the Colonel's secret army—if he was still speaking to her.

She had a lot to think about. It appeared Jax had been doing some thinking about this future too. "I'm not going back in the field for a while. Maybe never. I don't know yet."

"I've heard through the company grapevine that the Colonel has some plans for you that I think you'll like. I just want to clarify that I support whatever you decide. As long as I'm in the picture."

Well, wasn't that interesting? Both that her boss was making plans for her and that Jax wanted to be in her world, no matter what those plans were.

"Let's get back to you," she said. "You've got the itch for medicine again, for real?"

"Well...here's the deal. I want to be wherever you are. But, yeah, I want to finish my education and get licensed. It won't take much, Beatrice already looked into it. But you come first, Ruby."

Was he saying what she thought he was saying? "I'm not sure I understand."

"I'm pretty sure you do."

She narrowed her eyes at him. "Spell it out for me, big guy. I want to hear the words."

"Jesus, woman, you're a ball buster."

"You love it. Now define what *you come first* means in Jax Sloan terms."

He shifted his weight, looked around. "I kinda forced this whole situation on you and Hayden, and it backfired big time.

I'm not forcing anything else. Our future—and I do want us to have a future—is going to be up to you. Beatrice wants a doctor on staff and I'm the most likely candidate, but you call the shots on what happens with us, and I'll..."

His gaze dropped to the bed, to their intertwined fingers.

"You'll follow?" She chuckled. "You're a control freak, Jax. You'll never be happy letting me call all the shots. And, yes, I want a future with you too, but..."

Now she was the one who couldn't finish. *Dammit.*

Why was it so hard to talk to this man. He'd saved her life, more than once if she guessed correctly. He obviously loved her, and she loved him.

"For God's sake, Jax, just say it. Say the words I need to hear."

He closed his eyes for a second, rubbed his knuckles along his jawline.

Her pulse did another jump, the monitor behind her head jumping along with it. Jax opened his eyes and frowned at her. "You're stressing." He started to rise, pull away. "Are you in pain? I'll get the nurse. It's time for your morphine."

Tightening her grip, she yanked him back toward her. He lost his balance and ended up falling onto the bed, catching himself so he wouldn't smash her.

"Jaxon," she said, "I fucking love you, and I want to hear that you love me too."

A cocky grin. His eyes lit with mischief. "That's some fine swearing there, Agent McKellen."

He was going to be the one who needed pain meds if he didn't tell her what she wanted to hear. She grabbed him by the collar of his shirt and jerked his face close to hers, ignoring the break-through pain in her ribs. "Say it."

He set his elbows on either side of her face, peering down at her with that heart-melting grin of his, and gently stroked her hair. "I love you, Ruby."

"About time you admitted it."

He kissed her then, a soft peck against her lips. "I've screwed up a lot of things in my life, I don't want to screw this up too."

"Ditto. And honestly, being perfect is too damn much work."

"So you're in? On us?"

She kissed him back, letting him know she was very much in. "You're going to need someone to play doctor with."

He waggled his eyebrows. "You volunteering?"

Wrapping her good arm around his neck, she nodded. "I probably need a consult right now, don't you think? Want to feel me up? The bandages are a killjoy, but we can pretend we're into kinky shit."

"Jesus, Ruby." But he was laughing.

"Hey, no kink-shaming. You're a doctor and I'm a willing patient."

His belly vibrated against hers, his laughter filling her with happiness, which was better than any pain killer. "You just underwent major surgery. We should probably wait a day or two."

"Party pooper."

"Believe me, once you're able, sweetheart, I'm going to do more than feel you up. I have this fantasy of you dancing for me naked except for one of those jingly lap skirts. Like you did in Marrakech."

"You can have anything you want, Dr. Sloan."

He kissed her again, deep and long, and Ruby knew her new partner was going to be the best one she'd ever had.

Epilogue

One hour later

The jet cut through the deep night sky, the lights of Chicago far behind them. Beatrice sat in the comfy, leather seat with a fruit smoothie in her cup holder. Strawberry-kiwi. Her new favorite.

"I don't feel anything," she told Maria, who had a single finger dug into the bottom of Beatrice's bare foot.

The midwife, a former Mossad agent whom Beatrice had helped relocate to the US with a new identity, smiled knowingly. "You will."

Beatrice hated hospitals. She'd spent too much time in them lately. Deciding to take an alternative route for her first pregnancy, she'd hired a midwife.

Maria's new identity had included an old profession—one as ancient as her Israeli roots. The ex-agent's great-grandmother had been a midwife and passed it down to the next generations. Maria had grown up with the community of female companionship and mothering, but had turned her back on it, yearning for adventure. The violence and death she'd endured during her time in Mossad damaged her soul enough, she'd had to get out. Mossad had refused to let her go, and Beatrice, her own experience at leaving a government intelligence agency still fresh in her mind, had helped Maria to "die." Maria's resurrection was two-fold: a new identity in America, as well as a return to the profession she knew so well.

From the moment she'd found out she was pregnant, Beatrice had investigated, researched, and learned all she could about birthing a child, and against all Western logic, had decided on a home birth. She even had a special bathtub Cal had installed in case she decided to birth the baby in water, as Maria had recommended.

Now as yet another day past her due date loomed, she had second thoughts. Maybe she should check herself into the hospital and let them inject her with oxytocin to start contractions. She might even undergo a C-section.

She shuddered at the thought. Surgery, drugs, the harsh lights of the hospital rooms... It all made her squeamish.

She never got squeamish.

Was it wrong to hope for a gentler welcome for her child in this unforgiving world?

Cal, seated next to her and looking like death warmed over, took her free hand and rubbed the back of it with his thumb. "Patience, B. The baby is healthy. You're healthy."

"And you need some sleep. Close your eyes and rest."

"I'm not letting you out of my sight until the baby is born."

She loved his dedication. His resolve. His utter neuroticism. "I'm several thousand miles above ground, flying through the night sky with you. I'm not going anywhere except home."

"Hunter!" Cal shouted, and Trace popped a head up over the front seat.

"Yes, sir?"

"Keep an eye on my wife. For real. She moves one iota in that seat,"—Cal pointed at her—"I don't care if she's going to the head, you wake me, got it?"

Trace stood and moved to a seat across the aisle from Beatrice. "Got it, sir."

Trace Hunter. Always the good soldier.

Sighing, Beatrice looked over at him and gave him a *sorry* smile. He winked at her.

At least having Trace next to her gave Cal enough peace of mind to shut his eyes.

Maria released the acupressure on Beatrice's foot and rose from her spot on the floor. She'd already done a few other places on Beatrice's back and lower legs. "Should just be a few minutes now."

A few minutes. Right. After waiting all these months, all these extra days, the baby was going to suddenly kick things into gear because Maria had poked at the underside of her foot?

Beatrice understood algorithms, matrices, logistics, and the psychology of the human mind. She even understood what made the former SEALs around her tick most of the time and could more often than not outguess what they were going to do—or not do.

But there were some things in the world Beatrice didn't understand. Things that didn't fit into any matrix or psychological profile. Feelings, desires, how the physical, emotional, and mental aspects of each person were so intertwined, it was nearly impossible to separate them.

Her phone buzzed with a text from Jax.

An update from her star operative: Agent McKellen was still doing fine. Her boss had arrived at the hospital to talk to her about her future and Jax was waiting not so patiently in the hall. He was staying with her until she was well enough to fly back to Arlington, then who knew?

Georgetown, she typed back. *Or Johns Hopkins. Your choice. I'll make the arrangements.*

Jax's response was a thumbs-up emoticon. In her head, though, she could hear him swearing and telling her to back off for one good goddamn minute.

Leaning her head back, she relaxed. It would be good to have a physician on board who already had the field experience necessary to handle himself on missions while taking care of his teammates. Jax had been filling that role unofficially. Once he became a full-fledged doctor, she'd bet he'd have plenty of groups sniffing around, wanting to take him from her.

Let them try. She knew her men, and she knew Jax. He was loyal to a fault. The only thing—*person*—who might hold sway over his decisions would be Agent McKellen.

Beatrice was willing to let Jax go for her. Begrudgingly, and it wasn't as if she wouldn't fight for him, but if he was happy, then so be it. Happiness, like all the other emotions Beatrice struggled with, didn't fit into any algorithm she could understand.

Shifting, she no longer felt like drinking her smoothie. Her belly felt so heavy, so full. Why wouldn't this baby come?

The twinge below her navel barely registered. A gas bubble, no doubt. Beatrice shifted again, trying to take some of the pressure off her back.

Beside her, Cal issued a soft snore, and she froze, not wanting to wake him. There was just no getting comfortable, and at least he was catching up on missed sleep. He still hadn't told her how his meeting with the new president had gone. A slender finger of fear slipped under her collarbone.

How was she going to keep up with running the teams? What if Cal started shipping out on top-secret missions for the country? She might not know where he was or when he'd be back. He wouldn't be there to head his SFI team and she'd have to pick a new leader.

"You okay?" Trace murmured from across the aisle. He'd been meditating, but had picked up on her movements as if he were hardwired into her.

Or maybe he'd simply felt her anxiety. He seemed to read energy as easily as he read facial expressions and body language.

We're all energy, he'd told her. *Nothing but energy.*

He'd been helping her understand and tune into people's energy, more and more. The tool helped her pick up on other's emotions, and acknowledge her own.

Another twinge, this one deeper in her womb, brought her upright. She took a breath, let it out, keeping her voice low in order not to wake up Cal. "Just a muscle cramp. Nothing to worry about."

His frown was incremental. First his brow drew together, his eyes narrowing. A crease appeared across his forehead. The corners of his mouth drew down.

"Let's put your seat back and raise your feet," he said, pushing himself out of his chair. "I'll get you a pillow and a blanket."

Holding up both hands in a stop sign, she shook her head, then tilted it toward Cal. "I don't want to wake him."

A hand grasped hers, pulled it back. Cal, eyes shut, said, "Put your feet up and let Hunter get you a pillow, B."

So much for him getting some sleep.

Trace did as instructed, Cal helping him prop up her feet and tuck her in under a blanket. For a long second, Trace studied his work, studied her, as Cal kissed her and instantly fell back asleep.

Maria had her eyes closed and Trace frowned at her. Seconds passed. Then minutes. Finally, convinced Beatrice was all right, Trace resumed his seat and began meditating once more.

Beatrice started counting the twinges. Minutes passed between them, random, no rhythm to them.

Yet, anyway.

They were like cramps, only lighter and quicker. Only on occasion did one really grab her, her belly feeling like it was being pulled down toward the floor.

Was this labor?

Her water hadn't broken yet. She'd read about Braxton-Hicks contractions. *Maybe that's it.*

No reason to get everyone stirred up. She could use a few minutes of peace.

Her phone buzzed with a new text from Jax. He must have still been in the hallway waiting for Ruby to finish talking to her boss.

Having that baby yet?

Actually, she typed back, *I believe it's a possibility.*

A long pause, then, *seriously??? That foot thing works???*

She wished he were there. Not that she didn't respect and feel confident with Maria nearby, but there was something about Jax that gave her an additional boost of assurance.

I'm experiencing an odd sensation in my lower abdomen.

It's called a contraction. This was punctuated with a smiley face emoticon she didn't understand, and yet…

He was making fun of her. *That* was apparent.

Do your breathing exercise. Imagine a white room.

Definitely goading her. Beatrice wondered if there were a middle finger emoticon. *It's more like a twinge.*

She saw the bubble that meant he was responding. *The twinges will grow in intensity and become closer together. How long till you land?*

She didn't know. They'd been in the air less than an hour and the flight usually took around two.

Not long.

More silly emoticons danced across her screen. *Don't worry, boss, with the first child, labor usually lasts hours, even days.*

She knew that from the books she'd read. *Wish you were here.*

Another long pause, so long, she thought he might not answer at all.

And then, three words. Just three words that surprised her.

So do I.

Oh, yes. Jax was part of their team. Part of their family. He knew where he belonged as much as she did.

Ruby needs you more right now. You did the right thing, staying with her, but hurry home. SFI needs you.

She didn't really expect him to respond this time. He did, though. A string of emoticons, creating some kind of coded message her brain couldn't fathom, but her heart understood.

Jax was coming home.

As her belly contracted with renewed urgency, lifting her upper body from the pillow, she pinned her lips together to keep from making any noise.

Trace was beside her in a fraction of a second, his hand landing on Cal's shoulder, waking him.

Which was a dangerous thing to do since her husband was a light sleeper and suffered from PTSD.

Cal, as expected, came out of his seat like his ass was on fire, grabbing Trace's hand and nearly breaking his arm.

As cognition dawned, Cal released Trace. "Shit, man. Don't do that to me."

Trace grinned and both men glanced down at Beatrice, who was now gripping the armrests and trying to find her breath.

"Thought you might want to be awake for this, sir," Trace said.

Cal's face blanched and he fell to his knees in front of her. "Is she coming? Is our baby coming?"

Beads of sweat popped out on her forehead and Beatrice gritted her teeth. Definitely more than a twinge.

"Of course, she's coming." Maria appeared, medical kit in hand. "I told you it would work."

Beatrice was about to say something when her water broke. Liquid gushed down her legs, over the seat, onto the carpeted floor.

Her phone buzzed with an incoming text from Jax, Trace ran to get towels from the kitchen, and Cal let out a whoop, grabbing her hand and squeezing it.

"It's a boy," she huffed over the commotion. She looked at her husband and smiled through the ache in her belly. Somehow everything had once again worked out perfectly. "Sloan. Our son's name is going to be Sloan."

The End

Thank you for reading FATAL COURAGE.

Stay tuned for FATAL LOVE, a Shadow Force International novella, coming January 2017, and featuring Beatrice, Cal, and their new baby.

If you enjoyed meeting Colton Bells, aka Shinedown, he'll be featured in the upcoming full-length SFI story, FATAL VISION, due out Spring of 2017. He'll be finding new love with his ex-wife, and things are going to get hot and dangerous!

ABOUT THE AUTHOR

USA TODAY Bestselling Author Misty Evans has published nearly forty novels and writes romantic suspense, urban fantasy, and paranormal romance. She got her start writing in 4th grade when she won second place in a school writing contest with an essay about her dad. Since then, she's written nonfiction magazine articles, started her own coaching business, become a yoga teacher, and raised twin boys on top of enjoying her fiction career.

Misty likes her coffee black, her conspiracy stories juicy, and her supernatural characters dressed in couture. When not reading or writing, she enjoys music, movies, and hanging out with her husband, twin sons, and two spoiled puppies. A registered yoga teacher, she shares her love of chakra yoga and energy healing, but still hasn't mastered levitating. Get your **free Super Agent story** and sign up for her newsletter at www.readmistyevans.com. Like her author page on Facebook or follow her on Twitter. Bloggers and reviewers, if you'd like to join Misty's Rockin' Readers review group, send her a message at misty@readmistyevans.com and she'll hook you up!

Made in United States
North Haven, CT
07 June 2023`